DO I
REALLY
KNOW
YOU?

BOOKS BY SHERYL BROWNE

DO I REALLY KNOW YOU?

SHERYL BROWNE

bookouture

Published by Bookouture in 2022

An imprint of Storyfire Ltd.
Carmelite House
50 Victoria Embankment
London EC4Y 0DZ

www.bookouture.com

ISBN: 978-1-80314-329-3
eBook ISBN: 978-1-80314-328-6

For my family and friends.
We are stronger than we know.
xx

Your own mind is a sacred enclosure into which nothing harmful can enter except by your permission.

Arnold Bennett

PROLOGUE

Every creak of the floorboards is magnified a thousand times as I feel my way down the stairs. Part way down, I freeze as someone raps hard on the front door. Quickly I glance back, needing to know my children are safe, that my little boy has been as mature as I know he can be and has persuaded his sister away from the landing, and then, terror clutching my chest, my fear of the dark threatening to choke me, I continue on down.

The silence now so profound I swear I can hear the beat of a moth's wings, I pause in the hall, my eyes fixed to the opaque glass in the door and the dark silhouette that looms beyond it. My heart flutters like a frantic bird in my chest, and then lurches violently as he moves suddenly, pressing his face to the glass and trying to peer through it. 'You should open the door,' he says, his tone flat, devoid of any emotion. 'You must be petrified in there.' He *knows*. He's known about my phobia since he first met me.

I take a stumbling step back and then, fear driving me, fear for my babies, I spin around and fumble my way towards the kitchen. I have to get to my phone. I picture it on the work surface where I left it, and a hard knot in my stomach tightens as I realise I will have to negotiate my way there in the dark.

I've reached the kitchen door when the letter box flaps behind me. I stop, ears straining for any movement or sound, and then jump as there's a thud. The heel of a hand against the front door? I try to place it. A fist? I wait, interminably long seconds turning to minutes. There's nothing more. Is he regrouping? Trying to think what his next move should be? How he can trap me? Silence me?

Grasping the door handle, I push the kitchen door open and find my way to the worktop on the inside wall. Where is it? *Please* ... Hands trembling, I feel my way along the surface. Where *is* it? A ragged sob escapes me as I swipe a cup to the floor. Frantically I sweep both hands over the worktop, then whirl around as another bang echoes through the house. *Shit!* Turning back, I try again – and part of me dies inside as I realise the crash right next to me is my phone hitting the floor.

God, please help me. Dropping to my knees, I crawl and palm my way around. Jubilation crashes through me as my hand falls on the phone, and I snatch it up and pull myself to my feet. Praying with all my might that it isn't broken, I open the casing and almost wilt with relief. I've never been so grateful to see blue light in my life. I turn on the torch, spin back around – and my blood freezes.

My skin crawling with revulsion, I step towards the jam jar on the middle of the kitchen island. The kind my boy collects his bugs in. It's full to the brim. Packed with spiders, too many to count, hunched legs and bodies entangled as they crawl over each other, searching instinctively for escape. Horror and fascination drawing me to it, I reach to pick it up. Are they poisonous? I have no way of knowing, no way of identifying them. I know why he's left them, though. He's delivering a clear message: *I'm not going to kill you. I'm going to petrify you until your fear does the job for me.*

For my family and friends.
We are stronger than we know.

xx

Your own mind is a sacred enclosure into which nothing harmful can enter except by your permission.

Arnold Bennett

It's a game. Bile rises hotly inside me. I will *not* let him win. A mother's instinct is to kill before she will let any harm come to her children. He knows I will fight. I won't die fighting, though. Can't. If need be, *he* will.

Trembling with rage and terror, I'm lowering the jar back to the island when there's another loud crash behind me. The back door splintering. The jam jar shatters as it slips from my hands, sending sharp shards of glass and scurrying spiders across the floor.

My heart stops beating. 'Why?' I whisper, turning to face him. '*Why?*' Disbelief and deep visceral fury unfurl inside me. 'If you don't care anything for me, at least think of the children.'

He drops his gaze, rubs the thumb of one hand against the palm of the other as if considering. Finally he looks up. 'You don't know me at all, do you?' he says quietly. 'I would never harm the children. It's *you* I've come back for.'

ONE

Maddie

'I wish I had wings.' Kiara glanced longingly heavenwards. 'That would be real freedom, wouldn't it, soaring across the skies, all your cares and worries left behind you.'

Apprehension prickled Maddie's skin as Kiara looked back at her, the light from the bonfire dancing spookily in her eyes. She'd obviously had too much to drink. Maddie had been worried about her since her split with Jake, who was basically an arsehole. The word on the student grapevine was that Jake had been put out because Kiara *wasn't* putting out. It had been just over five months since she'd been attacked, stalked by some sicko and raped on the university campus, and unbelievably, Jake had considered his sexual gratification more important than her psychological welfare. At least it had peeled the scales from Kiara's eyes. Good-looking and aware of his own attractions, Jake had always been full of himself. He must have been severely pissed off when she'd dumped him in front of his mates in the refectory.

'Okay, Kia?' Maddie called across to where her friend sat opposite her.

Kiara appeared not to hear her. 'I'd be a hawk.' She sighed wistfully. 'Or a big, bold eagle, beautiful and graceful.'

'Small problem, Kia.' Jake, who was sitting with his arm wrapped around the girl he'd had the nerve to bring with him tonight, glanced amusedly in Kiara's direction. 'You don't have wings. You might be a bit pushed with the bold bit, too, since you seem to have turned into a timid little recluse lately.'

'Jake! *Stop*,' Maddie hissed.

Kiara dropped her gaze, obviously hurt. Plucking bits of grass from her jeans, she didn't say anything for a second. Then, finding her courage, she lifted her head to glare at him. 'I don't need you to tell me what my limitations are, Jake,' she growled. 'In my heart I can fly. And at least I've bloody well got a heart.'

'Yeah, whatever.' He shrugged moodily. 'It might interest you to know that other people do too.'

'For God's sake, Jake ...' Maddie shot him a scathing glare as Kiara scrambled up and hurried back to the house. 'Pack it in, will you?'

'What?' Jake splayed his hands innocently. 'She needs to chill out. Shit happens. She should get over it and stop taking everything so seriously.'

Maddie stared at him, incredulous. Did he actually believe that being raped was something people just got over? He had no idea, did he? None at all. Kiara had been *pregnant*. She'd done the maths and decided not to have the baby. She'd had the abortion two months after the attack and been utterly devastated, yet she'd felt unable to tell Jake, the boy she was supposed to be able to trust. Maddie could see why. God, he really was a piece of work.

'Like her relationship with *you*, you mean?' she said witheringly.

'Yeah, well, she obviously didn't take *that* very seriously, did she?' Jake shrugged indifferently again.

Disbelieving, Maddie jumped to her feet and eyeballed him furiously. 'You know, there's a really unpleasant smell around here. Why don't you just go, Jake, and do us all a favour?'

He shook his head. 'That the best you can do, Mads?'

She was about to reply with a suitable retort when Nathan came out from the kitchen and caught hold of her hand. 'Leave it, Mads,' he urged her. 'If you two start arguing, it will only upset Kiara.'

He was right, but Maddie was so angry for her friend. 'If you dare upset her any more, Jake ...' she warned him.

Jake yanked himself to his feet, pulling his clearly impressionable girlfriend up with him. 'You know, you should do as Nathan says,' he suggested, his face tight. 'And maybe take a chill pill while you're at it. Kiara can look after herself.'

'In the absence of the bastard she was going out with, who clearly doesn't look after anyone but number one,' Maddie growled back.

Jake ignored her, turning to his girlfriend instead. 'Come on, Sophie,' he muttered. 'We're obviously not wanted here.'

'You're not,' Maddie assured him. 'Kiara's fragile, vulnerable. You *know* she is. Why would you turn up with your latest pathetic conquest and start poking fun at her?'

'That's out of order, Madeline.' Jake looked wounded, unbelievably. 'I don't want to upset her. I *care* about her. I've always cared about her. I love her, for Christ's sake, but what was I supposed to do when she shut me out? Beg her to talk to me?'

Bemused, Maddie squinted at him, and then glanced at Sophie, who didn't seem quite so impressed by him suddenly. She looked crestfallen, and Maddie felt bad for her.

'We're going,' Jake muttered, grabbing hold of Sophie's arm.

Sophie clearly took exception to that. Her face flooding with indignation, she snatched her arm from his grasp. Her expression was one of pure venom as she looked him over contemptuously before turning to stalk off.

'Cheers, Mads.' Jake ran a hand agitatedly through his hair. 'You ended that relationship nicely, didn't you?'

'I'd say you managed that all by yourself, Jake.' Nathan stepped forward. 'Might be a good idea if you leave before you upset anyone else, don't you think?'

Jake laughed scathingly. 'I'm going, don't worry. In case it escaped your notice, though, pretty boy, I live here. I'll be back.'

'Hasta la vista,' Nathan replied drily as they watched him strut towards the gate.

'Don't rush,' Maddie shouted after him. Wishing he would realise that his housemates didn't want him living here any more and that he would find someone else to share with, she turned away to go and check on Kiara.

'What's up with him?' she heard David say behind her. Coming back late after an evening lecture, he'd obviously passed Jake on the path.

'He's a prat,' Nathan supplied, heading after Maddie.

'Apart from that,' David commented drolly. 'He pushed past me with barely a grunt.'

'That would be because he's also a pig,' Maddie called as she went through the back door. If Jake hadn't already put a damper on Bonfire Night, the drizzle that had started was about to. 'He's being his usual caring self,' she told David as the boys came in behind her. 'Turning up with his new girlfriend, upsetting Kiara.'

'How?' David asked, frowning.

'Belittling her. Being generally obnoxious,' Maddie supplied.

'Bastard,' David muttered, not quite under his breath.

That surprised Maddie. David rarely swore. He was an

entirely different beast to Jake, lacking in confidence if anything. It had taken everyone by surprise when he'd found the courage to ask Kiara out recently. She'd accepted, albeit a bit reluctantly. Her self-esteem had been shattered after the attack, and being shy, David wasn't the most scintillating of conversationalists. She'd reported back that she'd had a good evening, however. She'd welcomed being able to just be, she'd said, feeling for the first time that she didn't have to make an effort to impress. The conversation had flowed because David hadn't felt awkward in her company, and Maddie hoped that the two of them might get together. She had a soft spot for David. She felt he was right for Kiara, caring and undemanding, never making crass advances. If Kiara was going to date again, someone like David was just what she needed.

Maddie understood why her friend had become so withdrawn. Believing her assailant to be a fellow student, wondering why he'd targeted her, hadn't helped her recovery. He'd been wearing a face covering, a balaclava of sorts, which must have been terrifying. He hadn't spoken, carrying out the brutal attack in complete silence. Kiara had no idea who it might have been, and as the corner of the campus where the attack had taken place wasn't covered by CCTV, the police had had little to go on. He'd taken her locket, too, ripping it from her neck during the struggle. Kiara hadn't said much about it, but Maddie knew she'd loved that locket. It would take courage for her to trust a man again, even David, who Maddie was sure would never hurt a fly. He might not be the sort who would set the world on fire, but he was dependable. And he wasn't bad-looking, in that dark, brooding way that was undeniably attractive.

'I should go up and see her.' His brow creased with concern, he started towards the stairs.

Placing a hand on his arm, Maddie stopped him. 'I'd leave it a while. It might seem a bit ...' She searched for the right word.

'Too heavy?' David provided intuitively.

Maddie smiled. She wasn't wrong about him. He knew it would take time for Kiara to process all that had happened, and he was prepared to give her that time. She did hope Kiara would let him in a little. 'I'll go and check on her,' she said. 'It would be helpful if you and Nathe could maybe get some food together, though,' she suggested. 'We were going to do burgers and eat them around the bonfire, but I forgot to pick up buns.'

David nodded thoughtfully and went across the kitchen to check out the supplies. 'I'll rustle up a surprise,' he said with an assured nod.

It would certainly be that. With most of them having spent the last of their student loans on clubbing and cheap booze, the contents of the food cupboard were meagre. 'Thanks, Dave.' Maddie was grateful.

Glancing around for Nathan, she headed for the hall, peering into the lounge as she went. There was no sign of him. Had he gone on up to see Kiara? Swinging around the newel post, she flew up the stairs and then stopped. She was being ridiculous. Yes, Kiara was extremely attractive, though she was trying hard not to be lately, wearing baggy sweatshirts and unflattering jeans. Petite, with lustrous ebony hair and huge brown eyes that reflected a thousand flecks of gold, she had an air of vulnerability about her that made you want to protect her. The attack on her had certainly brought David's protective instinct to the fore. Nathan's too, which was why he was constantly checking with Maddie that she was okay.

He'd once asked Kiara out. Just before Maddie and he had got together, not knowing that she was already going out with Jake. It was silly, but Maddie couldn't help wondering whether he might still have feelings for her. She felt guilty thinking it, but she'd noticed the way he'd looked at Kiara a couple of times; not lecherously – Nathan wasn't like that – but contempla- tively, as if considering what might have been. He'd looked at her with sympathy and kindness since the attack, but that was who Nathan was, a kind, thoughtful person. He was aiming to become a medical entomologist, studying insects that transmitted chronic disease in poorer communities, which proved how caring he was.

She needed to stop this. She was being unfair – on everyone. She, Kiara and David, even Jake before he'd turned into someone too immature to care for anyone but himself, had all become close. Sharing a house, they'd had no choice. It was more than that, though. They'd formed a tight friendship. They didn't really have to make an effort to get along any more, and Nathan had fitted in easily. He was genuinely nice, trustworthy, something not all people were, as Kiara had found to her terrible cost.

Despairing of herself for doubting him, which she knew was due to her own insecurities, her conviction that she wasn't worthy of love – that she couldn't be for her mother to have done the terrible thing she'd done – Maddie tapped on Kiara's door. 'Only me,' she called.

When she stepped into the room, an icy chill greeted her. 'Kia?' Trepidation knotting her stomach, her gaze shot from the small bed to the open window. 'Kiara!'

Kiara was perched on the window ledge, her legs dangling into space, her eyes fixed downwards, tears streaming down her face.

'Kia, what are you doing?' Stopping a foot away from her, her heart banging a warning in her chest, Maddie spoke softly.

Kiara didn't answer, gulping back a breath instead.

Maddie edged further towards her. 'I don't think it's a great idea to fly tonight, sweetheart,' she said, her own breath catching in her chest. 'It's raining and you only have your PJs on.'

Kiara emitted a strangled laugh and wiped a hand under her nose.

Don't let go! Please don't let go. Maddie felt the blood drain from her body. 'Come inside, Kia,' she urged her. 'It's bloody freezing in here.'

'Can't,' Kiara murmured.

Maddie inched further forward, placing her hand over Kiara's, which was gripping the ledge. 'Why, lovely?' she asked kindly. She wanted to weep.

'There's a sp ... sp ... spider,' Kiara stammered. 'It's hiding.'

Hiding? Maddie's heart turned over. She knew Kiara was scared of spiders, but she was trembling, truly petrified. Was this something to do with the rape? Some primal thing making her believe the spider was going to leap out and attack her? 'I don't see any spider, Kia,' she said. 'I'll check, shall I, but please come—'

'It's there! It's *waiting*,' Kiara sobbed, wiping at her nose again.

'Okay,' Maddie said quickly. 'It's okay, lovely,' she repeated, relief crashing through her as she heard David behind her.

'Kia?' he whispered, his tone shocked.

Maddie shook her head, indicating that he should give them some space. 'It's all right, lovely. I'm right here. I'm not going anywhere,' she assured Kiara. Praying hard, she risked threading an arm around her friend's shoulders. 'David's here too.' And Nathan, she realised, as she heard him mutter, 'Bloody hell,' behind them. 'They'll find the spider.'

TWO

'Put it out! *Now!*' Kiara begged as Maddie led her towards the door after finally persuading her off the windowsill.

'It will die if I drop it out there.' Nathan looked alarmed – for the spider. 'They have exoskeletons. Their bones are on the outside. That's why people think they look ugly, but they're harmless.'

'It can't hurt you, Kiara. Honestly,' David tried to reassure her. His face was deathly pale. He was clearly still in shock.

Kiara wouldn't be comforted. She was physically shaking. 'Throw it out,' she whimpered. 'Please.'

'Get rid of it, Nathan.' Maddie drew her friend protectively towards her. 'Just because you love insects doesn't mean everyone does.'

'Spiders aren't insects, they're arachnids, which is a separate group to insects,' Nathan pointed out. 'I concede they're not exactly pretty, but you can't help but feel sorry for them when people's first reaction is to want to kill them.'

'Nathan.' Maddie shot him a warning glance as she and Kiara stepped out onto the landing. 'Just do it. Okay?'

Nathan sighed. 'Okay, okay. I'll take it downstairs. I can't just chuck it out the window. I'm not a murderer, sorry.'

Once Maddie had helped Kiara bunk down in her room, where she thought she would feel safer, she went back downstairs. Nathan was coming in through the back door, the spider presumably released into the wilds of the overgrown garden. 'Job done,' he said, glancing around. 'Where's Kia?'

'My room. I think she'll feel better with some company tonight.' Maddie nodded at the ceiling, then shook her head in despair as she looked back at Nathan.

He frowned in puzzlement. 'Did I do something wrong?'

'That was a bit thoughtless, wasn't it?' she said.

The furrow in his brow deepened. 'I've lost you.'

'That "I'm not a murderer" comment. She thinks everyone believes *she* is now.'

'Oh come on, Mads.' He walked across to give her a hug. 'I didn't mean anything by it. She obviously has a phobia.'

'She had me terrified there for a minute.' David cleared some of the cooking debris from the table and sat wearily on a chair. 'She's not having a great time of it, is she? First Jake showing up with his new girlfriend, then the spider.' He glanced worriedly at Maddie as she sat opposite him.

Maddie sighed. 'No. You can understand her thinking it was lying in wait for her. She's probably waiting for bad things to happen after all she's been through.' Poor Kiara, she was like a different person. Maddie thought back to the end of the spring term, when the two of them had rented a caravan for a week and gone off to Cornwall. They'd had a brilliant time, walking trips and beach by day, pubbing and clubbing at night. The little harbour towns were a charity-shopper's paradise. Maddie had bought Kia the locket there. They'd found it in a tiny second-hand shop. It wasn't fancy, but Kia had loved it. They'd taken loads of photographs together that week, both of them pulling faces and laughing hysterically. Where had that Kia gone?

Grabbing beers from the fridge, Nathan glanced across to her with a look of bemusement on his face. 'It was a house spider, Mads. A big bugger admittedly, but it was just wandering around its natural habitat.'

'For God's sake, don't tell her that.' Maddie looked horrified as he passed a beer to David and sat down next to her.

'What?' Nathan seemed utterly confused.

'That it was wandering around. That it was in its natural habitat,' Maddie spluttered, astonished that he couldn't see the obvious. 'She'll think it's on its way back in as we speak.'

'Ah.' Nathan closed his eyes in a wince. 'I get it. Sorry. I didn't mean to be dismissive of her feelings. Or yours.' He caught hold of her hand and gave it a squeeze. 'I know tonight was a big thing for you, that you were doing it to try to cheer Kia up.'

Maddie knew he meant it. He was aware of her background. Nathan and David both knew that she had a fear of the dark and fireworks that banged in the night. Everyone did, in fact, thanks to her almost having a heart attack when the fuse box had blown one night last year. Jake had been kind, she recalled, springing into action and finding the one torch they had in the kitchen. Had she been a bit harsh on him? It was possible that he had tried to reach out to Kiara but just hadn't known how. Now she was in danger of being moody with Nathan. She didn't mean to be. 'You're forgiven,' she said, glancing apologetically at him.

'I'm not in the doghouse then?' he asked hopefully.

'No, but you're on the sofa.' She gave him a rueful smile. 'Sorry.'

He sighed. 'Not a problem,' he said good-naturedly.

'I'm glad you got to her quickly,' David said, his expression dour. 'I dread to think what might have happened if you hadn't.

I'd probably have been useless. I'm not great with heights,' he added with an embarrassed shrug.

'It's a painful way to do it,' Nathan mused sombrely. 'If you were intending to kill yourself, I mean. The results are unpredictable. You could wake up in a world of pain. Personally I'd prefer sleeping tablets, or a car window hose job or something. Mind you, death by carbon monoxide poisoning is not necessarily pain-free. It depends on how much of it you inhale.'

Maddie blinked at him, astounded. He was clever, soaking up information like a sponge, but facts on how best to commit suicide? 'You sound as if you've been doing some research on the subject.' She looked him over worriedly.

'Nah, you're not that bad, Mads.' Nathan wrapped an arm around her and pulled her to him.

'So what would be painless?' David asked. 'If, say, there was a meteorite on a devastating collision course with the world and you didn't want to stick around for the big bang, how would you do the deed?'

'I actually think that would be pretty awesome to stick around for.' Nathan considered. 'If I had to choose, though, leaping off the Grand Canyon. At least the trip down would be exhilarating. Still not painless, though. Once you hit the water ... *splat*. Considering terminal velocity, it would probably be like landing on concrete.'

David shook his head. 'What's your phobia then? The situation you'd rather die than face?'

Taking a glug of his beer, Nathan thought about it. 'I don't have any. Well, enclosed spaces maybe. I get a bit claustrophobic. I'm not sure it's an actual phobia, but—'

'Will you two just stop?' Maddie interjected. 'I mean, don't you think this is a really morbid conversation to be having?'

Laughing, Nathan squeezed her to him. 'Don't worry, Mads, I'll make sure to keep a torch handy when we're in our own place.'

THREE
PRESENT

Maddie

'Nathe, could you get the door, please?' Hearing the doorbell, Maddie called from the bathroom, where she was attempting to brush their daughter's hair and encourage their seven-year-old son to get dressed for school. She wished she hadn't succumbed and taken a sleeping pill last night. She felt more disorientated and tired than ever.

She shouldn't have gone to visit her mother yesterday. Even catching sight of the building, grey and featureless, made her feel empty inside. Her mother was still in denial that she'd been responsible for what had happened to Maddie's father on that long-ago night, the evil, cruel thing she'd done. Maddie so wished *she* could remember what had happened. She had no real memory of events, nothing but the hazy images that haunted her dreams. The counsellor she'd consulted in her teens had explained that she'd repressed the memories because her childhood mind would have been unable to process the

Maddie smiled uncertainly. She was pleased he'd mentioned them getting somewhere together, but she wished he wouldn't be quite so light-hearted. 'Look, I know you two are just fooling around,' she tried not to look too reprimanding as her gaze travelled between them, 'but the fact is, Kiara could have killed herself tonight. I was there for her this time, but what about if there's a next time and I'm not?'

horror of what she'd seen; that her recollections as she tried to deal with them later in life would seem real but might not be. She'd been right. In her nightmares, Maddie felt as if she were living and breathing the chemical smell emanating from her mother, sweet and putrid in the confines of the car; the scorched smell of wood burning; the plume of smoke on the air as she'd twisted in her seat to peer through the back window; the sparks popping like fireworks.

She'd jerked awake last night as she always did, sweat wetting her body. Nathan had held her, shushed her, suggested she should leave off the sleeping pills, which played havoc with her concentration, making her forgetful and, even by her own admission, slightly delusional and paranoid. Snuggling up in his safe embrace, she'd assured him she would. Still, though, her mind hadn't been able to switch off. *Were* her memories false? Her mind painting vivid pictures to fill in the gaps? She would never know unless her mother told her.

She'd lain awake for the rest of the night, worrying about it. About Kiara, too, who'd been inexplicably distancing herself from her for months before she and David had split up, which to Kiara also seemed inexplicable when they'd seemed so strong together. She'd been furious with her friend. Yet she hadn't known all the facts. She still didn't. She did know, though, that after their split a few weeks ago, David had been devastated.

'I can't find my trainers,' Josh moaned from his bedroom, bringing her back to the present and the realisation that they were going to be horribly late for school. 'Someone's moved them.'

Maddie sighed. 'No one's moved them, Josh. They're in the hall where you left them. Get your uniform on, please. We're leaving in five minutes. Nathe!' she called more loudly as the bell rang again. 'The door!' It would be the new builders come to give them an estimate on finishing the refurbishing of the second floor, she guessed, arriving early as workmen tended to. With the previous builders having let them down, they needed the work done as soon as possible, but the renovations seemed to be taking forever. She and Nathan had both fallen in love with the ramshackle Victorian house with its long, rambling back garden, woodland at the bottom of it and glorious views of the Malvern Hills beyond, but constant restructuring was terribly disruptive. Plus, even with access to the second floor blocked off, she was always worrying about the children going up there and falling through rotten floorboards.

'I'm going,' Nathan called back, sounding exasperated. 'I heard you the first time.'

'So why didn't you answer me?' Maddie buried her frustration. It wasn't his fault she'd slept so badly. He would no doubt also be exhausted, thanks to her waking him up.

'I was in a Zoom meeting, Mads, remember?' he said. 'I did mention it.'

Hell. She'd forgotten he was talking to some of his entomologist colleagues at the university tropical medicine faculty this morning. It was all very important, she was sure, but she did have a job to get to. Teaching children who took longer to achieve what other children found easy required dedication and understanding. She had to be patient with them, but above all, she had to encourage them to be patient with themselves. Arriving late and stressed wouldn't kick off the day well. 'Sorry,' she apologised, feeling guilty nevertheless. It couldn't be easy for him working from home, which he often had to when he wasn't out at a project. With all the works going on, a Labrador that refused to outgrow the puppy stage and two children who demanded full-on attention, the distractions were many.

'No problem.' He sighed. 'I suppose I could always apply for a job as a doorman if the grant from the Vector Control Consortium falls through. Boomer, down!'

The dog had beaten him to it, Maddie gathered, hearing a

distinct thud as Boomer launched himself at the front door, barking frenziedly.

'Boomer, *sit*,' Nathan tried, clearly not getting that the dog thought commands were issued to be disobeyed. 'Okay, you've had your chance. On your bed, mate,' he ordered him.

Maddie's mouth curved into a smile. Had he remembered, she wondered, that the only way of getting Boomer into the kitchen was to entice him there with a treat, throw it across the room and then outsprint him back to the door?

Finally securing Ellie's hair in a messy bun, out of necessity rather than design given the time, Maddie was urging her along the landing to find her shoes and about to poke her head around Josh's door when something in Nathan's tone stopped her in her tracks.

'Kiara? Are you sure?' he said, sounding stunned.

A chill of apprehension prickling her skin, Maddie ushered Ellie into her room. 'Put your shoes on, sweetheart, and stay here a sec while Mummy has a quick word with Daddy.'

'I don't have any clean football shorts.' Josh emerged, his cheeks red with frustration. 'I can't miss PE again. I'll be in big—'

'They're in the ironing basket,' Maddie told him, as she did on a regular basis. 'I'll bring a pair up with me. Stay with your sister a minute, Josh. I need to see who's at the door.'

Josh's mouth gaped open. 'But we're late,' he said, boggle-eyed.

'One minute.' Maddie gave him a stern look. 'Help Ellie put her shoes on, okay?'

'Oh *Mum*.' Josh's shoulders drooped. 'Omar will be waiting for me in the playground.'

'No he won't,' Ellie piped up. 'He'll get fed up and go in with Ben. And anyway, I can put my own shoes on.'

'Yes he will,' Josh retorted. 'He always waits for me. He's my mate. And you can't. You're useless at buckles.'

'Can,' Ellie scowled.

'Can't,' Josh taunted.

'Enough,' Maddie cut in firmly, startling them into silence. 'Behave, both of you. And make sure you're ready to go when I come back up, or else.' Fixing them with her best no-nonsense look, she skirted around the workman's ladder the previous builders had left sitting on the landing and hurried down the stairs. She stopped halfway down, her stomach tightening as she saw a police officer standing in the hall, another man with him who, although he was wearing a suit, also looked like a police officer.

'What's happened?' she asked, dread pooling in the pit of her tummy as she noted their solemn expressions. 'Nathe?'

'You might want to sit down, Mads,' he suggested, his tone tight.

Noting that his complexion was pale even beneath his semi-permanent tan, Maddie felt trepidation travel the length of her spine. Clutching the stair rail hard, she continued on down. 'What is it?' She scanned the officers' wary faces for some indication of why they were here. But she knew. Some part of her already knew why they'd come.

The plain-clothed officer produced his identification. 'I'm Detective Sergeant Paul Fletcher and this is PC Andrew Simons. Could we just confirm that you are Madeline Anderson?'

Maddie nodded, though she wondered why he was asking, since he'd just spoken to Nathan.

The detective smiled sympathetically. 'Are you sure you wouldn't like to sit down, Mrs—'

'I'm fine.' Maddie felt every sinew in her body tense. 'Could you please just tell me what on earth is going on?'

'Mads, the kids.' Nathan indicated the stairs.

Understanding that he didn't want Josh and Ellie overhearing, Maddie turned quickly to lead the way to the lounge. Once inside, she drew in a sharp breath and faced the officers. Her legs felt leaden, but she didn't sit. If she did that, she would have to offer them a seat too, and she didn't want to. She didn't want them here. She simply needed to hear what they had to say. *Now.*

'We found your details on Kiara Beckett's phone,' DS Fletcher started hesitantly. 'You're listed on her lock screen as her primary contact in case of emergency.'

'Emergency?' Maddie's stomach turned over.

'I'm afraid I have some very bad news,' he went on, his expression grim. 'I'm sorry to tell you that Kiara Beckett was found dead last night.'

FOUR

'*Dead?*' Maddie felt the blood drain from her body. 'But ...' Her mind refusing to digest the incomprehensible news, she shook her head. Then, 'I have to go to her,' she said, moving determinedly past the two men who were standing between her and the door.

'Mads ...' Nathan caught her arm.

'I need to go to her.' Maddie shook him off. 'I have to be with her. She'll need me. I can't just—'

'Maddie!' Nathan swung around in front of her, placing his hands on her shoulders. 'There's no *point.*'

She struggled to pull away from him. 'I have to *be* with her,' she cried, bewilderment and frustration bubbling up inside her. 'She'll need someone to talk to. She—'

'Maddie, for God's sake, she can't talk! She's not *here* any more!' Nathan fixed his gaze hard on hers. 'She's not here any more, Mads,' he repeated more quietly.

Stupefied, Maddie searched his face. He was frightened. She could see it in his eyes.

'She won't know you're there. She's dead, Maddie.' He forced the point painfully home.

Dead. The finality of the word hit her, leaving her winded. A turmoil of emotion churning inside her – shock, confusion, most of all deep, empty desolation – she pictured the woman she felt she'd known for ever. Someone she'd once shared all her secrets with, cried with, laughed with, danced with, fallen out and argued with. Out of nowhere, another stark image emblazoned itself on her mind, leaving her reeling: her beautiful, animated friend lying still and broken; unsmiling, unmoving. Lifeless. 'No!' She pressed a hand to her mouth.

'Mads?' Concern etched into his brow, Nathan studied her uncertainly and then pulled her towards him. 'It's okay, Mads,' he whispered. 'It's okay.'

But it *wasn't*. She looked at him in disbelief. Things would never be okay again. Pulling away from him, she gulped back the nausea rising hotly inside her. 'How?' she asked, her voice a hoarse whisper.

'A post-mortem examination will need to be completed to establish probable cause of death,' DS Fletcher informed her efficiently, 'but we believe it was suicide.'

'Suicide?' Maddie felt as if he'd just hit her with a sledgehammer.

'The decision made by the coroner is based on a number of factors, so we can't know for certain yet,' he went on, 'but it would appear that Mrs Beckett sadly took—'

'Wait.' Nathan stopped him. 'Maddie, you need to sit down.' He threaded an arm around her as she felt the floor tilt beneath her.

'Deep breaths,' he said, helping her down onto the sofa and then crouching in front of her to take hold of her hands. He twisted to look at the detective. 'Have you contacted her husband? I'm assuming you would have done that before coming here.'

'We were told by Mrs Beckett's neighbour that they were separated.' DS Fletcher looked at Maddie as if for confirmation.

'We're trying to locate him, but as you were listed as her prime contact, we made the decision to inform you first.'

Maddie stared at him, stunned for a second. 'They are,' she confirmed falteringly. 'He's staying with his parents for a while, I think. Kia has a father,' she went on through the whirl of confusion in her head. 'She doesn't have any contact with him, though. She lost her mother a few years ago.' She stopped, a mixture of raw grief and excruciating guilt kicking in sharply. She and Kiara hadn't seen much of each other, hardly anything since their last get-together at New Year. Once they were inseparable, but recently a void had opened between them, and Maddie had no idea how. No idea how she would get through knowing she would never see her again. She couldn't believe it. She just couldn't.

'Mads,' Nathan jarred her from her thoughts, 'the detective asked you a question.'

Maddie looked confusedly at him, and then back to DS Fletcher.

'I was wondering how long Mr and Mrs Beckett had been separated?' the detective said.

'Weeks.' Cursing the fogginess in her head, the sleeping pills that caused it, Maddie tried to think back. 'A month or so. I never really understood why. David, her husband, didn't either. He's still in love with her. He's always been in love with her. He doesn't deserve this.' Her voice cracking, she glanced tearfully at Nathan, who moved to sit next to her, wrapping an arm around her shoulders. 'I should have gone over there. I should have been there for her. She obviously needed someone.'

'You can't be everything to everyone, Mads.' Nathan eased her close. 'Please don't start blaming yourself.'

Maddie caught a sob in her throat. 'I should have called her. I was going to. I *should* have.'

'It wasn't your *fault*.' Nathan tightened his hold around her. 'You tried.'

'Not hard enough,' she cried wretchedly.

'We've both known David and Kiara for years.' Nathan addressed Fletcher throatily. 'Their split came as a bit of a shock. We thought they were strong together. Christ, poor Dave.'

'Do you have his parents' address to hand?' Fletcher asked.

'They're in Evesham. They recently moved to a retirement apartment there. I have the address on my phone,' Nathan answered. 'How did she ...?'

'It's believed she fell from the balcony,' Fletcher provided. 'It appears that she had been drinking. As yet, we haven't been able to establish whether there was anyone else at the property, but we haven't formally closed our investigation.'

Meaning there might be some doubt? Maddie's heart skidded to a stop, her gaze shooting back to Nathan. His thunderstruck expression told her his thoughts were on a par with hers. That he too was back there at that long-ago Bonfire Night, when, terrified by a house spider, Kiara had been perilously close to jumping from her bedroom window.

They'd all revealed their phobias that night, a night that could have ended in similar tragedy. It would appear to be a coincidence on the face of it, but was it? An icy shudder ran through her as she imagined something driving Kiara to the balcony. The same fear that had driven her then. She closed her eyes as she pictured her again, lying face down on the cold concrete, her limbs splayed at impossible angles, the life blood seeping from her body.

'While we're here, it would help if you could provide any information regarding Mrs Beckett's last movements,' Fletcher said, bringing her attention back to him.

Maddie tried to focus. Was she imagining a link between what had happened to Kiara back then and this? She was aware that zopiclone had side effects. Nathan was too, which was why he tried to persuade her away from the sleeping pills. The metallic taste in her mouth she'd got used to, but the memory loss, the delusions she struggled with. She needed to stop taking them. But without them, she was so sleep-deprived she didn't know what she was doing half the time. She would never sleep again now. Poor Kiara and what she might have been going through, her last moments alive, would be forever on her mind. She would have to talk to her GP, look at alternative medication.

'Mrs Anderson?' Fletcher reminded her he was waiting for an answer.

'Sorry.' She shook herself. 'I'm afraid I can't be of much help,' she said, glancing towards the hall. Boomer was scraping at the kitchen door, the noise, like fingernails against a blackboard, jarring her nerves. The children were mysteriously quiet upstairs. Her heart squeezed inside her as she thought of them. Kiara had been like an auntie to them. They loved it when she came over while Nathan was away, which she had done regularly up until recently. Josh and Ellie would stay up a little too late, dining on pizza while watching animated films. How would Maddie break the news to them?

'So you didn't see her yesterday?' Fletcher asked.

'No.' She swallowed back the tears that were rising. 'I was visiting my mother,' she said, and didn't elucidate.

'And you came straight back here afterwards?'

'Yes,' Maddie answered uncomfortably.

'Which would have been what time?' Fletcher checked. 'Sorry,' he added, with a small smile. 'It's just routine, to make sure there's nothing we might have missed.'

Still Maddie felt uneasy. The truth was, she hadn't come straight back home. She'd driven around, trying to come to terms with something her mother had said: 'I wouldn't be here if it wasn't for you.' She'd held Maddie's gaze calmly as she'd said it, no malice in her eyes, no feeling. Nothing. And Maddie had had to suppress an urge to reach across the table and shake her.

It was true to a degree, though at six years old, she couldn't have known it would be her who would seal her mother's fate. Would she have answered the questions the police had asked her back then differently if she had?

She pictured herself, small and scared, sitting with strangers. Strangers who smiled at her kindly but still frightened her. 'Is there anything you can tell us about the car journey with your mummy before the fire, Maddie?' the pretty lady policeman had asked. 'Anything that sticks in your mind?'

Her recollections weaving in and out of each other, fluctuating between those in her nightmares and the graphic images of Kiara she was picturing now, Maddie flinched inwardly. Were they images made up by her subconscious? Or were they real?'

'The car smelled funny,' she heard herself say, her child's voice wary and small.

'Funny how? Could you describe the smell, Maddie?' the pretty lady urged her. 'Was it a nice smell, like perfume or flowers, or a horrible smell?'

'Like smoke?' Maddie had asked worriedly.

'Yes.' The lady had glanced at the other nice lady who was holding her hand, and then smiled encouragingly back at her.

Maddie had thought about it. 'No,' she said. 'It was a nice smell, but not flowers. It was like when we go to the garage and Daddy puts petrol in the car.'

Her mind came lurchingly back to the present. She couldn't remember how long she had driven around. What time she'd come home. Feeling the detective's eyes on her, she swallowed and licked her dry lips.

'It was around nine,' Nathan supplied, taking hold of her hand. 'I'd just got back after taking the kids to a birthday party at McDonald's.'

Maddie glanced at him, surprised. Nathan kept his gaze fixed firmly on the detective.

'And you didn't see Mrs Beckett either?' Fletcher asked him.

Nathan shook his head. 'No. Like I say, I was at a birthday party with the kids. It was a late one, past their bedtime – the parents of the birthday boy couldn't get an earlier booking, apparently.'

'They needed your full attention then?' Fletcher commented, a knowing look on his face.

Maddie sensed he empathised, meaning he had children. She had a sudden blinding image of being taken away from her own.

FIVE

SIX YEARS AGO

Kiara

'So, where are we off to afterwards?' Nathan asked, pushing his dessert plate towards Maddie so she could finish what was left of the tiramisu they were sharing. 'I thought we could hit Bushwackers or Tramps maybe?'

Maddie almost spat her tiramisu out. 'Nightclubbing?' She looked at him with boggle-eyed astonishment. 'You must be joking. I think my days of strutting my stuff are long gone.'

'But it's supposed to be a double celebration.' Nathan splayed his hands as if he didn't get her reluctance. 'Dave and Kia's upcoming fifth wedding anniversary, our upcoming addition to the family.'

He had that look in his eye, Kiara noticed, that little twinkle that told her he was winding them up. Pity. After what had happened to her at university, she'd stopped going to nightclubs, or indeed anywhere very much, other than the cinema or the pub with Dave, and Mads and Nathe, of course, who she considered her safe circle. With David being a home bird, she probably wouldn't go anywhere very much now if not for them. She could quite fancy letting her hair down now that running her own business had given her some of her confidence back. David, though, she guessed wouldn't have been up for it even if Nathan were serious. His sort of thing was quiet meals out, or staying home cosied up in front of the fire.

'Precisely.' Maddie gave Nathan a look. 'Do you really want me to jiggle about after eating a plateful of pesto followed by tiramisu? There could be an awful mess in the car.'

'Ugh.' Picturing it, Kiara screwed up her nose.

'Er, maybe not.' Nathan smiled, placed a hand on Maddie's small bump and kissed her temple. 'I'll just have to settle for a night of wild passion instead.'

'Nathe!' Blushing furiously, Maddie eyed the waiter who was collecting their plates and who now had a knowing smirk on his face.

'Congrats, you two.' Smiling, David raised his glass in a toast. 'He or she couldn't have nicer parents.'

He meant it, Kiara knew, but she guessed he was wishing they were the ones celebrating an impending happy arrival. Dave wanted children. Kiara, though, wasn't ready, not yet. There'd been a time in her life when she hadn't felt able to look after herself, let alone be responsible for a whole other human being. She might not have emerged from that dark period if it hadn't been for Maddie and Nathan. And David, of course, who'd been endlessly patient. She hadn't told him about the baby she'd aborted after the attack; she hadn't told anyone except Maddie, who she'd sworn to secrecy. Racked with guilt and grief, she simply hadn't known how to. She was sure he would have been sympathetic, but he would have treated her as if she were fragile. Damaged. More damaged. She couldn't have borne that.

She felt stronger now. Less like a failure. She hadn't been

able to tell anyone about that either, that that was how she'd felt, as if somehow she could have prevented what had happened. Little by little, since she'd made up her mind not to be defined by her past, to rid herself of the ghosts that were holding her back, she was growing, feeling more able to cope with the everyday things other people took in their stride. She'd been tempted to try for a baby, especially after meeting little Josh for the first time, who was just so gorgeous she could eat him. She'd been there when he'd taken his first teetering steps, and again she'd wavered. But she still needed a little more time to find herself, to be absolutely sure she could cope. Thank goodness David was understanding. He was always that, which was why she'd married him.

'Cheers,' Nathan said, clinking glasses with David and then Kiara in turn. 'To the baby and best friends.'

'For ever.' Maddie caught hold of Kiara's free hand and gave it a squeeze.

Kiara squeezed back. She couldn't imagine a time when they wouldn't be best friends. She'd thought they might drift apart once Maddie became a mum. They hadn't, which had to make their friendship very special.

'Coffee, anyone?' Nathan asked. 'Before us boring old farts wend our way home?'

'Less of the old,' David said. 'Boring, yes, but then I'd rather be that than look like a prat on the dance floor.'

'Oh I don't know,' Nathan mused. 'I still have some moves.'

'True,' David conceded, furrowing his brow. 'Unfortunately, your John Travolta moves emptied the dance floor, as far as I recall.'

He was talking about their wedding. Kiara remembered it had done the opposite, encouraging everyone up to strut their stuff.

'They were standing back in awe,' Nathan countered with an unperturbed smile as he signalled to the waiter.

Maddie gave him a nudge. 'Ask him for extra choccy mints,' she whispered, looking guilty.

Kiara smiled. Maddie was obviously over the morning sickness and making up for lost time. She looked really well, despite the fact that she still slept as badly as she had at university. In fact she'd confided that her insomnia, which she'd always suffered from, was getting worse. Kiara hoped that, weighed down by excellent cuisine, she would get some sleep tonight.

Nathan was giving the waiter their order when she noticed two staff emerging from the kitchen with a cake festooned with candles. Her mood plummeted. Nathan had already booked the table for tonight when David had told her about the meal. She hadn't said anything. Maddie had clearly been desperate for a night out after weeks of feeling awful, and David was keen. Now, though, she didn't think she could sit and listen to everyone singing happy birthday to whoever the recipient of the cake was.

Waiting until the waiters had passed their table, she pushed her chair out. 'Back in a sec,' she said, heading for the corridor leading to the loos.

Nathan was coming into the corridor as, having composed herself, she headed back to the table. 'Okay?' he asked, concern crossing his face. 'You looked a bit upset just now.'

Typical Nathan. He always was perceptive. 'I'm good,' she said with a small smile. 'It's just ...'

'Just?' he urged her.

She drew in a breath. They were all aware she'd lost her mum just under a year ago after a battle with cancer. They couldn't know how poignant this date was for her, though. 'It's my mother's birthday.' She shrugged wanly. 'It's fine,' she added quickly. 'I mean, it was until I saw the cake. It reminded me, obviously.'

'Christ.' Nathan squeezed his eyes closed. 'I'm sorry, Kia.

You should have said something. I could easily have changed the date.'

'No, honestly, it's okay,' she assured him. 'David was obviously keen to come. It's not a big deal. I just needed a minute to, um ...' *Shit.* She stopped, the tears welling up again before she could stop them. It was the way he was looking at her, with such sympathy in his eyes.

'Hey,' he said, wrapping an arm gently around her shoulders and easing her to him. 'It *is* a big deal. It's okay to talk about it, you know, especially to us. It wouldn't have spoiled anything. Grief isn't something you just get over, and nor should you be expected to.'

Kiara couldn't help thinking it would have spoiled things. That she would have dragged everyone's mood down. She didn't want to be that person any more. But she was grateful for his kindness.

Nathan held her for a minute, until the door from the restaurant swung open behind them. 'I wondered where you two had got to,' David said, his eyes narrowed in bemusement. 'I don't want to interrupt anything, but I needed to pay a visit.' He nodded past Nathan to the toilets.

'You're not,' Nathan assured him, giving Kiara's shoulders a squeeze and then easing away. 'Kia was in need of a cuddle. It's an emotional day for her.'

'Oh, right.' David knitted his brow. 'Well, thanks for obliging.' He stepped towards them. He was smiling as he placed his arm around her, but Kiara couldn't help noticing a flash of annoyance in his eyes.

SIX

FOUR MONTHS AGO

Kiara

.

Kiara was checking the chocolate pecan pie when a distinct smell of charred minced beef told her the chilli con carne was burning. 'Damn.' Closing the oven door, she grabbed the pan from the top of the Aga, and then – '*Shit!*' – clanged it back down, splashing sauce all over her new cream cashmere top in the process.

Could she be more disorganised? Mads and Nathe were due any minute for their annual New Year's Eve dinner, and she was hopelessly behind. Despairing, she was halfway across the kitchen to run her smarting hand under the cold tap when she froze, terror clutching at her chest.

She'd *known* it was there, lurking. How had it appeared out of nowhere without her noticing? Her heart pounding, she stepped carefully sideways and snatched a spatula from the work surface. Sweat prickled her skin as she moved cautiously towards the spider, which seemed almost to be taunting her. *Do it*, she willed herself, desperate not to lose sight of it. She couldn't be here with it and not know where it was. Her throat dried as she stared at it; it was *huge*. Her stomach clenching, she inched closer. It would run if she didn't get it. And then it would appear again when she least expected it, stark against the white tiles, petrifying her. A mixture of anger and fear twisting inside her, she raised her arm, and then almost had heart failure as it shot across the floor, its thick legs gambolling towards her at the speed of light.

A blood-curdling scream escaping her, she fled in the opposite direction. 'David!' Slamming the kitchen door behind her, she screamed louder. '*David!*'

'What?' He swung around the post at the top of the stairs so fast he almost fell down them.

'Get it!' she begged him.

'Christ, I thought the house was on fire.' Shaking his head, he glanced down to where she was now perched precariously on the antique chair next to the umbrella stand.

'Quick,' Kiara urged him tearfully. 'Before it disappears.'

'Okay, okay, calm down.' He sighed kindly. 'It's only a spider, Kia. It can't hurt you.'

'It *can*,' she insisted, as she had done so many times before. 'It scared me half to death!' She knew she was being ridiculous, that she looked ridiculous. She knew her debilitating fear was irrational, that it was born of some primeval instinct buried deep in her subconscious. She was aware she was sensing threat where there was none, overexaggerating that threat, but she couldn't help it. The bloody things appeared as if by magic. She'd tried everything, vinegar and citrus spray, cayenne pepper, all the supposed repellents she could buy online, to no avail. Their house was a barn conversion. They'd evicted the spiders when they'd renovated the property, and now they were moving back in, every single one of them, plus their extended families.

'Stay there.' David smiled half-heartedly. 'I'll get it.'

'Don't put it out,' Kiara warned him as he reached for the door handle. 'It will come back. They *always* come back.'

'I'll put it in the fields. Miles away. It won't come back.'

'It *will*,' Kiara cried as he closed the door, but her plea fell on deaf ears. He couldn't bring himself to kill them, and she understood. She was always racked with guilt whenever she squashed one, but it was far outweighed by the fear, a fear that had grown worse after she'd been attacked, and which left her physically trembling. He insisted they only came in during mating season, which in itself sent a shiver down her spine. But in that case, what was this one doing here? Visiting for New Year? They were everywhere.

'Got it,' David called triumphantly after a minute. 'You can climb down now before you do yourself an injury. Back soon.'

Kiara waited for the sound of the back door closing, then, her eyes darting around the walls – because spiders always seemed to come in threes – she stepped gingerly down. *Oh no.* Her gaze fell on the hall clock. Mads and Nathe would be here in five minutes, and she looked like a dog's dinner, with chilli stains all over her jumper. *Dammit.* She'd really wanted to make an effort tonight. The Christmas period wasn't a great time for her, with no family of her own to speak of since her mum died. Even after six years she still missed her, especially at this time of year. She'd met up with her father again at the funeral, and they were at least talking now following years of silence after he'd gone off and left her mum for a younger model. She couldn't ever envisage spending Christmas with him, though.

David's parents were lovely. Aware of her circumstances, they tried to make things homely for her over the Christmas holiday. They'd produced a banquet for Christmas lunch this year, traditional turkey with all the trimmings, but still she sometimes felt lonely, even in a room full of people. She'd always found that difficult to explain to David. When they came home, with just him for company, that loneliness was exacerbated. She didn't really know why. It wasn't his fault. He was who he was, someone who more than ever now preferred quiet nights in to going out anywhere rowdy. She'd once loved his quiet thoughtfulness, his dependability, but lately she just wanted to let her hair down and do something exciting. Dance until she dropped. Stand on top of the Eiffel Tower and scream. David wouldn't be into that either, though, since he didn't like heights.

She'd been determined not to be down tonight; to be organised and in control. Mads always seemed to be organised, making a huge effort around their get-togethers. She always had done, even as far back as university. Kiara would never forget that bonfire party she'd organised for her, which of course she'd managed to ruin. Sensing that her confidence had dwindled after the attack, Mads, Nathan and David had all made an effort for her. She wanted to be upbeat now, the life and soul of the party, not someone who needed treating with kid gloves because she might be emotionally vulnerable. And then along came a spider.

Sighing despondently again, she was halfway to the stairs to get changed when she remembered the chilli. Hell, she'd left it on the hob. Whirling around, she dashed back to the kitchen. She took a breath before opening the door, then, her eyes skimming the walls and the floor for unwelcome visitors, flew to the hob. Too late. Her heart dropped as she peered inside the pan to find the mince cremated and clearly unsalvageable.

Feeling exceptionally incompetent, she was heading to the bin, her mind whirring, trying to think of what she could conjure up from the freezer, when the doorbell rang. Maddie was always bang on time, a super-efficient multitasking mum with a flair in the kitchen. It had been her turn to cook at their last New Year's Eve do, and she'd produced haute cuisine: salmon en croute served with roasted crushed potatoes, broccolini and sautéed leeks, with Key lime pie for pudding. Kiara hadn't got a hope of competing with that.

Now she was being a jealous cow. Reminding herself that Maddie had her own share of heartbreak to cope with – losing her father under unimaginable circumstances, her mother in prison – she chastised herself. Maddie struggled with her ghosts too. Her friends were important to her, which was why she went to such efforts to make sure their get-togethers were fun and enjoyable. Pulling herself up, she braced herself and headed for the front door.

'Happy New Year!' Nathan smiled, waggling a bottle of wine and leaning in to wrap her in a firm hug.

'You too.' Kiara squeezed him back, then turned to give Maddie a hug.

'Smells good,' Nathan said, a curious look on his face as he set the bottle down on the hall table and shrugged out of his coat.

'You're a liar, Nathan Anderson.' Kiara laughed. 'But thank you. Unfortunately, if you want to taste it, you'll have to lick it off my jumper.'

He raised an eyebrow, his gaze travelling downwards. 'I'm game if you are,' he quipped.

Maddie looked taken aback. 'Nathe.'

'Joking, Mads.' He shook his head and rolled his eyes jokily at Kiara.

Kiara glanced at Maddie. Her friend actually looked a little bit miffed. She would have to be careful. The last thing she wanted was for her friend to think she fancied her husband.

SEVEN

'Takeaway,' Nathan announced half an hour later, holding up bags of food that would save the day.

'Cheers, mate.' David carried the plates that had been warming in the oven through from the kitchen.

'No problem,' Nathan assured him, placing the bags on the table and tugging off his coat for a second time. 'We're used to fire-fighting with two kids making life interesting, hey, Mads?'

'Definitely.' Maddie rolled her eyes. 'That's why I make sure everything I serve is prepared beforehand and freezable. I'd poison the guests otherwise.' Her cheeks flushed with embarrassment as she obviously realised that that didn't make Kiara feel much better. 'I have a fabulous freezer-to-table recipe book,' she offered with an encouraging smile. 'I'll let you have it when we meet up next week.'

'Great, thanks.' Kiara smiled back, but she couldn't help feeling even more incompetent. Why hadn't she thought of that rather than risk cooking before her guests arrived, which was always a disaster waiting to happen? Sighing inwardly, she turned her attention to the takeaway, taking the cartons from the bags and arranging them on the table. At least she could do that competently.

'We're used to fire-fighting too.' David filled the awkward pause, setting the plates down and swinging across to the drinks cupboard for the bottle of red he'd opened earlier. 'Our little ones are slightly less appealing, though.'

Parking the wine in the middle of the table, he sat down next to Maddie, winking at Kiara as he did, which Kiara found distinctly unamusing.

'Ah.' Nathan nodded and reached for a spoon to serve the rice. 'I take it you had an uninvited house guest?'

'Several,' Kiara confirmed, another chill running though her as she helped Maddie to some korma.

'One,' David corrected her. 'I keep telling her they can't hurt her, that she sees them everywhere because she's subconsciously looking for them, but—'

'I'm not subconsciously doing anything of the sort!' Kiara refuted. 'They just appear. I swear to God sometimes you're encouraging them in.'

David heaved out a sigh. 'Yep, that's right. I sent them an invitation.'

'To be fair, they do terrify her,' Nathan pointed out as Kiara looked down at her plate. She was being silly, but she did wonder sometimes if David was quietly pleased that she was dependent on him to save her. At least Nathan had never tried to convince her they couldn't hurt her and that they were more scared than she was, not since he'd first witnessed her encounter with her worst nightmare all those years ago at uni.

'What I don't get is why you would choose to live in such an old property,' Nathan said, glancing from her to David.

Kiara didn't get that either. Their previous house hadn't been brand new, but at least it hadn't had a thousand dark corners. She had no idea how Maddie lived in her ancient property while it was actually undergoing renovation. There must be creepy-crawlies everywhere. 'It was Dave's choice, not mine,' she answered shortly.

'You fell in love with it.' David looked across at her, his expression defensive.

'Yes, but I didn't realise it would be infested with the things. You know how much I hate them, yet you're still dead set against moving somewhere safe. I sometimes think you want me to die of fright.'

'Don't be daft, Kia.' David eyed her in despair. 'I'm not dead set against it.' He stirred his food moodily with his fork. 'It's just …'

'You don't want to live somewhere without a huge garden. Did it never occur to you that those old outhouses out there are perfect breeding grounds for them?' Kiara finished with a huff. Then, realising she'd killed the conversation, she dropped her gaze, playing with her own food, which she now had no appetite for.

'Tell me about this safe place.' Nathan attempted to rescue the situation.

Kiara's gaze slid towards him. 'You're taking the pee.'

'I'm not, I promise.' He smiled sympathetically. 'Look, Kia, I understand why you're scared of them, honestly.' He reached to give her hand a squeeze. 'I'm not the greatest fan of some of the insects I find myself up to my armpits in.'

Kiara shuddered. 'Somewhere modern,' she said, glancing hopefully at David. He didn't meet her gaze. Obviously she'd made him feel uncomfortable. 'An apartment,' she ploughed on, wanting to know if Nathan and Mads thought it was such a ridiculous notion. 'One of the girls who works at the salon lives in a fourth-floor apartment and she says she never has any spiders there.'

'It's a bit of a drastic move, though.' Maddie eyed her curiously. 'He's not great with heights, are you, Dave?'

'I know that, but he said himself that being inside a high-rise building doesn't affect him in the same way being outdoors does.' Kiara sighed. She could see how this looked, as if she didn't care about David's feelings. She did. 'You don't honestly think I would force him to move somewhere *he* would be terrified on a daily basis, do you?'

'Er, hello, subject of discussion in the room,' David interjected.

'Sorry.' Realising she was making their guests feel extremely awkward, particularly Maddie, who looked as if she didn't know where to put herself, Kiara reached for the wine to top up the glasses. 'I just wish you'd consider it,' she said, 'rather than dismissing it out of hand. It feels like I don't have any say in the matter.'

'You do. Of course you do.' David looked surprised. 'I just worry that it won't solve the problem, that's all. And we have put a hell of a lot of work into this place.'

'I know.' Kiara understood his reticence, but she couldn't help the way she felt. She wished she could. What she wanted most in life was to be able to live it to the full, to be free of the things that were holding her back, her insecurities, her fears, which had been majorly exacerbated by the attack. It had reduced her confidence to nil, her trust in men, in herself. She'd fought hard to get her life back. She was still fighting, but this place seemed to be setting her back rather than allowing her to move forward. Surely David could see that?

'Look.' She searched for a way to make him feel better. She was making him seem like the bad guy here, and she didn't mean to do that. 'I did love it at first, when we viewed it, while it was being refurbished, but ...' She faltered, noting his gloomy expression, as did Nathan and Maddie, judging by the embarrassed glances passing between them.

'You're not so keen on the uninvited house guests.' He drew in a breath. 'Okay,' he nodded, 'I'll think about it.'

'Really?' Kiara's hopes soared.

'Really.' He smiled, though he clearly wasn't that enthusiastic. 'I love you, Kiara. You know I do. I don't want you to be unhappy.'

'Thank you.' She emitted a sigh of relief. David was never going to climb a mountain. He had no aspirations in life other than to be a school teacher, which she sometimes found frustrating, but she was sure he wouldn't let her down.

Giving her another small smile, he turned his attention to Nathan. 'So, Nathe, tell us about your latest trip to exotic climes.' Kiara guessed he was attempting to thaw the uncomfortable atmosphere.

Nathan clearly realised as much too. 'I'd hardly call it exotic.' He shrugged. 'I'm mostly based in villages in rural regions, poking around in people's homes.'

'What are the homes like?' Kiara asked, trying to imagine how anyone could live in houses that weren't made of solid bricks and mortar. This one was bad enough.

'They're largely built from wood or thatch, which makes it pretty stifling work in the heat, but they're perfect places for insects to live.'

'Poor communities then?' David asked interestedly as Kiara shivered afresh at that thought.

'Very,' Maddie picked up. 'You'd have to be passionate to do it: leaving your nice comfy bed for an airless hotel room in a tropical climate for weeks at a time. Either that or mad.' She smiled with mock bemusement in Nathan's direction.

Nathan smiled back, a little uncertainly, Kiara thought. Not long ago, when Nathan's job had started taking him overseas more often, Maddie had confided to her that although she admired what he did, they sometimes had words about him being away at some crucial time, a school event or a child's birthday. It was obviously a bone of contention between them.

'The villagers are usually subsistence farmers,' Nathan

continued. 'They try to make a living by selling surplus crops, so yes, they would be extremely poor.'

'I'm not sure I could make that journey on a regular basis,' Maddie chimed in again, plainly feeling obliged to keep the conversation flowing. 'The flight from Heathrow to Ecuador is twelve hours alone, then there's another twelve hours' drive after that to whatever region he's working in, lugging suitcases crammed with clothes in case there are no laundry facilities. And he has to make space for lab equipment. It can get him into trouble at the airport, as security tends not to understand that a microscope isn't a deadly weapon and that he does have all the necessary paperwork for the biological reagents he's transporting. Can you believe he was stopped for cocaine testing last time?'

'I was travelling with coffee,' Nathan explained, looking amused at Maddie's appalled expression.

'It's not funny, Nathe,' she scolded him. 'I almost had heart failure when you rang me.'

'I bet Nathe almost had heart failure when they stopped him,' David pointed out.

'Pretty much.' Nathan shrugged. 'I travel without the coffee now.'

'So what exactly are you poking around in people's homes for?' David asked, clearly fascinated.

'*Rhodnius ecuadoriensis*.' Nathan reeled off the Latin name. 'Commonly called the triatomine bug or kissing bug. They live in the domestic environment and can be found in the cracks and crevices between wood and adobe. They come out at night and feed on humans, often biting on the face, frequently at the corner of the mouth, hence the name.'

'Oh yuck.' Kiara screwed up her nose, her stomach curdling at the image that conjured up.

'And are they dangerous?' David asked. Kiara wished he

wouldn't. Like Maddie, she admired Nathan's dedication, but she wasn't sure she wanted all the details.

Nathan nodded. 'Extremely. They transmit a disease commonly known as Chagas disease. Not everyone infected shows symptoms, but those that get chronic disease are infected for life. There is no known cure and it can be fatal, hence the research.'

Kiara could see why he was passionate about his work, having a natural predilection to help people, but still she didn't want to hear any more. Indicating to Maddie, who was half on her feet to help her, that she should stay where she was, she gathered up dishes as Nathan started describing how they collected the bugs. 'They're about half the size of a man's thumb,' he said, demonstrating. 'We shine a light on them and then pluck them out of their crevices and drop them into a glass jar.'

Ugh. Her mind immediately conjuring up an image of the leggy things crawling all over each other, she beat a hasty retreat to the kitchen.

She was loading up the dishwasher when she heard someone come in behind her. Thinking it was Maddie, she turned around and was surprised to see Nathan, who'd obviously collected up the takeaway cartons.

'Thought I'd lend a hand,' he said, placing them on the work surface. 'Mads is deep in conversation with Dave about how exhausted I am when I get home, so ...'

'She's just worried for you,' Kiara assured him. 'She probably thinks the travel is a bit much.'

He nodded. 'Leaving her to run everything at home's a bit much, but I don't have a lot of choice,' he said with a disconsolate shrug.

'Mads understands. She knows that what you do is who you are, and she wouldn't have you any other way.'

'You reckon?' Nathan smiled doubtfully. He really did have

a lovely smile. And he was generally always smiling. Kiara liked that about him. He tended to lighten things somehow, unlike David, who took everything so seriously.

'I do. She would only be miserable if she thought you were miserable, stuck here not doing something you love. Sorry about all that, by the way,' she added, nodding towards the dining room.

'All what?' Nathan furrowed his brow diplomatically.

'The awkward conversation,' she reminded him, as if she really needed to. 'It's just, I know Dave loves the country life. That he's determined to live in a roses-around-the-door cottage where everything is pollution-free and perfect. The thing is, it's not perfect, not for me. It's been torture.'

'Hey, come on.' Nathan moved towards her, threading an arm around her shoulders as she blinked back her tears. 'He's agreed to think about moving, hasn't he?'

Kiara locked her gaze on him. 'He has to. It's going to kill me, Nathan. I keep trying to tell him, but he's not listening.'

Nathan studied her in confusion, then, 'You're serious, aren't you?' he said, concern crossing his face.

'Deadly.' Kiara nodded hard. 'I had to go to the hospital. My GP sent me. I didn't bother David with it because he was busy with exam preparation at school. I had a pain in my left arm, which frightened me. They did some blood tests and found a raised enzyme that might indicate heart trouble. They said it had settled down and that my ECG was normal when they took a second test,' she added quickly. 'But I'm scared, Nathe. I've tried to tackle my phobia, but I just can't.'

'Christ, Kia.' Nathan circled his arms around her and eased her to him.

Kiara rested her head on his shoulder, feeling safe in his comforting embrace, as if he really did understand her. 'I haven't told David yet,' she whispered. 'You won't mention anything to him, will you?'

He shook his head. 'I won't,' he said. 'But you have to tell him, Kia. He needs to know.'

'I will. It's just ...' She hesitated. 'There's something else that's been worrying me.' She knitted her brow, wondering what his reaction would be. 'You'll probably think I'm mad.'

'I won't, I promise.' He smiled encouragingly.

She took a breath. 'I really do wonder sometimes if he's doing it on purpose,' she said. 'Bringing the spiders in, I mean. You know, so he can be my hero and save me.'

Nathan emitted a bewildered laugh. 'He wouldn't do something like that. Dave's straight down the line. He thinks the world of—' He stopped, pulling hastily away from her as Maddie appeared in the doorway.

'Not interrupting anything, am I?' she said.

A little over-brightly, Kiara perceived.

EIGHT

Maddie

Maddie squeezed David tight as they said their goodbyes. 'Happy New Year,' she whispered. What was he thinking? she wondered. He hadn't said anything, but he'd followed her to the kitchen in time to see Kiara and Nathan looking somewhat flustered. He'd seemed unperturbed, unlike Maddie. Avoiding eye contact with Nathan, she'd talked incessantly for the rest of the evening rather than risk causing further upset, which she'd felt perilously close to doing.

'You too.' He gave her a hard squeeze back.

Nodding, she swallowed and stepped away to give Kiara a hug. She could hardly not. She had no idea what was going on, but demanding answers when both she and Kiara had been drinking probably wasn't a good idea.

'I'll call you tomorrow,' Kiara promised.

'Do that,' Maddie said, forcing some enthusiasm into her voice.

'But not too early,' Nathan added, giving Kiara a playful wink as he leaned to kiss her cheek. She turned her head so that her lips met his.

Maddie tried to reassure herself. It was a kiss between friends, that was all. She was reading too much into it. Was she, though? He'd once asked Kiara out. It was years ago now, but still Maddie felt an undeniable surge of jealousy.

'Don't do anything I wouldn't,' Nathan joked, turning to shake David's hand warmly.

David's mouth twitched into a semblance of a smile. 'Doesn't leave much then,' he replied, an unusually acerbic edge to his voice.

Nathan arched an eyebrow curiously as he moved away. 'Plenty, I should think,' he said wryly. 'Catch you soon.' Turning to the car, he waved over his shoulder. 'Our place next time.'

'Brilliant. Mads and I will fix a date,' Kiara called as Maddie followed him.

Slipping into the passenger seat, Maddie waved as they drove off. She waited for Nathan to say something, but he kept his eyes on the road and didn't utter a word.

She couldn't stand it a second longer. 'You're not going to tell me what was going on with you and Kiara then?' she asked him, her voice tight with a mixture of hurt and anger.

'Ah,' was all he said.

She couldn't believe it. Surely he must be aware that he owed her an explanation? 'Was it appropriate, do you think, to be embracing her quite so closely?' she asked as evenly as she could.

Nathan didn't reply, merely looked awkward, which exacerbated her frustration. 'I noticed the glances you two were exchanging at the table before you followed her, by the way,' she went on, feeling horribly betrayed and confused.

He sighed heavily. 'Don't be ridiculous, Mads. We were

doing no such thing.' She could hear the irritation in his voice. 'You're imagining things.'

That stung, horribly. He knew how worried she was about the things her mind conjured up. '*Me* ridiculous?' She turned in her seat. 'It seems to me it was you two who were being ridiculous. I mean, copping a quick grope in the *kitchen*?'

'Copping a quick ...' Nathan laughed. 'Are you serious, Mads? I mean, really?' Shaking his head, he looked despairingly at her, then fixed his eyes back on the road.

That got to her. He was being dismissive of her, facetious. She was upset, as she considered she had every right to be, and he was laughing at her. The least he could do was apologise, offer up some excuse for being so intimate with her best friend.

'You know, sometimes this "everything's a joke" attitude you have can be really annoying, Nathan,' she retorted, angry tears springing to her eyes. 'There are some things that need to be taken seriously. Our relationship, for—'

'She has a heart condition,' Nathan cut in bluntly.

Maddie felt her own heart turn over. *Kiara?* But she'd never said anything. Never uttered a word. 'What condition?' she managed after a stunned second.

Nathan pulled in a tight breath. 'I don't know exactly. Something about a raised enzyme they found when she was sent to the hospital with pain in her arm. She said they'd repeated the test and that it might not be anything to worry about. She hasn't told David yet, though.'

Which was why Nathan hadn't said anything while they were at the house. Maddie closed her eyes, devastated for Kiara, and filled with a deep sense of shame that she'd pounced on Nathan. And while he was *driving*. Could she have acted more irresponsibly? It had clearly all been in her overactive imagination. But ... 'Why didn't you say something as soon as we drove off? Why wait for me to ask?'

'I didn't want to worry you.' Nathan glanced at her again, his expression contrite. 'I don't think Kiara does either. I suspect it just kind of came out when I offered her a shoulder. And that's all it was, Maddie,' he assured her, hurt obvious in his voice, probably because she'd leapt to conclusions, which said a lot about her trust for him. 'I accept it might have appeared as if there was more to it, though, and I apologise.'

Maddie felt worse by the second. He was just being who he was, caring, naturally affectionate. What had she been thinking?

'There's something else,' he continued, as she suppressed an urge to ask him to turn the car around so she could go back and give her friend a proper hug, one she obviously badly needed. Kiara had been upset when they'd arrived, more so than Maddie had realised. That was why she'd been on edge, sniping at David. And all Maddie had done to try and dispel the tension she'd felt between them was rattle on like a bloody runaway train.

Angry now with herself, she swiped a tear from her face. 'What?' she asked tremulously, wondering what else there could possibly be.

'This really is going to sound ridiculous.' Nathan paused, his gaze flicking again towards her. 'She seems to think that David's manipulating her.'

'What?' Maddie almost laughed at the absurdity of that notion. David was one of the nicest people she knew. He wasn't capable of being manipulative or deceitful. 'How?'

Nathan hesitated. 'She has a ludicrous idea that he's bringing the spiders into the house deliberately.'

'Oh for goodness' sake.' Maddie stared at him, astonished. 'Why on earth would he do that?'

Nathan shrugged uncertainly. 'She said something about him wanting to be her hero. To make sure she needs him, I suppose she meant. Like I say, it's pretty ridiculous. I am concerned for her, though, particularly with this heart thing.'

Maddie was really concerned now. The idea of David, of all people, trying to manipulate Kiara seemed preposterous. Was it possible that her phobia was making her paranoid?

NINE

David

David poured two fingers of brandy, swirled it around the glass and contemplated the rich amber colour of it. Should he say anything, he wondered, or just leave it alone? Would Kiara? She must have realised that the clinch she'd been in with Nathan had looked compromising. Judging by her bewildered expression, Maddie had certainly thought so. Why hadn't Kiara mentioned it once she'd come back to the table? Why hadn't Nathan, come to that?

Swallowing his drink, he poured another stiff measure, knocked that back too, then placed the glass down on the drinks tray. He studied it for a second, frowning, then reached to line it up precisely with the other glasses. He didn't like things out of order. Off centre. Right now, his entire world felt off centre.

Kiara was in the shower when he went into the bedroom. He walked across to the chair where she'd abandoned her clothes. The underwear was new, he noticed, picking up the bra she'd taken off and feeling the soft silk of it between his finger-tips. It was sexy, but not overly racy. Tasteful, in fact, soft pastel pink with pretty scalloped edging. Had she worn it this evening for him? He thought not, since she'd now taken it off. Had she ever loved him? he wondered. She'd liked him, he'd known she had, but had she ever really loved him the way he'd loved her, passionately? From the second he'd first set eyes on her, he'd hoped to find a way to make her want to be with him. From the way she'd talked to him tonight in front of Maddie and Nathan, from the way she'd been with Nathan, he wasn't very confident she wanted to be with him any more.

Placing the garments back on the chair, he walked across to the dressing table where she'd left her phone and picked it up. His thumb hovering over the screen, he hesitated, then drew in a tight breath. No, he wasn't going this route. He was desperate, yes, fearing she was pulling away from him. Spying on her, though, how pathetic would that make him? He was placing the phone back when the bathroom door opened behind him.

'Oh my God,' Kiara said, her expression alarmed as he turned to face her. 'You almost gave me a heart attack.'

'That scary, hey?' David shrugged disconsolately.

Which clearly irritated her. He seemed to be doing that a lot lately. He put it down to the fact that she was obviously unhappy here, but still it was hurtful.

'You might have announced your presence or something,' she said, clutching her towel tight to her chest as she walked across the room.

Gathering that she wanted access to the dressing table and that he was in the way, David moved aside. 'I didn't realise I had to announce myself. I do sleep here, Kia,' he reminded her with a sad smile.

'You caught me by surprise, that's all.' Selecting her night attire from her drawer, she walked past him to the bed.

David watched as she discarded the towel. 'You and

Nathan seemed very cosy tonight,' he commented after a second, his eyes travelling down the soft curve of her back.

Quickly she fed her feet into her shorts, wobbling a little as she did. 'What's that supposed to mean?' she asked, picking up her top and pulling it over her head as she faced him.

'Nothing.' He shrugged. 'You just looked cosy.'

Kiara laughed. 'You are joking, aren't you? He's a friend. *Our* friend.'

'As is Maddie,' David pointed out.

'Oh for goodness' sake.' Kiara gathered up her hair, tying it into a haphazard knot on top of her head. 'Are you seriously telling me you're jealous of Nathan? We've known him for years. He's also a happily married man, in case you haven't noticed.'

He continued to watch as she yanked down the duvet ready to climb into bed and then snatched up her water glass from the bedside locker. She was clearly irritated now. Didn't he deserve an explanation of some sort, though?

'It just seemed a bit intimate,' he pushed, wishing she wouldn't be so flippant about his feelings, as if they were inconsequential. 'Maddie noticed it too.'

She stopped and turned around, her expression now one of disbelief. 'You're being ridiculous, David. We were just chatting. I'm tired. I need to go to bed.' She shook her head in exasperation and turned back to the bathroom.

Stepping quickly after her, he caught hold of her arm. 'Nice underwear,' he said, nodding towards where it lay on the chair. 'Is it new?'

'Yes, it's new.' She looked up at him curiously. 'I bought it with the token you gave me for Christmas.'

He scanned her eyes. Soulful deep umber eyes shot through with iridescent flecks of gold, they'd been so full of vulnerability after she'd been attacked. All he'd ever wanted to do was protect her. To protect her from herself. It was clear to him that she fell for the wrong kind of men. That arrogant prat Jake she'd been going out with was evidence of that. But now he was upsetting her, and he didn't want to do that. 'You smell nice,' he murmured, burying his face in her neck, breathing in the musky, feminine scent of her under the rose blossom shower gel she liked to use.

'David, stop it.' Kiara tried to squirm away from him as he sought her lips with his. 'David! Let go!'

TEN

Kiara

Glancing towards the door as someone came into the salon, Kiara was not entirely surprised to see it was Nathan. She shouldn't have called him. She'd been worried after David had mentioned that Maddie had noticed them in the kitchen together. She would hate for her friend to read too much into it. Realising that Nathan was tied up with the children and that her timing was bad, she'd told him that David and she had had a few words but assured him it was nothing to worry about. Nathan had clearly been concerned, though, enough to come here today.

Catching his eye, she mouthed, 'One sec,' then gestured one of the girls who was in between customers to come across. 'Do you mind if Rose finishes your blow dry, Ally?' she asked, turning back to her client. 'Someone's just dropped in unexpectedly and I have to have a quick word with him.'

'No, no problem. I'm loving the colour.' Ally smiled, eyeing her new lowlights enthusiastically in the mirror.

'It's fab, isn't it?' Rose said. 'Really suits you.'

Kiara left her client in Rose's capable hands and hurried across to Nathan. She couldn't help overhearing Ally's stage whisper as she went. 'Cor, he's a bit hot, isn't he? He could drop in on me any time.'

She hid a flicker of annoyance and fixed a smile in place. The last thing she wanted was rumours flying around, especially with a certain person now working here. 'To what do I owe the pleasure?' she asked Nathan, who was looking her over curiously.

'I tried to call you back and I couldn't get hold of you. I was in the area so I thought I'd drop by,' he said with an awkward shrug. He was worried. Of course he would be.

'I'm fine,' she assured him, glancing quickly over her shoulder for ears flapping in the hope of juicy gossip. 'Do you fancy a coffee?' She indicated the kitchen, where they could talk in private.

Nathan checked his watch, appearing to deliberate, then, 'Why not?'

Kiara led the way into the kitchen, then turned to close the door.

'So what happened?' he asked as she walked across to fill two mugs from the coffee filter jug.

She hesitated. 'Nothing,' she said, turning back to him with a tremulous smile.

'Right.' He arched his eyebrows, unconvinced. 'So why the call?'

Kiara hesitated. 'David got a bit ... well, jealous, I suppose, and we argued. But obviously you gathered that much.'

'Badly?' Nathan asked, his forehead creasing into a troubled frown.

She handed him his coffee, strong and black the way she

knew he liked it. 'Badly enough.' She sighed and glanced down. 'He said some things and, um ...' She faltered. 'He's acting strangely,' she blurted, and then stopped, unsure how much Nathan would believe.

'Strangely how?' He narrowed his eyes.

'Differently. I can't quite explain.' Kiara hesitated for another second, and then, 'Do you think he might be seeing someone else?' she asked.

'David?' Nathan laughed dubiously. 'I'm sorry, but I can't see him for one minute being interested in anyone else. In any case, when? Who? As far as I'm aware, he goes from home to work and back again. Has he been out a lot lately? Have you noticed any suspect phone calls?'

'No.' Kiara shook her head. 'But it could be someone at work, couldn't it? Another teacher, perhaps. Someone he feels understands him. They would have a lot in common. More than David and I have had lately, at any rate.'

Nathan was silent for a moment. Kiara could see from the wary look on his face that the wheels were going round, that he was considering the possibilities. Then he laughed again, incredulously. 'No,' he said with an adamant shake of his head. 'You're way off the mark, Kiara. There's no way Maddie would become involved with David. They're just friends.'

'No,' Kiara said quickly. 'Of course not. I just thought ... They've always been very close, but ... Forget I said anything. I was racking my brains, looking for reasons he would seem so unlike himself.'

Nathan looked somewhat subdued, but the hand rubbing his neck indicated his agitation. 'Have you considered that there might be something else troubling him?' he asked after a loaded pause. 'The fact that you're not sharing things with him, possibly? He's a sensitive bloke, Kiara. He'll know there's something going on with you. Don't you think it might be an idea to try to put his mind at rest?'

She drew in a breath. 'You're right. And about what I just said. It's only that his behaviour has been so odd. I don't know, I jumped to conclusions, I suppose.'

'Wrong ones,' Nathan said firmly, but there was a flash of something in his eyes, just briefly; a flicker of uncertainty. 'I should go. Maddie's expecting me back.' Taking a gulp of his coffee, he planted the mug back on the work surface, studied it for a contemplative second, then looked back at Kiara, his expression now somewhere between cautious and disappointed.

She'd upset him, planted seeds of doubt in his head. He clearly wasn't impressed. She should have thought it through before shooting her mouth off. What was wrong with her? 'You won't tell her what I said, will you?' She stepped after him as he turned to the door. 'About my doubts.'

Nathan smiled, but it wasn't his usual easy smile this time. 'No, I won't. It might be a good idea if you talk to her, though. You promised to ring her,' he added, walking away with a shake of his head.

He was at the salon door when one of the girls called to him and gave him a wave. He squinted in her direction, but it was clear from his face that he didn't recognise her.

Watching him go, his head bent and clearly deep in thought, Kiara thanked God for small mercies. She *had* to be more careful. Things were complicated enough as they were. She was in danger of blowing her relationship with Nathan if she allowed her emotions to get the better of her. The last thing she wanted was for him to start pulling away from her.

ELEVEN

Maddie

Maddie checked her phone for missed calls. There were none. Kiara hadn't rung her as she'd promised she would. Maddie had left a couple of messages on her voicemail, the last suggesting they meet up for a pub meal and a good chat. She hadn't called back. Maddie had wondered at first if it was because she didn't recognise her new number, but she'd texted her since, telling her she was concerned about her. A new frustration growing inside her that her friend hadn't felt able to confide in her and now seemed to be avoiding her, she rang Kiara's salon, and was relieved when the girl who answered said they'd had a cancellation and could fit her in immediately.

She wasn't yet sure how she was going to get Kiara to open up, but she had to. She'd clearly been feeling extremely fragile on New Year's Eve. Too much alcohol had obviously caused her worries to come tumbling out, and she would need someone to talk to. David would be shocked to the core if he knew she imagined he was trying to manipulate her into staying with him by presenting himself as some kind of spider-catcher hero. It was ludicrous. Maddie had never known him to be anything but gentle and caring. Why wouldn't Kiara have told him about her hospital visit? It was all so odd.

'Bye, Boomer. Daddy will take you walkies soon.' She smiled reassuringly and patted the dog, who was panting hopefully. 'Off to the hairdresser's. Back later,' she called to Nathan, who was busy getting the children suitably wrapped up for their trip to the park.

'Don't do anything too drastic,' Nathan called back. He'd always said he liked her naturally curly boring brown bob, but actually, after being so shaken up seeing him with Kiara, she was considering something a bit more adventurous – highlights possibly. A new look might not transform her into the sexually alluring creature she felt Kiara was, but at least it might brighten her up a bit. Also, the length of time she would be there would give her plenty of opportunity to talk to Kiara. Hopefully her friend would have time for a coffee later and they could have a chat in private.

'Are you going to bring us some sweets back?' Josh asked, skidding into the hall as she reached for her coat.

'Hmm?' Maddie looked at him. 'What's the magic word?'

'Please.' Josh adopted his best angelic expression.

She couldn't help but smile. 'It depends how good you are. Best behaviour at the park, okay? And remember, Dad will be reporting back.'

'Yay!' Josh twirled around, clearly confident that Nathan would report back favourably. 'Haribo Starmix,' he said, heading happily to the kitchen with Boomer bounding excitedly alongside him.

'Kinder Surprise,' Ellie called.

'We'll see.' Maddie shook her head in amusement. It was too much to hope that the two would agree on anything. She would probably end up bringing both. Still, Saturday was sweetie day, and they hadn't had any major fallings-out for a whole two days.

Half an hour later, after picking up her repeat sleeping pill prescription from the chemist, she rushed through the salon door and stopped in her tracks. 'Sophie?' She squinted at the woman who had come to greet her. It was her, she was sure of it, the girl Jake had brought to their long-ago bonfire at university.

'Madeline! How lovely to see you.' Sophie smiled delightedly. Maddie wasn't sure why she would be delighted, since she'd been pretty awful to her back then. She felt herself flush with embarrassment as she remembered referring to her as Jake's latest pathetic conquest. 'You look absolutely amazing,' Sophie gushed, coming to help her off with her coat.

'You too,' Maddie said, meaning it. Sophie had been an attractive girl, she recalled, open-faced and pretty. Since then, she'd blossomed. Her once wild red hair was flowing in soft waves down her back. Her eyes, a myriad of forest greens, were dazzling and expertly made up. Wearing nothing but a sweep of foundation, and with her usual baggy sweater pulled on over a T-shirt and jeans in ten seconds flat, Maddie felt distinctly dowdy by comparison.

'Thank you.' Sophie accepted the compliment gracefully. 'Working here helps. Kiara and the other girls have been so lovely, giving me tips on my make-up and hair.'

Maddie blinked in surprise. Kiara had obviously decided to let bygones be bygones and befriended her, which was magnanimous of her. Sophie hadn't been to blame for Jake's unfeeling behaviour, but having her around had to be a reminder of one of the worst periods of Kiara's life. The awful attack she'd suffered had left her bruised, emotionally and physically. She'd made up her mind not to let it define her, but Sophie must surely be a reminder of all that she'd tried to leave behind her.

'So, how have you been?' Sophie asked, leading Maddie to a chair, a contemplative furrow forming in her brow as she ran her fingers through her unruly straggle of hair. From which Maddie gathered Sophie would be doing her hair, which was okay. She'd been happy to grab whatever appointment they had if it meant she could talk to Kiara.

'Busy,' Maddie answered, smiling in the mirror. 'Between two children and work, I scarcely have time to breathe.'

'Tell me about it,' Sophie said with an empathetic roll of her eyes. 'My two are a full-time job on their own.'

'You're married?' Maddie asked. Then cursed her clumsiness as it occurred to her she might not be.

'Fourteen years,' Sophie confirmed, waggling her ring finger.

'Wow!' Maddie quickly did the maths. That must mean she'd got married a year or so after that ill-fated Bonfire Night, which had definitely been one to remember.

'I know. You'd get less time for murder, right?' Sophie rolled her eyes. 'It's not all bad, though. The kids are at an age where they're full on, fourteen and twelve, a boy and a girl, fondly referred to as "Moody" and "Stroppy", but Jake's great with them, and he does do his fair share. So, what are we doing for you today?'

Stunned, Maddie simply stared into the mirror as Sophie looked at her expectantly. She'd married Jake? The boy who'd declared in her presence that he was in love with Kiara? Had she already been pregnant that evening – with his child? It was certainly possible. She tried to get her head around it, feeling another pang of guilt at having made such a derogatory comment about her.

'We worked things out,' Sophie said quietly, no doubt sensing her astonishment.

Maddie nodded and attempted to look less bewildered. 'Colour,' she said quickly, changing the subject, which was one that Sophie clearly didn't want to pursue. 'I thought blonde highlights and maybe some warm darker tones? And a trim, obviously.'

'Great idea. It will really suit you.' Sophie smiled encouragingly. 'I'll just go and grab some colour charts and you can have a browse. Can I get you a drink? Coffee? Tea?'

'Coffee would be lovely, thanks. White, one sugar.'

Maddie attempted to gather herself. What on earth was going on here? Why would Kiara have entertained the idea of employing Sophie knowing who she was married to? But then it was possible she hadn't known when she'd interviewed her. Where *was* Kiara, come to think of it? She'd been here earlier. Maddie had asked when she'd rung. Might she really be trying to avoid her? It was possible she had upset her in some way, she supposed. Muddled sometimes when she was on the sleeping pills and sleep-deprived when she was off them, she might have said or done something without realising or even remembering. But how could she put it right if she didn't know? Thinking she had no other choice, she decided to take the bull by the horns and ask her friend outright where she stood.

She was about to send her a succinct text when Kiara herself appeared, coming down the stairs from the treatment rooms on the floor above. She looked taken aback for a second as her gaze fell on Maddie. Then, stopping to give some instructions about a client's colour on the way, she came across to her.

'Sophie?' Maddie mouthed, eyeing her questioningly as she reached her. She was trying to keep it low-key, but she was sure Kiara would understand what she was asking, and why.

Kiara glanced over her shoulder, then turned back to her. 'I don't bear grudges,' she whispered. 'I'll give you a call and we'll chat later. I have to dash. I have a doctor's appointment.'

Maddie watched flabbergasted as she spun on her heel and hurried across the salon, grabbing her coat from one of the hooks and disappearing through the door without a backwards glance. She might be wrong here, but she had a distinct feeling that

Kiara didn't want to chat later; chat to her at all for that matter. Why? Why was she acting so strangely? Despite the intimacy she'd witnessed between her and Nathan, she didn't believe there was anything going on between them. Nathan had put her mind at rest. Hadn't he?

TWELVE

Kiara

Driving straight from the salon to the brand-new fourth-floor apartment for an exclusive viewing, Kiara tried to ignore a twinge of guilt. She felt bad for David, but for the sake of her mental health she had to get this ball rolling now he'd finally agreed to consider moving. She'd reached the point where she'd been considering moving without him, but there was no way she would have been able to secure a mortgage on such a perfect property on her own. She couldn't stay in the house. She simply didn't want to *be* in it, her nerves fraught and her stomach constantly churning.

David had tried to help her get over her fears, he really had. And he'd been right, at first she had loved the barn conversion with its homey feel and picturesque location. Once they'd moved in, though, closely followed by the original natural inhabitants, her dreams of cosy evenings around the fireside and dinner parties on the patio had evaporated. David still insisted the spiders only came in during mating season, but that just wasn't the case. 'They don't have a calendar! They drop in when they feel like it!' she'd once yelled at him. Knowing how terrified she was, he'd stopped short of calling her neurotic, but he had said she was only seeing them because subconsciously she was always on the lookout for them, that her brain was pre-programmed to send a message to her eyes, which would automatically dart around every room she entered. Kiara conceded that that might be the case, but that didn't stop them being there, appearing out of nowhere to petrify her. She simply couldn't understand why he didn't get that it had turned her dream home into a nightmare, that it was impacting on her day-to-day life.

He would try over and over again to reassure her, his patience seemingly endless. He was always that, patient, quiet and courteous. Also unadventurous and predictable. With no hobbies apart from the garden, which Kiara felt bad about depriving him of, he was always at home on the evenings and weekends. She wished he wasn't, that he would find something to do independently of her. He wouldn't be budged, though, maintaining that he was content to stay home. 'You can get pretty much everything on TV now,' he would say, settling in his armchair, remote in hand. 'And we have our own wine cellar, so what's the point?'

There were several points, but Kiara had given up trying to make him see that a) she wouldn't go down to the cellar to save her life, b) she needed something other than the four walls to look at sometimes, and c) whenever she suggested something to watch that interested her, he didn't object as such, but reaching for his Kindle was an unsubtle enough indication that he was bored. She'd even called him controlling in one heated argument. Yet he wasn't, not overtly. Certainly not in a way that anyone else would notice.

She'd been comfortable with the way he was when they'd

first started dating. She'd felt secure with him, protected. She hadn't wanted to go out much after being attacked in what she'd thought was a safe place. Dressing up to go out nightclubbing or drinking in bars just didn't appeal, and David had always said he preferred her natural look, so she hadn't felt she had to try too hard with him. Now, though she still cared for him, she felt stifled. Trapped. She wanted to go out, dress up for an occasion, stretch her wings and rediscover the part of herself she felt she'd lost, but somehow she felt David didn't want her to. It was terribly difficult to explain that she didn't need his protection any more. Didn't want to be thought of as fragile by anyone. She was a grown woman, running her own business. She needed her space, a degree of independence. But how was she to tell him all this without him perceiving it as rejection? David seemed to exist to make sure she was safe. To Kiara it felt more like being contained.

Perhaps she was being neurotic. Anyone who knew David would think she was. Maddie, who adored him, would certainly think so. Burying a sigh, she headed into the apartment block using the security code she'd been given.

She loved the whole feel of the place even before she'd reached the fourth floor. It was all so clean and white, like a little bit of heaven. Her idea of heaven anyway. Pulling out her phone as she walked towards the apartment, she was about to press call when the door to the stairwell opened behind her. He was here, bang on time. She'd guessed he would be.

'Hi.' He smiled, leaning to press a kiss to her cheek then producing the key from his pocket. 'Do you want to have a wander around on your own?' he asked, turning to push the key into the lock. 'Get a feel for the place?'

'Let's do it together,' she suggested, stepping in before him as he opened the door and held it for her.

The cleanliness hit her immediately, the vast light spacious-ness of even the hallway. Heading towards what she guessed was the lounge, she was immediately drawn to the wall-length patio doors, the view from which overlooked the cathedral, which would be stunning lit up at night.

'Big, isn't it?' he said as she twirled around taking in the pristine white walls with no dark corners where spiders might hide.

The kitchen was the same: airy and spotless, all white marble worktops with ultra-modern handleless cupboards beneath. No clunking pipes, rattling radiators or original beams that would harbour a host of unwanted visitors. No cobwebs.

'Shall we check out the bedrooms?' he asked, sliding an arm around her as she ran a hand over one of the surfaces, loving the smooth feel of it under her fingertips.

'Let's,' she agreed, nodding keenly.

She was standing at the large picture window of the master bedroom, looking at the view over the city skyline, when she sensed him approaching her.

'What do you think?' he asked, threading his arms around her.

'I love it,' she whispered, nestling into him.

'I thought you would,' he murmured, his lips finding the sensitive spot on the side of her neck. 'Do you think David will go for it?'

THIRTEEN

Maddie

'Like the hair,' Nathan said, coming into the kitchen, Boomer and the children charging excitedly ahead of him. Maddie had a sneaking suspicion the kids were rather more keen to get their hands on their promised sweets than to greet their mum.

'Thanks.' Her mind still on her brief meeting with Kiara at the salon this morning, she smiled distractedly and gave Boomer a fuss, then reached for his water bowl to top it up. As she did, she noticed the jam jar Josh had obviously parked on the worktop, inside of which was a caterpillar pupa. She didn't mind him collecting bugs and insects; he was fascinated by them, spending hours in their still untamed garden, or else delighting in finding some creepy-crawly thing that had emerged indoors with the renovations constantly under way. She was sure he was following in Nathan's footsteps, which was no bad thing. She did wish he wouldn't leave them in the kitchen, though.

Turning around, she sighed as the little man himself headed

for her bag on the island. 'They're mine,' he said, digging inside it and grabbing the Starmix before Ellie could.

'I *know*,' Ellie replied with a despairing roll of her eyes. 'I don't want them anyway. I have my Kinder Surprise and I'm going to keep the surprise all to myself.'

'There's one egg each,' Maddie intervened. 'And the sweets are to share, Josh, no arguing.'

Knitting his forehead, Josh did a quick mental calculation, and then obviously decided it wasn't a bad deal. 'Okay.' He shrugged and scooted back towards the lounge, the sweets in one hand, his egg in the other.

'And ask before helping yourself in future,' Maddie called after him. She wasn't keen on them going into her bag. She'd drummed into them never to put anything into their mouths they shouldn't, but there was always the possibility they could be tempted by something that looked enticing, such as her pretty blue zopiclone tablets. She'd recently renewed her prescription after another bout of insomnia, even though she really didn't like taking them. Nathan understood that she didn't sleep well without them – though she wasn't sure he knew to what extent – but he did worry about the side effects. She'd accused him of all sorts of things last time she was on them. Only little things, like moving her car keys, but it highlighted her forgetfulness, her tendency to be a little delusional. Still, she wasn't sure that lying awake most of the night with all sorts of random things running scattergun through her mind, plus the exhaustion that followed, which made her equally forgetful, was a better alternative.

'I give them five minutes before we need to referee.' Nathan sighed resignedly from where he was unloading the shopping bags he'd brought in with him.

'You've been a while,' Maddie commented, glancing curiously towards him as she filled the kettle.

'I dropped the kids off at my mother's while I went to get

the shopping and some stuff I'll need for my trip. Sorry, I probably should have called.' He smiled apologetically.

Maddie's heart sank more than it normally did at the thought of him going away again. She could usually rely on a couple of evenings in with Kiara to ward off the solitude, and a good chinwag over the phone in between if she needed someone other than the children to talk to, especially after visiting her mother, which always left her feeling hollow and broken. But with Kiara seeming to be distancing herself for reasons she still didn't understand, she would feel more lonely than ever.

'How is your mum?' she asked. She liked Nathan's mother. She still worked and had made a new life for herself after her divorce, so they didn't see a great deal of her, but she loved to spend time with her grandkids when she could.

'Good. She's off on some girls' trip to Portugal in a couple of weeks. God help the local male population.'

Maddie laughed. 'Good for her.'

'I picked up some things for a special meal later.' Nathan walked across to where she stood at the work surface and circled her with his arms. 'I thought we could snuggle up and watch a film together. And then maybe have an early night?' he suggested, pressing his lips lightly to the side of her neck.

Maddie twisted to face him as his kisses grew skin-tinglingly intense. 'Does this mean I'm on a promise, Dr Anderson?' she asked, threading her arms around his neck.

His mouth curved into a smile. 'Most definitely, Mrs Anderson,' he whispered huskily, his mouth finding hers.

But as his kiss grew deeper, his tongue pleasurably seeking hers, her mobile ringing on the worktop caused her to pull away. Quickly she scrambled to answer it, and then sighed inwardly. 'Right,' she said curtly. 'Thank you, Joe, but I'm pretty sure I didn't ring the Windows helpline, so why don't you bugger off?'

Cutting the call with a scowl, she glanced at Nathan, whose

expression was a mixture of curiosity and amusement. 'Scam call?'

Maddie nodded. 'I hoped it might be Kiara calling back,' she said. 'You haven't spoken to Dave recently, have you?' She was wondering whether he might have given Nathan some hint of what might be wrong. Kiara must be avoiding her because of something she'd said or done.

Nathan furrowed his brow. 'No. Why?'

Maddie hesitated. Was she getting things out of proportion? 'She's still not returning my calls,' she confided miserably.

'What, deliberately?'

'I don't know.' She shrugged. 'It's just not like her. Do you think it's something to do with New Year's Eve?'

'How so?' Nathan turned away to collect mugs from the rack.

'Well, I was upset finding you two together in the kitchen. Do you think she might have picked up on something and wondered if it was to do with the situation between her and David? The house move thing, I mean. I did appear to side with him, didn't I?'

Nathan considered. 'No. In fact, you pretty much kept the evening going,' he assured her. 'She's probably just busy, and possibly worried about those hospital tests.'

'But that's my point,' Maddie picked up. 'We've always talked about everything in the past. Why wouldn't she want to talk to me about that?' *Particularly as she's spoken to you*, she didn't add. 'I was at her salon today. She knew I was coming, yet she didn't find me to have a chat, which she always does. Oh. Sophie's working there, by the way. Do you remember her from uni, the girl Jake brought along to that bonfire party? You could have knocked me over with a feather when I saw her.'

'Really?' Nathan sounded surprised. His attention, though, was on making the coffee. It wouldn't be that riveting to him, Maddie supposed.

'She and Jake got married.'

Nathan missed the cup with the water. That had obviously got his attention. 'Blimey, that's a turn-up for the books.'

'Too right,' Maddie agreed. 'I'm assuming Kiara might not have known when she employed her. Even so, it's strange that she would have wanted her working there, don't you think?'

Nathan considered. 'I guess. But then the Jake thing was years ago now, wasn't it? And it was hardly Sophie's fault. Kiara obviously decided it was history.'

'I suppose.' Maddie pondered. He was probably right. Hadn't Kiara said she didn't bear grudges? But still, it did seem a bit odd.

'So did you get to speak to Kiara?' he asked.

'Not really. She was upstairs in the treatment rooms. It was almost as if she was avoiding me. And then when she did see me, she rushed out with barely a word. Do you think there's something else? Something I've done to upset her that she's reluctant to tell me about?'

Nathan frowned thoughtfully. 'I doubt it. Knowing Kiara, she would have said something. Did she say where she was going?'

'A doctor's appointment, but wasn't that a perfect opening to share anything she might be worrying about?'

'Except she was in a rush. Plus she was at work,' Nathan pointed out. 'I doubt she's avoiding you, Mads. You're probably just being oversensitive.'

Maddie searched his eyes. They were flecked with concern, and something else. Wariness. She glanced down and back. 'Imagining things, you mean?'

'I didn't say that.' He sighed in obvious frustration. 'The sleeping pills do make you a bit ...'

'Delusional?' Maddie suggested.

'Distracted,' Nathan corrected diplomatically. 'You're tired, that's all, not surprisingly with the nightmares on top of juggling the kids and your job. You need to worry more about yourself and less about other people. Give her some time. I'm sure she'll get back to you.'

'I suppose,' Maddie said, an uneasy feeling creeping through her nevertheless. She was tired, yes, but she wasn't imagining Kiara being off with her, not unless she was also imagining the unanswered calls and texts on her phone. Kiara had never behaved that way with her before. Her concerns were valid, she was sure they were, yet Nathan seemed keen to dismiss them. Or was she imagining that too?

FOURTEEN

THREE MONTHS AGO

Maddie

Maddie stifled a yawn and tried to concentrate on the paperwork she was hoping to get through in her lunch hour. Having decided to come off the pills again, she wasn't sleeping well, but she was wondering whether it was something she would just have to live with rather than become dependent on pills that clearly were making her delusional. Last week she'd imagined someone was at the front door and climbed out of bed to answer it. It was half past three in the morning. Nathan, who was due at the airport early for yet another trip away, hadn't been impressed. Forgetfulness was one thing. Hallucinating callers in the small hours was quite another. She wasn't sure how well she would function without the pills, but she owed it to Nathan and the children to try. Also the kids in her charge, who faced more challenges than those in mainstream schools and needed her to be focused.

She pondered the situation with Kiara, which wasn't

helping her state of mind. Her friend was at least returning her calls now, but they weren't having meaningful conversations. Maddie had asked her outright about her health, reminding her that she'd told her she was dashing off to the doctor's when she'd seen her at the salon. Kiara had brushed it off, saying she'd had some tests but that there was nothing to worry about. Still, though, Maddie was concerned. Should she ring her again? Try and get her to open up?

She reached for her phone, but then, realising the children were coming back into the classroom, reminded herself she needed to leave her personal worries at home and pushed it aside.

Once the children were at their desks, she decided to get them back into learning mode with a brainteaser, a fun activity that would stimulate their cognitive ability but not feel like work. She could certainly do with stimulating a few of her own sluggish brain cells.

'Right, children, settle down,' she said over the excited chatter. 'I need some help with this sentence.' Turning to the blackboard, she chalked up: *The yolk of the egg is white*, and then, underneath it: *the yolk of the egg is white*.

'So,' she turned back to them with a teasing smile, 'can any of you bright sparks tell me which is the correct sentence?'

'Neither, miss! Egg yolks are yellow!' was the unanimous answer.

'Correct.' Maddie grinned as a sea of delighted faces looked back at her. That had certainly refocused them, and also reminded her why she loved what she did. 'Right, how do you fancy doing some painting this afternoon?' she asked.

Minutes later, having set them the task of painting with white and yellow, plus one other colour, she was impressed with their inventiveness. There were green jungles with big yellow suns, a huge white ice cream outlined in the same brown as the cone so it would stand out against the white paper, and one sheet of paper that was blank apart from some strategically placed black blobs. 'I bet you can't guess what it is?' The boy whose masterpiece it was looked expectantly up at her.

'Ooh, I think I can,' Maddie said, perusing it thoughtfully. 'Now, let me see ... Eyes, nose, mouth,' she indicated the various blobs, 'and buttons. It's a snowman!'

'Correct!' He beamed her a smile and looked very pleased with himself.

After a fruitful afternoon, which had hopefully sent the children home feeling inspired, Maddie was busy clearing up ready for the next day when her phone alerted her to a text. Nathan. She smiled and checked it. She was so looking forward to him being back home. *Setting off for Quito shortly,* he'd sent. *Will probably have to wait for the airport to sign off on biological samples. May take some time. May also involve a bribe to make sure nothing confiscated. Wish me luck. See you in a couple of days. Kiss the kids for me.*

She felt a mixture of elation and fear. Elation because he was on his way home, fear because, although he'd already done the arduous boat trip from his base, he still had the long drive to the airport, avoiding traffic jams and, more worryingly, landslides. *Will do. Stay safe. Can't wait to cuddle up with you,* she texted back.

He pinged back a reply. *Close your eyes and imagine all the unspeakable things I'm going to do to you.*

Maddie laughed and felt a whole lot better for being in touch with him. *I would, but still at school. Might look a bit odd.*

Nathan sent back a crying-with-laughter emoji, followed by *Will call you.*

Realising she might be late to pick up Josh and Ellie from the childminder, she was rushing to collect her things when her phone rang. She answered quickly, purring, 'I hope this is an obscene phone call,' in her best sexy voice.

'Er, no,' a voice responded uncertainly. 'I'm not normally in the habit of making obscene phone calls.'

Hell. Maddie blushed furiously. 'Dave! How are you?'

'Confused.' David laughed.

'Sorry.' Maddie cringed. 'I thought you were Nathan.'

'I gathered. I think.' He was taking it in good humour. As he would. Maddie was glad it was him. It could have been anyone calling.

'He said he would ring and, um ...' She half attempted an explanation, then stopped before she embarrassed herself further. 'How are you?' she asked. With Kiara being so distant, she hadn't had much contact with David either. She missed him. Worried about him, too.

'Honestly?' David sighed expansively. 'I've been better.'

Maddie frowned, the thought occurring that her friend's evasive behaviour might be something to do with relationship issues. Kiara knew that Maddie cared very much for David and might be reluctant to confide in her. 'Problems?' she probed carefully.

'I'm not sure.' David paused, then, 'Can I ask you something, Mads? I'll understand if you don't want to break a confidence, it's just I'm going out of my mind with worry.'

'Of course,' Maddie replied, a knot of apprehension tightening her stomach. 'Ask away. I'll answer if I can.'

He hesitated. 'It's Kiara,' he said with a sharp intake of breath. 'It might be nothing of the sort, but ... is she having an affair?'

'What?' Maddie laughed in astonishment.

'Has she said anything to you?' David asked, a desperate edge to his voice. 'I know how close you two are, and I wondered ... I asked Nathe what he thought, but he said he very much doubted it. He thinks she loves me and that I'm imagining things.'

'She does,' Maddie replied quickly. 'I'm sure she does.' She tried to reassure him, but in reality she didn't feel so certain. She'd wondered on several occasions whether Kiara had stuck with David because he was a safe option. It had been clear from the outset that he thought the world of her. He would do anything for her. She couldn't imagine that Kiara would even consider cheating on him. If she was, it would have to be with someone pretty bloody special, that was for sure.

'She has a strange way of showing it.' David sighed heavily again. 'We barely communicate lately, let alone ...' He trailed off awkwardly, and Maddie felt awful for him. There she'd been, advertising the fact that she and Nathan were good together, and David's heart was quite clearly breaking.

'She's probably feeling a bit down,' she suggested. That might explain her odd behaviour. Perhaps she'd felt unable to talk to Maddie about how she was feeling for fear of things getting back to David.

'About the house, you mean?'

'Possibly.' Maddie knew that was a bone of contention between them.

'We're moving,' David announced. 'To the apartment she wanted.'

'Really?' Maddie was doubly astonished. He'd obviously realised just how unhappy Kiara was and moved things along swiftly. And if that wasn't proof enough of how much he cared for her, nothing would be. Kiara *couldn't* be cheating on him. It was incomprehensible that she would risk losing someone who would give his life to make her happy. 'But what about the house?' she asked tentatively, aware of how much he loved it there.

'I'm not happy about selling it,' he replied despondently, 'but I can't lose her, Maddie. I'll do whatever I have to.'

Would it be enough to mend their marriage, though? Maddie wondered. Clearly there were huge problems if it had come to this.

'That's why I rang,' David went on. 'Well, partly. I wondered if you and Nathe could help out. I have a removal company for the heavier stuff, so it's just boxes and anything that might be fragile. It's not a problem if you'd rather not, or you have something else on. I just ...'

Thought it would be less like a funeral and more like a celebration, Maddie guessed he meant. 'When do you move?' she asked him gently.

'Next weekend. It's all signed and sealed.' David sounded more dejected by the second.

'We'd love to,' Maddie said, mentally crossing her fingers that Nathan wouldn't mind. She was sure he wouldn't. He would be exhausted for a couple of days when he got back, but he'd be recovered by then and keen to help out.

'Thanks, Mads,' David said quietly. 'I could use the support.'

She would bet he could. Maddie felt wretched for him.

FIFTEEN

Nathan had been as shocked as Maddie was when she'd told him the news. He'd understood why she wanted to support David, and reluctantly agreed to help out with the house move, although he thought it was going to be an extremely awkward situation to be in.

He'd been right. Maddie had never felt so uncomfortable in her life. Far from not talking, Kiara was chattering on nineteen to the dozen, gushing about the apartment. She seemed to be on a high. Maddie tried to look enthusiastic, but she wondered what the point of all this was if she was having an affair. If it were true, which Maddie still couldn't believe, did Kiara intend to go on deceiving him? To leave him? To stay, hoping David would leave *her*, here in her dream apartment? And where would that leave David? Devastated. Utterly. That much was obvious from the hurt in his eyes when she grabbed the opportunity to have a quiet word with him out on the balcony.

'It's a beautiful view, isn't it?' she said, watching him looking out over it without seeming to see it.

'Spectacular,' he agreed. Clasping his hands over the balustrade, he took a sharp breath as he glanced towards the ground. 'Vertigo.' He smiled embarrassedly. 'I just hope I don't end up taking in the view on the way down.'

Maddie felt her chest constrict. His fear of heights didn't bother him when he was inside. Kiara had said it herself. It bothered him here, though, standing on his own balcony. He was going to hate it here. Did Kiara realise what David had done for her? The sacrifice he'd made? Did she realise what it would do to him if she were to cheat on him? It would kill him. 'Don't talk like that, David, please.' She reached to place a hand on his arm.

'Sorry.' He glanced apologetically at her. 'I'm being an idiot, feeling sorry for myself. Ignore me.'

She gave his arm a squeeze. 'Just promise you'll call me if you need to talk. Any time. Okay?'

He nodded and ran a hand over his face. 'I will,' he said, his voice tight. 'Thanks, Mads.'

'Do you have any proof?' she asked quietly as they both gazed out at the cathedral, which looked more sombre suddenly than spectacular.

David shook his head. 'Nothing but a gut feeling. The way she is with me. Generally. She's different. Pulling away from me. I can't really explain it.'

He didn't need to. Maddie felt the same. She quite clearly hadn't been imagining the way Kiara had been with her.

'We should go back in.' David nodded over his shoulder to where Nathan and Kiara appeared to be attempting to manoeuvre the sofa. 'Here, let me,' he said, stepping back through the patio doors and moving to take over Kiara's end. 'This thing weighs a ton.'

'Thanks.' Kiara smiled, but she didn't look at him, Maddie noticed. 'We thought it would be perfect opposite the patio doors, looking out onto the balcony, didn't we, Nathe?'

'Might as well take in the view at night,' Nathan said,

glancing awkwardly in Maddie's direction. He was obviously feeling uncomfortable. Maddie couldn't blame him.

'Is here okay?' David asked as they lowered the sofa to the floor.

Kiara knitted her brow. 'I'm not quite sure now.'

As Kiara pondered, David glanced at Maddie, giving her a small appreciative smile. Nathan kneaded his forehead, then shoved his hands in his pockets and waited.

Kiara cocked her head to one side, appraising the sofa thoughtfully, then, 'Could we have it a little more to the left?' She glanced hopefully at Nathan rather than David. With no one seeming to know where to look, awkward was about right. You could cut the atmosphere in here with a knife.

'Shall I go and get some drinks?' Maddie offered, twirling in the direction of the hall and the pristine white kitchen, which was a far cry from the homey farmhouse kitchen at the barn conversion. Clinical almost. Definitely not somewhere she felt David would feel at home, though Kiara clearly did, gushing about the spaciousness of the apartment as she'd showed Maddie around.

'Nothing for me,' Nathan said behind her. 'Driving, sorry. We'll need to leave pretty soon,' she heard him add. 'We should get back to the kids.'

Maddie was surprised. She'd booked the babysitter until late, meaning Nathan was making excuses to leave. He really must feel uncomfortable. 'Dave? Red or white?' she called. They'd brought both, along with some glasses, which they'd hoped might help relax things once the heavy work was out of the way.

'Red, thanks,' David called back. 'Just a small one.'

Feeling in need of a large one, Maddie carried on to the kitchen. Eventually finding the fridge amongst an array of featureless cupboards, she pulled out the white wine, fetched a red from the wine rack and was filling the glasses when Kiara followed her in.

'Is everything all right?' she asked, walking across to her.

Maddie wasn't sure how to answer. 'As far as I'm aware,' she opted for, hoping that Kiara might pick up on what she meant and finally talk to her.

'With you and Nathan, I mean,' Kiara added, taking her aback. 'You both seem a bit on edge, distant.'

Maddie set down the bottle and turned to face her. 'We're not *distant*.' She laughed, confounded. 'We're good. Better than we've ever been.'

'Really?' Kiara's expression was troubled. 'It's just that you've been a bit off lately and, well, I wondered if everything was all right between you two.'

Maddie was flabbergasted. 'I haven't been anything of the sort,' she said defensively. 'And what on earth gives you the idea that Nathan and I are—'

She stopped as Nathan appeared in the doorway. 'Everything okay?' he asked, his gaze travelling warily between them.

Hunky-bloody-dory. 'I think we should go.' Maddie turned to walk away before she said something she shouldn't, which would be grossly unfair on David.

'Mads?' Kiara came after her and caught her hand. 'I'm sorry,' she said, looking flustered. 'I didn't mean to upset you. Please don't go off—'

'But you *have* upset me.' Maddie whirled around, her frustration spilling over. 'You're speculating about things that are simply not true. I have no idea what's going on with you, but—'

'Me?' Kiara stopped her, astonished.

'Yes, *you*.' Maddie felt her temper rising. Did Kiara really think she wouldn't be upset? Not solely about the ridiculous comments she'd just made but about everything? 'You can't be bothered to answer my calls half the time. You cancelled our last get-together. You've been avoiding me like the plague.'

Kiara's eyes sprang wide in surprise. 'I have *not* been avoiding you. When?'

'All the time.' Maddie stared at her in disbelief. 'When I came to the salon, you couldn't get out fast enough. You couldn't have made it clearer you didn't want to talk to me.'

Kiara laughed, bewildered. 'That was ages ago. I had a doctor's appointment. I told you. Why would you think I don't want to talk to you, for goodness' sake? You're imagining things, Maddie. You're like a sister to me. You know you are.'

Maddie felt her heart sink. She was *not* imagining things. She *knew* she wasn't. 'I'm leaving,' she said, swallowing back the tears that were too close to the surface and turning away again. 'Oh, and by the way,' she glanced back at her over her shoulder, 'I know.'

'Know what?' Kiara called after her as she walked towards Nathan, who was still hovering in the doorway.

Maddie didn't know anything but what David had told her. Yet he seemed so convinced. 'Just don't hurt David,' she warned her.

They were in the car when Nathan finally spoke. 'What was that all about?' he asked her, running a hand over his neck.

Maddie stared at him. 'You know very well what it was all about. I told you.'

'Right.' Nathan drew in a breath. 'And do you think David would want us to intervene?'

'*Yes*, if she's cheating on him.'

'*If* she is,' Nathan countered agitatedly. 'David *thinks* she might be. There's no proof.'

'But he's our friend,' Maddie reminded him, not quite able to believe that it was her he seemed to be agitated with. Again. 'Are we supposed to just stand by and—'

'They're *both* our friends, Maddie,' Nathan said sharply. 'David's a grown man. He doesn't need you to fight his battles for him.'

She looked at him with a mixture of shock and disappointment. 'Which means what?'

He blew out a sigh of exasperation. 'Nothing,' he said. 'I'm just concerned, that's all. You care a lot about David, that's pretty obvious.' He glanced at her. 'The fact is, I think you might be taking sides where you shouldn't. Because of this idea you have that Kiara's avoiding you or whatever.'

Which he obviously *did* think she was imagining. 'I see,' she said, swiping a tear from her face. 'No doubt you'll be quick to point out it's all in my mind, but it sounds to me as if there's someone else taking sides here, Nathan. And since you seem to be Kiara's chief confidante and defender suddenly, forgive me for being *totally* paranoid, but I can't help wondering why that would be.'

Nathan was quiet for a second, then, 'Are you back on the pills, Maddie?' he asked bluntly.

SIXTEEN

Driving on autopilot to the school to pick up the children a couple of days later, Maddie racked her brains trying to think of anything she might have inadvertently said or done to upset Kiara. Any indication she or Nathan might have sent out that there were problems between them. Unless her memory was more elusive than she'd realised, she couldn't recall anything. Up until that fateful New Year's Eve dinner, when it had appeared that there might be problems between Kiara and David, everything had been fine between all of them. Or so she had thought.

She cast her mind back to when she and Kiara had met up just before Christmas. They'd arranged to take the children to the Victorian Christmas Fayre in Worcester and both Ellie and Josh were giddy with excitement, a handful, as children tended to be at that time of the year. Despite that, they'd had a lovely time, mooching through the local arts and crafts and festive gift stalls, sampling all the edible treats – until Ellie had let go of Kiara's hand and slipped off. Maddie felt her stomach clench afresh as she recalled how petrified she'd been losing sight of her child. Initially she'd told herself she couldn't be far away and tried to stay calm, searching through the bustling bodies around them, calling for her. But then, seeing no sign of her, sheer panic had ripped through her.

People had stopped, heads twisting in her direction, as she'd screamed for Ellie over and over again. Her mind conjuring up scenarios that caused the blood to drain from her body, she'd searched frantically, pushing people bodily out of her way. Then, 'There!' Josh had shouted.

She'd whirled around to see Kiara and Josh racing towards the stall where they'd sampled local toffee and nougat a few moments before, and felt herself go weak with relief. In an instant she was in front of Ellie, pulling her hard to her. 'Where *were* you?' she demanded, the fear that was still causing her heart to beat like a frantic bird in her chest overriding the sympathy she should have had for her little girl.

Shame washed through her again as she pictured Ellie's face. Her cheeks were wet with tears, her small body trembling as her confused eyes had held Maddie's. She'd obviously been scared. Scared by *her* screaming and shouting. 'I was *here*, Mummy,' she'd said, her bottom lip quivering. 'I stood still when I couldn't see you. Just like you told me to.'

She had. Maddie had drilled it into the children to stay where they were so she could retrace her steps if ever she lost sight of them. And that was what Ellie had done, sensibly, maturely, and she'd spoken sharply to her, compounding the little girl's distress. She'd clamped hard on her tongue, but she remembered the furious gaze she'd shot Kiara, wondering what in God's name she'd been thinking letting go of Ellie's hand for even a second. It had taken several seconds' deep breathing before she'd realised it wasn't Kiara's fault. Maddie knew only too well that you needed eyes in the back of your head to watch children every second of every day.

Might that have been what had kicked this all off? Had she made Kiara feel incompetent, untrustworthy? Nearing the school, she scrambled through her mind, trying to remember how the atmosphere had been between them when they'd parted. The shrill blare of a horn forced her thoughts to screech to a stop in her head. Her heart catapulting into her mouth, she stamped on the brake. Too late. She'd shot through a red light, the other car forced to a stop in the middle of the junction, the repeated raucous shriek of its horn drawing her attention to the fact that she hadn't been paying attention. Because after coming off the pills again, she hadn't slept a wink last night and her ability to drive was obviously seriously impaired.

She felt part of her die inside as she looked horrified towards the car that had skidded to a haphazard halt to her side. The woman at the wheel looked back at her, her face chalk white, her eyes wide with palpable shock. There were children in the back. She'd been coming away from the school, driving innocently along with her children. And Maddie could have killed them.

Her blood turning to ice in her veins, she pulled her trembling hands from the steering wheel. She wasn't capable. *She* was the incompetent one. This was her fault.

Her heart, which had been sinking steadily since she and Nathan had argued leaving the apartment, settled like cold lead in her chest. She'd almost killed this family. What else might she have done that her stupid, dysfunctional brain might not remember?

SEVENTEEN

PRESENT

Maddie

Hearing Boomer barking in frenzied excitement, followed by Nathan coming through the front door, Maddie braced herself. Apart from the words they'd had about Kiara earlier in the year, which she now bitterly regretted, she and Nathan rarely argued. Having gone into their relationship knowing his work would take him away from home on a regular basis, she tried not to mind about his absences, despite the fact that she missed him. That the kids did. This time, though, it was different. Important. To David. To her. She couldn't believe Kiara's funeral wasn't important to Nathan.

'You've definitely decided then?' she asked, glancing back from where she was preparing Boomer's dinner.

'I haven't decided anything, Mads.' Nathan sighed, kneading his forehead as he glanced into the dining area, where the kids were glued to the TV. 'The project is at a crucial point. There's a village overrun with—'

'Bugs,' Maddie cut in shortly and plonked the dish down, startling the dog. 'Yes, I know.' *Which are obviously much more important than people,* she restrained herself from adding.

'Mads, I am sorry. I want to be there. Of course I do.' Nathan stopped as the loud animations on the TV all but drowned him out.

'Can't the university get someone else to fill in?' Maddie asked, just as Ellie squealed in fright and Josh let out a whoop of delight.

'Go and play in your rooms for a while, kids,' she said, walking across to them. 'Your dad and I need to have a chat.'

'Aw, Mum, it's "The World Wide Spider",' Josh groaned, referring to the episode of *Danger Mouse* they were watching – ironically, given the subject she and Nathan had to discuss.

'Go, Josh,' Maddie said, her tone brooking no argument. 'You can download it later.' She would have to persuade him to watch another episode, though, she realised, as Ellie was clearly uncomfortable with the subject matter. Her heart twisted as she was reminded of Kiara. Her friend's debilitating fear might well have been exacerbated by the dreadful attack on her, yet Maddie had shown her little sympathy when she'd moved to the apartment to try to get away from it. She'd been awful to her, in fact.

'That sucks,' Josh grumbled, sliding moodily off his stool at the island.

'Josh, watch the backchat, please.' Nathan shot him a warning glance.

'But it was just getting to the interesting bit.' Josh splayed his arms defensively.

'No it wasn't,' Ellie mumbled, clinging to Nathan's neck as he lifted her from her stool. 'It was scary.'

'Was it indeed?' Nathan matched Ellie's scowl with one of his own. 'What say we do something different then?' he suggested. 'Play a game maybe?'

'*Yay!* Penfold: Clone Spotter.' Ellie was clearly up for it.

Josh, though, had other ideas. 'Full Speed Extreme Turbo!' he said excitedly.

Nathan closed one eye, appearing to debate. 'We'll play both,' he decided, lowering Ellie to the floor and giving Boomer a pat. 'Provided you play quietly upstairs for five minutes.'

'Okay,' Josh said cheerfully, clearly placated.

'And no arguing,' Nathan added as his son – a miniature of his father, apart from the seven-year-old's sulkiness – headed happily off to the hall, Boomer, who'd cleared his dish in five seconds flat, in close pursuit.

'We'll be as quiet as mouses,' Josh promised.

'Mice,' Nathan called after him.

'And them,' Josh quipped, already halfway up the stairs.

A smile twitched at Nathan's mouth.

'We'll whisper,' Ellie assured him, trotting after her brother and Boomer.

Not entirely sure that was reassuring, considering their two angels' ability to argue at any volume, Maddie shook her head in wry amusement. 'You should referee more often,' she suggested, and then felt bad. Judging by his downcast expression, Nathan obviously thought she was having a dig. She wasn't. It was just … 'It's Kiara's *funeral*, Nathan,' she reminded him. 'We've known her since we were in our teens. Can't you at least delay the trip?'

Nathan's expression was now contrite, from which she gathered he couldn't. 'I would if I could, Mads, you know that, but there's no other medical entomologist who can step in at short notice. I promise I've tried. I'm needed there.'

He was needed here too. He needed to chase the builders, which she'd done to no avail. They appeared to have abandoned the job, leaving the top floor half renovated, with loose floorboards and building materials everywhere, which was downright dangerous. But apart from that, *she* needed him. Surely he must know she did. 'It's a good job it's not my funeral,' she mumbled, tears welling as she turned away from him.

'Mads ...' She sensed him walk across to her, felt his arms around her. 'Please don't talk like that.' He buried his face in her hair. 'I can't bear it.'

She felt her throat close. 'I'm sorry,' she murmured, facing him and dropping her head to his shoulder. She knew he was hurting. She'd seen the tears he'd tried to hide after the police had gone, leaving them both stunned. He'd loved Kiara just as much as she had.

She recalled the pivotal point that had changed her relationship with her best friend: New Year's Eve, when Nathan had offered Kiara the comfort he was now offering her, holding her gently while she cried. She would never forgive herself for the way she'd reacted, ready to accuse him of cheating on her without any of the facts. To accuse Kiara. Things had soured with her friend after that. Maddie had tried to act normally, to carry on with the evening as if nothing had happened, but she felt sure Kiara must have sensed her anger. On top of what had happened at the Christmas Fayre, she was convinced it was all her fault. Kiara had distanced herself from her at a time when she'd quite obviously needed her more than ever. No matter what the situation was between her and David, Maddie should have tried harder to reach out to her, to be there for her.

'I just can't believe she's gone,' she said past the painful lump in her throat.

'Nor can I.' Nathan pulled her closer. 'Did the coroner's report throw any more light on what happened?' he asked softly after a second.

Maddie caught her breath, the same excruciating devastation crashing through her that she'd felt when she'd spoken to David after the inquest. She'd braced herself for what he might tell her about the autopsy report, but nothing could have prepared her for what they'd found.

'From what I could gather, her internal organs were normal for a woman of her age,' he had said. 'The hospital had been monitoring her for a suspected mild heart attack but hadn't found anything conclusive. She'd clearly decided not to mention it to me. I don't think I'll ever understand why.' Breathing in sharply, he'd paused, pressing a thumb and fore-finger hard to his eyes. 'Sorry.' He'd looked back at her after a second, his complexion ashen and his eyes those of a haunted man. His voice had been choked as he'd gone on, shocking her to the core. 'She'd obviously decided not to tell me about the baby either.'

'She was pregnant,' Maddie whispered to Nathan now, her grief for her friend almost unbearable. She knew that after all Kiara had endured years ago, she would have wanted the child. She'd tortured herself back then, agonising over whether the decision she'd made had been the wrong one. Quietly grieving while telling herself she had no right to.

'Jesus.' Nathan's arms tensed around her. 'David's?'

'I don't think he knows whether it was his.' Recalling David's expression, somewhere between bewildered and utterly bereft, Maddie's heart ached afresh for him. 'I'm not sure he would want to know.'

Nathan nodded and pressed a light kiss to her hair. 'There was nothing else, though? Nothing to suggest it was anything other than suicide?'

Wondering why he would think there would be, Maddie glanced curiously up at him. 'No,' she said as he wiped a tear from her cheek with his thumb. 'It was odd, though,' she added, knitting her brow. 'David didn't know about the heart problem.'

Nathan didn't answer for a second. 'She said she'd had a second test and that her ECG had been normal. I think she was thinking it was some kind of blip. She did say she would tell him, but she obviously didn't.'

Maddie nodded slowly. 'Why didn't she, though?' She

would certainly have spoken to Nathan if she'd received such potentially life-changing news.

Nathan frowned thoughtfully. 'I guess they weren't communicating very well.' He drew in a breath. 'Let's not allow that to happen to us, Mads.' He looked imploringly at her. 'I'm truly gutted not to be able to be there with you. You shouldn't have to go on your own.'

Maddie studied him. Seeing the deep sadness in his striking blue eyes – honest eyes, she'd always thought, where she could read his every emotion – she gave him a small smile. 'It's David I'm concerned about,' she admitted. She could only imagine the mental torture he must be going through. He'd left the apartment convinced she'd been with another man. He'd never said what it was that had convinced him, probably couldn't bring himself to. He'd been hoping Kiara would contact him, Maddie supposed. It seemed that she hadn't. 'I know they'd split up, but it wasn't what he wanted. I think he was hoping the affair would fizzle out. He would have taken her back, I know it. He's going to be so lost and lonely now.'

Nathan swallowed and nodded. 'I know. I'll ring him, try to organise some holiday once this crisis is over and spend some time with him. A couple of days away possibly?' He looked at her for approval.

Maddie gave him a squeeze. He wasn't uncaring. He tended to try to lighten things, that was all. It would be good for David to spend some time with him, to realise there were people there for him. 'He'd like that,' she said.

'I'll get it sorted,' Nathan promised. Closing his eyes, he moved to lean his forehead against hers. 'You know I'd be lost without you, don't you?'

Would he? Maddie felt a flutter of uncertainty inside her. He seemed to manage perfectly well without her while he was away. These last few months, when she'd really wanted to talk to him, he'd been inaccessible a lot of the time. Either travelling or unreachable in some obscure village in the far reaches of South America. Exhausted when he came home. Catching up with laboratory testing or paperwork at the university in the evening. When he wasn't exhausted, she was. Juggling work with home and family and not sleeping well had left her so drained lately it was all she could do to crawl into bed. The last time she'd made an effort to reach out to him, Ellie had woken with a nightmare and Nathan had fetched her into their bed. Maddie had missed him, missed the closeness that lovemaking brought them. She loved him. She could never imagine loving another man as much as she did him. She searched his eyes. Did he still feel the same?

'I do love you, Maddie,' he said, seeming to read her thoughts. His expression was almost anguished as he looked at her. 'I know I don't tell you often, but—'

It was enough. Maddie silenced him, pressing her lips softly to his.

Nathan looked surprised for a second, and then he reciprocated, closing his mouth over hers, his tongue seeking hers, his hands tracing the contours of her body, as if he too needed the reassurance physical contact might bring.

'Dad, it's been nine *whole* minutes,' Josh whined, bursting into the kitchen, Boomer bounding in with him.

'Dammit.' Nathan cursed quietly and pulled away. 'I'll be there in a sec,' he promised with an indulgent roll of his eyes.

'It's okay.' Josh sighed. 'I can see you're having a *really* important conversation.'

Nathan laughed in surprise and Maddie couldn't help but smile. 'He's a little replica of you, you know that, don't you? Who would Kiara's baby have looked like, I wonder?' she murmured, her heart wrenching again for both Kiara and David.

Nathan pressed his forehead softly to hers. 'We'll never know, will we?' he whispered throatily.

EIGHTEEN

'Has she settled down?' Maddie asked, looking up from the book she was attempting to read as Nathan came back into the bedroom. He'd been gone ages, making sure Ellie was convinced there were no bug-shaped monsters under her bed – an idea no doubt put there by Josh.

'Sleeping like a baby,' he assured her, and Maddie's mind went immediately to Kiara, to the tiny baby that had died with her. She squeezed her eyes closed. She'd been so angry with her friend, thought so badly of her. It would never stop haunting her.

Her thoughts went to the man Kiara had thrown away her marriage for. Had he known she was pregnant? Had he been married too?

There were things they would never know, as Nathan had said. Try as she might, though, Maddie couldn't stop thinking about them. Wired from lack of sleep since she'd come off the pills, her mind was obviously in overdrive. She would never sleep again at this rate.

'Okay?' Nathan asked her, smiling his twinkly-eyed smile as he slid under the duvet.

'Ish.' Maddie looked him over. How was it he was still as impossibly good-looking as he had been when she'd first met him, she wondered, while she was noticing telltale signs of ageing? She'd spotted a frown line this morning, which she suspected made her look grumpy even if she didn't feel it. She thought again of Kiara, who'd always looked immaculate, her complexion flawless. Her chest constricted painfully as she recalled her friend's startled expression the last time she'd seen her. She hadn't expected Maddie to be so furious with her. But Maddie simply hadn't been able to stifle it.

'Do you want to talk?' Nathan asked, moving towards her.

Maddie picked up the book she'd abandoned and placed it on her bedside table.

'You're reading. Sorry.' He eased away. 'I hadn't realised.'

'It's okay, I can't really concentrate on it anyway,' Maddie assured him, snuggling into him as he made space under his arm and cursing the insecurities that had stayed with her since she'd felt so abandoned and unloved as a child. She had to stop imagining she wasn't worth loving, stop looking for reasons to doubt Nathan.

'Sure?' he asked, giving her a squeeze. 'The light doesn't bother me that much.'

'I'm sure. I must have read the last page three times and not taken in a single word.' Sliding her arm over his torso, she rested her head on his chest, where she could listen to the reassuring thrum of his heartbeat, which somehow seemed to chase her monsters away.

Nathan ran his fingers through her hair, causing her skin to prickle pleasantly. 'How did it go at school?' he asked. 'Didn't you have a new pupil today?'

'Good.' She smiled, pleased that he'd remembered. 'He's settled in really well. His mum's relieved she's finally found somewhere that's a good fit for him.' She pictured Charlie's beaming face as he'd waved goodbye at the end of the day. The little boy had seemed shy at first, uncertain and tearful. His mother had been reluctant to leave him, which was fine; Maddie encouraged the parents to stay until they and their children were comfortable. The woman had been amazed when Maddie had managed to encourage Charlie out of his shell with some organised learning games, working on turn-taking with other children. She'd deemed it safe to slip off after a while, and Charlie hadn't even noticed she'd gone. He was mischievous and intelligent, Maddie had soon learned, reading out words in the Down syndrome education books, which surprised her. She'd uploaded some photos and sent them to his mum. Capturing one of him gleefully laughing, his eyes dancing with merriment, had been the highlight of her day.

Nathan squeezed her closer. 'You should be proud of yourself,' he said, kissing the top of her head. 'You're making a difference to people's lives.'

A small difference, Maddie thought, but yes, she was. It was hard work sometimes, but knowing she was helping a child towards reaching his or her full potential whilst giving the parents reassurance and some much-needed downtime was so worth it. She needed to stay focused. She had so much that was good in her life. She had to try to look forward, not back. Try to let go of her demons.

'Can I ask you something?' she ventured, trailing a fingernail over his chest.

'Anything. As long as it's not too personal,' Nathan joked.

Maddie hesitated. She should let this go, but she couldn't, quite. 'Have you ever been tempted by anyone else? Since we've been married?'

Nathan laughed in bemusement. 'Why would you imagine I would be?'

'I don't know.' She glanced up at him. 'People are, aren't they? Even the last people you imagine. Your work takes you away a lot, and I just wondered whether you might have been.'

He didn't answer immediately, studying her curiously instead. Then, 'Maddie,' he said, shaking his head, 'first off, the likelihood of the opportunity presenting itself in whatever inhospitable place I'm likely to be working in is slim to none. Secondly, if it ever did, I would most categorically not be tempted – why would I be when I have such a beautiful wife? Thirdly, after a hellish journey, probably ending up with my luggage in some other far-flung location, I wouldn't have the bloody energy. And finally, if this is you telling me *you've* been tempted,' his eyes darkened, and then he took her completely by surprise, somehow managing to flip her onto her back in a second flat, 'then I'm going to have to do something about it.'

His eyes held hers for a second, before straying to her mouth. 'Have you?' he asked sternly.

'Never.' She didn't flinch.

'Sure?' He kissed her lips lingeringly, then worked his way gently downwards, pausing to trail his tongue over the soft dip in her neck. 'Because if you have, I might just have to torture you,' he murmured, 'extremely slowly.'

Sweet torture. She gasped out her pleasure as he sought her breasts, his hand sliding up the inside of her thigh, sending a shock of sexual excitement right through her.

She must have been mad imagining he would cheat on her. He would never tear his family apart. Her back arched as he worked his way down her body, and she buried her worries, praying they would stay there.

NINETEEN

The service ended with the instrumental soundtrack from *Titanic*, a reflective, haunting melody that couldn't fail to touch even the most unromantic of hearts. Maddie knew why David had chosen it. If any music ever evoked love that would transcend time, this tune did. They'd watched the film together, she and Nathan, Kiara and David. Her mind flew back to the first ever New Year's Eve celebration they'd shared together as two couples. It had been the year after Kiara had been attacked, a significant moment when Kiara had said she wanted to look forward not back, and had set the agenda for every year thereafter.

'So what shall we do to pass the time until the midnight chimes?' Nathan had asked, clapping his hands together after clearing away the last of the takeaway debris. 'I vote strip poker.'

'Ha ha.' Kiara had rolled her eyes, unimpressed. 'I'll need a bloody good incentive to bare my all in this weather.' She'd shivered and pulled her chunky cardigan tighter around her.

'Er, me naked?' Nathan had suggested.

'How about watching a film?' Maddie ignored him, walking across to link arms with Kiara.

'Excellent idea,' Kiara enthused. 'Dave got me *Titanic* for Christmas. It's a real heartbreaker.'

'Mmm, Leo,' Maddie sighed ecstatically. 'He could pencil-sketch me naked any time.'

Heading to the lounge, she and Kiara exchanged amused glances as they heard David talking to Nathan behind them. 'How's your ego?' he asked him.

'Sunk,' Nathan answered despondently. 'Without trace.'

After the initial groans of protest at having to watch a romance, the boys had been as riveted as Kiara and Maddie were, sitting through the whole film without a single sarcastic comment. A sad smile curved her mouth as she recalled how David had hugged a blubbering Kiara to him, wiping a tear from his own cheek as the last scene rolled to a close to the music that was playing poignantly now. 'That's going to be us,' he'd murmured throatily.

At which Kiara had snatched her head from his shoulder. 'You're no good to me *dead*.' She'd stared at him aghast, thumped his arm and cried all the harder.

Maddie had thought they were made for each other. That their love would go on and on. That Kiara would. She'd never imagined a time when she wouldn't be here. And now she wasn't, and Maddie didn't think her heart could bear it, that David's would.

She watched as he walked from the church, his head bowed and his sister supporting him. Maddie was surprised to see her here. She'd thought she'd emigrated years ago. She recalled how she and Kiara had fallen out because Katie had been annoyed that David hadn't been seeing much of his family. She'd been at the pub they'd been drinking in one evening, accused Kiara outright of wanting to keep him all to herself. It was true, David hadn't tended to go home much during that first year they'd been together. That was hardly Kiara's fault, though. David had been besotted with her, concerned about leaving her. Also,

aware that Kiara had become a little introverted, unwilling to push her to go anywhere she didn't want to.

Now he was devastated. Maddie had watched him trying to stifle his sobs during the service. He'd obviously still loved Kiara, despite what she'd done to him. When Maddie had last spoken to him, he'd said he had no idea how he was going to exist in a world where Kiara didn't. Hearing the raw emotion in his voice, she wasn't sure he wanted to.

She still couldn't believe Kiara had taken her own life. David was struggling with that too. To him it was inconceivable. Even when she'd reached her lowest ebb after the attack all those years ago, she hadn't felt that way. She'd been depressed, but she'd fought it, determined not to become a victim. She'd learned to trust David, eventually to stop blaming herself. She'd grown in confidence over the years; running her own business was testament to that. Apart from the phobia that had dogged her, she'd laid all her ghosts to rest and been happy – or so it had seemed.

David was clearly blaming himself now because he hadn't been able to help her overcome her fear of spiders. Like Maddie, he thought her whole life had been affected by it, that she believed they were predatory creatures and could sense her fear, growing bolder because of it. Just like the man who'd attacked her. 'We should never have moved to the barn conversion,' he'd said, his voice laced with bitter regret. 'That's when things began to go wrong. Up until then, we were doing fine.'

'You didn't force her to move there, David,' Maddie had tried to reassure him.

'I know.' He had paused. 'We'd been trying for a baby before she left,' he'd confided wretchedly after a moment, and realising he thought the baby might well be his, Maddie's heart had jolted. 'Things had started to improve between us, or so I thought. And then this bastard comes along and ruins everything.'

David was destroyed. A broken man who felt he had no reason to go on. Maddie looked across to where he stood at the graveside under a fittingly charcoal-grey sky, his hand clamped over his eyes, his shoulders slumped, his demeanour diminished by a loss too heavy to carry. Seeing his sister thread an arm around him, she decided to wait before speaking to him. She felt she would be intruding on his grief if she were to approach him now, grief for the woman he'd loved; the child he would undoubtedly also be mourning.

She hung back until the crowd had dispersed before placing her own flowers at the graveside: a simple arrangement of yellow roses to celebrate their friendship. 'I know a bank where the wild thyme blows, where oxlips and the nodding violet grows,' she whispered, quoting Shakespeare, something she'd thought appropriate. 'I hope you're in that place now, Kiara. That you no longer have to search for the happiness that obviously eluded you.'

She looked to the skies and then back to the place where her friend's mortal remains lay, picturing her, so stunning in life, so still in death, her beautiful face bloodied and bruised. The image was so vivid she felt herself reel from the impact of it. 'Why, Kiara?' Her voice cracked, anger surging above her excruciating grief. 'Why did you do it?'

'Madeline?' said a quiet voice behind her.

Wiping quickly at her wet face, Maddie turned around and stared in surprise at the man standing there. She'd expected to see Sophie, but Jake? On his own?

He smiled hesitantly. 'It's been a while.'

With no idea how to answer, she simply nodded. Scanning his eyes, she saw none of the arrogance that had been there all those years ago. Nothing but sadness, which appeared genuine. Also guilt, she perceived. Clearly he'd revisited their university days and the awful Bonfire Night that now seemed so

prophetic, examined his conscience as Maddie had done endlessly since her friend's death.

'How are you?' he asked, for something to say, she guessed.

'Generally, fine,' she replied. 'Today, not good. You?'

'Shocked,' he said, tugging in a breath. 'Wondering why she would have ...' He stopped, swallowing hard as he looked past her to the grave.

'We'll never know,' she said softly.

'I wanted to pay my respects,' Jake went on after a second. 'Sophie couldn't face it, but I ...' He wavered. 'I did love her, Maddie.' There was something close to torture in his eyes as his gaze came back to hers. 'I treated her badly. I was an idiot, but I did love her.'

Maddie hesitated, and then, following her natural instincts, placed a comforting hand on his arm. 'We've all said and done things we regret, Jake. It's called being human.' God alone knew she had.

He nodded slowly, then pressed a thumb and forefinger to his eyes. 'I should go,' he said. 'Sophie's upset. I don't want to leave her on her own for too long.'

Maddie understood. Working so closely with Kiara, Sophie had obviously become friends with her. 'Give her my best,' she offered.

'I will.' Jake gave her a small appreciative smile and half turned to go. Then he turned back. 'Did they ever find out who attacked her back then?' he asked with a troubled frown.

Maddie shook her head. She was certain now, after talking to David, that Kiara had never really been able to move on from that. She wondered again whether she'd ever truly been in love with David, or whether she'd married him because she'd felt safe with him.

'If you ask me, it was him who drove her to this,' Jake muttered, a flash of fury in his eyes.

Maddie glanced over her shoulder to see David approaching. Confused, she turned back to Jake.

'For the record, despite what Kiara thought, I never told anyone what was going on in our relationship,' Jake went on before she could ask him what he meant. 'Whatever rumours were circulating back then about me supposedly being annoyed because Kia was struggling with physical intimacy, they didn't come from me. That's what I was talking about, by the way, when I said shit happens. I meant the gossip flying around, not what happened to her. I'd have to have been a right prick to have meant that, wouldn't I?'

Maddie eyed him uncertainly. Was that the truth?

'I should leave.' He glanced again at David. 'I doubt he'll want to see me here. Bye, Maddie. Perhaps we'll meet again soon under better circumstances.' Raking a hand through his hair, he turned abruptly and walked away, leaving Maddie feeling bewildered.

'Was that Jake?' Reaching her, David squinted disbelievingly after him.

'Come to pay his respects,' Maddie confirmed, wondering whether she'd misjudged Jake back then, as she seemed to be misjudging everyone now.

'His *respects*? After what he did to her?' David laughed cynically, and then his face grew rigid with palpable fury. 'The bastard should have been locked up.'

TWENTY

ONE MONTH AGO

David

David looked up from his laptop as Kiara raced into the kitchen. Sweeping his gaze over her, he noted the clingy knitted wrap dress and high heels she was wearing and couldn't help thinking she might be a little overdressed for a curry night out with the girls from the salon.

'Have you seen my phone?' she asked him, looking flustered as she scanned the work surfaces.

'Bedroom?' he suggested.

'I've tried in there.' She blew out a sigh of frustration and checked the fruit bowl, lifted the school curriculum notes he was working on to look underneath them, and then came around to where he was sitting to search the shelves under the island.

He caught the scent of her perfume as she did. He recognised it. It was the Dior one she'd hinted she wanted for Christmas. He recalled thinking how heady it was when he'd gone into Selfridges and sampled it before buying. It was distinctive, definitely her, he'd thought, warm vanilla 'with fresh citrusy notes and accentuated by a denser cocoa tone', as the sales assistant had informed him. She hadn't needed to sell it. David had made up his mind he would always buy his wife what she wanted rather than something that might disappoint her. Kiara had said she would use it sparingly, for special occasions only. She'd splashed it on tonight.

Realising he was in her way as she rummaged around him, now looking somewhat frantic, he dutifully climbed down from his stool and moved aside.

'Are you sure you haven't seen it?' she asked him, straightening up after a second and brushing her freshly washed hair back from her face, which was now creased into a scowl. Despite that, she looked stunning.

Swallowing back a tight knot in his throat, he shook his head. 'It can't have gone far,' he said. 'Did you check the lounge?'

'Of course I did,' she replied tersely. 'And the hall and the bathrooms and the balcony. I've even looked in the laundry basket. It's not anywhere.'

'Maybe you've left it somewhere? A shop maybe?'

'I haven't.' Kiara pressed a hand to her forehead as she scanned the kitchen again. 'I haven't moved from the salon today and I was using it earlier.'

'Might you have left it in the car?' David was trying to be helpful. He guessed she would be considerably frustrated. He would be if his phone was mysteriously missing.

'I've just said I've been using it this evening.' Emitting another despairing sigh, she whirled around, glancing at her watch as she hurried back to the hall.

David followed her, watching as she snatched up her car keys from the hall table and tugged her jacket from one of the hooks. 'I'll have another look around while you're out,' he offered, reaching to help her on with it.

'Thanks.' Her eyes flicked down and back. 'I'm sorry I was a bit snappy. It's just I'm running late now.'

'No problem.' He smiled understandingly. 'I'll make sure to have a thorough search, don't worry.'

She cupped a hand to his face. 'You have the patience of a saint.'

Did he? David wasn't so sure he did. He'd known when he'd first started going out with her that Kiara didn't love him in the way she'd loved Jake. He'd tried not to mind. That she cared about him and needed him had always been enough. He'd been understanding when she'd wanted to leave the house he'd hoped they might start a family in, a house that you could truly make a home in, with a garden full of established trees sturdy enough to support a tree house, which had to be every child's dream. Now, though, he felt his patience was wearing thin. Whatever he did, it didn't seem to be enough. But what else *could* he do? He wasn't going to confront her. That would only lead to an argument, which might give her the excuse she needed. His only option was to bide his time and hope that if his suspicions about an affair were accurate, it would run its course. And if it didn't? He had no idea what he would do if she left him. He'd only ever loved her. He wasn't sure he would know how to be without her.

'Have a great night,' he said, working to keep his emotions in check as he leaned to kiss her.

Kiara turned her face away as he did, meaning his kiss landed awkwardly on her cheek. 'I will.' She twirled around, waving a hand behind her as she headed to the door. 'We might go back to one of the girls' houses afterwards. Don't worry about waiting up.'

'I won't.' Thrusting his hands in his pockets, David stayed where he was until the front door closed behind her. Then he stayed there another minute as he considered which of the girls' houses she might be going to. He should have asked her, but then he would be guilty of questioning her, which, after New Year's Eve, when he'd acted out of character, he'd promised himself he wouldn't.

Sighing, he massaged the back of his neck, attempting to relieve the tension there, then went to the lounge. Crossing to the patio windows, he watched until she came out of the foyer and walked across the small car park to her car. He stood for a while after she'd driven off, looking out at the view across the river to the cathedral. Kiara thought it was spectacular. David felt it was soulless. Viewed from an apartment four floors up from the ground, it made him feel isolated, lonely.

Turning around, he went across to the sofa, glanced contemplatively down and then crouched to slide his hand underneath it. Finding the smooth surface of her phone, he drew it out and flicked to her home screen. Studying it for a second, he considered, then keyed in a set of digits.

Incorrect password flashed up. He'd thought it would. Was it likely she would have used his date of birth when his birthday had meant so little to her, she'd forgotten it?

TWENTY-ONE

PRESENT

Maddie

'What do you mean?' Maddie searched David's face. 'David,' she urged him, cold trepidation prickling her skin as he looked evasively away. '*Why* should Jake have been locked up?'

He seemed reluctant to answer.

'You think it was him who attacked her, don't you?' she asked, disbelieving. 'But why would he? They were going out together.'

David looked back at her finally. 'Not according to Kiara. She told me she'd been trying to end it with him for weeks, but that cocky bastard apparently wouldn't take no for an answer.' His eyes were burning with contempt. 'I mean, who would want to turn God's gift to women down after all?'

Maddie stared at him in incomprehension. 'You're joking.'

David drew in a terse breath. 'I wish I was. She didn't know for sure it was him, which is why she kept it to herself. I couldn't persuade her to report it and there's nothing I can do about it now, obviously. I didn't think the guy would have the balls to show up here, though. Sorry, Maddie. I'm a bit overwhelmed, as you might gather.'

'It's okay. I understand,' Maddie assured him, her chest pounding with a combination of raw grief and impotent anger. If Kiara had suspected it was Jake, surely she would have told her. Was he capable of doing something like that?

'Why did she do it, Mads?' David asked, inhaling sharply.

Maddie realised he was trying hard to control his emotions, and her heart bled for him. He wanted answers. Answers no one but Kiara could give him. 'I don't know,' she whispered. 'I clearly didn't know her as well as I thought I did.'

'No.' David squeezed his eyes closed. 'I suppose you can never really know a person, can you? What dark thoughts go on in someone's mind.'

Aware of her own dark thoughts, the scenarios her mind had conjured up, Maddie looked away. Seeing a bird soaring high across the sky, reminded again of that Bonfire Night, she felt her heart fracture another inch.

David turned his gaze skyward. 'Do you think that's her?' he asked after a contemplative moment.

'I hope so,' Maddie answered, catching a ragged breath in her chest. 'I hope wherever she is, she's left all her cares and worries behind her.'

'Me too,' David said, his voice thick.

Maddie looked back at him, saw the rise and fall of his throat as he swallowed and knew he was struggling. He'd lost weight. He was drawn, gaunt almost. 'Are you okay?' she asked him.

'I've been better,' he answered flippantly, as he had once before. His wry smile told her what a ridiculous question it was. How could he possibly be okay when he'd just buried his wife? And Kiara had still been that in his mind. Maddie was positive he'd decided to just wait it out, hoping the affair would blow over. That he would have taken her back.

'You're welcome to stay with us, Dave. You know that, don't you?' she offered, concerned for him. He was a man who bottled things up. He wouldn't easily ask for the support he quite clearly needed. 'Nathan's not home right now, as you know, but I'm a good listener.'

He smiled appreciatively. 'Thanks, Maddie. I'd love to, but—'

'Dave!' A voice called from the direction of the church, and Maddie turned to see his sister hurrying towards them. 'There you are,' Katie said, pulling him into a hug as she reached him. 'I was worried about you. Are you okay?'

David smiled faintly. 'Coping,' he said.

'That's a lie if ever I heard one.' Pulling away, she looked him over despairingly and then turned her curious gaze to Maddie.

'This is Maddie, Kiara's closest friend,' David introduced her. 'You met once, I think, years ago.'

'I remember.' Katie smiled, but it was such a brittle expression Maddie felt a distinct chill run through her. She supposed she couldn't blame the woman. Maddie had looked daggers at her that long-ago night in the pub, and had later caught up with her outside, telling her something similar to what Nathan had said not long ago, that David was a grown man and quite capable of making his own decisions. 'One of those being *not* to go home,' she'd added, looking Katie over pointedly, 'and quite frankly, I don't blame him.'

She hoped Katie had grown up in the intervening years. She'd been glad that David had decided to stay with his parents rather than at the hotel he'd gone to after realising Kiara was cheating on him. She wasn't sure that someone as possessive and anti-Kiara as his sister would help him get through this, though. In Maddie's experience, he needed to hold on to the good memories right now. The bad would eat away at him.

Was Katie aware of Kiara's affair? she wondered. David's parents hadn't come today because of his mother's angina, and David was such a private person, she wasn't sure how much he would have told them.

Katie appraised her for a minute and then looked back to David. 'I have to go,' she said. 'Will you be all right?'

'What, now?' David's expression was a mixture of surprise and alarm.

'I'm afraid so.' She shrugged apologetically. 'I've had an urgent call from the hospital. I'm a nurse,' she explained, glancing briefly again at Maddie. 'There's been a major road traffic accident. Several people critically injured.'

'Christ,' David murmured. 'Right, of course. Go. I'll be fine.'

'You're sure?' Katie didn't look convinced. 'It's not going to be easy for you.'

'I know.' He forced a smile. 'I'll manage, don't worry.'

'I'll look after him,' Maddie assured her. She was quietly relieved that Katie was leaving.

Her expression dubious, Katie nodded reluctantly and leaned to kiss David's cheek. 'Call me if you need me,' she said, squeezing his arm, then gave Maddie another short smile before hurrying off again.

'What's not going to be easy?' Maddie asked, though she had a feeling she knew.

'I have to go back to the apartment after the reception. There's paperwork I'm going to need regarding the business, other financial commitments. I'd rather not, but I have to start informing people. Katie was going to come with me, but now ...' David ran a hand through his hair. It was trembling, Maddie noticed. 'To be honest, I'm not sure how I'll manage, but I guess I'm going to have to.'

Maddie hesitated. The thought of going back to the apartment where Kiara had been so distressed when she'd last seen her caused a hard lump to expand in her chest. Seeing David's expression, though, the apprehension and anguish in his eyes, she knew she had no choice. 'Would you like me to come with you?' she asked him.

'Would you?' His look was now one of tangible relief.

TWENTY-TWO

As she looked through the jewellery box David had suggested she check, Maddie found an old strip of photographs. She and Kiara had been on their mad caravan trip to Cornwall. Posing cheek to cheek, arms around each other, they were both pulling ridiculous faces. Kiara was wearing the silver locket Maddie had bought her. The one that had been ripped cruelly from her neck during the attack. Maddie was wearing Kiara's polka-dot scarf. They were like sisters back then, never imagining they would ever be separated. Now Maddie felt as if half of her were missing. What would she do without her friend?

Thinking David might like to see the photos, she took a tremulous breath, rose from where she'd been sitting on the bed and walked across to where he was sorting through a box of paperwork at the dressing table.

He smiled fondly as he looked at them. 'She was happy once, wasn't she? Sadly, not so much with me.'

Knowing there were no words she could offer that could begin to ease his pain, Maddie placed her arm around him. Squeezing his shoulders, she held him for a second, hoping he would know she would always be there for him. As she did, her gaze fell on the legal documentation in front of him. Kiara's insurance documents and her will, she realised, her throat constricting. There were business documents pertaining to the salon too, along with paperwork for the apartment. It all seemed so cold, clinical and impersonal. The salon had been Kiara's life. Her identity in a way, the identity she'd felt she'd lost when her confidence and belief in who she was had been stripped away.

She couldn't help but notice the letter from the hospital David had obviously been looking at, which seemed to confirm what Nathan had told her. A fresh wave of guilt crashed through her as she recalled how she'd doubted her friend. It had even crossed her mind that she might have confided in Nathan to get his attention. She'd been wrong. Horribly wrong. Had David truly had no inkling about this, though? She wanted to ask him but didn't know how.

'I can't believe she didn't tell me.' Clearly aware that she'd seen the letter, David answered her unspoken question. 'It crucifies me that she wouldn't share something so important, that she wouldn't think I would want to be there for her whatever the circumstances between us. But then she probably didn't want me to be, did she?' he added with a heartbreaking smile.

Maddie had no idea what to say. She wanted to tell him that in her right mind Kiara would have wanted him there, someone she knew truly cared for her, but the truth was, she didn't know. Had Kiara's affair been just that? An infatuation? Or had she been in love with the man, whoever he was, hoping he would be the one who would be there for her? Neither of them would ever know the answer. 'I'll go and make us some tea,' she suggested after a second, thinking he might need a moment alone.

He answered with a small nod, and she eased away. Walking to the door, she noticed the gold locket David had bought Kiara to replace the one that had been taken lying on the chest of drawers. Glancing back, she paused, then carefully opened it, and her heart plummeted with a mixture of fondness and sorrow as her eyes fell on the photograph of the two of them Kiara had kept inside it. Again they were cheek to cheek, laughing this time, holding each other as if they would never let go. She couldn't believe she would never see her friend again, never talk to her. That they would never laugh together again, cry together, go on madcap holidays in the rain.

Wiping away the tears that spilled down her face, she headed for the kitchen. Noting the fresh fruit in the fridge, melon, grapes and strawberries, next to a half-eaten slab of chocolate, she smiled. And then felt like weeping. If that didn't sum Kiara up, nothing did. Her guilty pleasure, she called the chocolate she would always keep in stock. Had her affair been that? A guilty pleasure she'd felt she couldn't give up even for the sake of her marriage?

Quashing her tears for David's sake, she made the tea and went back to the bedroom to find him sitting on the edge of the bed. He had his back to her, the flat of his hand pressed to Kiara's pillow. She saw him draw in a breath and realised he was quietly weeping. She backed out. The tea wouldn't help. Letting go of some of his grief might, but she doubted he would want her to witness it.

Returning to the kitchen, she glanced around. They hadn't had much time to make the apartment their own. She couldn't help wondering whether they ever would have. It was all so clean and crisp. While she'd understood that Kiara's phobia was affecting her life, she couldn't help wondering again why she'd wanted to move here, to an apartment that although luxurious wouldn't be the best place to bring up a child. David, who loved the rural life, would never have truly been comfortable here. He'd tried to look enthusiastic the day they'd moved in, but there'd been deep disappointment in his eyes. Perhaps, embroiled in a relationship with another man and thinking she and David would split up, Kiara hadn't cared. Had she intended to buy him out? The salon had been doing well. It was possible. Maddie would never know what had driven her friend to such madness. Love, she supposed.

Wrapping her arms around herself, she wandered to the lounge, bypassing the sofa that Kiara had wanted positioned so that she could look out onto the cathedral. She could see why. The view was breathtakingly beautiful, the lighting around the historic building creating a mellow amber glow against the incoming night sky. Its reflection, like an impressionist painting, rippled on the softly undulating river beneath it.

Drawn towards the patio doors, she pulled them open, stepped out and edged tentatively towards the balustrade. What had Kiara been thinking as she'd plunged to her pointless death? she wondered, her heart catching painfully in her chest. She'd been drinking. That had been confirmed by the coroner's report. Was she thinking of the child growing inside her? The father? The people she would leave behind? Maddie would never know. She would never talk to her again, never hold her friend's hand when she needed her. Never be angry with her. Swallowing back the bitter taste of regret, she wished she'd been able to take hold of her hand that night and never let go.

Blinking away tears, she stepped back into the darkening lounge, and froze, her heart stalling, as the unmistakable silhouette of a huge spider scurried across the floor from the patio doors behind her.

Shocked, she flew to the far wall. Her own fear was of being alone in the dark, but this creature appearing out of nowhere had shaken her. It had stopped somewhere, she realised, her eyes darting around the room. Where? Her stomach constricted as it sprang from a corner, scampering for the underside of the sofa. *Shit.*

Her heart thrashed, panic rising inside her as she fumbled for the light switch. Surely the place wasn't so minimalist it hadn't got switches? As she slapped her hands along the wall, her gaze darting to the space where the spider had disappeared, she remembered that the lights were on some sort of ultrasonic sensor, which clearly wasn't working in here. Whirling around, she dashed to the bathroom, where it had definitely sensed her presence earlier.

Relief flooded through her as she was bathed in a soft white glow. She closed the door behind her, leaning heavily against it, and tried to slow her frenetic breathing. It was just a spider. It couldn't hurt her, she told herself, as David had so often told Kiara. She pulled herself away from the door to head to the sink for a drink of cold water.

Glancing in the mirror as she reached for the tap, she stopped dead. There in the middle of the vast expanse of white wall behind her sat another spider, bigger, leggier. Feeling the blood drain from her body, she spun around and fixed her gaze on it as she inched her way sideways towards the door.

Carefully, fearing she might startle it, she eased the door open, slipped through it and closed it again fast. 'David,' she called, hurrying to the bedroom. 'David?' She stopped inside the door. Where was he?

She headed to the kitchen, only to find he wasn't there either. Puzzled, she went back to the dark lounge. The patio doors were still open, and she hurried across to them. About to step outside, she almost had complete heart failure as something moved behind her.

'Are you okay?' David emerged from the shadows. 'You look as if you've seen a ghost.'

'Where were you?' Maddie stuttered, her nerves jangling.

'Just sitting on the sofa.' He nodded towards it.

She swallowed against the dryness in her throat. He might have said something. He must have heard her calling. 'I didn't see a ghost, no,' she answered shakily. 'But it might as well have been. There was a spider, or rather two of them. It scared me, seeing them here now, I mean.'

'Yeah.' David knitted his brow thoughtfully. 'I've seen a few myself. I'm guessing there must be an infestation somewhere. Kiara would have been petrified being here on her own. You never know, she might have realised I was worth having around after all,' he added with an ironic smile.

Maddie's heart leapt, cold foreboding creeping through her as she recalled what Nathan had said. *She has a ludicrous idea that he's bringing the spiders into the house deliberately.*

No, it wasn't possible. She scanned David's eyes fearfully.

'Sorry, I'm doing it again, aren't I? Feeling sorry for myself.' He shrugged sadly. 'I guess I'm just going to have to get over the fact that she fell out of love with me.' His voice cracked. 'It's bloody hard, though.'

Maddie watched him turn away to wipe at a tear, and her heart settled clunkily back into its mooring. It was *her* who was doing it again, allowing her imagination to run riot. She was growing paranoid with or without the sleeping pills. Without them, she lay awake thinking about Kiara and how she'd failed her, while every night she gave in and took a pill she was filled with graphic nightmares, which left her equally drained and growing ever more confused.

TWENTY-THREE

Maddie despaired of herself. She knew David. He wouldn't even hurt the spiders, let alone a human being. Still, though, she was perturbed, deeply. He and Kiara hadn't lived here that long. Surely spiders didn't breed so fast that the place would already be overrun with them? She would ask Nathan, she decided. Spiders weren't insects, he would no doubt point out, as he often did to Josh, but he would know all there was to know about them.

'All done?' she asked, poking her head around the bedroom door, where David was collecting up his paperwork. Walking towards her, he picked up the gorgeous hand-made classic teddy bear he'd given Kiara for their first Valentine's from the dressing table. She'd kept it, which must be heartbreaking in itself.

'It meant a lot to her,' he said, that same ironic smile curving his mouth. Clearly he was thinking it was the bear itself that was precious to her, rather than the memories it held. 'That's pretty much it for now. I'll have to come back, obviously, but I can't face going through her things right now.' He had a last glance around the room. 'Do you want to have her locket?'

Maddie hesitated. 'Are you sure?' she asked, concerned that

she might be taking something he would later regret parting with.

'Positive,' he said. 'I think she would have wanted you to have it.'

'Thank you.' She enclosed it in the palm of her hand as he passed it to her, then leaned to kiss his cheek. Part of her wished it was the old silver locket, but she was grateful to have it, something that had obviously been of sentimental value to Kiara and which she'd worn close to her heart.

She waited in the hall while David went to the lounge to make sure the patio doors were locked. Her mind was on Kiara, how terrified she must have been out there on her own in the dark, when the intercom buzzed, making her jump. His sister, she assumed. He'd said she would be coming to collect him.

Maddie told her to come up, then peered around the lounge door. David was out on the balcony, she realised, his mind possibly going where hers had, wondering what Kiara's last thoughts had been, whether she might have been thinking of him. 'Dave,' she called, reluctant to go in, not solely because the lighting wasn't working, but because of the wretched spiders. The notion that they were haunting her was ridiculous, but still she felt unnerved. She found herself scanning the floor and the walls. She could feel it, the same fear Kiara must have felt, as if the spiders really were hiding. She was almost positive that if she looked away, one would come scurrying out of nowhere.

'Dave,' she called again quickly, feeling hot and clammy suddenly in the confines of the hall.

He took a second to answer, causing her heart to falter, then, 'Coming,' he replied.

Relief sweeping through her, Maddie reached to open the front door. Katie looked tired, not surprisingly considering the medical emergency she'd been called to on top of the funeral. Maddie smiled at her as she stepped inside. However antagonistic the woman had been towards Kiara, the past was the past.

David would need his family and friends now. Maddie only hoped that Katie wasn't inclined to be as possessive as she had been before. At some point David would need to build up his confidence and move forward. He wouldn't manage that with people dictating what he should do.

'Long day?' she asked, an attempt at making conversation.

'Very,' Katie answered, appraising her with that same look in her eyes Maddie had seen earlier, as if she were measuring her up. 'How is he?'

'Not great.' Maddie glanced towards the lounge and then lowered her voice. 'I'm a bit worried about him, to be honest.'

Katie nodded. 'He's struggling.' She sighed. 'But then he's bound to be, isn't he, after devoting his life to a woman who clearly didn't give a damn about him.' The last words were almost spat out, her eyes hostile, accusing almost.

Maddie caught her breath. 'He told you?'

'Yes, he told me. Not that he needed to,' Katie hissed, her voice laced with contempt. 'I knew as soon as I saw him. He was still in shock, devastated by what that little trollop had done to him.'

'What?' Maddie stared at her in disbelief.

Katie looked contrite for the briefest of seconds. 'I'm sorry to speak ill of the dead,' she said, her stony expression indicating that she wasn't in the least bit sorry, 'but the fact is, she crucified him. Controlled him, used him and then tossed him aside like so much ...' She stopped as David came out of the lounge.

Maddie was absolutely staggered at the woman's vitriol. Was this something that had festered inside her over the years?

'How are you doing?' Katie turned to her brother, concern now etched into her face. David managed a small smile, and she wrapped her arms around him, drawing him to her. 'It will be okay,' she whispered as he rested his head on her shoulder. 'The worst is over now. Come back home. You need looking after for a while.'

After a second, David eased away. 'We'd better go,' he said, working to compose himself.

Katie nodded. 'Did you get everything you needed?'

'For now,' he confirmed.

'So what happens next? With the apartment?'

He shrugged and sighed heavily. 'I come back and go through her things, organise a charity collection, put the furniture in storage, and get an estate agent round, I guess. I'll probably have to get a fumigation company in first, though.'

Katie looked at him askance. 'Fumigation?'

'Spiders,' he explained, a frown crossing his face. 'There's been a few of them, an infestation of some sort. I think Maddie's wondering whether they drove Kiara over the edge.'

Maddie frowned, taken aback by his choice of words.

'Sorry.' David squeezed his eyes closed and pressed a thumb against his forehead. 'That was an unfortunate turn of phrase.'

Katie moved forward to take hold of his arm. 'Come on, let's get you home. You're not thinking straight, and no wonder after everything that's happened. You're obviously exhausted.'

Maddie watched them step outside, feeling more flummoxed by Katie's attitude by the second. She couldn't help thinking the woman might be the reason David had had so little confidence in the first place. 'I'll pull the door to after me,' she offered. 'I have to grab my handbag and coat from the kitchen.'

'Thanks, Mads,' David said, turning to kiss her cheek. 'For being here.'

'No problem.' Maddie gave him a hug. 'I'll call you,' she added, watching them walk to the lift.

She waited until the lift doors had closed, then sighed and went back inside, wandering distractedly to the lounge. Approaching the patio doors, she froze, a stark image jolting the breath from her body. She could feel her, see her: her friend glancing back at her, her face a mask of abject terror as she stumbled out, heading towards the fall that would kill her.

Maddie lurched forward, her hand outstretched, her fingers brushing Kiara's for the briefest of seconds, and then she was gone.

Her heart jarred. She'd seen this before. In her subconscious? In her nightmares? It must have been. But it felt so *real*. 'What happened, Kiara?' she whispered, tears of confusion and bewilderment clogging her throat. *I need to know. I need to understand.*

TWENTY-FOUR

Breaking her own Saturday rule, Maddie handed the sweets she'd brought as a reward for being good to a delighted Ellie and Josh, then mouthed, 'One minute,' to the childminder, who'd kindly given up her evening when she'd explained about needing to support David, and headed to the kitchen to call Nathan back.

'Hi,' she said, relieved when he picked up straight away. 'Sorry, I just needed to check on the kids.' Hearing nothing but silence, she sighed in frustration. He was obviously in a bad reception area. 'Nathe, can you hear me?'

'Not very well,' he replied, his voice breaking up. 'Hold on, I'll ...'

Guessing he was moving in hopes of improving the signal, Maddie waited as patiently as she could. She felt jittery and disturbed after the events at the funeral, to say little of the delightful Katie's attitude.

'Is that any better?' Nathan said after a minute.

'Yes. Can you hear me?'

'You're clearer, but it's still not great.' He sounded as if he was in a tunnel. 'How did it go? How was Dave? Did you get a chance to talk ...'

He faded out again, frustratingly. There was so much she needed to talk to him about. 'Nathe?' She waited, and was about to hang up when he came back on.

'Sorry,' he said. 'The reception here's rubbish.'

'I gathered. Dave's coping, though he's devastated, naturally.' She filled him in quickly in case the reception dropped again. 'I went back to the apartment with him to help sort through some things.'

'Directly after the funeral?' Nathan sounded surprised.

'He needed some paperwork,' Maddie explained. 'He has to sort out the business side of things as well as her personal affairs, doesn't he?'

'I suppose.' Nathan sighed. 'Christ, that must have been difficult for you. Are you okay?'

'I'm fine,' she assured him. 'It was upsetting, obviously, but he needed the support. His sister was going to go with him, but she got called in to work. I didn't want him to be on his own, so I felt I should go with him.'

'His sister?' Nathan sounded puzzled. 'I was under the impression she'd emigrated years ago. I'm sure Dave mentioned something about her being in New Zealand.'

'Possibly. I didn't get a chance to talk to her about that. She's obviously back now. She hasn't changed.'

Maddie couldn't remember David ever talking much about his sister. It was strange that Kiara hadn't mentioned she was back, though. But then she had hardly been talking to Maddie before she'd done the drastic thing she had. The realisation that she would never hear her friend's voice again hitting her like a tidal wave, Maddie closed her eyes, attempting to force back the acrid grief and the guilt that came with it, to no avail.

'Still charming, then?' Nathan said wryly.

'Definitely that.' Maddie smiled, but Katie's problem with Kiara was bugging her. 'Jake was there,' she added, wondering what Nathan's reaction would be. 'At the funeral.'

'Jake?' He was clearly astonished. 'Blimey, he's got some front, hasn't he?'

'He did know her,' Maddie reminded him. 'He was there on his own. Sophie didn't feel up to going, so he came instead to pay his respects.'

'Nice of him, considering,' Nathan muttered, a cynical edge to his voice.

'He was okay. Different,' she said, pondering again what Jake had said about David, which had left her mystified. 'He made himself scarce when David came across to us. David definitely wasn't impressed to see him there.'

'Unsurprisingly,' Nathan said. 'Jake was still in love with Kiara when Dave started going out with her, wasn't he?'

'Supposedly.' Maddie hesitated, wondering whether to repeat what David had told her. She hadn't thought much of Jake after the rumours about Kiara had started flying around, but now, since Jake had denied spreading them, and seeing how upset he'd been at her funeral, how genuinely contrite and angry, she felt troubled. Also hopelessly confused.

'David said he thought it was Jake who attacked her,' she said, deciding she needed Nathan's take on it. He'd known Jake as well as she had.

Nathan went quiet, then, 'You're kidding?' he gasped, obviously shocked.

'He said Kiara thought it might have been him,' Maddie clarified, 'but she wasn't sure, so ...'

'She didn't pursue it,' Nathan finished. 'Jesus. And she never said anything to ...'

The call broke up again, and Maddie sighed in despair. She wished he was home. She was desperate to talk to him properly.

From Kiara avoiding her to the friction between Jake and David, the spiders seeming to have taken up residence in the apartment and Katie turning up still so protective of David, everything just seemed off.

Realising that the signal had dropped out completely, she ended the call and went back to the lounge to find everything miraculously peaceful. Even Boomer was quiet, sitting obediently between Josh and Ellie as they stared at the TV and munched on their sweets.

'Watching anything interesting?' she asked. Clearly they were, judging by their mute responses.

'*The Good Dinosaur*,' Abi, the childminder, provided with a wry smile.

Ellie twisted to face Maddie. 'We watched it with Auntie Kiara. Do you remember, Mummy?' she asked, and Maddie felt as if someone had just punched her.

Her throat closing, she answered with a shaky smile. Kiara had told them it was a film about confronting and overcoming your fears, she recalled. Knowing that Ellie was scared of the imaginary bugs under her bed, she'd been trying to persuade her that she could surmount the same fear that had blighted her own life. If only she'd been able to do that herself. She'd wanted to. More than anything she'd wanted to conquer the things she felt were holding her back and stifling her emotionally. She might be alive today if she'd succeeded.

'Is Auntie Kiara coming again soon?' Ellie asked. Maddie had no idea what to say, how she would ever tell them. 'She's not cross with me for letting go of her hand, is she?' Ellie's eyes were filled with nervous uncertainty as they searched hers.

For a moment, Maddie couldn't speak. Then, 'No, sweetheart. She would never be cross with you,' she whispered, kneeling beside her children to place an arm around each of them and press soft kisses to their heads.

Apart from that time all those years ago when Kiara had

found the courage to stand up to Jake, Maddie couldn't remember her being outwardly angry with anyone. Not even David's bloody sister. She certainly wouldn't have been angry with Maddie, not in the sustained way it seemed she had been. There was more to it. It simply didn't add up. Any of it.

TWENTY-FIVE

ONE MONTH AGO

Kiara

'I've missed you,' he murmured, pulling her into his arms as soon as he stepped through the apartment door. His kiss was deep, sensual, his tongue plunging into her as if he was making love to her mouth. She caught a gasp in her throat, her breasts tingling in anticipation as he trailed his lips down her neck, his hands sliding the straps of her camisole over her shoulders.

'Bedroom.' He nodded her towards it.

Kiara hesitated, the nagging thought occurring that his mind might be more on the clock and how much time he could afford to spend with her than on actually spending time with her. Still, she didn't resist as he steered her that way. In the face of his potency, his obvious desire for her, it was as if her will to resist didn't exist.

Once inside, he wasted no time, tugging off his clothes then helping her hurriedly out of hers. She felt a tinge of disappointment that in his haste to free her of her lingerie, he'd barely noticed it was new, provocative and chosen especially for him.

His eyes dark and intense, he swept his gaze over her body as she stood naked before him, seemingly unaware of the imperfections Kiara knew were there. 'I want you,' he whispered, his voice thick as he reached for her again, one hand sliding down her back, the other up the inside of her thigh.

His kiss was tender yet possessive, absorbing all her senses as he guided her backwards towards the bed, urging her down onto it. His tongue finding hers, exploring, probing, he pressed himself over her, the firmness of his flesh expunging the breath from her body.

His own breathing heavy, he paused, easing away from her, a mixture of guilt and lust now in his eyes. 'Look at me, Kia,' he instructed hoarsely. 'I want to see you.'

She wanted him to see her too. All of her. She wanted him to want her, to take her like this, urgently. She wasn't sure she would ever have found the courage if he hadn't instigated it that first time. She wanted him to find it impossible not to be with her. She wanted him so much it was excruciating.

Difficult though it was not to close her eyes, she did as he asked, watching him, watching her as he entered her.

Aware of her sharp intake of breath, he paused, checking, and she smiled through her immense guilt. She couldn't help but love him more for that.

He smiled in return, a relieved, impossibly irresistible smile, withdrawing from her and thrusting slowly again. His gaze locked on hers, he increased the pace, deep, sure strokes, weaving his hands through her hair, kissing her hungrily. 'Tell me when, Kia,' he whispered. 'Come with me.'

'Now,' she cried as a white-hot spasm clenched her muscles around him, followed by another as he emitted a throaty moan and jolted inside her.

'Christ,' he said, exhaling hard and resting his forehead against hers. 'Okay?' he asked, concern now clouding his eyes.

Kiara nodded, incapable of speaking.

'We shouldn't be doing this.' His gaze flicked down. '*I* shouldn't.' Dropping his head to her shoulder, he swallowed hard.

Feeling his breath warm against her neck, Kiara swallowed in turn, bitterly disappointed, with him, with herself. Would she ever be anything more to him than a guilty secret? Would she ever find the courage to tell him she couldn't be that any more? Her hand went to the soft round of her growing tummy. She had to tell him.

'Won't be a sec,' she said, easing herself from under him to go to the bathroom. She should do it now, before the nagging voice in her head telling her she might lose him changed her mind.

Quickly she freshened up, then took a long breath and studied herself in the mirror. She didn't look any different. She *felt* different, though, scared, excited, extraordinarily sad. She glanced down at her stomach, placed the flat of her hands over it. She hadn't told him about the baby she'd aborted after the attack. She hadn't told anyone except Maddie, who she'd sworn to secrecy. Racked with guilt and grief, she simply hadn't known how to.

Taking another fortifying breath, she pulled open the bathroom door and froze. He was fully dressed. Already? She eyed him in disbelief as he came towards her and hooked a finger over the front of the towel she'd wrapped around herself.

'Suits you, but I prefer you without it,' he said, a smile playing at his mouth.

'You're leaving?' she asked, moving away from him.

'I have to,' he said, checking his watch. 'I promised the kids—'

'You promised *me* we would go out for a meal,' she cut in, a mixture of hurt and anger unfurling inside her. She hadn't wanted to go anywhere fancy. They would drive out somewhere, he'd said, somewhere deep in the countryside. It meant a lot to her that he would spend time outside of the bloody bedroom with her. 'I feigned a stomach bug to be with you,' she reminded him.

He shoved his hands in his pockets and glanced away. 'I didn't ask you to, Kia. It was your decision,' he said, his expression awkward as he looked back at her. 'I promised I would never pressurise you, and I don't.'

Right. Except he did. He knew she loved him, that she was desperate to be with him. He'd said he was desperate to be with her. But of course there was always some family drama meaning it wasn't the right time to announce he was leaving. 'I should have gone with David,' she pointed out, tears rising hotly inside her. 'His mother's ill and I lied to him to be with you.'

He massaged his forehead. 'Look, Kiara, you know how things are. You came into this with your eyes open. We both did. You know I'm married. I can't just do as I please when I please.'

'Really?' She eyed him with contempt. 'It seems to me that you do exactly that.'

'I have to go,' he said, his gaze flicking past her to the door. 'I can't let the kids down. That wouldn't be fair.'

That was a low blow. 'But you can let me down,' she replied, disappointment crashing through her.

'I don't want to.' He looked her over imploringly. 'You know I don't. I don't have a lot of choice, though, do I?'

'You said you were leaving her. You said you would *tell* her.' Her voice wobbled and she bit back her tears. She didn't want his children to be hurt in all of this, but didn't the fact that *she* was hurting, that she was incredibly hurt every time he found an excuse to run out of the door, count for anything?

Clearly it didn't. She gulped back a bitter taste in her throat. He was using her, that was all. And she was letting him.

'I will tell her. Soon.' He shrugged. 'I just need more—'

'Don't you *dare* tell me again that you need more time.' She eyeballed him furiously, feeling truly naked now in front of him as the tears fell. And cheap, like some common little bit on the side.

Heaving out a sigh, he shook his head and walked past her to the hall. 'I'll call you,' he said. 'Assuming you want me to.'

'You have to tell her!' Kiara followed him. 'If you don't, I will!' She regretted the words as soon as they'd left her mouth.

More so when he replied, 'That wouldn't be smart, Kiara.'

'Which means what?' Faced with his back, she couldn't see his expression, but his shoulders were tense, his tone tight.

'Just don't, I'm warning you,' he grated, yanking the front door open and walking out.

Kiara felt a cold emptiness spreading through her. He'd threatened her. She stared after him, bewildered. Because she'd threatened him, she tried to rationalise it. He'd been angry. He had a right to be. She *had* gone into this with her eyes open. But things had changed. Yet she hadn't told him. How could she have been so stupid, giving in to her emotions without thinking it through? He wouldn't call her. Why would he now?

Wiping a hand across her wet cheeks, she went back to the bedroom. She was trying to think what to do, whether to text him, distraught at the thought that he might not reply, when her phone rang from the dressing table.

Shit! Sure it was him, she dashed to snatch it up.

'Hey,' David said. 'How are you?'

Her stomach flipped over. 'Fine,' she said brightly, and then cursed silently as she remembered she was supposed to be ill. 'Much better, thanks,' she added quickly.

'Sure?' David checked, sounding confused.

'Positive.' She changed the subject. 'How's your mum?'

'She's improved quite a lot actually,' he said, clearly pleased. 'She's been discharged. Dad says he can manage, so I thought I'd come home. I'm a couple of minutes away.'

Kiara felt the blood drain from her body. Her heart banging, she flew to the kitchen window, which looked down on the car park.

Dread pooling inside her, she watched him drive away, David's car coming through the entrance a good minute later. He parked and climbed out, collecting his overnight bag from the boot seemingly unperturbed. He hadn't seen him. Thank God. She finally allowed herself to breathe out.

TWENTY-SIX

David

'Hi,' David called as he came through the front door. Getting no answer, he checked the lounge, and then went to the kitchen, where he placed the flowers he'd bought on the draining board. 'Anyone home?' he asked, going to the bedroom.

'In here,' Kiara called back from the en suite. 'I'm in the shower. Won't be long.'

'Right.' He walked across to drop his overnight bag by the wardrobe, then turned to scan the room, trying to quash the suspicion that had wormed its way into his head when Kiara had sounded so bright on the phone. She'd been quite unwell earlier, so much so that he'd been worried about leaving her. It was a stomach bug, she'd said. It was going around at the salon and she was concerned about passing it on to his mother. She certainly seemed to have made a quick recovery. His gaze falling on the underwear draped over the stool in front of the dresser, he walked across to it and picked it up. Oyster in colour this time, it was evocative, silky, expensive. He pressed it to his face. It reeked of perfume, the perfume he'd bought her.

His throat tightening, he draped it carefully back over the stool, studied it for a second and then, swallowing hard, walked across to the bed. His heart dropped as he looked down at the duvet. It was the wrong way round, the broderie anglaise embroidery at the foot end of the bed rather than the pillow end.

His stomach knotted as he stared down at it, trying to come up with an explanation as to why she would have remade the bed. *Shit!* Squeezing his eyes closed, he clenched his teeth hard, fighting back the tears that were dangerously close to the surface. If she thought this little of him, he doubted his breaking down would stop her ripping his heart from inside him. He needed to stay calm. Wait. For *what?* Was it likely to blow over? He very much doubted it. Reaching for the duvet, he yanked it off, tried to think what to say, how to act. As if everything were normal? He really wasn't sure he could do that.

He was repositioning the duvet, noting the small stain on it – a smear of foundation? – when she emerged from the bathroom.

'Hi,' she said, behind him. 'Sorry, my temperature has been all over the place. I was a bit hot and sweaty so I ...' She wavered. 'What are you doing?'

He didn't look at her. 'The duvet was on the wrong way round,' he said. Had she slept with him on top of it? he wondered, sure he could smell aftershave and now trying very hard to keep his emotions in check.

'Oh,' she said uncertainly. 'I must have thrown it back on like that. I was tossing and turning so much in the night the chain on my locket broke and I lost it in the bed,' she went on quickly. Lying. David could sense it.

'Did you find it?' he asked, straightening up and looking her over curiously. How many lies would she tell him? Just how little did she care for him?

'Eventually,' she said, her back to him as she stuffed her arms into her dressing gown and pulled it on.

'Good.' He forced a smile. 'Did we have any visitors while I was out?' he asked, willing her not to humiliate him further with yet another lie.

'No. Why?'

'Just wondered.' He shrugged, confusion and anger writhing inside him.

She kept her back to him. 'No one apart from the postman. Tea?'

'Coffee, thanks,' he replied, struggling to keep his voice on an even keel. 'Be with you shortly. I'll just put my stuff away.'

He watched as she hurried out, tying her belt tightly around her as she did. He was struggling to believe she could be so calculatingly callous. He'd always loved her, been obsessed with the idea of a future with her even before he'd spoken to her. He'd done everything within his power to make her happy, look after her and protect her. It wasn't enough, was it? He'd been kidding himself, hoping that she would grow to love him, that she would want to be with him, especially after she'd experienced the worst kind of torture a woman could at a man's hands. It had *never* been enough.

Leaving the bag, he went across to the dressing table. He debated for a second – did he really want to know? – then lifted the lid of her jewellery box. The locket was inside, where it usually was. He plucked it out. Examined the chain and the clasp. Tested it. It wasn't broken. Allowing the chain to slide through his fingers, he dropped it back into the box and tried to decide what to do.

She was back in the bedroom, painting her toenails, probably trying to avoid him, when he saw an opportunity. Her phone was still on the kitchen work surface where she'd left it while making the coffee. He wondered why she wasn't worried about leaving it there. But then it was locked, so she would imagine she was safe.

He picked it up, his thumb hovering over the screen, and then keyed in the PIN he'd had in mind, the month and year of her mother's death. *Bingo.* He'd cracked it. He didn't feel elated, though. Didn't feel anything very much, other than the pain where his heart should be.

Scrolling quickly through her texts, he paused at one that tightened his gut like a slip knot. *Miss you,* it read. *Can't stop thinking about you. Call me when you get a chance.*

He scrolled further down, finding several similar messages. *Please call me,* the previous one said, and then another, *Are we meeting up next week?*

He sucked in a breath, faltered for a second and then called the sender's number. It rang for a while. He was expecting the message to kick in when it picked up. 'Hello?' a male voice said.

David cut the call and put the phone back. Then picked it up again and muted it, in case the bastard called back.

So what now? Hopelessness washing through him, he glanced around, wondering whether he should challenge her. His gaze fell on the flowers he'd bought her, which were still on the draining board. White roses; he'd selected them carefully to complement the decor, the minimalist soulless decor he couldn't stand. He walked across to them, studied them pensively. She hadn't even put them in water. What had he expected? That she would appreciate the gesture? That they would mean something to her? He laughed scornfully. Not from him they wouldn't.

Cautioning himself to remain calm, he went to the utility cupboard to extract a vase. There weren't that many to choose from. Kiara had thrown out most of the stuff she considered clutter, including a decorated ceramic vase given to them by his mother, which she'd deemed ugly. She'd got rid of anything she felt was surplus to requirements, in fact. How long would it be before she decided *he* was surplus to requirements? Until she was sure she didn't need him any more, emotionally, financially?

Going back to the sink, he placed the vase next to it, then reached for the kitchen shears from the utensil rack and began snipping the ends from the stalks. He was part way through the task when the blade sliced through the thin flesh on his finger.

Turning to swill it under the tap, he watched, mesmerised, as the blood plopped into the bowl, clouding the water like rich red ink from a squid. Then he reached for the roses and stuffed them head down into it. It wasn't a grand gesture, considering how he was feeling, but it would make the point.

The message he scrawled in huge crimson capitals on the clinical work surface before leaving her to fend for herself would make the point more profoundly. *I KNOW, YOU FUCKING WHORE!*

TWENTY-SEVEN

Kiara

When she heard a rap on the door, Kiara's heart jolted. He was here. She'd known he would come when she'd told him how terrified she was. He'd been incredulous at first that it was David she was terrified of, but as soon as she'd mentioned the message written in blood, which had frozen her own blood in her veins, he'd said he would come straight away. He cared. He loved her. She knew he did. Almost wilting with relief, she raced to the front door and wrenched it open. She regretted not looking through the peephole the second she saw who was standing there.

'You thought you were safe, didn't you?' The last woman in the world she wanted to see stepped uninvited into her hall, her expression hard and unforgiving. 'You were wrong.' She paused, looking her over with a mixture of contempt and palpable anger. 'I know your darkest fears, Kiara. Remember?'

Hearing the threat in her voice, Kiara swallowed back her racing heart. How much did she know?

'Where? When?' Hostile eyes drilled into hers. 'How many fucking times?'

With no idea how to answer, Kiara stood mute, struggling for something to say. There was nothing, nothing that would placate her.

'Did you really think you wouldn't get found out?' The next question was almost spat in her face. 'That it wasn't obvious from your skulking around, *his* skulking around?'

How did she know? They'd been so careful. Had he told her? Finally? Had Kiara's frantic call to him prompted some kind of confrontation?

'I'm sorry,' she murmured, her heart squeezing at the thought of the pain she'd caused a woman who didn't deserve it. Her cheeks burning with deep shame and humiliation. 'It wasn't planned. We—'

'Ha!' That was met with a sneer. 'Spare me the "it just happened" bullshit.'

'It *did*!' Kiara blurted. 'We didn't mean to hurt anyone. We ...' She stopped, feeling flustered and angry. Why hadn't he rung her? Why hadn't he prepared her for *this*? 'You can't help who you fall in love with,' she murmured tremulously.

'You can help who you sleep with!' her friend, no longer her friend, raged, stepping towards her.

Kiara moved back, trembling under her contemptuous appraisal.

'How long has it been going on?'

She dropped her gaze.

'Months? Years?'

She had no way to answer. She couldn't defend it. 'A while,' she admitted guiltily.

Silence prevailed for an excruciatingly long moment, and then, 'You've been seeing him here, I assume?'

'No,' Kiara denied quickly. Then, 'Not often,' she added awkwardly.

'It's difficult for him, I suppose.' The response was filled with bitter-edged sarcasm. 'Since he has to make excuses and lie to his *wife*.'

Kiara dropped her gaze further.

'What is *wrong* with you? Can't you see what he's doing, manipulating two women he clearly cares nothing about? It's the getting away with it that turns him on. The thrill of illicit sex, surely you must realise that? Why would you do it? Risk your own marriage to a good, caring man for a seedy affair with someone who will never be there for you?'

'It's more than that,' Kiara retaliated defensively. 'I love him. He loves me. He wants to be with me.'

'Oh, right.' A scornful laugh. 'For God's sake, wake up, will you? He's not going to leave his children. Did you really imagine he would? Men cheat because they can. Because women like you bloody well allow them to. He's stringing you along, telling you what you want to hear until the gloss wears off. He's never going to walk away from—'

'I'm pregnant!' Kiara cried, tears springing to her eyes. 'It's his. The baby, it's his.'

Her revelation was met with complete silence.

'You need to go,' she said, panic climbing her chest.

'And *you* need to stop,' the woman who now clearly hated her seethed. 'Before I do something I might regret.'

TWENTY-EIGHT

PRESENT

Maddie

After leaving work early thanks to a water pipe bursting, Maddie sat for a while in her car, going over things yet again. She'd been thinking long and hard since the funeral. Almost a week had passed, and she was still of the same opinion. Feeling the need to prepare the children, she'd told them that Auntie Kiara was poorly. She still had no idea how she would tell them the truth.

The thing that was bothering her was that Kiara *hadn't* been ill. She hadn't had much time to digest the contents of the letter from the hospital she'd seen when she'd been at the apartment, but it had seemed to confirm what Nathan had told her, that Kiara's first ECG wasn't normal but her second was. She just couldn't understand why Kiara wouldn't have told David about the tests, though. She supposed it was because they'd already drifted apart, but even so ... *Had* he known? He'd said after the inquest that he hadn't, yet that letter had been there, sitting amongst Kiara's paperwork. Maddie might be being delusional, again, which was entirely possible with so little sleep, but she was sure that a man who suspected he was being cheated on would have searched through his wife's things, possibly turned the apartment upside down looking for evidence to substantiate his suspicions. Wouldn't he have come across it?

And what about the man she'd been seeing? Anger burned inside her as she considered that Kiara's death was probably no more than an irritating inconvenience to him. That he would simply go on with his life after glibly ruining other people's. Had *he* known she was undergoing hospital tests? That she was pregnant? Assuming he was married, might he have been worried that his own marriage would be under threat?

She breathed out a frustrated sigh. The fact was, she couldn't know what had gone on between David and Kiara, between Kiara and her lover; what had been going through Kiara's mind. She did know, though, that Kiara hadn't seemed like a woman who was depressed. She recalled David's comment about her being driven over the edge, a decidedly odd thing to say, Maddie had thought, considering how she'd died.

Had it really been suicide? Try as she might, Maddie still couldn't accept it. There were so many questions, all of them buzzing around in her head like demented bees. What were the spiders doing at the apartment? One she could have ignored, but two or more of them? If Kiara had seen them, she would have been terrified. Her natural instinct would have been to flee. But what if her exit through the front door had been blocked? In her panic, might she have run towards the balcony, somewhere she perceived to be outside of the apartment, just as she'd climbed through the window to escape a spider all those years ago? In which case, might her death have been an accident?

Whatever had happened, Maddie should have been there for her, instead of which she'd left her a few messages, sent her a few texts and then given up. A fresh wave of guilt crashed over her. She might be overthinking things, but she couldn't get the baby Kiara had been carrying out of her mind. She would have wanted that child. She would have loved it unconditionally, been the best mother she could be. The way she'd been with Ellie and Josh was proof of that. The way she'd grieved over the baby she'd decided not to have after that brutal attack was also proof in Maddie's mind that she would have wanted the child. She would have done anything to keep it safe. She would have seen it as a reason to live, not to …

She breathed in hard. Reaching for the locket she now wore next to her own heart, she stroked her thumb over the casing, then prised it carefully open. The tiny image of her and Kiara laughing together looked back at her, seeming to confirm her thinking: that she *had* known her friend. That she would have sensed something if Kiara were so depressed she was contemplating suicide. She had been down in the past, so down Maddie had worried she would never find her way out of it. But she had, she'd clawed her way back to the surface, found the strength to go forwards, to try not to look back. Had she really slipped back down the precipice? So far that Maddie wouldn't have noticed?

Leaning back against the headrest, she closed her eyes, and then snapped them open as the image she'd seen at the apartment seared itself on her mind. So real this time she felt she could reach out and touch it, it assailed every one of her senses. She could almost smell the rain in the air, carrying the musty aroma of the river; Kiara's perfume, vanilla mingled with warm chocolate. Why did she keep seeing her? What was it that was evading her? Had Kiara been expecting some kind of emergency when she'd listed her as the person to contact in case of one? Surely, though, it should have been David's contact details on her lock screen?

She gasped and clutched the steering wheel as it occurred

to her that if Kiara hadn't listed Maddie's details, then whether or not they were separated, David would have been the first point of contact. They were still married, so the police would have made every effort to contact him.

Kiara clearly hadn't wanted him contacted. She *didn't* jump. She'd been pregnant, and Maddie was growing more and more certain that she wouldn't have taken her own life. It was far more likely that she would have tried to protect a life, that of her unborn child.

She made a decision. There were unanswered questions around Kiara's death, things within that apartment that the police might have missed. No matter how muddled her thinking, she couldn't let it rest. She had to try to do something about it. She had to talk to the police.

But she would need more. What, though? The neighbours! She needed to speak to them. David had said he thought there might be a spider infestation. Was that possible in a newly built apartment four floors from the ground? If someone else had had similar problems, then it would put at least one nagging doubt to rest.

Twenty minutes later, she was at the front door of the apartment next door to Kiara's. 'Sorry to bother you,' she said, relieved when the woman who lived there recognised her, opening the door with a smile. 'There's something I hoped you might be able to help me with.'

'No problem at all. How did the funeral go?'

'As well as it could,' Maddie answered with a sad smile.

The woman nodded, understanding. 'Such a tragedy,' she said, shaking her head.

Maddie was grateful she didn't pursue it as she'd expected she might. She wasn't sure she felt emotionally strong enough to start speculating with anyone else about why Kiara would have taken her own life. 'I just wondered ...' She hesitated. 'This is probably going to sound a bit mad, but you don't have spiders in your apartment, do you? More than the odd one, I mean?'

The woman raised her eyebrows in surprise. Maddie guessed she probably did sound mad.

'It's just that Kiara's apartment seems to have attracted a few, and I wondered if you'd noticed any?' She was actually wondering whether she'd put the spooks up this poor woman. She hadn't considered that she might be scared of them.

'No.' The woman furrowed her brow thoughtfully. 'They don't really bother me that much, but I haven't come across any. We've never had any, come to think of it. I think it's because we're so high off the ground. It's a bit odd that Kiara has ... had ...' She glanced away, clearly feeling awkward.

'That's what I thought.' Maddie nodded in agreement. 'David was worried about an infestation, but I think they're more likely to have arrived with one of the moving boxes. Thanks. I know it sounded like a crackers thing to ask, but he's been worrying about it on top of everything else, thinking he might have to get a pest control company in. At least he can stop worrying about that now.'

'Like I say, no problem at all. I haven't seen David since he left. Please give him my condolences.'

'I will,' Maddie assured her. 'I'd better go. My childminder will be waiting to get off.'

As she turned away, she recalled with a sinking heart David's remark regarding the spiders. *You never know, she might have realised I was worth having around, after all.* His ironic smile as he'd said it.

She desperately wanted to ignore Nathan's comment, which also played ominously through her mind – *She has a ludicrous idea that he's bringing the spiders into the house deliberately* – but she just couldn't.

TWENTY-NINE

THE NIGHT OF THE FALL

Kiara

Paralysed with fear, she kept her eyes fixed forward. It was just sitting there. She could see it in the corner of her peripheral vision, hunched, tensed, waiting. Her heart palpitating furiously, she tried to think of a way to get past it and out of the bedroom. But that was no good. It would still be here, hiding, lurking. She had to kill it. A mixture of guilt and sheer terror swept through her at the thought, leaving her hot and clammy in its wake. But *how*? She had nothing to hit it with, no magazine or book, not even her slippers. If she moved from where she sat petrified on the edge of the bed to find something, it might sense her and run. If she tried to hit it and missed it, she would die; her heart simply wouldn't survive it.

Reaching blindly for anything that might be to hand on her bedside table, she managed to topple the lamp. Her whole body jumped as it crashed to the floor, her worst nightmare simultaneously springing from its lair, its four pairs of legs alternating as it covered an expanse of the floor at least thirty times its body length in one second flat. A raucous scream escaped her, and she shot from the bed and flew to the door, following her primal instinct to run.

Tears squeezed from her eyes as she slammed the door behind her and took a stumbling step back. Where would it go? Panic rose so fast she thought it might choke her. Wherever it went, it would creep out. They always did. Fixing her gaze on the small gap under the door, she backed away, waving an arm frantically in the hope that the sensor would turn on the light. It refused, leaving the hall bathed in dark shadows where other monsters might lurk. *It can't hurt you. It's more scared than you are.* She silently repeated what people insisted on telling her, trying to mollify her and calm her hysterics. But it *could* hurt her. Wasn't the fact that she *was* hysterical evidence of that?

Cold fear and nausea constricting her throat, she groped a coat from the hooks, shoved it quickly against the bottom of the door and then backed towards the kitchen. Going straight to the work surface, she pulled a second bottle of wine from the fridge, the first being shut in the bedroom with that ... thing. She wouldn't have much, just enough to calm her nerves. She would have a small glass and she would wait. They'd argued on the phone, a heated argument full of accusation, but he'd promised he would come. She would wait in the lounge. She had no choice. Having also left her phone in the bedroom when she'd fled, she couldn't call him again, or anyone else either. And she could hardly leave the apartment dressed in only her underwear.

Trying to still her incessant shaking, desperately attempting not to picture the thing in her mind's eye, she turned to the cupboard for a glass. But what if it found a way to escape and appeared in the lounge with her? The thought sent another chill of terror right through her. Imagining it crawling silently down a wall behind her caused the hairs to rise icily over her body. She would stay here instead. Sit at the kitchen island, her bare feet tucked safely up on the stool. It would be a vantage point away from the walls where she would have a good view of the floor space around her.

Grabbing the glass, she headed back to the island – and froze. The bottle hit the floor a millisecond after her heart slammed full force into her ribcage.

THIRTY

PRESENT

Maddie

Maddie debated the wisdom of coming to the station as she waited for DS Fletcher, who would undoubtedly think she was mad. Was she? The dreams had been relentless recently. Even without the pills, her subconscious seemed to be in overdrive while she slept, conjuring up scenarios that seemed so real she could almost reach out and touch them.

'Are you sure you want to wait? He'll be tied up for a while. I could get him to call you.' The desk sergeant glanced across to where she sat, and Maddie wondered whether she should leave, try to put all of this behind her and get on with her life. But how could she? As surely as the dreams of her childhood haunted her, so would dreams of her friend.

Deciding to stay, to trust her intuition, she shook her head. 'Thanks, but I'd rather speak to him face to face if that's okay.'

'He knows you're here.' The officer smiled and went back to his paperwork.

Maddie checked the time and then texted her childminder again to make sure she was still okay to hang on after picking the children up from school.

All good, Abi texted back. *Just back from walking Boomer. About to play Hungry Hippos game. Cookie reward for winner. See you later.*

Maddie felt a surge of relief. Also a bit guilty. She made a mental note to spend more quality time with Josh and Ellie playing real-world games. She considered learning games aimed at improving children's interaction with other children crucial at school. Being more hands-on with her own kids was something she really should make more time for. She and Nathan both. It would be fun. Bring them all closer together. She wished she could have spoken to him before doing this. He might have helped her put things into perspective.

She was about to try his phone again, which hadn't even rung out the last time she'd tried, meaning he was somewhere with a weak signal, when DS Fletcher appeared.

'Mrs Anderson.' He glanced at her curiously and gestured her through the security door. 'Sorry to have kept you waiting. I was tied up in an interview.'

'I gathered.' Maddie followed him as he led the way through a large general office. 'Thanks for seeing me.'

'Not a problem,' he said, showing her into a small office to the side. 'Can I get you a coffee? Tea?'

'No thanks. I'm good,' she assured him, taking a seat in the chair he indicated.

The detective perched himself on the edge of the desk. 'So, I'm told you have some information about Kiara Beckett?'

'Not information exactly,' Maddie started awkwardly. 'More questions really.'

'Oh?' DS Fletcher arched an eyebrow, and Maddie saw him glance at his watch. He was obviously busy, or else keen to get off, possibly having a young family of his own to get back to.

She wavered, wondering again if her imagination wasn't getting the better of her, then steeled her resolve. She was here now. If DS Fletcher thought she was playing amateur detective, then so be it. She needed to know that they'd investigated thoroughly. 'I don't think Kiara took her own life,' she blurted, causing the detective to raise both eyebrows.

'I take it you have a reason for thinking that?' he asked, looking her over quizzically.

'I'm not sure.' Maddie faltered. 'Are you absolutely positive she was on her own when she ...?' Trailing off, she looked at him imploringly, hoping he wouldn't dismiss what she had to say, however ludicrous it might sound.

He paused before answering, his eyes narrowed as he scrutinised her. 'There was no sign of forced entry, Mrs Anderson. No visitors to her apartment we've been able to establish prior to her death.'

'So David, her husband, didn't go back there that evening?' Maddie realised what that might sound like, but she had to ask. 'I mean, did his parents confirm he was with them?' She hurried on, feeling uncomfortable under the man's puzzled gaze.

DS Fletcher folded his arms, probably to stop himself checking his watch again. 'They did.' He nodded.

Maddie felt her conviction wane. Of course they did. Of course David was there. And she must be losing her mind to have come here.

'Mrs Anderson,' Fletcher kneaded his forehead, 'why do you ask? There's clearly something worrying you.'

Maddie hesitated. Should she tell him? He'd have her down as the local loony. Did it matter? 'Spiders,' she said, feeling slightly ridiculous. 'In the apartment.'

'Spiders,' he repeated. He closed his eyes and breathed in. Maddie guessed he was trying hard to suppress his despair.

'They were *in* the apartment,' she emphasised, careless now of how ridiculous she sounded. 'More than one, in an environment they wouldn't normally be attracted to, a spotless apartment four floors up. How did they get there?'

She saw a faint smile curve his mouth and felt immediately irritated.

'Her neighbour says she's never seen one in her apartment.'

'Mrs Anderson, I'm sorry, but I fail to see—'

'She was terrified of them!' Maddie's voice rose. 'Not just scared, but petrified. She had a phobia. She'd had it for as long as I can remember. She would have run from them. If she couldn't get to the front door, she could easily have placed herself in danger.'

To her frustration, he didn't comment.

'She's done it before. Almost fallen from an upstairs window trying to escape one,' Maddie pressed on, trying to make him see what she could see. Kiara, so stricken with terror she would have done anything to get away from the cause of it.

'When?' he asked, his expression more alert. 'This prior incident. When was it?'

'Years ago, back at university. But she's still as terrified now as she was then. Was.' She breathed in sharply.

'I see.' He nodded.

Did he?

'DS Fletcher, you're aware she was attending the hospital regarding a possible heart problem.' She tried to compose herself. 'Don't you think it might just be possible that someone who knew all this might have put the spiders there? That Kiara's death might not have been suicide?'

He thought about it. 'Anything's possible,' he conceded.

Maddie sighed with relief. 'She wasn't depressed,' she went on. 'I'm sure of it. She was having a baby. She would have wanted that child, DS Fletcher. She would never have chosen to end her life.' She stopped, her emotions spiralling all over again.

'You seem very sure about this,' he said, his sharp grey eyes searching hers.

'Yes.' She nodded. 'I hadn't seen that much of her lately, because of her personal circumstances.' She wavered, unsure how much the detective knew.

'The affair,' DS Fletcher picked up.

'Yes.' Maddie glanced down, her eyes welling up. She didn't know who she felt she was betraying more, Kiara or David.

'Do you know who it was she was involved with, Mrs Anderson?' Fletcher asked, his expression curious.

Maddie shook her head. 'I wish I did,' she replied angrily. 'I take it you don't?'

'Unfortunately, no.' He sighed. 'One of her colleagues suspected she might be seeing someone, but she didn't know who.'

'But what about her phone?' Maddie couldn't believe they hadn't gone through that with a fine-tooth comb.

'We found it on the ground a short distance away from her. Damaged, unfortunately. We weren't able to access any information other than the details on her lock screen. Our technical people are still working on it, but we haven't been able to retrieve any significant data. We've also requested records from her mobile service provider. Our request hasn't yet been met.'

'Meaning the records might have been deleted?' Maddie's heart sank. That information might have been crucial.

'Possibly.' A flicker of annoyance crossed DS Fletcher's face. 'You say you don't think she was unhappy, apart from with her marriage, obviously?'

Maddie hoped he wasn't judging her. From his face, she couldn't tell. 'She was unhappy living in her previous property, a barn conversion, which wasn't ideal for someone with her phobia, but she seemed better when I last saw her,' she answered honestly. 'Will you look into it?' she asked him.

He thought about it. 'The file isn't closed yet,' he said at length, looking as if he might be offering information he shouldn't. 'I'll run it by my superior. See if we can get the apartment checked over again. I can't make any promises.' He got to his feet.

Guessing he was indicating he needed to get on, Maddie stood too.

'I'll be in touch.' He smiled and extended his hand.

'Thank you.' She shook it and hoped that he would. 'Can I ask you one more thing?'

'Ask away.' He shrugged, looking resigned to the fact that she would anyway.

'I know the CCTV cameras in the foyer aren't installed properly yet, but I just wondered, did you check the images on the camera in the car park?'

THIRTY-ONE

Finding a parking spot outside the salon where she could keep an eye on the car, Maddie turned to the children. 'I'll be two minutes,' she said. 'Stay in your seats.' Noting that they were both glued to their tablets, she suspected they would barely blink, let alone move.

'Back soon,' she said, grabbing her bag from the passenger seat.

'Uh-huh,' Josh answered without looking up.

Ellie nodded, her eyes still fixed to her screen.

Maddie smiled indulgently and climbed out. Board games, she reminded herself, where eye contact and communication would be essential.

The salon was busy, as it would be on a Saturday. Sophie was with a customer. Chatting and smiling away, she didn't look particularly upset, but then Maddie supposed she would have to put on a brave front for the sake of the business. The business that Kiara had built up from nothing. Having failed her degree, which wasn't surprising considering all that she was coping with emotionally, she'd been determined to prove herself. David had supported her while she trained. He'd been hands-on helping her refurbish her first shop. An overwhelming sadness swept through Maddie as she recalled how she'd walked in to find them both covered in paint, exhausted but happy as they'd shared a takeaway. 'I'm proud of her,' David had said, wrapping an arm around Kiara's shoulders. Kiara had blushed, but it had been obvious she was proud of herself. Maddie had been proud of her too. How had they gone from sharing everything in their lives to sharing nothing?

After a few seconds, Sophie spotted her and came across. 'Maddie, how are you?' Looking her over sympathetically, she hesitated and then pulled her into a fierce hug. 'I'm so, so sorry.'

Her throat closing, Maddie nodded and hugged her back.

'I can't believe it,' Sophie whispered, wiping a hand across her eyes as she eased away. 'She didn't seem down or upset. I just don't understand it.'

'Didn't she?' Maddie couldn't know how Kiara had really been in those confusing last few months of her life, but she held on to the fact that people who weren't so emotionally involved also felt she hadn't been down enough to take her own life. Perhaps her lover, whoever he was, had been the one who might have made her truly happy. If it had all gone horribly wrong, though, if he'd ended the relationship, could her actions on the night of her death have been some awful impulse?

'Not that I was aware. She did seem a bit preoccupied.' Sophie knitted her brow. 'But she did have a lot going on. She had so many plans for this place, we couldn't keep up with her. We even joked about it, do you remember, Anna?' She turned to the woman on reception.

'I do.' Anna shook her head sorrowfully. 'I don't know where she got her energy from. I remember telling her I'd have some of what she was having.'

Picturing the banter, recalling her friend the way she used

to be, Maddie smiled. That sounded like Kiara, a woman who would dwell for a while and then push herself on, determined to look forward not back.

'She wanted to extend the salon to make room for some massage tables,' Sophie went on. 'She was thinking about offering Botox. She'd even organised a couple of interviews with qualified practitioners. That's why I can't believe she ...' She trailed off, her throat catching.

'There was nothing specifically bothering her then? Nothing she might have mentioned?' Maddie asked. She was hoping Sophie might share with her what she'd told DS Fletcher about Kiara being involved with someone. But then it might not even have been Sophie who'd given him that information, and Maddie had no idea how to ask.

'No. Nothing, as far as I know,' Sophie replied.

'Apart from the spiders,' Anna added.

'Oh yes, those.' Sophie nodded thoughtfully.

'There was one in the kitchen a few weeks back. Poor Kiara almost freaked out, didn't she, Soph?' Anna went on, smiling brightly at a customer as the door opened behind Maddie.

'She certainly wasn't very happy about it,' Sophie said, moving aside to allow the customer to get to the desk.

'Soph was her nominated spider catcher.' Anna continued chatting while she showed the customer to a seat. 'Just as well. The salon would probably have been vacated in three seconds flat if that one had got loose. We have some really big spiders here,' she added with a shudder. The customer's eyes grew wide with alarm.

'Shush.' Sophie gave Anna a look, then turned back to Maddie with a roll of her eyes. 'I'd better get back. Do you want me to ask someone to make you a coffee?'

'No thanks. The children are in the car.' Maddie declined with a smile.

Sophie nodded. 'See you at your next appointment.' She gave Maddie another quick hug, then returned to her client.

Maddie watched her go with mixed emotions. Sophie was Kiara's hero then, it seemed. The two women had clearly been quite close. How much of Kiara's life had she been privy to? she wondered.

THIRTY-TWO

Dashing through the front door in a bid to grab the TV control before Josh did, Ellie skidded to a stop in the hall. 'Daddy's home!' she squealed delightedly. Following her in to see Nathan's rucksack in the hall, Maddie was surprised. She'd been expecting him to ring her from the airport.

'In here, kids,' he called from the kitchen.

'Yay!' Josh whooped, hurtling after Ellie, both of them ignoring poor Boomer, who was so ecstatic with joy at having all his humans home he didn't know who to greet first.

'Hi, Boomer.' Maddie paused to give him a fuss, though she was quite keen to get to Nathan herself.

Going into the kitchen, she smiled, her heart melting at the sight of her weary-looking husband sweeping Ellie up and then ruffling his son's hair as Josh locked his arms around his waist.

'So, what have you two been up to while I've been away? Behaving yourselves, I hope?' he asked, appraising each of them carefully.

'Yes,' Ellie answered with a confident nod. 'We haven't argued once, have we, Josh?'

'No.' Josh shook his head adamantly. 'Abi said we were like little angels.'

'Did she now?' A smile curving his mouth, Nathan exchanged glances with Maddie.

'We won a prize for being nice to each other, didn't we, Josh?' Ellie went on importantly.

'Ah, I see.' Nathan chuckled. 'So I guess that means you've been well behaved enough to deserve the surprise I brought back with me then?'

'Yes!' Ellie jiggled excitedly.

'Promise?' He eyed her narrowly.

'Promise.' The little girl quickly crossed her chest.

He smiled and kissed her nose. 'You'll find it on the coffee table in the lounge,' he said, lowering her to the floor.

The two of them scooted excitedly towards the hall, Boomer close on their heels.

'The guide to good parenting. If all else fails, try a little bribery.' Nathan winked at Maddie. 'I grabbed the Pictionary Air game from the airport. I thought it might keep them out of mischief for a—'

He staggered back a step as Maddie all but threw herself at him.

'I am *so* glad you're home,' she murmured into his shoulder, realising how much she'd missed him. How much she loved him. Only Nathan could have thought to bring an interactive game before she'd even mentioned it.

'I gathered.' He laughed bemusedly, circling his arms around her. He smelled different, sweet and musky, like a botanical garden, a combined scent of vegetation, moisture, soil and wood. The smell of the rainforest. The smell of life, he called it.

'Why didn't you call me to collect you from the airport?' she asked, easing back to scan his face. He looked exhausted.

'The flight got in early. I grabbed a taxi rather than drag you out. I hoped you might be having a lie-in.'

'Would that I could.' Maddie sighed wistfully.

'Still not sleeping?' Nathan looked her over, concerned.

'Not much, no.'

'Your mind on Kiara, I take it?' He frowned sympathetically.

'I can't stop thinking about her,' she admitted.

'How have things been?' he asked softly.

Maddie hesitated. 'Complicated,' she said, moving away to add milk to the tea he'd been making when the kids charged in. Should she tell him about the latest developments? He would be so jet-lagged. She'd hoped to hear something back from DS Fletcher, but now that Nathan was home, she needed to fill him in.

'Complicated how?'

She glanced back at him. He really did look dead on his feet. 'It can wait,' she said. 'You need to get some rest.'

'True.' He ran a hand tiredly over his neck. 'I'd rather you told me now, though. It's clearly something that's worrying you.'

Maddie fished the tea bags out and stirred the tea slowly. 'They're reinvestigating Kiara's death,' she said cautiously.

'What?' Nathan almost dropped the mug she'd passed to him. '*Why?*'

'I went to see DS Fletcher,' she went on, nervous butterflies taking off in her tummy. She guessed he wouldn't be thrilled that she'd spoken to the police without discussing it with him first.

He frowned and placed his mug on the work surface. 'Because?' he asked. 'Did you remember something? Something you thought they needed to know?'

'Not exactly.' She glanced away and back again.

'So?'

Maddie searched for a way to tell him without it sounding

ludicrous. But it shouldn't sound ludicrous, not to someone who knew Kiara's history as well as they did. 'It's just ... things seemed odd,' she started hesitantly.

'Odd?' Nathan's expression was wary. 'Odd how?'

She drew in a breath. 'There were spiders in the apartment. I couldn't help wondering—'

'Spiders?' Now he looked astonished.

'David said he thought there must be an infestation, but in a new apartment? Four floors up? I checked with the neighbours and—'

'Whoa, slow down.' Nathan looked at her askance. 'Is that all? You went to the police because there were *spiders* in the apartment?'

'Yes,' Maddie answered guardedly. Why was he looking at her like that, as if he thought she'd taken leave of her senses? 'I was concerned. Obviously I would be, knowing how terrified Kiara was of them. And after what you told me about her thinking that David might have been bringing them in, I thought ...' She faltered. 'I don't know. I just had a feeling.'

'A feeling?' Nathan squinted at her, bemused. 'They moved stuff from the barn conversion,' he reminded her. 'There were at least a couple of boxes from the loft with Christmas decorations in. Don't you think it's more likely the spiders moved in with them?'

'Those boxes were still taped up,' she said, feeling suddenly defensive. 'I saw them in the spare room. They clearly hadn't got around to unpacking them.'

Nathan shook his head. 'Kiara was struggling emotionally. We can't know her reasons for doing what she did, but we *do* know David. You probably better than anyone. What Kiara said was absurd. She was clearly becoming irrational way before she ...' He stopped and kneaded his forehead.

He thought she was getting things out of proportion. Was she? Might she be looking to blame someone because she couldn't bear the thought of her friend being so desperate, so lonely, she would have taken her own life? But she was sure something wasn't right. It was more than a feeling.

'David said he thought the spiders might have driven Kiara over the edge,' she told him. 'That they might have made her realise he was worth having around after all. Don't you think that was an odd thing to say, considering?'

Nathan closed his eyes. 'No, Maddie, I don't.' He sighed despairingly. 'Look, I understand you're worried, but don't you think you might be letting your imagination run away with you?'

No, but you obviously do. Maddie eyed him with bitter disappointment. 'She was *pregnant*, Nathan. She would have wanted that child. She would have been looking forward to the future. I *know* she would,' she said, wishing now, for the first time ever, that she hadn't confided in him about any of this. He evidently wasn't taking her seriously.

'You *don't* know, Maddie. You can't know what was going on in her head.'

'I *can*. I did!' she insisted. 'She'd been pregnant before. She couldn't have the baby; how could she after being raped? But she grieved for the loss of it.'

Nathan looked at her as it he'd been struck by a thunderbolt. Then, 'I didn't know that,' he said, obviously shaken.

'No one did. She only ever confided in me. I *did* know her.' Maddie was feeling more defensive by the second. Also angry that she needed to be. She had doubts. She might be wrong. But surely it wasn't a crime to be concerned about what might have happened to her friend. To *his* friend. 'There are so many things that don't add up. I couldn't just leave it.'

'What else?' Nathan asked. Maddie could hear discernible tones of exasperation in his voice, despite what she'd just told him, and couldn't quite believe it.

'I went to see Sophie,' she said.

'And?' Nathan waited, his expression curious but wary. Wary of her, she guessed.

'And she said Kiara didn't seem down. That she was thinking of extending the shop.'

'Maddie ...' Nathan sighed again.

'She wasn't depressed, Nathan.' Maddie tried to quash her growing frustration. 'She was making plans for the future. Does that sound to you like someone who's about to end their life?'

'People who are serious don't tend to advertise their intentions,' he pointed out. 'They're afraid that someone will try to stop them, don't you see? They try to act normally.'

Maddie's conviction was starting to wane in the face of his credible reasoning. But Kiara *hadn't* been acting normally. Because she was having an affair? Was it just that, though? Was that the whole reason she'd avoided her? Maddie couldn't believe that. She just couldn't.

'You're struggling to accept it,' Nathan went on, his tone softer. 'You're bound to be feeling guilty, blaming yourself. You shouldn't.' Moving towards her, he took hold of her hand. 'Maybe you should give coming off the pills another go,' he suggested.

So he did think it was all in her mind. She eyed him cautiously. 'I am off them,' she informed him quietly. 'If you were ever here instead of finding every excuse you can to leave, you would know that.'

Seeing his wounded look, she immediately wished she hadn't said it. The fact was, though, it was the truth. He *was* away a lot, following up on research when he was here. But he was right to worry. She was forgetful and confused when she was on the pills, distracted through exhaustion when she wasn't. She'd wondered herself whether she was imagining things. This wasn't just her, though. Hadn't DS Fletcher said he would look into it? Why would he if he didn't have doubts?

'I don't believe she committed suicide,' she said deter-

minedly. 'It's not about guilt, it's about what I feel here, inside.'
She pressed a hand to her heart. 'My instinct tells me there's
more to it. I intend to find out what. I certainly intend to find
out who this bloody man was Kiara was involved with.'

Nathan tugged in a tight breath but didn't say anything.
Feeling alone, abandoned almost, Maddie turned away.

'How?' he asked behind her, frustration evident in his voice.
'You don't have a clue who he is. Don't you think you should
just leave it?'

Her heart plummeted. 'Someone will know,' she assured
him. 'And no, I don't think I should leave it. I think I would
prefer to be able to live with myself.'

THIRTY-THREE

She can hear him breathing as he walks purposefully towards her, feel her heart pounding – thud, thud, thud, a prophetic drumbeat in her chest – as she scrambles to get away from him.

'You shouldn't have told,' he murmurs, reaching out to her, hands touching, fingertips brushing as she teeters, the cathedral lights simultaneously fading, the fast-flowing river slowing. For an instant, time freezes. Nothing moves against the silence of the night but her breath mingling with his as their eyes lock. And then she's falling. Her body landing, her bones jarring. The cathedral bells ringing. Mournful. Urgent. Insistent.

Maddie jerked upright. 'Nathan.'

'What is it?' He was beside her in an instant. 'Are you okay?'

'Yes,' she gasped, then, realising the ringing wasn't in her head, untangled herself from the duvet and climbed out of bed.

'Where are you going?' he asked, as she hurried across the bedroom. He was still half asleep and clearly confused, not surprisingly. Nothing short of an earthquake would normally wake him from his first full night's sleep after his long journey home.

Tugging her dressing gown from the hook, she shoved her arms into it and pulled the bedroom door open. 'There's someone at the front door,' she told him, as Boomer broke into frenzied barking.

Outside the bedroom, she leaned against the wall, pinpricks of sweat beading her forehead, her body trembling as she scrambled to hold on to the fragments of her dream. Her mind was fuzzy, a headache forming, pinpricks of sharp white light scorching her eyes, but still she could see his silhouette advancing through the darkness, feel the threat emanating from him as he came towards where she stood on the balcony, the cold steel of the balustrade pressing into her body.

It was him. The features were his, but the eyes were cold, flat, unfeeling; the eyes of the devil.

It was a nightmare. A bad dream, that was all. All in her mind. Her bloody, *bloody* mind, which was obviously in complete overdrive. Pressing the heel of her hand to her forehead, she hurried down the stairs, tightening her robe as she went.

'It's okay, Boomer,' she called through the kitchen door as the dog, keen to greet their caller, whined wistfully and pawed the other side of it. Then, drawing in a breath, she reached for the front door latch and inched the door open.

'Mrs Anderson.' DS Fletcher nodded shortly. 'Sorry it's so early. I wanted to catch you and Mr Anderson before you left for work.'

'Oh, right.' Maddie blinked, confused. 'Nathan's just back from a work trip abroad. He's jet-lagged. Still in bed.'

'Ah.' Fletcher nodded understandingly. 'I wonder if we might disturb him? I'd quite like to have a word with both of you if that's okay.'

'Of course. Come in.' Opening the door wider, Maddie moved back, scanning the detective's face as he stepped in. His expression gave nothing away. 'Would you like to wait in the lounge? I'll just go and fetch him.'

'Mads, who is it?' Nathan appeared on the landing, looking disorientated. 'Oh.' A furrow formed in his brow, then he continued on down, tugging on a sweatshirt.

'I hear you've just arrived back in the UK?' Fletcher said.

'That's right.' His expression somewhere between cautious and curious, Nathan nodded him towards the lounge. 'What can we do for you, Detective?' he asked, pushing the door to behind Maddie.

'It's nothing to worry about,' DS Fletcher assured him. 'You're aware that Mrs Anderson came to see me?'

'I am.' Nathan nodded, casting a wary glance in Maddie's direction.

'We did another sweep of the apartment,' Fletcher said.

'And?' Nathan urged him, irritation in his tone. He was tired, Maddie reminded herself, and bound to be as wary about the early morning call as she was.

'We found some fingerprints.' Fletcher's gaze travelled between them. 'There's probably a simple explanation, but we're obliged to follow it up.'

Nathan's frown deepened. 'Fingerprints?'

'Yours specifically. There are quite a few, actually, throughout the apartment.' Fletcher paused, his expression enquiring.

'As there would be,' Nathan answered, a small tic playing at his cheek, indicating his agitation. 'Maddie and I helped David and Kiara move in.'

'Ah, that would probably explain it.' Fletcher nodded thoughtfully.

'Is that it?' Nathan asked, moving towards the door.

'There is just one more thing.' Fletcher stopped him. 'Did you have occasion to handle a bottle of wine at all?'

Nathan's expression was now one of bemusement. 'We took wine with us,' he supplied. 'As you do when you visit people.'

'Of course.' The detective smiled, seemingly satisfied. 'I imagine Mrs Beckett must have selected that particular wine to take into the bedroom with her. That's where we found it the night she died.' He fixed his gaze on Nathan's. 'The bottle.'

Nathan regarded him coolly. 'We took more than one bottle,' he said, breaking eye contact and turning to open the door. 'If that's everything, Detective Fletcher?'

'For now.' Fletcher offered him a short smile and headed for the hall.

Apprehension creeping through her, Maddie waited while Nathan showed the detective out. 'What was he implying?' she asked as soon as he shut the door.

Nathan sighed wearily. 'I really have no idea.'

'The wine. He said it was in the bedroom.' Her stomach tightened as she looked at her husband, who appeared to be pointedly not looking at her. 'Why would—'

'For Christ's *sake*, Maddie,' he snapped. 'What are *you* implying precisely? Would you like to tell me, because I don't have the slightest clue what the *hell's* going on here?'

Seeing the unmistakable flash of anger in his eyes, Maddie studied him, bewildered. 'I'm not implying anything. I just don't understand—'

'*We* took the wine when we went over there. I've just told Fletcher that.' Nathan spoke over her. 'I didn't even want to go, incidentally, you might recall. But we went because *you* didn't want to let David down. Which begs the question, why exactly are you two so chummy?' He narrowed his eyes.

'What's that supposed to mean?' she asked, flustered.

'You talk to him constantly, make arrangements without consulting me—'

'I do not.'

'*You* made the arrangement that night, Maddie. We went

because you wanted to. We left when you wanted to. Presumably the extra wine we'd taken with us was in the wine rack. Kiara clearly selected it to take into the bedroom the night she died. It doesn't mean *I* was in the bloody bedroom!'

Why was he so angry? Come to think of it, why had he been so reluctant to go that evening? Maddie felt her own hackles rising. 'Right.' She eyed him levelly. 'And she just happened to choose that one to take into the bedroom with her? To drink dressed in her underwear?'

'What?' He squinted hard at her. 'This is fucking—'

'Nathan!' Maddie's eyes swivelled to the stairs. The children weren't in evidence yet, but they might well be any second.

He followed her gaze, then lowered his voice. 'It's ridiculous, Maddie. All of it.' He ran his fingers through his hair. 'I have no idea what's going on in your mind, but if it's what I think it is, you're wrong.'

'Why did you lie about the time I came home on the night Kiara died?' she asked, growing more confused by the second. Why would he do that? Why was he doing *this*? One minute protective of her, the next seeming to turn against her. It made no sense. Nothing did.

Nathan shook his head and walked past her to the kitchen. Maddie followed him.

'Nathan, why did you *lie* for me?' she demanded.

He spun around to face her. 'Because you weren't here! You *didn't* come straight home from seeing your mother. You were popping those bloody pills and I was concerned. You had some absurd notion in your head that Kiara was avoiding you for some reason. You even accused me of taking sides with her. Christ only knows what your thinking was there. I panicked, okay? I told Fletcher you were here because I was worried that you might have gone to see her. That you two might have argued and ...' He stopped, breathing hard.

Maddie stared at him, icy realisation crashing through her. He hadn't needed to finish his sentence. It was right there in his eyes, a combination of doubt and fear. Fear for her.

'Your mind's all over the place when you take those things.' Nathan drove his point home hard. 'You need to stop, Maddie. Not just for a few weeks. Permanently.'

THIRTY-FOUR

Thinking they needed some space between them, perhaps thinking she would find answers to her own questions about her constantly troubled state of mind, Maddie had left the children with Nathan for the afternoon. Now that she was here, she wasn't sure why on earth she'd come. No matter how many times she'd been here, everything about the prison was a shock to her system. The constant noise, the banging of doors, the shouting, which could be heard as visitors filed across the yard. The screaming. Often a single shrill scream would pierce the air, chilling her to the bone as it triggered flashes from her childhood, raised voices, loud crashes. There were no images, though. No picture in her mind of what had happened. Back then, she'd closed her eyes, blocked it out. And had nightmares ever since.

Her mother was waiting when she went into the visitors' room. Her appearance was always shocking too. She dressed in her own clothes, the clothes Maddie had brought her, along with her cigarettes, but other than that, she made little effort with her appearance. Thin and frail under the tracksuit bottoms and loose-fitting tops she preferred, she looked older than her fifty-seven years. There was little left of the young woman Maddie remembered, the woman who'd run the local flower shop and been a mummy to her, pretty in her make-up, smiling as she shared magical stories with her at bedtime, as Maddie herself did with Ellie and Josh. Until the day she'd stopped smiling.

Maddie caught her breath as a wispy memory floated back, her mother sitting alone in her bedroom, quietly weeping. 'Go back to bed. I'm fine.' She'd spoken sharply as Maddie had approached her, wanting to comfort her mummy as a little girl would. Maddie had crept back along the dark landing to her room, knowing her mummy wasn't fine. She'd seen the crimson stain on the tissue she'd had pressed to her nose. She hadn't known where her daddy was. She'd never seen him again. She'd learned later, through a careless comment made by her father's sister, who'd taken her in, that they'd found his charred carcass alongside the burned garden shed. He'd obviously been trying to escape the inferno, her auntie had added, unaware of Maddie's presence as she'd listened from the stairs.

'How are you?' she asked her mother as she sat awkwardly opposite her. She guessed her mother would be evasive, answering her questions almost monosyllabically, avoiding anything that might allow Maddie to understand, which she desperately wanted to.

'Fine,' her mother replied, her gaze skimming over her. She never looked directly at her. Because she felt guilty, Maddie surmised, because she'd robbed her of both her parents on that dark night. Or was the guilt because, despite her claims to the contrary, she did remember buying the petrol, carrying the can home in the car, planning to murder the man who, drenched in accelerant, had stood no chance?

'Are they treating you well?' Maddie asked. To ask what she wanted to would be pointless. She never got answers.

A faint smile crossed her mother's face. 'As well as they did yesterday and the day before that,' she replied with a fatalistic sigh. 'Nothing changes here. How are things with you?'

'Fine,' Maddie lied. 'Nothing much to report there either.'

Her mother nodded. 'How's that husband of yours?'

Maddie wondered why she would ask. 'He's good,' she said. 'Back home at the moment.'

'I bet the children are happy to have him back.'

'Ecstatic. They almost trampled the poor dog underfoot dashing to greet him.' Maddie was relieved that her mother seemed to be in a talking mood. Time dragged slowly when she wasn't. With nothing but stilted conversation punctuated by long silences, minutes seemed like hours.

'And you?' Her mother looked at her, making actual eye contact. 'Are you glad he's home, Madeline? Were you happy to see him?'

Maddie blinked, taken aback. 'Yes,' she said with a confused shake of her head. She'd given her mother no reason to think she wasn't happy. 'Why on earth would you ask?'

'No particular reason.' Her mother looked away.

Maddie wondered whether she should just leave. This was a bad idea. Had she really expected her mother to open up to her? Imagined that if she could only understand the past, the horrors that were haunting her now might miraculously make sense? She was clutching at straws because she was scared, because Nathan was scared. For her. There were gaps in her memory, just as there had been when she was a terrified child, lost and alone and afraid of things that went bump in the night. She'd squeezed her eyes closed, burrowed under the duvet, closed off her mind.

Now she felt as if it was happening all over again, nightmares jolting her awake, flashes of images that might or might not be real. Strive as she might to remember certain events, her time spent driving around after leaving this godawful place the last time, she simply couldn't. Nathan knew all of this. That was why he was scared for her. In being scared, though, he was terrifying her.

'You loved your daddy,' her mother commented abstractedly.

Maddie looked at her in shocked disbelief. After all this time, year after year visiting her, willing her to talk, she suddenly came out with this? 'Why are you mentioning this now?' she asked shakily.

'It didn't stop him destroying you, though,' her mother went on as if she hadn't heard her. 'That's what he did when he decided to destroy me. And he did. They claim not to understand that cheating on the woman who's loved them, cared for them, supported them through thick and thin, given birth to their children leaves them bereft, questioning their sexuality, their very identity. They do understand, though, mark my words.'

She paused, a faraway look in her eyes. 'It was the lies I found so cruel,' she continued after a second, her tone flat. 'His constantly telling me it was all in my mind, until I began to think it might be, that I might be going mad. He would get angry if I called him a liar, but he was, of course. It's that that hurts most, the fact that they think you can't see through the lies. It's an insult to your intelligence, do you see?'

Her gaze met Maddie's, her eyes searching hers – for understanding, it seemed. Maddie laughed with bewildered incredulity. 'So you killed him?'

Her mother looked away. 'I didn't strike the match, Maddie,' she murmured.

'You *murdered* him.' Maddie stared at her, incredulous. 'You bought petrol. I was with you. I could smell it in the car. You burned him *alive!*'

Her mother hesitated before answering. 'I drove an old van, Maddie. It was usually filled with flowers to restock the shop. I didn't think you ever noticed the petrol smell that lingered in the back when it was empty.'

Maddie was speechless. Did she not realise what she was doing, calling her a liar almost, denying what she'd done still? Did she not understand the enormity of it, the devastating impact it had had on her, her *daughter*?

'He was violent, Maddie.' Her mother drew in a breath. 'I tried to shield you from it. His death was no loss to the world, I assure you.'

Maddie had no idea how to react. Was this an attempt to justify her actions? 'Why didn't you just leave him?' she asked, her throat dry.

Her mother smiled sadly. 'And go where? My parents loved him. Everybody loved him. He was so amiable in company, the life and soul of the party. It was only me who saw the other side of him. I called him the smiling executioner. I said it once to his face. He laughed at me. And then he got angry. He always got angry. I used to hide from him. You probably wouldn't remember that either. I would sometimes come into your room. Whenever he drank so much he fell into a stupor, I would curl up next to you. You felt safer then, I think.'

Maddie felt her heart catch, saw her six-year-old self on the landing, peering worriedly around the bedroom door, trying to understand what the loud crashes in the night were. She did remember how her mother would creep into her room. How she would sit on the window ledge, the window pushed partially open, and smoke a cigarette before coming into her bed. Maddie had been scared of the dark even then, but she'd felt comforted by the white light when her mother struck the match, the warm glow of the red tip of her cigarette. Had she known? As a small child, had she known her daddy wasn't always the smiling, friendly man he'd seemed?

'I hear your friend died,' her mother said jarringly. 'It was on the news,' she added when Maddie stared at her in shock.

'You must have been devastated, losing her in such an awful way. I know you two were close.'

Maddie shook her head, attempting to keep up with her. 'What's that got to do with anything?'

Her mother scrutinised her thoughtfully. 'Was it her he was having an affair with?'

'Who?' What was she *talking* about?

'You seemed so distracted when you last came, so unhappy. I assumed that might be the reason,' her mother went on.

It took a second for the penny to drop. When it did, Maddie felt her world shift violently off kilter. 'Are you talking about Nathan?' she whispered, astounded.

'I just wanted you to know I would understand if you felt driven to do something about it. I'm possibly the only person who would,' her mother continued, her brow creased with sympathy.

What utter *rubbish*. Maddie felt like laughing. But for the fact that Nathan had been acting so strangely, she might have. She saw him again comforting Kiara on that fateful New Year's Eve, his arms circling her, his eyes holding hers as he gently lifted her chin, his lips a whisper away from hers. Kiara had been evasive with her. From that night right up until she'd died, she'd avoided her. She'd been having an affair, David had confirmed it.

Fear pierced Maddie's chest like an icicle. There were parts of her memory missing, time she couldn't account for.

'Madeline, don't go.' Her mother reached for her as she scrambled for her bag and jumped to her feet.

Maddie whirled around, her blood pumping so fast her head swam.

'I'm here for you, Madeline,' her mother called as she flew to the exit.

Maddie's heart stalled. She stopped and turned slowly to face her. 'You're not *there* for me.' She glared at her, a tsunami of raw emotion crashing through her, deep, visceral anger, acrid grief for all that she'd lost, all that she might still lose. She closed her eyes as, out of nowhere, an image of the long-ago night her father died crashed into her mind. She saw herself, her child's hand clutching a matchbox. She'd been scared, terrified by the shouting and screaming coming from the garden. Frightened of the dark.

Gulping back the sharp stone in her throat, she tried to do the simplest thing of all in life and just breathe. There were gaps in her memory. With or without the tablets, there had been since that dreadful day. She'd seen Kiara in her dreams looking back at her, her face a mask of unadulterated terror. She'd seen through her eyes before the fall had snatched the life from her body; sensed someone emerging from the shadows. She'd thought she hadn't been there for her. But now ... Her stomach lurched, nausea rising hotly inside her. *Had* she been there after all?

THIRTY-FIVE

Nathan

Nathan watched as Fletcher, a man about the same age as himself, who looked as exhausted as he felt, closed the door of the interview room he'd suggested they have an informal chat in. 'Thanks for coming in,' he said, walking across to him and extending his hand.

Nathan hesitated, then shook it. 'No problem,' he assured him. 'I'd rather that than you turn up at the house.' He'd rather not be having chats, informal or otherwise, with the police at all, but he'd guessed that to refuse when Fletcher called him would have looked suspicious. 'The kids pick up on things,' he explained as the man appraised him curiously.

'Ah, of course.' Fletcher pulled out a chair and sat opposite him. 'I have two little ones myself. My wife prefers me not to share too much around them. So,' smiling congenially, he glanced down at the notes he placed on the table, 'as I mentioned on the phone, this is just an informal interview to clear up one or two points that are troubling us.'

Lacing his hands in front of him, Nathan leaned back in his chair and tried to relax. He had no idea where this was going, but the fact that the police had been digging around worried him. With things the way they were with Maddie, he was going to have to be careful. 'If I can help, then obviously I'm happy to.'

'Is your wife aware that you're here?' Fletcher enquired.

Nathan's guard went up at the mention of Maddie. 'Should she be?' He shifted uncomfortably.

'No, I just wondered,' Fletcher answered with an easy shrug.

'She's visiting her mother,' Nathan provided. His inclination was to tell the man as little as he needed to, but he guessed he'd probably done his homework and knew that Maddie's mother was serving an indeterminate sentence for murder. Plus, he didn't want him to think he was being deliberately evasive. 'Will this take long? It's just that I've had to leave the kids with the childminder at short notice.'

'No more than a few minutes. I've no doubt you'll be keen to get back.' Fletcher flicked through his notes, then settled his gaze back on Nathan. 'We found evidence of blood,' he said, getting bluntly to the point. 'On the kitchen floor.'

Shit. Nathan's gut turned over. 'Jesus,' he murmured, looking away. He hadn't meant to. His aim had been to hold the man's gaze and remain as calm as possible. Now he was feeling far from calm. 'Whose? I mean ...' He forced his gaze back to him. 'Is it Kiara's?'

Narrowing his eyes, Fletcher scanned his face, which really didn't help the nervous tension he could feel building inside him. 'It belongs to Kiara Beckett, yes,' he confirmed.

'Christ.' Nathan resisted wiping away the trickle of sweat he could feel beading his forehead. 'So how come you're only mentioning this now? Shouldn't it have been picked up before?'

he asked, playing for time. His throat was dry. He wanted to reach for the coffee he'd been supplied, but folded his arms across his chest instead. His hands shaking would definitely indicate he might be hiding something.

Fletcher nodded as if it were a fair point. 'We had no reason to believe Mrs Beckett's death wasn't suicide,' he replied, scrutinising him carefully. 'Until your wife came to us, that is.'

Nathan said nothing. There was nothing he could say that wouldn't draw further attention to Maddie, to him. He wished to God she'd spoken to him before talking to the police. She obviously hadn't factored in that the first people they would look at if they had any doubts about the way Kiara had died would be those closest to her. And the first thing they found when they went back in there: a wine bottle with his prints all over it. He doubted very much they would just dismiss it as coincidence.

'The blood had been thoroughly cleaned up,' Fletcher went on. 'Not quite meticulously enough to eliminate specks that had bled into the grouting, however.'

Nathan frowned thoughtfully. 'But it could have been there for a while?' he asked. 'From an old injury maybe?'

'Possibly,' Fletcher conceded. 'We also found blood in the lounge,' he continued, 'which gives us further cause for concern. Again only specks, but enough to warrant further forensic investigation.'

'I see.' Nathan felt a cold knot of apprehension tighten his stomach.

'I don't suppose you have any idea how the blood got there?' Fletcher asked.

The knot tied itself tighter. 'No. Why would I have?'

'I just wondered, as you were close friends, whether you might have been aware of any incident or accident that might have accounted for it.'

Nathan studied him for a second. What was he saying here?

'No. Sorry, none,' he said, making a show of checking his watch as he glanced away. 'Is there anything else? I should really get back.'

'Just a couple of things. Shouldn't take long.' Fletcher consulted his paperwork. 'You mentioned that Mrs Anderson came straight home after visiting her mother on the evening of Mrs Beckett's death.'

Nathan felt himself tense. 'That's right,' he confirmed, running his free hand tightly around the wrist of his watch arm.

Fletcher nodded and made a note. 'Did you have any reason to contact Mrs Beckett on the evening in question?'

Nathan took a second. 'No,' he answered. 'Not that I remember.'

Fletcher made another note. 'We've retrieved certain data from her mobile,' he informed him, and let it hang, no doubt to make him sweat. It was working. Nathan swallowed back the panic rising inside him.

'There were several texts from your wife,' the detective went on. 'It seems the two women had had a falling-out.'

Nathan furrowed his brow, as if that were news to him. Why was it so bloody hot in here? Had they banged the heating up on purpose? He desperately wanted to take off his jacket, but didn't dare.

'Mrs Beckett didn't reply to many of them,' Fletcher continued, 'although there was a short phone call made from Mrs Beckett's phone to your wife's phone, which I believe was a recent purchase?'

'A Christmas present, yes,' Nathan replied shortly.

Fletcher wrote that down too, then, holding Nathan's gaze, got to the question he'd obviously been taking his sweet time over. 'Interestingly, there was a text on her phone sent from you at eight ten p.m. on the evening she died. Did you send that text, Mr Anderson?'

Nathan glanced down, rubbed his thumb against his forehead. 'Yes,' he replied. 'Sorry, I'm afraid with all that's gone on since, it completely slipped my mind.'

'Understandable.' Fletcher nodded. His expression told Nathan he didn't believe a word of it.

'I was trying to get hold of Maddie,' Nathan added. 'I thought she might have gone to see Kiara.'

'Strange.' Fletcher frowned. 'The text, I mean. I would have thought you might have sent something like "Is Maddie with you?" rather than "Are you okay? Call me."'

'Yes, I, er ... She hadn't been much in touch with Maddie. I wondered—'

'She arrived home on time, though? Maddie?' Fletcher interrupted.

Nathan paused before answering. He was under suspicion here, or at least he might soon be. 'There's no "on time",' he pointed out, working to keep his voice on an even keel. 'Maddie visits her mother out of a sense of duty. The meetings are never easy for her. She leaves when she's had enough, basically. Then there's the drive back. Sometimes, if she's feeling particularly emotional, she'll stop for a coffee. She said she'd come straight home that evening. What I actually said was that she was there when I arrived at around nine.'

Fletcher acknowledged the point with another short nod. 'But you needed to get hold of her urgently?'

Nathan held his gaze. 'Not urgently exactly, no. One of the kids wasn't well.'

'Too many treats at the birthday party?' Fletcher said understandingly. Then, 'Did you drive to the party, Mr Anderson?' he asked him.

'No.' Nathan guessed he knew that already, but buried his frustration and answered anyway. 'It was at McDonald's in the city centre. There's not much parking, so I left the car in the car park and we took the train. It's just a couple of stops away.'

And the deceased's city-centre apartment is within walking distance of McDonald's, he half expected the detective to say.

'And did you have any reason to leave the party?' Fletcher asked, inevitably.

'No,' Nathan stated categorically.

Fletcher made yet another note. Nathan was beginning to feel nauseous. Also irritated. He needed to get out of here, back to his kids.

'And when you arrived home, one of the children wasn't well?'

'Ellie,' Nathan confirmed. 'I just needed to know where the Calpol was.'

Fletcher eyed him quizzically. 'Strange thing to worry her with considering where she was, the emotional toll on her you mentioned.'

Nathan considered him thoughtfully in turn. 'I also wanted to let her know Ellie was off colour. She would have wanted me to. Wouldn't your wife want to know if one of your children was ill, Detective Fletcher?'

'She would.' Fletcher conceded that point. 'But you couldn't get hold of her?'

'I'd forgotten that she would have had to hand in her phone before visiting her mother,' Nathan said. 'Where is this going, DS Fletcher?'

'Just making sure we have all the information we need,' Fletcher answered. 'We have to be thorough in our investigation. I'm sure you understand.'

Nathan nodded slowly. 'Pity you weren't so thorough in your initial investigation,' he said flatly. 'I need to go. I take it I'm free to?'

'Of course.' Fletcher gathered up his papers and got to his feet. 'We'll be in touch should we need to corroborate anything further.'

Nathan hesitated. 'Can I also assume I'm free to do my job,

DS Fletcher? I'm due to leave the country again shortly. Are you going to ask me not to?'

Fletcher eyed him carefully. 'No,' he said after an interminably long minute. 'I would ask that you make sure to leave all your contact details, though.'

THIRTY-SIX

Maddie

'*Blood?*' Maddie stared at Nathan in bewildered astonishment. He was packing his case. He'd just told her that her friend's, *their* friend's, blood had been found in the apartment, that he'd been questioned about it at the police station, and now he was travelling abroad again? Tomorrow morning? Her stomach roiled, panic taking root inside her as she watched him going from the wardrobe to the drawers. 'But how? Where was it found? And why wasn't it found before?'

On his way back to his case with a handful of garments, Nathan shrugged. 'I have no idea,' he said, stuffing the clothes inside. 'It was cleaned up, according to Fletcher.' He paused, glancing briefly in her direction, before continuing his task, seemingly oblivious to the fact that he would be leaving her alone with all of this. 'There were specks left behind, I gather, in the grouting on the kitchen floor, some in the lounge. They're looking into how it might have got there. They have to be *thorough* in their investigation, apparently.'

Maddie noted his scornful tone. 'But it would have been from an accident, surely?' She searched for an explanation. 'She must have cut herself with a kitchen knife or a glass.'

'That, I imagine, is what they're trying to establish,' Nathan said shortly.

Why was he acting this way? He seemed so angry. Nothing like the light-hearted Nathan she knew. *Everybody loved him. He was so amiable in company, the life and soul of the party. It was only me who saw the other side of him. I called him the smiling executioner.* Her mother's voice floated back to her, the look in her eyes one of interested curiosity as she'd studied her, as if assessing whether Maddie knew her own husband.

A hard lump expanded in her chest. 'Why did they ask you about it specifically?' she asked shakily. Why did they want you to go to the station? I don't—'

'I have no idea about that either.' He slammed the lid of his case shut, then drew in a breath and turned his gaze to the ceiling. Finally he looked at her properly. 'I'm sorry,' he said, his tone more subdued. 'I have no idea why they wanted to talk to me specifically, Maddie. The fact is, though, they're bound to want to, aren't they, after you went to them asking them to reopen the investigation.'

Maddie squinted at him, a confusion of emotion swirling inside her as she noted his unimpressed expression. Was he blaming her? She felt he was, but she didn't know why. 'They wouldn't have reopened the case if they hadn't thought there was good reason to,' she pointed out, willing him to talk to her, to tell her what he was thinking.

'No,' he conceded. 'I know. I just …' He fell silent.

'Kiara's death might not have been as it seems. Doesn't that concern you?' Maddie searched his face, willing him to reassure her in some way.

He sighed heavily. 'I *am* concerned. Of course I'm concerned, but my fingerprints are all over the apartment.' He looked at her in despair. 'On the assumption they're looking at someone else being there that night, and since there was no evidence of anyone having broken in, they're looking at me, don't you see? How soon do you think it will be before they're gathering other DNA evidence? Microscopic particles of clothing. Christ only knows what they might come up with.'

Like what? Maddie was growing more bewildered by the second. 'But we've explained that we helped them move in. They'll soon establish that you weren't there that evening.'

'Right,' Nathan answered tersely. 'How?'

'I don't know.' He *was* scared. She could feel it. 'Witnesses,' she said. 'The parents at the party. They'll all corroborate you were at McDonald's, won't they?'

Nathan didn't answer, causing fear to slice through her. 'You don't get it, do you, Maddie?' he said, his expression one of disillusionment.

'Get what?' Her breath stalling in her chest, she watched as he dropped heavily down on the bed. 'Nathan?'

He dragged his hands over his face. 'I texted her that night. I hoped she might talk to me, tell me what the hell was going on between you two. I wondered whether you might even be there.'

Maddie tried to digest this. 'You know where I was,' she said, apprehension and nausea churning inside her.

'Do I?' He studied her, the look of mistrust in his eyes causing her heart to turn over. 'I'm not worried for myself, Mads,' he said, his voice thick with emotion. 'It's *you* I'm—'

'Daddy,' Ellie said from the doorway. 'There's bugs under my bed. I can hear them scratching.'

Nathan swiped an arm across his eyes and got to his feet. 'Coming, sweetheart.'

Glancing again at Maddie as he walked past her, he bent to

sweep Ellie up. 'There won't be any,' he assured her, pressing a soft kiss to her forehead. 'You were probably dreaming, but how about I check anyway?'

'But there might be.' Ellie's fearful tones drifted back as he carried her along the landing. 'They might be hiding. Josh said they hide in dark places. If I can't go back to sleep, can I sleep in the big bed, Daddy?'

THIRTY-SEVEN

Sensing someone leaning over her, Maddie woke with a start.

'It's just me,' Nathan whispered. 'I have to go. My taxi's here.'

'What time is it?' She blinked, confused. He couldn't be leaving already. She was desperate to talk to him since their fraught conversation last night had ended so abruptly.

'Early. Five o'clock. Go back to sleep.' He reached to ease the duvet up over her and Ellie, who couldn't be persuaded back to bed and was now sleeping soundly curled up close to Maddie. 'I'll call you,' he promised. 'I shouldn't be gone for more than a few days. We've managed to get hold of someone in the US who can take over. Will you be okay?'

Maddie nodded uncertainly. He was suspicious of her. He truly was. He didn't trust her. The frightening thing was, she wasn't sure she trusted herself. Her nightmares, the images her dysfunctional mind conjured up, seemed as real to her as the bugs under the bed were to Ellie.

'I'll be back before you know it.' Nathan leaned to kiss her forehead.

Panic mushrooming inside her, Maddie reached for his

hand as he straightened up. 'Don't go,' she almost begged him. Since visiting her mother, a sense of foreboding had settled icily inside her, and try as she might, she couldn't make it go away. Something was going to happen, something bad, she could feel it.

'I have to.' He squeezed her hand. 'There are children getting sick, Mads. I can't just abandon them. You know I can't. I'll be home as soon as I can, I promise.'

She listened to the bedroom door close. She heard him pause on the landing, pictured him peering through Josh's partially open door to make sure his son was okay. He loved his children. He would die before allowing any harm to come to them. She was sure of that. *She* loved *him*, the caring man she knew him to be. She could never envisage a day when she wouldn't, how she would ever survive without him.

Hearing the front door open, she eased herself carefully away from Ellie and went across to the window. Drawing the curtain back, she watched him climb into the taxi. Shivering in the cool morning air, she wrapped her arms tightly about herself as she waited for it to pull away. She knew what it was like to be alone. She'd felt it the second the police had taken her mother away. Standing here now, though, she felt more alone than she'd ever felt in her life.

Guessing that sleep was out of the question, that if she did drift off her mind would wander to unbearably dark places, she checked Ellie was still sleeping, then collected her dressing gown and crept out of the room.

Sitting at the kitchen table with Boomer warming her feet and her laptop in front of her, she decided to pass the time until the children woke up flicking through images of happier times, those on her Facebook page of Nathan and herself with Ellie and Josh. There were many of away days and holidays where Nathan was either building sandcastles with the children or else being buried in the sand. Further back, beautiful pictures capturing perfect moments in time, Nathan cradling his newborn babies, his face filled with awe as he studied them, counting fingers and toes, pressing soft kisses to tiny noses. She came across one that caused her breath to catch. With Ellie nestled in the crook of his arm, Nathan had looked up as Maddie snapped the shot, and the love and pride shining in his eyes had touched her to the very core.

She'd felt so safe with him, so emotionally protected. Did he realise how much she loved him? Had she told him lately? She was working hard now to hold the tears back, something Boomer instinctively picked up on and immediately jumped up to place his big paws on her lap. 'It's okay, sweetheart,' she assured him, looking into his anxious chocolate-brown eyes as she stroked his head. 'Mummy's just a bit tired.'

Placated, Boomer settled back down with a wag of his tail. Never more grateful to have his comforting presence close by, Maddie made a mental note to buy him a special treat on the way home from the park later, and continued to scroll through the memories she and Nathan had made together, which were inarguably real. She couldn't believe those she'd posted of the two of them early on in their relationship. Nathan had hardly changed. He had the odd extra crinkle at the corners of his eyes, but he was still unfairly young-looking. She, on the other hand, definitely wasn't the carefree young woman she'd been then. Had she ever been carefree, though, really? Photographs supposedly didn't lie, but Maddie thought that perhaps she'd had to work hard at being happy. She hadn't wanted to be someone with baggage that Nathan might also be forced to drag around. Yet now here he was, weighed down by it. Could she blame him if he were to seek the company of someone less encumbered?

He hadn't. He wouldn't. Quashing her baseless suspicions, she moved forward through her posts. There were endless photos of her and Kiara: on girls' nights out together, out shop-

ping. Many more of them both with David and Nathan, celebrating birthdays and special days. Always New Year's Eve.
Her heart folded up inside her as she realised she hadn't taken
any this year. She'd meant to.

Flicking through the photos, she noticed how Nathan
always seemed to be smiling. He was frowning in a few, but
even then there was amusement dancing in his eyes. *Amiable in
company, the life and soul of the party.* Maddie breathed in
sharply. Scrolling further, she couldn't help noticing how often
his arm was draped around Kiara.

Rubbish. She was feeding into her mother's nonsense.
There were just as many photos where Nathan had his arm
around *her* shoulders. Several where he was giving David a
matey hug. That was who he was. Why then did she
suddenly feel she didn't know him? That he didn't
know her?

Ridiculous. All of it. Her mind was obviously on a roll,
conjuring up things that simply didn't exist. There was nothing
wrong with their relationship, or at least there hadn't been until
now. Had there? Of course there hadn't. She would have
known. But he was away such a lot, often disappearing off to the
university in the evenings.

She willed herself to stop before she really did drive herself
mad. Quickly she exited the site, then jumped as her mobile
buzzed to her side. Thinking it might be Nathan ringing from
the airport, she snatched it up, ready to ask him point blank
what it was *he* was imagining. She was about to answer when
she realised it wasn't Nathan. She hesitated, and then tentatively accepted the call.

'Mrs Anderson, sorry to disturb you,' DS Fletcher said. 'I
was trying to get hold of your husband, but his phone's going to
voicemail.'

Perturbed, Maddie glanced at the kitchen clock. It was still
early. Too early for the police to be calling. 'He's away,' she said,

a knot of trepidation tightening inside her. 'On a work trip. He left a few hours ago.'

'Ah, that would explain it. Most likely he's just boarded the plane.'

'Probably.' Maddie felt a fresh wave of loneliness wash through her. 'Is it something I can help you with?'

DS Fletcher hesitated, then, 'Actually, yes,' he said. 'I'm just trying to ascertain Mr Anderson's movements within the Becketts' apartment.'

Maddie gripped the phone hard.

'He mentioned you were there on the day they moved in,' Fletcher went on. 'That you took wine with you, which might explain the fingerprints we found on the bottle in the bedroom. I was just wondering, though, whether he had occasion to go physically into the bedroom; to help move some piece of furniture perhaps? We've found further fingerprints. Obviously I need to establish when they might have been left.'

'I don't know,' Maddie stammered. 'He did help David move various bits and pieces,' she said, the knot of trepidation in her tummy twisting itself tighter. 'I honestly can't remember. Have you asked David?'

'I've left a message on his mobile. He mentioned that his mother isn't well, so I thought it might be a bit early to ring his parents' house. Not to worry, I'm sure he'll call back and confirm it one way or the other,' Fletcher assured her. 'Oh, incidentally, we found one or two of those spiders you mentioned scurrying around. I did think it was a bit odd, I must admit. There aren't enough of them to qualify as an infestation as such, but enough to terrify someone who has a phobia.'

'Yes, that's what I thought.' Maddie swallowed. Wished to God she'd never mentioned them, or spoken to him at all, in fact. She'd felt she owed it to Kiara. Now she wasn't sure what she felt, other than petrified. The nagging worry in her head was growing more persistent. *Had* Nathan and Kiara ...? No, it was ludicrous. As was the notion that she herself had been there on the night Kiara died. Nathan didn't think it was, though. Hadn't he told her he thought she might have been? He would never have done that unless he believed it.

'I'll be in touch if I have any further information,' DS Fletcher said. 'Again, sorry to have disturbed you.'

'No problem.' Maddie took a breath. 'Could you just tell me, the furniture you found the fingerprints on, what was it?'

'They were on the chrome headboard in the main bedroom,' Fletcher provided after a pause, 'as if it had been gripped onto tightly.'

THIRTY-EIGHT

Maddie gave it an hour after DS Fletcher had rung, using the time to get the children's breakfast, and then made the call she knew she had to. *Please pick up.* Pressing her phone to her ear, she glanced through the kitchen window to see Ellie and Josh racing around the garden playing ball with Boomer. At least they were happy, oblivious to the fact that the foundations of her life seemed to be crumbling. Was her marriage falling apart without her even having noticed the cracks? She couldn't believe that was true. That Nathan would ever deceive her. But what if he had? What if he'd been deeply unhappy and hadn't told her? She swallowed back a hard lump in her chest. She would have to deal with it. Somehow she would have to maintain a sense of normality for the children's sake. *David, please, please pick up*, she willed him. He knew Nathan. If anyone could put her mind at rest, David could.

She was about to hang up before his phone went to voicemail again when, mercifully, he answered. 'Mads?' he said, a curious edge to his voice. 'Everything okay?'

'No. I don't know.' Her voice quavered. 'I've been trying to get hold of you for ages. DS Fletcher has too. Where were you?'

'Out,' David replied, clearly puzzled. 'I took my parents into town. I thought it would do my mother good to get some fresh air. Sorry. I forgot my phone. I haven't had a chance to check it yet.'

'No, I'm sorry,' Maddie apologised, realising she'd spoken to him sharply and had no right to ask him where he'd been. After all he'd suffered, didn't he deserve a little normality in his life? 'I wouldn't have bothered you, but there's something I need to ask you.'

'It's no bother, Maddie,' David assured her kindly. 'You can call me any time, you know that. It's always good to hear from you.'

Maddie wasn't sure he would think so when she asked him what she needed to. She would much rather not. The last thing she wanted to do was plant the same seeds of doubt in his mind that seemed to be gnawing insidiously away at hers, but what choice did she have? She'd opened a can of worms around Kiara's death, and now they were spilling out. Nathan was suspicious of her, she of him. She felt as if she really might be going insane. And the worst thing was that it was Nathan who seemed to be causing her to question her sanity.

Making sure the children weren't about to charge through the back door, she steeled herself. 'It's about Nathan,' she said.

'Nathe?' David sounded surprised. 'Is that what Fletcher was calling me about?'

'He found more fingerprints.' Maddie got straight to the point.

David paused. 'You mean other than those on the wine bottle?'

Hearing the wariness in his voice, Maddie hesitated. How did she do this without dredging up painful memories for him? 'They're probably still there from the day you moved in,' she suggested carefully.

'Right.' David paused again and Maddie almost changed

her mind. But DS Fletcher would ask him anyway. And she needed to know, though she really didn't want to. 'So where were they?' he asked.

'In the bedroom,' Maddie answered reluctantly.

'I see.' David went quiet.

Maddie hesitated. 'Do you remember whether Nathan helped move anything in there? Or whether he went in there for any other reason? Other than when you were showing him around, I mean.'

David took a second. 'To be honest, I can't,' he replied uncertainly. 'He carried a couple of boxes up for Kiara from the car, but ... Where were they exactly, Mads, these fingerprints?'

Maddie wavered. This was unbearable. If her suspicions turned out to be true, it would kill her as surely as if Nathan had driven a knife through her heart. And it would utterly destroy David. 'On the headboard of the bed,' she told him, her tone flat, defeated, even to her own ears.

David drew in a sharp breath. 'Can I ask you something, Maddie?' he said eventually.

Maddie felt her stomach plummet. She knew what it was before he spoke.

'Do you think it was Nathan Kiara was having an affair with?'

'I don't know.' She squeezed her answer past the constriction in her throat.

Another long silence followed. Then, 'I'm not entirely sure what you're asking me, Mads,' David said, his voice tight. 'Are you asking me to tell Fletcher that Nathan did go into the bedroom on the day we moved in?'

THIRTY-NINE

After dropping the children off at school, Maddie had rung Sophie and was relieved when she'd agreed to meet her. She wasn't sure whether Sophie would be able to offer any more information than she already had, but she was praying she might. With every hour that passed, she was growing more convinced she was going slowly out of her mind. Either that or she'd been hopelessly blind.

Leaving work promptly at lunchtime, she was sitting in the café opposite Kiara's salon when her phone rang. She reached for it. *Nathan.* Breathing deeply, she hesitated and then rejected the call. She would have to speak to him, but not yet. She wasn't ready.

Her stomach knotted with nerves, she switched the phone to silent and glanced back to the salon, to see Sophie emerging. She looked radiant, her glossy red hair piled artistically on top of her head, leggings and a short biker jacket complimenting her slim figure. Wearing her staple jeans with a simple shirt, Maddie felt dowdier by comparison than she ever had.

Seeing her in the window, Sophie smiled and waved enthusiastically, then came across the road. 'Hi,' she said, hurrying through the door and snatching up the menu as she sat opposite her. 'Sorry I'm a bit late. Things are hectic at the moment. I have a lot of Kiara's clients now, so I'm run off my feet.'

Maddie ran her eyes over her, feeling both irked and saddened. Sophie probably just wasn't thinking, but she seemed unperturbed by the fact that Kiara having died was the reason she was so busy. 'That's a good thing, though, isn't it, that you've been able to take over her client list?' she commented, working to keep any pointedness from her voice.

'Hell.' Sophie squeezed her eyes closed. 'That was really tactless, wasn't it? Sorry, Maddie. I can't say I'm not relieved to be building up my own list. With Jake having lost his job and two children demanding the latest trends in everything, money's a bit tight. But obviously I'm devastated about the circumstances.'

'Oh, I'm sorry. I didn't realise.' Maddie felt bad for her. She also empathised. Things had been tight for her and Nathan while they'd both been completing their training. She certainly couldn't blame Sophie for being relieved at having some extra income coming in.

'It's fine. Or I'm sure it will be. He has some interviews lined up.' Sophie glanced back to the menu. 'They have triple-layer chocolate cake,' she said, looking slightly flustered. Embarrassed at having to admit things were tight, Maddie supposed. 'Shall we treat ourselves?'

Reminded of the half-eaten chocolate bar she'd found in Kiara's fridge, Maddie felt another wave of raw grief wash through her. Her friend would never have been able to resist chocolate cake. 'Just a coffee for me. I had an early lunch,' she lied. She had very little appetite anyway. Now, she doubted she could eat a morsel.

'Oh.' Sophie looked her over, her forehead creasing into a concerned frown. 'Are you okay?' she asked. 'You look upset.'

'I am,' Maddie admitted, glancing again towards the salon.

She'd sat at this very table with Kiara once, looking across at the empty shop as Kiara had outlined her plans for it. Sitting here now, she could feel her heart breaking as she considered how Kiara had died, the fact that they'd barely been communicating. She'd been desperate to know why before she'd learned of her death. She was still, but she didn't think she could bear it if the reason was what she was beginning to dread it was.

'Of course you are.' Sophie reached across the table for her hand, squeezing it gently. 'And here's me chuntering on nineteen to the dozen. I'm really sorry, Maddie. You must think I'm awful.'

'Of course I don't. It's fine, honestly.' Maddie gave her a small smile. 'I know you'd rather not have built up your client list like this, but I'm pleased that things are working out for you.'

'Thanks.' Sophie smiled back. 'So, you said you had some questions for me when you rang. I'm happy to answer them if I can,' she said with an uncertain shrug. Maddie noticed there was a sudden guardedness in her eyes.

'Not questions exactly,' she started, and paused while the waiter took their order. Once he'd gone, she drew in a breath and pushed on. 'I gathered you and Kiara had grown quite close and I just wondered if you could tell me a bit more about how she seemed generally.'

Sophie looked thoughtful. 'I wouldn't say close, but we were friends, yes. I'm not sure how much else I can tell you, though.' She sighed regretfully. 'Like I said, she seemed to be okay. A little manic recently maybe, but I think that was to do with the fact that she was planning to extend the salon. You know, drawing up the plans, interviewing people.'

'Did she seem happy?' Maddie asked. She really wanted to ask whether it was Sophie who'd told Fletcher Kiara might be having an affair, and if so, did she have any idea who with, but she could hardly do that.

'She seemed to be, certainly for a few weeks before she ...' Sophie trailed off awkwardly.

'And before then?

She thought about it. 'Well, she wasn't *un*happy, but I noticed a definite change in her. I think we all did.'

'Did she mention David much?' Maddie fished. She was probably being too obvious, but she had to gather as much information as she could before talking to Nathan. Her chest constricted painfully at that prospect.

Sophie knitted her brow. 'Thinking about it, she didn't really. I did wonder whether there might be a few problems there before they split up, to be honest. She sometimes avoided taking calls from him, and that seemed a bit peculiar. Oh, and she once nipped out the entrance at the back of the shop when he came in. She said they'd had words, but she didn't elaborate.'

Maddie's heart twisted. They obviously had had words if David had suspected Kiara was having an affair. Poor David. What must all this have done to his confidence?

'We all do it, don't we?' Sophie added with another sigh. 'Have moments where avoiding our dearly beloved is the preferable option to killing them.'

That comment jarred. It was just a glib remark, though, Maddie told herself. Sophie clearly wasn't one to pause for thought. 'Did you ever notice anyone else popping in?' she asked as casually as she could.

Sophie eyed her curiously.

'I wondered whether there might have been someone in her life who'd upset her in some way,' she added with a hopeful shrug. 'I'm looking for explanations, I suppose.'

Sophie narrowed her eyes as she studied her. 'Not really,' she said, after a pause. 'Nathan dropped by, I recall. Other than that, no one apart from plumbers or electricians. The water pressure is always dropping for some reason. Oh, and more recently, a few tradesmen came to offer estimates on the building works for the extension.'

Maddie hardly heard the rest of what she'd said. 'Nathan?' she asked, her throat suddenly dry.

'Just after New Year,' Sophie provided. 'Something to do with your birthday, Kia said. She was thinking of planning a surprise for you.'

'Oh, right.' Maddie's heartbeat ratcheted up. It certainly would have been a surprise, considering her birthday wasn't until much later in the year. Anger tightened inside her. Why hadn't Nathan mentioned this?

FORTY

After a long afternoon forcing herself to focus on the job she was not only paid to do, but which she needed to do well for the children in her care, Maddie was walking towards the car park when her phone rang. Still feeling unable to talk to Nathan, she checked it and found it was from an unknown number. Thinking it might be a sales call, she debated for a second and then hesitantly answered.

'Madeline, it's Katie,' a woman's voice said. 'David's sister,' she added, as if her brusque tone wasn't enough to remind Maddie who she was. 'You do realise how upset he is, don't you?'

Maddie was taken aback. 'Of course,' she said, not sure what else to say. 'He's bound to be, isn't he? I was going to call him later. I'm just on my way—'

'Do you really think you should?'

'Sorry?' Maddie slowed to a stop.

'Have you any idea what you're doing?' the woman demanded angrily.

'I'm not sure what you mean.' Maddie frowned, confounded.

'I'll speak plainly then, shall I?' Katie said, a definite acerbic edge to her voice. 'David doesn't need people calling him right now for their own selfish reasons. He has enough problems to be dealing with, as *you* should be well aware.'

What on *earth*? 'Of course I'm aware,' Maddie replied, disbelieving. 'David's a dear friend to me. Of course I'm going to stay in contact with him. I'm very concerned about him.'

'Are you? Are you really?' Katie asked. 'Or is it yourself you're concerned for?' she went on before Maddie could answer.

Maddie took a breath. She didn't need this. She didn't want to have a conversation with a woman who clearly had some kind of a problem with anyone David was close to. 'I really have no idea what you're talking about, Katie,' she said, her anger mounting. 'Now, I really have to go. I have to pick up—'

'You're trying to manipulate him!' Katie seethed over her.

'What?' Maddie laughed, astounded. Was the woman on something? No. Remembering how she'd been with Kiara all those years ago, Maddie realised that her first impressions had been right. Katie was simply not a very nice person, which was surprising considering that David was the complete opposite.

'After all he's been through, I can't believe you had the gall to actually ask him to lie for you,' Katie went on.

'I did no such thing,' Maddie started furiously, only for Katie to talk over her again.

'Hasn't he suffered enough?' she asked her. 'He's already consumed with guilt, thinking he wasn't good enough for a woman who was *never* good enough for him. That he was the reason the selfish cow took her own life. Now he has to feel guilty if he doesn't compromise himself and lie for his so-called friends!'

Finally Maddie had some inkling of what she was talking about. She was referring to the conversation she and David had

had about the fingerprints in the bedroom. But Maddie hadn't asked him to lie for Nathan. She would never have done that.

'His mental health has been deteriorating for years at the hands of that trollop, who did nothing but use him, taking advantage of his good nature right from the outset,' Katie went on, spitting vitriol. 'He's better off without her, if only he would realise it. As for you and that husband of yours, he doesn't need friends like that in his life. If you care for him at all, as you claim you do, I suggest you stay out of it.'

Maddie stared at her phone as she realised the woman had ended the call, leaving her absolutely staggered. She'd thought *she* was going mad, but Katie was on another level. Maddie had assumed she was overly protective of David. In fact, she'd seemed to be seething with jealousy. It was no wonder David was so unsure of himself. His sister had obviously kept tabs on him wherever she'd been in the world.

FORTY-ONE

'Maddie?' Maddie heard someone calling her name as she stood where she was for a moment. She was so shocked, so bloody angry, she was literally shaking. She was of half a mind to call Katie back, but for the fact that might make things worse for David, who she was sure would be unaware that his sister had taken it upon herself to call her. She would certainly be ringing David. And when she did, it would be to offer him the sympathy and support she doubted very much Katie had ever provided.

'Maddie!' Whoever it was called again.

She looked up and was astounded when she realised it was Jake who was hurrying towards her.

'Sorry to leap on you.' He stopped as, uncertain what he wanted, how on earth he'd found her, Maddie took a step away from him. 'Are you okay?' he asked. 'You look a bit shocked.'

'An emotional conversation.' She brushed it off, thinking that Jake wouldn't be the best person to confide in. 'What are you doing here, Jake? How did you know where I worked?' She tried to calm herself, though her nerves were churning. She was very aware that there was no one else about. She had no idea whether what David had said about Jake was true. After seeing him at the funeral, she was struggling to believe that it might have been him who'd attacked Kiara, but still, she felt wary.

'I, er, checked out your social media accounts. Your FB profile says you're a special needs teacher and I made some calls,' Jake admitted with an embarrassed shrug. 'I'm not stalking you, I promise,' he added quickly, now looking worried. 'I just needed someone to talk to, I guess. Someone who knew her.'

Maddie hesitated. She wasn't sure she was the greatest judge of character, certainly lately, but she could see he was struggling. 'Someone who couldn't believe how she died?' she ventured, wanting to see his reaction.

He dropped his gaze. 'Doesn't make much difference, though, does it?' He shrugged again, a defeated, hopeless gesture. 'However it happened, she's still dead.'

Maddie wasn't sure what to say. He looked angry, as confused as she felt, and was clearly grieving. 'Do you want to go for a coffee?' she asked him. 'It will have to be a quick one, but there's a café down the road if you'd like to.'

'I would.' Jake looked relieved. 'Thanks, Maddie.'

'No problem.' She wanted to talk to him, but not here in the middle of the empty car park.

Checking in with the childminder, she told her where she was and that she wouldn't be long, then led the way to the café.

'I'll get them. What do you fancy?' Jake offered as they went in.

'A straight black coffee for me. I could use the caffeine,' Maddie said, heading for a table in the corner. She felt so tired, she was sure one of these days she would fall asleep on her feet.

He was soon back, carrying two steaming mugs. 'I asked them to put a dash of cold water in there so you don't scald yourself. Hope that's okay?'

'Perfect.' Maddie took a grateful sip. And thoughtful. She

glanced at him over her mug. He looked as exhausted as she felt. As if he hadn't slept for a week. There was no hostility in his eyes. Still some anger, but the same kind of anger that burned inside her, she perceived. Anger born of frustration and confusion. She was relieved that he appeared approachable. She'd never imagined he would be that until she'd seen him again recently. Surely David had been wrong about him?

'Do you mind if I ask you something?' she said.

Jake frowned pensively, then wrapped his hands around his mug and fixed his gaze on it. 'No.' He sighed. 'I guessed you'd have questions.'

'About before you split up with her ...' she started hesitantly.

'Thanks to some bastard spreading rumours around the campus to make sure we did split up,' Jake said agitatedly. 'Sorry about the language. I was angry then. I'm still angry.' He glanced apologetically at her and then back to his coffee.

It was obvious that he really had loved her. Maddie felt for him. He'd clearly been badly shaken by her death. 'Did she ever seem down to you back then?' she asked him carefully. 'Did she ever suffer any depressive episodes? I'm sorry,' she apologised in turn as he looked at her curiously again. 'I'm just trying to understand what happened.'

Jake tugged in a breath. 'I get it.' He nodded. 'Yes, there were depressive episodes after the attack, but if you want my honest opinion, they weren't solely because of it.'

Maddie frowned. 'I'm not sure I'm following.'

'If she were here, I think she would tell you it was more to do with the perception other people had of her. She didn't want to be treated like a victim after that bastard attacked her. I know everyone was trying to help, but it seemed to me that they were doing precisely that, being careful of her feelings. It was natural, I know, people were concerned for her, but ... I don't know. I think she lost sight of herself, if that makes any sense.'

It did, perfectly. 'Is that what you meant by what you said about David driving her to it?' she asked him, because she had to.

Jake hesitated. 'I just think that by treating her as if she were made of porcelain, he was emotionally suffocating her.' He shrugged and fell silent.

Maddie studied him for a long moment. 'Did you see Kiara before she died? Did you speak to her?'

'No, not for years. I would have liked to have talked to her, asked her whether she was happy. I suppose I thought that if she was still with David, she must have been. Christ, how wrong can you be?'

Maddie noted the bitterness in his tone. The fingers he was now drumming agitatedly against the tabletop. 'What makes you think she wasn't?' she asked carefully.

Jake glanced at her bemusedly. 'With a man who was reluctant to move house even though he knew how desperate she was? Someone who stipulated what she could and couldn't take with her when he eventually agreed? The bloke has a problem, that's all I'm saying. It was one hell of a bid for freedom, wasn't it, if she really did jump to her death?' he added angrily.

Maddie studied him carefully. He seemed oblivious to what he'd just said. How could he know that David had been reluctant to move? That he'd told Kiara what she could take with her, which didn't sound like David at all? Through Sophie? Possibly. But even assuming Kiara had confided in Sophie, was Sophie likely to have repeated all this to her husband, a man who she knew had once been in love with Kiara? Wouldn't she have been fearful of reigniting the flame?

'What did you mean when we spoke at the cemetery, Jake? About the rumours that were circulating?' She tried to keep her tone concerned rather than accusing. 'Did you think it was David who might be spreading them?'

Jake laced his fingers on the table and stared down at them. After a second, he shrugged in that way he did, and looked back at her. 'I'm not the person you want to talk to about all this, Maddie,' he said tightly. 'It's David.'

FORTY-TWO

'Thank Christ.' Nathan heaved out a sigh of relief when Maddie finally answered one of his many calls. 'Is everything okay? Are the kids—'

'The kids are fine,' Maddie assured him.

'So why haven't you been returning my calls or texts?' he asked apprehensively. 'I've left three messages today alone. Has something happened?'

'I wanted to wait until Josh and Ellie were in bed before speaking to you.' Maddie avoided his last question, though she wanted to scream at him that yes, something had happened, that her life seemed to be disintegrating and she would quite like to know why, but what good would that do? She didn't want to make accusations based on suspicion. And what if she did and he lied to her? There would be no going back from that. But in not telling her he'd been to the salon, hadn't he already lied by omission? If he'd been seeing Kiara, hadn't he been spinning her a web of lies? What else might he have lied about? She closed her eyes, seeing again the wariness in his before he'd left. He'd told her it was her he was concerned for, that he was worried about her whereabouts on the night Kiara died. Why would he do that? *To deflect attention from himself,* whispered a nagging little voice in her head.

'But why?' He sounded bewildered. 'I've been going out of my mind.'

'I'm sorry. I needed some time,' she told him honestly.

Nathan didn't say anything for a second. Then, 'What's going on, Maddie?' he asked flatly.

Maddie braced herself. 'Did you speak to DS Fletcher?'

'I did. Can we not talk about that now, though? It's whatever's going on with you that's worrying me. Why you're acting so strangely. I know my coming out here wasn't great timing, but I'm doing my best to get back, I promise.'

She gasped in disbelief. Did he really think it was about his being away, as if she were incapable of coping without him? 'They found your *fingerprints*!' She almost laughed, incredulous that he would seek to evade the real issue. 'In the *bedroom*.'

'I gathered,' Nathan replied wearily. 'But my fingerprints would be all over the place, wouldn't they? Yours too. We were both—'

'On the fucking *headboard*!' she hissed over him.

'Jesus, Maddie.' He was clearly shocked by her language. 'What the hell?'

'What were they doing there, Nathan? You need to tell me. And please do *not* lie to me,' she warned him.

Nathan laughed, astonished. 'I've never *lied* to you in my life. Maddie, where's this coming from. I have no idea what—'

'What were they *doing* there?' Maddie demanded, working now to keep her voice down. The children were just upstairs. She didn't want them involved in any of this.

Nathan went quiet again. Then, 'Are you serious, Maddie?' he asked. 'You were right there with me. You know damn well what they were doing there.'

'They were on the *headboard*.' Humiliation climbing hotly inside her, she pointed out this apparently unimportant detail again.

He inhaled sharply. 'I helped move the furniture,' he reminded her, anger rising in his voice. 'Including the bloody headboard. Did David not tell you that?'

'Did you ask him to?'

'What? No. I just assumed he would—'

'When did you move it?' Maddie spoke over him. 'I didn't see you go in there other than to drop a box by the door.'

'No. That would be because you were busy having a cosy conversation out on the balcony with David,' Nathan retorted.

'*Cosy?*' She baulked. 'What on earth are you talking about?'

'You talk to him a lot.' It sounded like an accusation.

'He's our friend. He's lost his wife,' she countered, disbelieving. 'Of course I talk to him. Would you rather I didn't?'

'No.' Nathan sighed. 'Of course not. It's just, you think a lot of him, it's obvious you do, but ...'

'But *what?*' she pressed him, interested to hear how far he would go. 'You might as well spit it out now you've started.'

He hesitated again, infuriatingly. 'Kiara thought he might be seeing someone else,' he said eventually. 'She said he was acting oddly, and I ... I didn't know what to think.'

Maddie felt as if he'd slapped her. 'You thought it was me?' she said, now truly incredulous.

'No. I ... Yes,' he admitted, with another heavy sigh. 'I dismissed it, tried to. But then the way you were after she died, so stuffed with remorse and guilt, I just didn't know. I didn't want to think that way.'

Maddie was shocked to the core. She couldn't believe that he would actually think *she* was having an affair – with David. 'That's ridiculous. Absolute rubbish,' she almost spat. Had Kiara thought she was? Was that why she'd avoided her?

'I *know*. I know that now,' he tried to assure her. 'I trust you, of course I do.'

'That's very magnanimous of you.' She couldn't keep the scorn from her voice.

'That's hardly fair, Maddie, when you've just as good as accused me of Christ only knows what.' He stopped. Maddie could feel his frustration. 'Look, I'm sorry,' he said, his tone contrite. 'I wish I hadn't said anything. It was stupid. My insecurities at play, that was all. Please let's not argue. I'll be back soon. We can sit down and talk properly then.'

Her head whirled with confusion and frustration. Just how much had gone on that she wasn't aware of? Why did the conversation keep coming back to her and her supposed faults? 'Is that why you went to see Kiara?' she asked, pushing the conversation back to him.

'See her? When?' Nathan sounded guarded.

Do not lie to me, Nathan. 'At the salon,' she reminded him, just in case his recollection was faulty.

'Ah, right.' He sounded awkward. 'Yes, I went by just after New Year. She rang me and I called in after dropping the kids off at school. I suggested that David's odd behaviour might be because she was shutting him out, that they should sit down and talk.'

'But you didn't think to tell me any of this?'

'She asked me not to,' he said awkwardly. 'To be honest, I didn't think it was a good idea either. I said she should talk to you too. And then when you said she was avoiding you ...'

'You thought she might have reason to,' Maddie finished. 'Strange interpretation of trust you have, Nathan.'

'I know. I'm sorry,' he said again. 'I don't know what else to say.'

Maddie's emotions churned. *Was* this the truth? All of it? 'And you didn't see her other than then?'

'No,' Nathan said emphatically. 'Apart from New Year and then when we both saw them at the apartment, I've had no contact with her.'

'The New Year dinner where I found the two of you having an extremely cosy conversation,' she reminded him.

'We've been over that, Maddie,' Nathan replied despondently.

'And when we saw them at the apartment, you mysteriously left your fingerprints on the headboard.' She reminded him of that too, a subject he seemed determined to sidetrack.

'Kiara asked me to help move the dressing table,' Nathan answered exasperatedly.

'So you moved the bed?' Maddie hoped he could hear the facetiousness in her voice.

'She thought it was off centre,' he expanded, not very convincingly. 'Maddie, I know what you're thinking, but you're wrong, I promise you. I've never looked at another woman.'

Maddie didn't respond. That had to be a lie. Men had eyes in their heads. She did, and hers would stray in the direction of a good-looking man. They'd strayed in Nathan's direction. It was human nature.

He obviously gleaned from her silence that she wasn't impressed by his noble declaration. 'Well, okay, I've looked, but I'm not interested in anyone else. For God's sake, why would I be? We're good together. Happy. Or at least I thought we were.'

Still Maddie didn't comment. She didn't feel very happy right now. But he'd no doubt gleaned that much too.

'You're right to doubt me,' he went on after a second. 'I know it sounds like a pathetic attempt to explain things away. The thing is, it was awkward. I felt obliged on one hand. On the other, once we were in the bedroom, I wanted to run a mile. Kiara seemed ... let's just say overfamiliar. That's why I didn't want to stick around. I was beginning to realise their relationship was a mess, that she might have engineered the situation to try to make David jealous, and I wanted to get out of there.'

'But how could David have verified your explanation?' She pointed out the obvious hole in his story. 'Presumably he wasn't witness to all of this?'

'He made some joke about hoping I wasn't sleeping on the job as he came out of the main bathroom. He must have known I was in there.'

Maddie breathed in hard. Was he lying? Shifting blame? Deflecting? Again? Nausea and uncertainty swirled inside her. How could she tell if she couldn't see his eyes? Would she even know then, though? He'd sworn he'd never lied to her. She didn't think he had. But the amusing comments he made. His glibness sometimes. Was that all a front? A facade that hid a darker side of his character?

Steeling herself for his answer, she asked the question she had to. 'Did you see Kiara the night she died, Nathan? You need to tell me honestly.'

'You really are serious, aren't you?' He laughed in exasperated bewilderment. 'I was with the *kids*, Maddie. At McDonald's. You know I was.'

'But did you leave the party?' Even though her heart drummed a warning in her chest, she pressed on. He would know what she was implying. He might hate her for it, but she had to know. 'There were plenty of people there who could have kept an eye on the children after all, weren't there?'

Nathan fell silent for another agonisingly long moment. 'You think I had something to do with her death, don't you?' he said eventually, his voice filled with hurt and bitter disappointment.

She had no idea what to say. She wanted to take the words back. To hold him, have him hold her and tell her everything was okay. But she couldn't. Everything wasn't okay and he was a million miles away.

'I'm coming home,' he said quietly after another loaded pause. 'I'll see you soon, assuming you haven't judged me, found me guilty and changed the fucking locks.'

'Nathan? *Nathan?*' Maddie's throat closed, her heart constricting painfully as she realised he'd hung up.

FORTY-THREE

Maddie was sick with worry. She'd wondered at first whether Nathan might be giving her a taste of her own medicine, not answering her calls, ignoring her texts, but now, with three whole days having passed without a word, she had no idea what to think. He'd said he was coming home. She had no way of knowing whether he was, where he was.

Finding a parking space close to the school, she checked her phone again, hoping for a message from him or one of his colleagues in Ecuador. She found none, and the knot of fear that had taken root inside her twisted itself tighter. He wouldn't do this. No matter what was happening between them, he wouldn't leave her to worry like this. He would always be in touch, if only for the sake of the children.

'Mummy, we're going to be late,' Ellie said from the back seat, where she and Josh had spent the entire journey to school playing with their Create a Car apps and arguing over whose vehicle was coolest. They were both fractious. They were bound to be with her so obviously distracted. Ellie had had a bad dream last night. Maddie had fetched her into her bed, but still the little girl had been fearful. 'I don't feel safe without

Daddy here to catch the bugs,' she'd whispered, her voice small and tremulous as she'd snuggled up to her. 'When's he coming home, Mummy?'

'Soon,' Maddie had murmured, stroking her hair softly, lulling her to sleep, fear running like ice through her veins as she'd wondered whether he would be coming home at all.

Shaking herself, she reached for the door handle. 'Grab your bags, kids,' she said, injecting some enthusiasm into her voice. 'Ellie's right. We need to get our skates on.'

'I'm trying, but Ellie's sitting on my rucksack strap,' Josh moaned. 'Shove over, stupid.'

'Josh, enough,' Maddie warned him, opening the back door and reaching to unbuckle Ellie. 'You do not to talk to your sister like that.' Helping the little girl out, she gave him a stern glance.

'Sorry,' Josh sighed, undoing his own belt and scrambling out too.

'To Ellie, please.' Maddie nodded in her direction.

'Sorry,' Josh repeated, a world-weary look on his face. 'You're not really that stupid.'

'It's okay.' Ellie shrugged benevolently. 'You're only jealous because my fire engine is way cooler than your digger.' So saying, she twirled around to saunter off towards the school, leaving Josh gawking after her.

'Sisters are such a pain.' He sighed, shaking his head as he trudged after her.

Maddie took a breath and warned herself not to overreact. Josh was just acting up. She knew he loved Ellie. She recalled how one day shortly after Ellie had started school, she'd found him sitting in the reception class with his arm around his sister's shoulders. Ellie had been homesick. Josh had been trying to reassure her. 'I'm never going to be far away, Els,' she'd heard him say as she'd quietly approached them. 'I'll look out for you, don't worry.' Realising how much he reminded her of his father, she forced her tears back. Nathan would never do anything that would hurt his children. He would always be there for them. If she wasn't sure about anything else, she could be sure of that.

'Maddie, hi.' One of the other mothers waved across to her as she went through the school gates. It was Kim, she realised, the mother of the girl whose party Ellie and Josh had gone to on the evening that Kiara's life had ended and her own had begun to fall apart.

Swallowing back a surge of pain, she waved cheerily back, then bent to kiss Ellie and give Josh a hug. She watched until they were safely through the school doors, then hurried across to Kim before she headed off. 'Hi. How are you?' she asked.

'Good,' Kim assured her. 'You?'

'Fine,' Maddie said, smiling brightly. 'I can't believe how much Leah has grown.' She nodded towards Kim's little girl as she disappeared through the school entrance.

'I know. She's six going on sixteen, I swear.' Kim sighed. 'Growing up way too fast.'

'Tell me about it.' Maddie gave a sympathetic roll of her eyes. 'How did the birthday party go, by the way?' she asked casually. 'I'm sorry I couldn't be there.'

'We hardly missed you,' Kim assured her. 'Seriously, I can't believe how great that husband of yours is with the kids. They all seemed to gravitate towards him. Leah told me it's because "Ellie's daddy makes us laugh". He certainly kept them entertained while he was there.'

Maddie's radar went on red alert as she picked up on the last few words. 'That sounds like Nathan.' She drew in a breath and took a gamble. Kim would either confirm her fears or quell them. Either way, she had to find out. 'Were my two okay while he popped out?' she asked. 'Josh mentioned he'd had to.'

'Oh.' Kim closed one eye in a wince. 'They were fine, yes, but Nathan asked me not to say anything.' Maddie's heart boomed in her chest. 'I'm guessing you know now, though?'

'Well, he had to tell me once the cat was out of the bag,' she managed, her throat tight.

Kim sighed again, wistfully. 'What a lovely romantic gesture. I wish my Chris was half as thoughtful. He's as likely to book a surprise anniversary holiday to exotic climes as I am to sprout ...'

Maddie had stopped listening. With everything going on, their anniversary had come and gone. There'd been no exotic holiday. No mention of one.

FORTY-FOUR

Her mind ticking feverishly, Maddie drove home on autopilot. He'd been lying. About *everything*. He'd been trying to convince her that she'd been at Kiara's apartment that night. Why? So she wouldn't suspect that he had, quite obviously. Did he realise she'd almost convinced herself she was going insane? No. *He'd* been convincing her she was. Why would he do that? She'd thought he'd loved her. She loved him, still, with her whole heart, and he was breaking it, crushing it. She couldn't believe it. It must all be some terrible, awful mistake. All in her mind.

Ha! Emitting a half-hysterical laugh, she screeched the car onto the drive, stopping an inch away from the garage door. She waited a second, her hands curled into white-knuckled fists as she gripped the wheel. *Breathe.* She drew air into her lungs, blew it out slowly, then shoved the car door open, scrambled out and rushed to the front door.

Inserting her key into the lock with trembling fingers, she pushed it open, slammed it shut and leant against it. She was stuck in a nightmare. There could be no other explanation. Where *was* he?

Her legs leaden, her chest pounding, she headed towards the kitchen, digging into her bag for her phone as she went. She tried Nathan's number again. Her blood ran cold when she got a 'the subscriber you have dialled is not in service' message. What did that mean? Had he switched the phone off? Was it faulty? Lost?

Hurriedly she searched for the number of the person she'd spoken to in Ecuador, then jumped as her phone rang. An international call. She fumbled to answer it. 'Hi, this is Melissa Bowers from the South American Entomologist Society project,' a woman with an American accent said. 'Is that Madeline Anderson?'

'Yes,' Maddie confirmed quickly. 'This is she. Are you calling about Nathan?'

The woman hesitated. 'I take it you still haven't heard from him?' she asked cautiously.

'No, nothing.' Trepidation twisted Maddie's stomach. 'His phone's been going to voicemail and now it's out of service. Do you know where he is?'

'I'm afraid we've no idea,' the woman said apologetically, and Maddie felt her blood run cold. 'As far as I was aware he was travelling home. He said there was a family crisis. That he had to get back urgently.'

'And you've heard nothing from him since?' Maddie gripped her phone tight.

'No. I'm sorry.'

She squeezed her eyes closed. 'When did he leave?' she asked past the hard stone in her throat.

'Three days ago,' the woman supplied. 'He was hoping to catch a cargo boat, but there was a problem, engine trouble, I gather. The guide we generally use was due to bring some supplies in the day after. He would have taken him as far as Quito, but Nathan said he couldn't wait.'

'So what did he do?' Maddie pictured the scene, felt the

stifling heat, the humidity. He'd been angry, palpably. Filled with despair and confusion after their last conversation. She recalled how that conversation had ended, his last biting remark. *I'll see you soon, assuming you haven't judged me, found me guilty and changed the fucking locks.*

He'd acted impulsively, broken his own rule never to take risks while he was travelling. Why had she tackled him over the phone? She felt a part of her die inside. It could have waited until he was home safely. What had she done?

'He paid a local for the use of his boat. A large sum of money by local standards, I gather. Madeline, I have to be straight with you,' Melissa said, a warning edge to her voice. 'He set off on his own, said he knew the route well enough and that he had his GPS. These boats are no more than wooden canoes, however. The local people basically strap an outboard motor on the back and use them as private transport or local taxis. They're not meant for tourists to navigate the complex network of rivers and tributaries that comprise the Amazon. With heavy rainfall forecast, the journey would have been perilous. I'm extremely concerned for his safety.'

FORTY-FIVE

Once Melissa had rung off, having promised her she would alert the embassy and organise an immediate search mission, Maddie stood frozen to the spot. He'd been desperate. Of course he would have been after the things she'd said to him, the accusations she'd made, which weren't substantiated and might never be. Couldn't possibly be if her husband was the man she knew him to be.

Had he been desperate to get back to her, though? Or to get away? Even as she thought it, she hated herself for it, hated that she doubted him, that he'd given her cause to. He'd said he'd never left the party that night – the darkest night of her life alongside the night of her father's death, which was still a muddled mess in her head. She was still no closer to finding answers to anything. Why had Nathan done this? Where was he?

Blinking through the tears streaming unchecked down her cheeks, she hurriedly hit call receive as her phone rang again. DS Fletcher, she realised, her breath stalling as he spoke.

'Sorry to bother you, Mrs Anderson,' he began, as he usually did. 'There are one or two things I wanted to bring you up to speed on.'

'What things?' Did he know Nathan was missing? Of course he didn't. She'd only just spoken to the woman from the project. She felt a fresh wave of fear crash through her.

'We've consulted with our technical people regarding the footage we have from the camera in the car park,' the detective went on. 'We have a couple of grainy images of someone entering the foyer shortly before the time Kiara fell.'

'Are you able to identify who?' Maddie asked, her mind whirring.

'Unfortunately not,' Fletcher replied. 'The area isn't well lit, and the angle of the camera doesn't give us much. From the weight and height, we think it was a man, but we can't be one hundred per cent certain. The build does approximate to that of David Beckett, although he has an alibi provided by his parents. It could equally fit any number of men, of course ...' He paused, and Maddie's world reeled.

'It could also be Nathan,' she whispered. The two men were similar in build and there was nothing to choose between them height-wise.

'Possibly,' Fletcher confirmed. 'Equally, it could be someone completely unrelated, but I thought I should let you know.'

Know what? That he suspected her husband had been cheating on her? That he was a murderer? Her emotions a whirl of hopeless confusion, she tried to process the new information. Even if Nathan had been seeing Kiara, it didn't mean he was involved in her death. She had to believe he wasn't. Had to believe in him. If she didn't hold on to that belief, she felt she would crumble.

'Are you sure this person was visiting Kiara's apartment?' she asked, looking for some small shred of hope.

'We can't be certain of anything yet. We have been able to eliminate a number of residents or visitors entering the building around the time of Mrs Beckett's death, however. That narrows it down somewhat.'

'I see,' Maddie said, her hope fading.

'There's one other thing,' Fletcher continued. 'A few details I hoped you could confirm about your visit to your mother.'

Maddie's heart stuttered. 'Of course,' she managed. 'My mind's all over the place right now.'

'It's bound to be.' Fletcher's tone was sympathetic. 'We've verified you were there – naturally we would do that, you understand?'

'Yes.' Maddie clutched her phone tighter.

'You mentioned you came straight home. Can you just confirm that was actually the case?'

Maddie had no doubt that if he'd verified she was there, then he already had his answer. 'No,' she admitted. 'I'm sorry. What I meant was I didn't stop off anywhere, but I did drive around for a while. It helps clear my mind. The visits to my mother tend to leave me unsettled, and I didn't want to upset Nathan or the children.'

'Ah, that would explain it,' DS Fletcher said. 'We've checked the time you signed out, you see, and it doesn't quite tally with your arrival home.'

Maddie felt a cold hollowness spreading through her. He didn't believe her. She could hear it in his tone, his scepticism loud and clear. But why would he tell her all this? Was he trying to prompt her into some kind of action? Did he think Nathan was involved in Kiara's death? Was he preparing her for that fact? Did *she* think that? Truly? Did she really believe there was a side to her husband she'd never known?

FORTY-SIX

David

Outside Maddie's house, David pressed the doorbell for a third time. Still getting no answer, he pulled out his phone and tried her mobile again. He was sure she was home. Her car was on the drive, and he'd heard the dog barking. He was also sure he could hear her phone ringing somewhere inside the house. She wasn't likely to have gone far without it.

Stepping back from the door, he glanced at the front windows, his eyes travelling upwards to the bedrooms and then further up to the second floor, which still looked to be in a state of permanent restoration. That was a shame. He'd always liked this house. With its spectacular views over the Malvern Hills and plenty of land adjoining it, it would be paradise for him. Such a pity it was still so far from reaching its full potential. But then Nathan hadn't had much time in between work trips to give it much attention. He didn't know how lucky he was, married to a woman who loved him enough to put up with his constantly being away from home.

Though maybe he did. David checked the text Nathan had sent him before he'd left for his latest trip. *Could you keep an eye on Maddie for me?* he'd asked. *I'm worried about her.* David intended to. There were things he hadn't been able to confide to her, naturally, things between him and Kiara that were better kept private, but Maddie had always been a good friend to him, concerned for him. David was sure she would have been the same whether or not he'd been with Kiara. He would make sure to be there for her as he knew she would always be for him.

Growing concerned at getting no answer, he was sizing up the garden gate, debating whether to climb over it and check the back door, when the front door opened. A surge of relief swept through him. He guessed she must be beside herself, suspicion about what Nathan had been up to eating away at her until she thought she was going out of her mind, especially after he'd felt unable to confirm that Nathan had been in the bedroom on the day they'd moved into the apartment. He knew how that felt, the frustration of not knowing, of possibly being lied to compounding the hurt and soul-crushing humiliation.

'David?' Maddie blinked at him in confusion, obviously surprised to find him on her doorstep.

Pocketing his phone, he smiled and walked towards her. 'Nathe asked me to keep an eye on you before he left. He was worried about you. I've been trying to get hold of you.' He stopped, squinting quizzically at her. 'Have you been crying?'

Maddie answered with a small nod, then moved back from the door.

'Hey.' Stepping into the hall, David ran his eyes over her; then, his heart jolting as he watched fresh tears sliding down her cheeks, he moved instinctively towards her. 'What is it, Mads?' he asked softly, drawing her to him. 'What's happened?'

A sob catching in her throat, Maddie didn't answer. David

waited, holding her as she cried hot, heart-rending tears. 'He's missing,' she finally blurted, burying her face in his shoulder.

David felt a shock wave run through him. 'Nathan?' He took a second to digest the news. 'Since when?'

'Three days ago,' Maddie choked. 'He took a boat out on the Amazon, a flimsy wooden thing. There was torrential rain and ...' She looked up at him, something close to torture in her eyes. 'Three *days* ago, David. I can't get hold of him. No one's heard from him. And it's all my fault. He left after I spoke to him on the phone. He was upset, trying to get home, and now he's missing. I said some awful things to him. He sounded so bewildered and angry, and still I kept on, making it obvious I didn't believe him. Why couldn't I have just waited until he got back safely?'

'Hey, hey. Come on.' David held her closer as another ragged sob escaped her. 'It's not your fault, Maddie,' he tried to reassure her. 'You're bound to be worried and confused.'

'What am I going to do?' she asked wretchedly. 'What am I going to tell the children?'

'Shush.' He stroked her back, trying to soothe her. 'Okay?' he asked as her sobs slowed to a shuddery stop.

She didn't respond. He guessed it was a ridiculous question.

'Sorry,' she murmured, easing away after a second. 'I shouldn't be crying all over your shoulder. You have enough to deal with.'

'Don't be. That's what friends are for.' David smiled softly. 'The people he's working for have notified the authorities, I assume?'

Maddie nodded. 'They're mounting a search.' She wrapped her arms about herself, clearly imagining all sorts of scenarios.

'In which case, I wouldn't tell the kids anything for the moment. Give them some time to get the search under way. I'm sure they'll find him.'

She answered with another small nod. 'I'm glad you're

here,' she said. Then, wiping her cheeks with the heel of her hand, she turned towards the kitchen.

Following her, David made an effort to pat Boomer, who was watching him carefully. The dog had never warmed to him. He was sure it could sense the fear that had stayed with him since he'd been bitten by one as a child.

'Why did I tackle him over the phone?' Maddie flicked the kettle on and turned to look at him, her eyes filled with self-recrimination. 'What did I think he was going to do when I as good as accused him?'

David straightened up, grabbed some paper towel from the roll on the work surface and handed it to her. 'Accused him of what?' he asked.

'Everything.' She took the towel and dabbed her eyes. 'I more or less said I thought he was lying about the fingerprints. About his reason for going to see Kiara at the salon days after we found him "comforting" her in your kitchen. It just sounded so implausible, I—'

'Hold on,' David interrupted, confused. 'He went to see her at the salon?'

'Oh no.' Maddie closed her eyes. 'David, I'm so sorry. You obviously didn't know either. I should have thought.'

'No.' He tugged in a breath. 'No, I didn't. And he went because?'

She glanced away uncomfortably. 'According to Sophie, Kiara claimed it was to discuss a birthday surprise for me, which is ridiculous considering my birthday wasn't for months. Nathan said it was because ...' She faltered, eyeing him nervously.

'You might as well tell me, Mads,' he urged her. 'It can't be much worse than what I already know, can it?'

She breathed deeply. 'Kiara thought you were having an affair,' she announced.

'Me?' He laughed, astonished.

'With me,' she added awkwardly.

'Jesus.' He shook his head in bewilderment. 'The plot thickens. I hope we enjoyed it.'

Maddie emitted a strangled laugh.

'The mind boggles, doesn't it?' He smiled with wry amusement. 'O, what a tangled web we weave ...'

'There's something else,' she went on cautiously.

David braced himself. From her reluctant expression, he was guessing this was also going to be something she considered shocking.

'The footage on the camera,' she said.

'What camera?' He eyed her warily. There was a camera in the foyer of the apartment building, but as far as he knew, the lazy bastards at the security company hadn't got around to actually installing the system.

'The one overlooking the car park. DS Fletcher told me they managed to get a couple of images from it on the night Kiara died. He said they were grainy and that it could be any number of men, including you, but ...'

'He thought it might be Nathan?' David finished. 'Christ.' Dragging a hand over his neck, he glanced away, tried to assimilate. Might they be able to make an identification? he wondered, his gut tightening. 'But ...' he looked back at her with a puzzled frown, 'wasn't Nathan at a birthday party with the kids?'

'He was.' Maddie dropped her gaze. 'He told me he hadn't left for any reason, but according to one of the parents I spoke to, he did. To book an exotic holiday for our anniversary, apparently.'

'Shit,' David muttered. He wished he could make this less painful for her, but there was no way to do that. 'I'm guessing there was no holiday?' he asked gently.

She shook her head.

'Maddie, I'm so sorry.' He drew her back to him. She looked so defeated, so vulnerable. She'd been one hundred per cent loyal to Nathan. Seeing the way she'd looked at him all those years ago, it had been obvious she was completely besotted. Just as David had been besotted with Kiara. For all that she'd done to him, his life was empty without her. He understood, therefore, exactly how Maddie was feeling. 'Are you going to be okay?' he asked.

She took a second, then nodded determinedly. 'I have to be for the children. Can I ask you something, David?'

'Anything,' he assured her.

'I know you said you didn't remember seeing Nathan moving anything into the bedroom, but do you remember seeing him in there at all at any point?'

He debated before answering. He would be dropping Nathan further in it, but judging by what she'd told him, it appeared the man was already sunk without trace. 'I don't, Mads, I'm sorry. I wondered whether he might have gone in while we were out on the balcony, but as I recall, he was moving the sofa at that point.'

'Did he ask you to lie for him? To tell Fletcher that you saw him in the bedroom?' she asked, such bewilderment in her eyes David felt an overwhelming urge to protect her.

'He texted me,' he said. 'Asked me to confirm he'd been there. The thing is ...' He hesitated. 'I honestly don't recall seeing him in there. In the end, I told Fletcher he might have been. That I couldn't remember everyone's movements.'

Squeezing her a touch closer, he felt her stiffen. 'You were right,' she said, inhaling sharply. 'They were having an affair, weren't they?'

'Truthfully?' He hesitated again, aware he would be driving another nail into Nathan's coffin. 'The evidence does look pretty damning, yes.'

She eased away. 'And there's an awful lot of it, isn't there?' Wiping a hand under her nose, she glanced around her kitchen, looking lost and disorientated, as if she didn't know where she was, and then breathed in hard. 'I have to pick up Ellie and Josh from the childminder,' she said, clearly trying to pull herself together for her children's sake.

David had no children – he'd wanted them, so much it ached – but he got it completely. 'I'll fetch them,' he offered. 'How about I take them for a bite to eat, give you time to get yourself together?'

Maddie thought about it. 'I'll be okay, Dave,' she said with a tremulous smile. 'I have to be, don't I?'

'For your kids, I know. And you will be.' He smiled back reassuringly. 'You don't look very okay right now, though, if you don't mind me pointing out. The kids will pick up on it. Give yourself a break. Take a hot bath, do whatever you need to. I'll make sure Josh and Ellie are fed and order a takeaway for the two of us. We can eat later if you don't feel up to it yet. I could give the dog a run when I get back if you'd like. How does that sound?' Glancing in Boomer's direction, he fancied the dog didn't look too enamoured of that suggestion. He needed to try to befriend the animal, though, if it was going to accept him being around.

Maddie reached to squeeze his hand. 'Like you're a saint,' she said. 'Thank you.'

'I'm here for you, Maddie. For as long as you need me to be,' he assured her.

He didn't want to leave her like this. His being here wouldn't go down well with a certain person, but it was high time he stopped giving in to the whims of women who'd never truly cared for him and applied himself to caring for a woman who did.

FORTY-SEVEN

Maddie

Why had Nathan asked David to keep an eye on her? Because he really was worried for her, or because he wanted to draw attention to her? Maddie's thoughts yo-yoed back and forth so fast she couldn't keep up with them, her emotions seesawing between anger and incomprehension. *Why* would he have done that? Had he asked DS Fletcher to keep an eye on her too? Was that why Fletcher had rung? Did Nathan really think she was involved in Kiara's death, just as she was becoming sure that he was? She didn't know what to believe any more, who to trust, whether she could even trust herself.

She hadn't yet told DS Fletcher that Nathan was missing. She wasn't sure why until she'd acknowledged the thought that had wormed its way into her head. *Is he missing, or might he be running?* Fletcher would presumably find out soon enough. What would he make of her not passing that information on to him?

Hearing Josh and Ellie hurtling through the front door, she tried to push her worries aside and went to the hall. 'Hey, you two. Did you enjoy your food?' She crouched to wrap her babies in a firm hug as they came to greet her, David smiling behind them.

'Uh-huh.' Josh and Ellie both nodded enthusiastically.

'We had pizza,' Ellie said. 'It was delicious.'

David smiled. 'I took them to the pub in the village that serves all day. They didn't have the healthiest choice on the menu, but I think they had a good time, hey, kids?'

'We saw a boat trying to turn around. It got stuck,' Ellie said, her eyes wide. 'David helped them, though, didn't you, David?'

'I did.' David flexed his muscles jokingly. 'They'd have been sunk without me.'

'Obviously.' Maddie rolled her eyes in amusement. 'And how was school?' She turned her attention to Josh.

'Same.' Josh shrugged and wriggled to free himself of the arm she still had around him, hugs not being his thing.

Maddie sighed good-naturedly and allowed him to escape to the lounge.

'And what about you? Did you have a good day?' She kissed Ellie's forehead. The little girl looked tired. Even in the big bed she'd slept fitfully. She always did when Nathan was away. She missed him. Maddie's heart squeezed painfully. *She* missed him too, so much she wasn't sure how she would bear it. How she would begin to tell the children.

Swallowing back the jagged knot in her throat, she tried to quash the graphic images that were now haunting her every waking second. Nathan lying injured in some unimaginably inhospitable place. If he was conscious, he would be aware of the wildlife foraging around him, snakes, venomous insects and deadly spiders. *Anacondas.* She recalled him describing them to Josh, telling him how they were one of the most feared and revered species in the rainforest. How they lived in swamps and marshes, remaining almost completely submerged as they waited to strike unsuspecting prey.

Josh had been awestruck, Ellie too, as Nathan told them tales of his adventures. They loved him, worshipped him. What was she going to tell them? That Nathan was on a plane, destination as far away as possible, everything they'd done together, everything they had together, their children, meaning little to him when measured against his freedom? *No.* That wasn't her husband, the man she knew intimately. The man whose hopes and dreams she'd shared, who'd shared hers. He wasn't capable of deserting his children. He wouldn't. *He'll come back.* She repeated the mantra over and over. He would end her nightmare. He *had* to.

'It was okay,' Ellie said. 'I was a bit scared, though,' she added, a worried little frown forming in her brow.

Forcing herself to focus on what was important in this moment, Maddie scanned her little girl's face. 'Why, sweetheart?' she asked, noting that Ellie's eyes were clouded with worry.

'Because we were telling stories at playtime and I told a story about the bugs under my bed and one of the big boys said there were millions of bugs *in* my bed, and I said he was lying, and he called me a sissy.' She stopped, her bottom lip quivering.

Maddie squeezed her gently. 'There are no bugs, darling,' she murmured, breathing in the perfect innocence of her. 'Daddy gets them all, doesn't he?' Her throat closing even as she said it, she glanced up at David, who looked sympathetically back at her.

'That's what Josh said.' Ellie sniffled. 'He told the boy he was a bully and that he should grow up.'

'Did he?' David's eyes grew wide in admiration, while Maddie felt like bursting into tears there and then. 'Well, good for him.' He placed an arm around Ellie's shoulders. 'I tell you what, how about we go into the lounge and play a game to take our minds off it?'

'Yay! Pictionary Air,' Josh called. He'd obviously heard his name and was listening intently to the conversation.

'Okay with you, Ellie?' David asked.

'Uh-huh.' Ellie nodded, looking slightly less anxious. 'Daddy bought it for us. He's coming home soon, isn't he, Mummy?'

Maddie felt her throat tighten. 'Yes, sweetheart,' she murmured, her heart going into freefall. 'Soon.'

David caught her hand as she got to her feet. 'I'll play with them for a while,' he said, 'assuming you have something else you need to do.'

Maddie smiled and squeezed his hand, grateful for his thoughtfulness.

Listening to her children laughing as she put the takeaway food David had brought back from the pub into the fridge, she quietly thanked God for him. Despite the betrayal he must feel, the emotional pain he must be in, he was big enough to be a friend to her, to be here for her, helping her maintain some semblance of normality for her children, whose lives would be devastated by all of this. He was a kind, caring man. She'd always known that. She had no idea what she would do without him to turn to. No idea why Kiara would have chosen to destroy him. Destroy her. Why Nathan would.

Had he, though? She backtracked again. He'd been so adamant, sounded so hurt that she would even think he would cheat on her, let alone commit murder, which was what she'd accused him of when she'd asked him if he'd left the party. She wanted to believe him incapable of things she could never have imagined in her worst nightmares, but knowing he'd lied to her, there was a part of her that now thought he might be. A seed of doubt that was growing steadily, no matter how hard she tried to quash it. A bigger part of her, though, was terrified for him. What if he was innocent? What if he'd taken that boat, knowing it was risky, because he was desperate to get back to assuage her suspicions – because, in accusing him, she'd made him think his world was falling apart and, thousands of miles away, he could do nothing about it?

She was looking at Google Earth, trying to imagine where he might be, and only succeeding in worrying herself more when David came back to the kitchen. 'Teeth brushed and bedtime story done,' he said, having offered to read to the children before bed. 'Nothing scary, don't worry. We made a tent and invented our own story, each of us adding a bit as we went. To be continued tomorrow.'

Maddie glanced at him curiously. They hadn't discussed him staying over.

'Sorry. I'm not assuming it's okay for me to stay.' He clearly caught her look. 'I, er, just thought you might need some company, but if you'd rather I didn't stay, it's no problem.'

Now he looked embarrassed. Dear David, he really was the sweetest man. How could the person he loved most in the world have hurt him so badly? The two people he loved most in the world. Her chest constricted with guilt at what Nathan had done. Might have done. *He'll come back. Please come back, Nathan. Please come home.*

She swallowed hard and made herself smile. 'I'd love you to stay, as long as you're happy with the spare room, which is a bit of a mess until the second floor is habitable.'

'More than.' David smiled, clearly relieved. 'To be honest, I could use the company too.'

Of course he could. Maddie felt another pang of guilt. She'd been so preoccupied with her own problems, she hadn't given any consideration to David's, the fact that his grief would still be so painfully raw. 'Thank you,' she said, turning from the work surface to press a grateful kiss to his cheek. 'For being here for me and for being so brilliant with the kids. I'm not sure how I would have got through today without you.'

He looked pleased. 'I'll always be here for you, Mads, as long as you want me to be. I guess we have a lot in common, both bereft and lonely.' He shrugged and glanced down. When he looked back at her, there was such deep sadness in his eyes, Maddie's heart bled for him. 'Only we can know how much we're hurting, the depth of the betrayal we're struggling to come to terms with,' he added. 'We need to be a friend to each other.'

His words shook her, but they were true. As much as she might not want to admit it, she did feel bereft, and so very lonely, even with the children for company. How must David be feeling, having lost the woman he loved and the child she was carrying? A child he would have wanted and loved without question. She moved to give him a hug, because he looked as if he badly needed one.

He hugged her back hard. Then, 'Careful,' he said, easing away after a second. 'We'll have the neighbours talking.'

'Not unless they're walking their dogs in our back garden,' Maddie joked, attempting to lighten things. 'That's the beauty of this place. We're not overlooked.'

'Not that we were doing anything untoward,' David added with a wry smile.

'No.' Maddie reflected. Hadn't this been exactly what Nathan had been doing on that fateful New Year's Eve, hugging Kiara, comforting her? An innocent, caring gesture that could easily have been misinterpreted. Had been, by her. She'd judged him guilty then. How much was she judging him guilty of now that might prove to be completely wrong? She needed to stop. She needed to sleep, deep and dreamless, to prevent her mind from shooting dark thoughts scattergun through her head. He *would* come back. It had been three days, that was all. Three days too many. Tomorrow it would be four.

'I'll finish up here,' David offered as she felt her heart

plummet another inch. 'Why don't you go up and say goodnight to the kids?'

Feeling very much in need of a hug from her children, Maddie gladly took up his offer. Miraculously, she found Ellie already fast asleep and was immensely relieved. She prayed she would sleep through tonight. Pressing a light kiss to her forehead, she made sure the duvet was snug around her and then tiptoed to Josh's room.

He was still awake, though from his wide yawn as Maddie went in, she guessed he would sleep soundly. 'Snuggle down,' she said, relieving him of his iPad and tucking him in.

Gazing down at the little boy who looked so like his father, a combination of cold dread and deep longing ran through her. *Please let him come back safely. Whatever he might have done, please don't let him be hurt.* She swallowed back a hard lump of emotion and reached to smooth Josh's unruly fringe from his forehead. 'Thanks for looking after Ellie today,' she said.

'That's okay.' Josh shrugged as if it were no big deal, but Maddie thought otherwise. He was by no means the tallest boy in his class, and he wasn't confrontational by nature. It must have taken some courage to stand up to a bully.

He paused for a second, then, 'I think it's my fault she's scared,' he said, his eyes flickering guiltily. 'I tried to tell her that insects are good for the planet because they pollinate plants and eat dead animals and stuff, but I think she's too young to understand.'

Maddie smiled. Josh had a good heart. Just like his father. She had to try to hold onto that. 'I'm proud of you,' she told him, leaning to kiss his cheek.

For once, he didn't wriggle away, sitting up to give her a firm hug instead, which touched and surprised her. 'Don't worry, Mum. I'll look after you and Ellie if Dad can't get home soon.'

Realising that David had taken it upon himself to tell her son that Nathan might be delayed, a spark of annoyance flared inside her. She couldn't believe he'd done that without checking with her first.

Once Josh was settled, she took a steadying breath and went back down to the kitchen. She had no choice but to tackle David about it. He should have consulted her before talking to her children. She hadn't wanted them to know anything until they had to. It was quite clear that Josh was quietly worrying.

She found him carrying the takeaway food from the microwave across to the island. 'It's not haute cuisine, but it's sustenance.' He gave her a smile as he put the plates down. 'You need to eat,' he added, reaching for the wine he'd also placed there.

Maddie knew he was right, but her appetite was nil. 'Why did you tell Josh that Nathan had been delayed?' she asked, her tone tinged with the anger and frustration she felt. The complete bloody powerlessness.

David looked at her, surprised. 'Because he asked when he was coming back. I thought it might be better to prepare them.' He knitted his brow quizzically as Maddie almost glared at him. 'I probably shouldn't have said anything without speaking to you first,' he admitted, 'but Josh is shrewd. He caught me on the hop. I apologise. On reflection, it might have been better to say I didn't know.'

Maddie felt the bluster leave her sails. 'I'm sorry,' she said, blowing out the breath she hadn't realised she'd been holding. 'I'm so wound up. So worried about Ellie and Josh. I desperately don't want them upset.' Yet she knew they would have to be. She bit back the useless tears that were constantly threatening.

'I get it.' David risked a small smile. 'I was only trying to help, though, Maddie. I'm not the enemy here. I'm your friend.'

She squinted at him, a turmoil of conflicting emotion creeping through her. Was he implying that Nathan was the enemy? The man she'd always considered to be her best friend? Above all else, the two of them had always been determined to be friends, to be there for each other. But he wasn't here, was he? She had no idea where he was. And if he was running rather than missing, it was clear he had no intention of being here for her or his children.

None of this was David's fault, though. She was about to apologise for jumping down his throat when his mobile rang. Before he cancelled the call, she glimpsed the name on the screen. Why would Sophie be calling David?

FORTY-EIGHT

Feeling drained, Maddie listened to the sounds of the dawn chorus. The birds were clearly keen to greet the day – blackbirds, thrushes, sparrows, nightingales, an abundance of birds that had made their homes in the overgrown trees and shrubs in their rambling garden. She'd often accused Nathan of wanting the garden to grow wild rather than evict them from their habitats. He *had* wanted that, of course, a natural space that would allow wildlife to thrive. She'd accused him of so much, outright and in her head, and hadn't given him a chance to explain. Might he have been able to?

Her heart caught as she realised she was using the past tense, and she grabbed her phone from her bedside table. She'd checked it a hundred times during the night. There were still no messages. No texts. She selected his number, her thumb hovering over it. To hear him speak even on his voicemail message would offer her some small comfort. Listening to the monotone voice that intercepted her call instead, telling her the phone was no longer in service, her heart folded up inside her. She couldn't talk to him, had no way to contact him. Might never hear his voice again. The most painful thing of all was that she couldn't *feel* him. Wherever he'd been in the world she'd been able to do that. And now she couldn't. She had no idea how she would survive this.

Clutching the phone to her chest, she fell back on the bed, her hand straying to the empty space where her husband should be, and allowed the tears to slide silently from her eyes. He'd only been missing a short while, but already her world was empty without him. Shuffling across the bed, she nestled his pillow to her midriff and curled herself around it. She could smell him, the essence of him, the piny, citrusy scent of his after-shave, mingled with earthy, woody smells that evoked his image. She gasped as the smile in his electric-blue eyes faded, giving way to a dull, lifeless gaze. *No. Please no.*

She was in another garden, sucked by exhaustion into her childhood nightmares, where a different smell assaulted her senses, a chemical smell, sweet and putrid. Her body jolted as someone shouted. Her father. 'Madeline! Go back inside!'

'Don't you *touch* her!' Her mother's voice, desperate. 'Don't you *dare* touch her!'

Banging, Maddie can hear it. The shed door rattles in its frame. Her terrified eyes snap towards it. There's someone inside. Her daddy is on the outside, the petrol can in his hand, his other gesticulating wildly at her as he bellows, 'Go back to the house. Now!' But the kitchen light isn't on, and Maddie's scared of the dark, scared of her father, who's turned into a snarling monster. She glances down at her own hand, her small child's hand, at the box of matches her fingers are curled around. For an instant her mind goes blank and there's nothing but the dark, all-encompassing, suffocating, closing in on her, forcing the breath from her body. And then the strike of a match. A bright light scorches her eyes. A new smell permeates the air, like when Mummy burned the bacon on Sunday. Not wood burning. *Him* burning. Blood-curdling screaming. Sparks popping like fireworks ...

'No!' Maddie fought to block out a new, terrifying sound. A dull thud, a body landing, limbs splayed at impossible angles. *Kiara.* Undiluted fear gripping her, she struggled to wake up. She didn't hear it. Didn't see Kiara. She *didn't*. She was filling in the gaps!

She yanked herself upright. Breathing deeply, long, slow breaths that did nothing to calm her, she glanced at the alarm clock and was shocked to realise it was almost ten o'clock. How? She hadn't taken a sleeping pill. She didn't want to depend on the damn pills. She needed to depend on herself. To be there for her children. It was a *school* morning. Scrambling out of bed she raced to the bedroom door, yanked it open and flew along the landing, to be met with complete silence. No bathroom taps running, no loos flushing. No children arguing.

'Josh!' Her mouth dry, her legs leaden beneath her, she stumbled towards his room and shoved his door open. His bed was empty. Her gaze shot to his dressing table. No iPad. He wouldn't go anywhere without it.

'Ellie!' Nausea roiling inside her, she whirled around, and then froze as she heard the back door bang. Her blood pumping, she crept towards the stairs. Cold fear constricted her stomach as she heard someone talking. A male voice. *David.* Relief flooded every vein in her body.

About to descend the stairs, she stopped as he came along the hall. 'Sorry about that,' he said, speaking into his phone. 'I'm at Maddie's house. I didn't get a chance to call you back.' He paused, then, 'No, everything's fine,' he went on. 'There've been some developments, though. I'll catch up with you later at the salon.'

The salon? Maddie frowned, watching him walk to the foot of the stairs, his eyes on his phone as he ended his call.

'Jesus.' He jumped visibly as he glanced up and noticed her. 'You almost gave me a heart attack. Are you okay?'

'Ellie and Josh, where are they?' She squeezed the words out, her heart thrumming a frantic drumbeat in her chest.

He squinted at her curiously. 'At school,' he said, as if she should be aware of this fact. 'You were dead to the world.' He started up the stairs. 'Did you take a sleeping pill? I noticed some in the bathroom cabinet. Sorry, I wasn't poking around. I went in there last night looking for toothpaste.'

'Why didn't you wake me?' she asked, her voice tight. 'I was petrified when I found the children weren't here.'

'Christ, of course. Sorry.' He shook his head. 'I did knock on your door. You didn't answer and I didn't like to come in.'

Maddie felt another wave of nausea swill through her. The banging she'd heard in her sleep. Had that triggered the flood of memories she hoped to God weren't real?

'I thought I should make myself useful.' David shrugged awkwardly. 'Josh didn't want to be late, and to be honest, I thought you could use the rest. I went to the apartment after dropping the kids off to pick up a few personal things. I left you a note by the kettle. That was stupid of me. I should have realised you'd find them gone before you saw it.'

Maddie studied him narrowly for a second, then pulled herself up. She was judging him now, imagining him uncaring when he was anything but. 'It's okay,' she said shakily. 'My fault. I should have checked the alarm.'

'I'll make sure to knock a bit harder next time.' Coming level with her, David ran his gaze over her. Realising she was standing in front of him in nothing but a skimpy vest top and shorts, she quickly folded her arms. His gaze flicked embarrassedly away and then back to her face. 'You look pale,' he said. 'Are you sure you're all right?'

'I will be when I've showered.' She nodded. 'Thanks for taking the children.'

'No problem. I'll go and put some fresh coffee on. You look as if you could use it.'

Maddie breathed a sigh of relief as he turned away. She felt uncomfortable, which was her fault for running about half naked, but still, she'd never imagined she would feel that way around David.

'By the way,' he stopped part way down and glanced back up at her, 'I was up early this morning, so I made a start on clearing the weeds in the garden. Some of them are three feet high, and there's a hell of a lot of cutting-back to do out there. I couldn't make out where your land ended and the woods started.'

Maddie was taken aback. She hadn't asked him to do that. She might not have wanted it quite so natural as Nathan did, but now she felt that the garden was all she had left of him. 'You won't go too mad, will you?' she asked him uncertainly. 'It's just that that's Nathan's thing and I'd like to keep it the way it is until he comes back.'

David nodded pensively. 'I won't.' He sighed, and somehow Maddie felt she might have upset him by seeming unapprecia-tive of his efforts.

She was wondering whether to say something when he spoke again. 'Oh, I bought some toothpaste on the way back. I'll bring it up in a sec.'

'Oh, right. Thanks.' He obviously wasn't upset. It was her being neurotic, her mind in irrational overdrive thanks to sleep deprivation. He was trying to be helpful, that was all, but still she felt a flutter of apprehension that he seemed to be making himself so at home.

'David.' She stopped him before he reached the kitchen. 'Was that Sophie you were talking to on the phone? It's just that I saw her name come up on your phone last night, and when you mentioned the salon just now, I wondered whether there might be a problem.'

Nodding, he ran his hand over his neck and then looked

back at her. 'She wants to take the salon over,' he said with a sad shrug.

Maddie was surprised. There was no reason Sophie shouldn't go for it, but she couldn't help feeling that once again the woman was sliding into Kiara's shoes. First Jake, all those years ago. And now this. It seemed a bit peculiar.

'Are you okay with that?' she asked.

'I suppose.' He sighed.

'Did you know before Kiara died that Sophie was working at the salon?' she said carefully. 'Sorry,' she added when David shot her a quizzical glance. 'I was wondering how long she's worked there and whether she might have noticed any other times Nathan had dropped by. I suppose I'm trying to understand when exactly he ...'

'Became involved with Kiara?' he finished when she couldn't.

'If he was.' Maddie's heart squeezed afresh. She had to defend him. Not to do so would be to give up hope. She couldn't do that.

'I think we have to assume he was, Maddie,' David said with a sad smile. 'And to answer your question, no, I didn't know she was working there until recently. I can only assume that Kiara decided not to hold her responsible for anything Jake had done.'

He was talking about the attack. Since meeting Jake again recently, though, Maddie was struggling to believe he had been responsible for that.

'Perhaps he contacted Kiara and convinced her it wasn't him,' David suggested. 'He always was a smooth-talking bastard, wasn't he?'

FORTY-NINE

David

Flicking the switch on the filter machine, David set about clearing up the kids' breakfast bowls. He wanted to be helpful. He enjoyed being here, in a house that felt like a home, as the barn conversion had to him. He would get to grips with the garden while he was here. It was well over an acre of land and really did need some serious work. Maddie would soon see the improvement once he started to make some headway.

The two of them had always got along, each seeming to know how the other was feeling. They'd had a lot in common at university, neither of them the most confident of people. They definitely shared a lot in common now, both of them deceived in the cruellest way possible by the people they'd given their lives to try to make happy. That was what really stuck in David's craw, the thought of his wife and his so-called best friend getting some perverse kick out of fucking each other behind his back, behind Maddie's. She didn't deserve that.

He would stay, he decided. He'd collected a few things in case Maddie needed him to, and it was clear that she did. He was beginning to have doubts about the new start he'd been planning anyway. He needed a woman who would respect him. Maddie had always done that. She'd been aware he'd been obsessed with Kiara and had encouraged him to go for it. She knew almost everything there was to know now about their relationship. He could talk to her, and she would undoubtedly want to talk to him about Nathan. They would be good for each other. Had things been different, they would have been perfect together. Now, here they were – together. Fate worked in mysterious ways.

He would look after her. She clearly needed someone to do that, make sure she ate sensibly, help her establish a routine that would give her a sense of purpose. He would have to try to help her establish a healthy sleeping routine, too. She was a pretty woman – she possibly didn't realise how pretty – but she was clearly exhausted.

He felt bad about lying to her about Sophie, but to have admitted that he had known she was working at the salon before Kiara had set her sights on buying the apartment might have led to more questions, which would have been awkward. It was Sophie who'd confirmed that Kiara was cheating on him. He'd been surprised to find her working there when he'd dropped by just after New Year. Definitely surprised when, after asking her how things were, she'd told him she'd married Jake. 'So how is he?' he'd asked out of politeness.

'Still Jake.' She'd sighed, a look in her eyes that told him she wasn't impressed with her husband. David hadn't been surprised. He could never have imagined Jake metamorphosing into a man who gave a damn about anyone.

'If you've come to see Kiara, I'm afraid she's not here,' Sophie had gone on, a flicker of nervousness in her eyes that David hadn't immediately understood.

'Oh, right.' He'd nodded as if it wasn't an issue, though actually it was. Kiara had been aware he was coming. He'd offered to take her out for lunch. After his deplorable behaviour following their New Year's Eve dinner, he'd been desperate to make it up to her. He'd been mortified at the way he'd reacted, but try as he might, he hadn't been able to shake his mind free of the image of her and Nathan together in the kitchen. Maybe if she had shown a little more enthusiasm for being with *him*, in bed or out of it, things might have been different.

A moment later, once Sophie had confirmed where Kiara had gone, he'd gathered why she'd been nervous. 'Her friend Nathan came in,' she said, looking at him guardedly. 'I think he must have wanted to talk to her about something important, because she left her client to one of the other girls to finish up, a generous tipper too.'

'I suppose he must have,' David replied, trying for casual but sounding choked even to his own ears. Kiara had been wearing her new expensive underwear that morning, the underwear *he'd* paid for. Did she think he was blind?

'She spoke to him out back.' Sophie waved a hand in that direction. 'I think he was a bit cross when he left. He certainly looked moody. Kia dashed off shortly after him. I hope there's not a problem.'

'No. No problem,' he'd assured her, thinking there was very much a problem. And that problem was Nathan. The signals were all there.

Hearing Maddie coming down the stairs, he grabbed up the filter jug, managing to burn his hand in the process.

'Ouch.' Maddie winced as he clanged it down. 'Quick, run your hand under the cold tap,' she said, hurrying across to turn it on. 'Do you mind if I ask you something?' She glanced tentatively at him as she held his hand under the running water.

Reaching for the towel, she wrapped it around his hand, her

fascinating hazel eyes, a myriad of autumn colours, flecked with worry as she looked up at him. David wished it was within his power to make her worry go away. 'Anything,' he told her.

'Sophie,' she said, and hesitated. 'Do you trust her?'

He felt a flicker of apprehension. 'I've no reason not to. Why?'

She sighed. 'I'm not sure. It's probably me, suspicious of everyone, but … I don't know.' She looked so broken and confused David felt his heart ache for her. 'She didn't hesitate to tell me that Nathan had been in the salon, and she seemed almost thrilled at the prospect of taking over Kia's clients.'

David nodded slowly. 'I think she's the sort who doesn't think things through. I doubt she means any harm, but if you think back to how we first met …'

Maddie nodded in turn. 'I suppose.'

'I get why you would be suspicious of everyone, Mads. Trust me, I was the same at one point, even of the bloody post-man.' He smiled despondently. 'Sadly, it was Nathan we should have been suspicious of.'

Maddie's gaze hit the floor and David felt like a bastard.

'I'm sorry, Maddie,' he said sympathetically. 'I loved him too, but you have to admit him leaving that party when he said he didn't sounds dubious. There's no evidence of a holiday being booked after all.'

Maddie wrapped her arms around herself, kept her eyes fixed firmly down.

'Did he really not admit he'd left when you spoke to him?'

Maddie took a second. 'He put the phone down,' she murmured. 'He said he was coming home. And now …'

'He's missing.' David didn't want to, but he felt he had no choice but to remind her of that too.

Seeing she was close to tears, he circled her with his arms. 'I'm sorry, Maddie,' he murmured, easing her close. 'I know you're struggling to accept that he clearly doesn't care about the suffering he's caused. Just hold onto the fact that it's nothing to do with you or anything you've done. It's him. We'll get through this together. I promise you we will.'

FIFTY

Maddie

Letting herself into the hall after a day at work where she'd barely been able to concentrate after another night of very little sleep, Maddie was greeted by a jubilant Boomer. 'Hello, gorgeous boy.' She caught his paws as he jumped up, tried not to mind the lolloping tongue licking her face and gave him a good fuss. None of what was happening was his fault. He couldn't understand. Yet he did, sensing her moods as only dogs could, being there for her as only dogs could, consistent and loyal. Unlike humans, who could make considered decisions to destroy people. She still couldn't believe that Nathan would do that. Yet there had been no sightings of him according to Melissa at the project, who'd rung to keep her up to date. No reports from the authorities. Where was he? *Running scared*, said the persistent voice in her head. Not half as scared as she was.

Would DS Fletcher think he was? She'd heard nothing from him. Did he know yet?

Inhaling deeply, a shaky attempt to contain her emotions for the children's sake, she glanced towards the kitchen as she tugged off her jacket and hooked it on one of the pegs. The door was closed, she realised. She cocked an ear for sounds of the TV, and a kernel of panic took root inside her as she realised the house was eerily quiet. 'David?' she called. 'Kids?'

Nothing but silence greeted her. It was so complete you could hear a pin drop. Her stomach tightened. David had said he would pick them up from school and she'd contacted the school to tell them he would. They should be back by now, though. Surely he hadn't taken them off somewhere without telling her?

Glancing up the stairs as she hurried to the kitchen door, she tried to tell herself she was overreacting, waiting for something else bad to happen, but why *was* Boomer in the hall? She'd told David they always left him in the kitchen, where he had access to his water bowl and his bed.

'Josh? Ellie?' she shouted. She pressed down the handle and shoved the kitchen door open – then almost had complete heart failure as two gleeful faces popped up from behind the kitchen island.

'Surprise!' they chorused, clearly delighted.

'Happy birthday, Mummy!' Ellie giggled, flying towards her, arms outstretched.

Attempting to slow her rapid heartbeat, Maddie swept her up, glancing past her to where Josh stood, the expression on his rosy face full of expectancy as he eyed the food on top of the island.

'We made you a party,' Ellie said proudly. 'We couldn't fit all the candles on the cake, but David said you would be happier with one. Are you?' She searched Maddie's face with a worried little frown.

Maddie laughed and swallowed back a lump of emotion. Nathan wasn't often away on her birthday. If he couldn't avoid it, he would always have something special delivered. He should have been here today. He'd said they'd found someone from the US to take over. That he wouldn't be away for more than a few days. Had he ever intended to come back?

'I am. Definitely,' she assured the little girl, then, kissing her cute button nose, she glanced towards David, whose expression was a mixture of pleased and bashful. 'Thank you,' she said, gathering now why he'd wanted to pick the children up. They'd obviously gone to the supermarket on the way home.

Could anyone have been more thoughtful? *Nathan could.* Her mind went to the little romantic gestures that would make her feel special. The flowers he would bring home, sometimes leaving a single red rose on her car seat. The texts he would send: *Thinking of you and smiling* or *I love you because* ... Where had that man gone? The man she knew him to be.

'My pleasure,' David assured her with a smile. 'The kids picked the cake.'

Seeing it was a *PAW Patrol* cake, Maddie had guessed they might have.

'And I picked the pizza.' Josh nodded importantly towards the slices of pepperoni.

As she checked out the jelly and custard and marshmallow kebabs on offer, Maddie laughed again. She had a sneaking suspicion Ellie and Josh had chosen all their favourites between them. 'Perfect,' she said, moving to give her little man's shoulders a firm squeeze.

'I picked the balloons, too, Mummy,' Ellie said, her eyes travelling upwards.

Maddie followed her gaze to where a bunch of Minions balloons bobbed against the ceiling.

'They escaped, unfortunately, just as you came through the

door,' David explained, walking across to pick Ellie up so she could grab them.

Balloons rescued, he swung her onto a stool. 'We'd better eat some of that food before Boomer does,' he suggested, nodding towards the dog, whose doleful eyes and nose were an inch away from the pizza.

'Yay!' Josh heaved himself up next to Ellie as Maddie encouraged Boomer away with a dog treat. 'We're playing party games after, aren't we, David?' Grabbing a pizza slice, Josh glanced hopefully towards David as he stuffed it into his mouth.

'We are indeed. But only if we eat slowly, otherwise we'll have indigestion.' Taking the seat opposite him, David gave Josh a mock scowl.

Maddie was impressed with his parenting skills, but also filled with a sudden overwhelming grief. He meant well, but seeing him sitting in Nathan's place doing what Nathan should be doing only sharpened the pain of his absence.

'I thought hide-and-seek?' Clearly sensing her change in mood, David reached for her hand and gave it a quick squeeze. 'They wanted Pictionary Air, but maybe we should give that a rest in favour of some exercise. What do you think?'

'Good idea.' Maddie nodded and managed a smile, but she couldn't help remembering the last time they'd played hide-and-seek as a family. She and Nathan had started to panic when they couldn't find either of the children. Nathan had been outwardly calm, but the fear in his eyes had been palpable. He'd imagined they'd ventured off into the woodland. They both had but hadn't dared voice it. They'd finally discovered them in the disused coal bunker on the patio. Nathan had been shaking as he'd scooped Ellie up and hugged Josh close. He wouldn't do this. It wasn't *in* him to do this. He would never leave his children. So where was he?

FIFTY-ONE

Maddie had opted to read the children's bedtime story herself tonight – to give David a break, she'd said. Seeing him in Nathan's place had stirred up too much emotion, but she couldn't bring herself to say that. He was clearly finding being here with the children therapeutic, and since he had some holiday owed to him, he'd offered to stay for a few more days. Reluctant to hurt his feelings or make him feel unwanted, which he must have felt so acutely with the breakdown of his marriage, Maddie had agreed. The children liked having him around, and he'd been right about the hide-and-seek. Ellie and Josh had loved it. They were absolutely worn out now, both of them almost dropping off before she'd finished the story, which was a first.

Going into the kitchen, she found that David had cleared up all the party debris, and though she was grateful, the desolation she'd felt earlier came flooding back. He was in the lounge now, waiting for her. But it was Nathan she wanted. She wanted her husband back so much she physically ached. He wasn't coming back, though, was he? She'd had no further reports from the project regarding his whereabouts. No contact of any kind from Nathan himself.

Breathing in hard to hold back the tears, she went to the fridge to extract the white wine. She filled a glass and took a large glug, then poured David a red and carried the glasses through to the lounge. 'I got us some wine,' she said. 'I think we've earned it. Oh.' She stopped, noting the ice bucket on the table, the open champagne, two flutes already filled on the coffee table.

'A birthday treat,' David said, as she looked at him with a mixture of surprise and uncertainty. With David and the children having gone to so much effort, she'd had no choice but to join in. To be drinking champagne, though, while Nathan was missing, felt too much like a celebration.

He clearly noticed her hesitancy. 'Have a couple of sips at least,' he urged her. 'It's open now. Shame to let it go to waste.' Straightening the scatter cushions, he patted the sofa beside him, looking so hopeful Maddie hadn't the heart to disappoint him.

She placed the wine glasses down with a weary sigh and went to fuss over Boomer, who was parked in front of the fire. He was watching proceedings carefully, she noted. She was sure he was missing Nathan too.

David waited until she was seated and passed her a flute. 'Here you go. I know you probably don't feel like celebrating, but it might help you relax a little.'

She mustered up a smile. He was just trying to cheer her up, but what would Nathan think of all this?

She pressed the flute to her lips and took a hefty gulp, the bubbles fizzing on her tongue and up her nose, evoking the memory of the first time she'd drunk champagne. He couldn't afford it, but Nathan had bought a bottle when he'd proposed to her. Uncertain that she would accept, he'd hidden it in the back of the fridge at the house share. When she'd seen the nervousness in his eyes as he'd got down on one knee, she'd been giddy with love for him, giddy with champagne. She was beginning to feel giddy now, this time with exhaustion rather than euphoria. Would it matter if she drank herself into oblivion? She wouldn't, she was responsible for two children, but she was sure there were many worse things she could do than get drunk given how much she was hurting.

'Happy birthday.' David picked up his glass and clinked it against hers.

Maddie dropped her gaze. There was nothing remotely happy about today. She shouldn't be doing this.

He placed his glass back on the table. 'I know it's not the best birthday, Mads,' he said softly. 'Just try to take it one day at a time, hey? You never know what tomorrow might bring.'

Maddie felt she did. Knowing how David must now feel about the man he'd once considered his best friend, part of her didn't want to talk to him about Nathan, but she so needed someone else's take on things. Taking another fortifying swig of her drink, she drew in a breath. 'He still hasn't been in contact.'

David frowned. 'Nothing at all? No texts or messages?'

'No,' Maddie admitted wretchedly. She wanted Nathan back. Felt she would take him back whatever he'd done. But she wouldn't, would she? If he'd done the terrible thing she was beginning to believe he had, then he would be gone from her life, from his children's lives. Just like her mother, he would be behind bars, existing rather than living, possibly never admitting what he'd done, to himself, to anyone. She saw it again, the terrifying image that had come to her in her dreams and was now scorched indelibly on her mind, her small child's hands clutching the box of matches, the blinding white light. What had she unconsciously forgotten? How much was her mother keeping from her? How much had Nathan been keeping from her?

'Maybe you need to stop hoping, Maddie,' David suggested, inhaling sharply.

Stop hoping? She peered at him, tried to focus through her confusion, a sudden sickening wooziness that seemed to hit her out of nowhere. He looked angry, his face tight and white.

'Why would I stop hoping?' she asked, bewildered. 'He's my husband, the father of my children. You think he doesn't care about us, but I just don't believe that. I know him. He wouldn't do this, David.' She wished now that she hadn't opened the conversation. She didn't think she could handle this. She felt dizzy, disorientated, more devastated than she'd ever felt in her life. And so desperately lonely, despite David being here, her children sleeping upstairs. She just wanted to crawl under the duvet where the nightmare couldn't touch her. Except it could. There was no escape; even in her sleep her past haunted her, the present, the future.

David blew out a breath and ran his hands over his face. 'But you don't *know* him, do you? Neither of us do. He isn't coming back, Maddie,' he said with a shake of his head.

Maddie eyed him, confounded. 'But—'

'He's not, Maddie. You *know* he's not. He would have contacted you by now if he was. I don't believe for one second that he wouldn't have. And nor do you. He's not coming back,' he repeated. Maddie wasn't sure who he was trying to convince, himself or her. 'We have to accept that he's either running or—'

'What?' She stopped him. '*Dead?*' Did he really believe that? Did he want her to believe it? Imagine that she would, ever, until she had irrefutable evidence?

'I'm sorry, Maddie,' he went on, seemingly oblivious to her feelings, 'but I think we have to accept it.'

How could he say that? Maddie's head swam, nausea now rising rapidly inside her. How *could* he? Nathan wasn't *dead*. For a while, she hadn't been able to sense him. But now she could. She *could*. She pressed a fist against her chest. It felt so empty, yet at the same time stuffed with so much hurt she couldn't breathe.

'Maddie, I'm truly sorry. I can't tell you how much.' David's voice reached her, muffled as though through water. He reached for her hand. 'I'm here for you. I'll always be here, but you have to—'

'No!' A jolt of pure rage shooting through her, she snatched her hand away and jumped to her feet. 'He's *not* dead!' Her chest heaved with impotent fury. Who she was furious with, she didn't know. Nathan? Herself? Her mother? Kiara? 'He's *not!*' She backed away as David got to his feet and moved towards her. 'He *can't* be.' She felt herself reel, the walls around her swimming out of focus as surely as her world was. David was next to her, trying clumsily to hold her. She pulled away from him. 'He's not!' she insisted vehemently. 'He might have run, but ...'

Why? Why had he run? Why was he doing this? *She* couldn't do this. She *couldn't*. She pressed her hands over her face, trying to stifle the moan that seemed to come from her soul.

'Maddie, please calm down. You're upset. In shock. I didn't mean to ...'

She flinched away from him as he reached for her again. It wasn't his fault. He'd lost his wife. He'd lost her twice over. He was a good man, a caring man. She knew he was. Why then did she feel so betrayed by him?

David ran his fingers through his hair. 'I'm sorry,' he said again, his voice strained. 'I don't mean to be so blunt. I ...' He faltered, agony in his eyes.

'He's not dead,' Maddie repeated tremulously.

David nodded, his expression a mixture of sympathy and indulgence. 'You accept that he's run, though?' He seemed to be driving the point home like a knife straight through her heart.

'Either way, he's not here, is he? I was just trying to be realistic, Maddie, to prepare you, that's all.'

'Prepare me? It's almost as if you want me to just accept it and move on.'

'Christ.' David shook his head. 'I don't. Of course you can't just bloody well move on. Don't you think I know that? I'm just trying to be here for you, Maddie. Like you've always been for me. We have something special. We always have. Please don't keep backing away from me. I can't bear it.'

She didn't understand. What was he talking about? She squinted at him, wondering whether she was hearing him right, whether he could understand the implication of what he was saying. Her stomach churning, her body suddenly hot and clammy, she attempted another step towards the door, and stopped as the room swayed violently around her. What was happening to her? She felt so light-headed, but she'd hardly drunk anything. 'I need to go. I don't feel well,' she mumbled, her words emerging elongated and slurred. 'I need to go to bed.'

'Whoa, steady.' He caught her as the floor tilted beneath her. 'Come on, I've got you.'

She felt his arm circling her waist, holding her so tight he seemed to be squeezing the last of the breath from her body. 'I'm okay,' she protested. 'If I could just ...' She reached out a hand, flailing uselessly for something to hold on to.

He held her closer. 'Lean on me. Don't want you falling over your feet going upstairs or getting undressed, do we?' he whispered, close to her ear. 'I'll always be here for you, Maddie. I promise I'll never leave you.'

FIFTY-TWO

Maddie woke with a start, her eyes springing open, a flutter of panic in her chest as she wondered what time it was. Her stomach heaved, reminding her she'd been drinking last night. Closing her eyes again, she swallowed back the stale taste in her mouth and tried to recall through the thick fog in her head how she'd actually got to bed. She couldn't. How much had she drunk? Panic spiralling as her mind flew to the children, she struggled to pull herself to sitting, then froze, her skin prickling icily as she heard the unmistakable sound of heavy breathing.

For a split second she imagined she'd woken from some terrible nightmare and that Nathan was there. Then it hit her like a thunderbolt. She recalled David's arms around her. Her head had been reeling, the room spinning. Trying to still the nausea swirling inside her, she twisted to face him. He was lying on his side, his face turned towards her, one arm under his head, his other draped over her. *Oh God, no.* She felt what was left of her world shift off kilter.

Was he dressed? Was *she*? Gliding her hand over her body, she felt a smidgen of relief when she found she appeared to be wearing a shirt, that her underwear was still intact. But that didn't mean ... Carefully she eased herself from under his arm and attempted to find the floor with her feet.

'Maddie?' he said behind her, causing her heart to leap into her mouth. 'Is everything okay?'

She couldn't believe her ears. *No!* she wanted to scream. *Everything is very much not okay.* Getting unsteadily to her feet, she turned slowly to face him.

'You look like death,' he said, pulling himself to sitting. 'It's early yet. Why don't you lie back down for a while?'

She stared at him in bewilderment as he patted the space next to him. 'Did we ...?' She faltered, the words sticking painfully in her throat. 'Did I ...?'

'What?' David frowned in confusion, and then his eyes shot wide with alarm. 'Christ, no.' Throwing the duvet back, he swung himself out of bed.

Maddie closed her eyes, sweet relief flooding through her. He was dressed. His shirt was open, but he was still wearing his jeans.

'What do you take me for, Mads?' he asked after a second, his voice thick with emotion.

She looked back at him, feeling wrong-footed and horribly judgemental. 'I thought we ...' She stumbled over her words under his wounded gaze.

'It's pretty obvious what you thought,' he said, anger creeping into his voice. 'You were drunk, Maddie. Out of it. Do you think for one minute that I would have taken advantage of that?' Shaking his head, he laughed scornfully. 'Clearly you do.'

'No. I don't,' she blurted. 'I don't, David.' She *had* thought that. He knew it. And in thinking it, she'd as good as accused him.

'Just so we're clear, *nothing* happened,' he said tightly. 'You were having nightmares. Not just shouting, but screaming out in your sleep. I came in to check on you. I was worried, not least because I thought you might be ill in the night. My only crime was being so exhausted I fell asleep. I slept next you, Maddie, not with you.'

Her face burning with shame, Maddie dropped her gaze. She had had nightmares, the incomprehensible twist on the night her father had died creeping back to haunt her again; a recollection too chilling to contemplate, her six-year-old-self complicit in her father's death. Another of herself in Kiara's apartment on the night she'd died, the brush of her friend's fingertips against hers. She could still smell Kiara's perfume, see the fear in her eyes. Was it possible she *had* been there? That she might have buried the memory because it was too painful to bear? That that was why Nathan had felt compelled to lie for her?

'I'll go and put some coffee on,' David said, hurt and humiliation obvious in his voice.

'David.' Maddie spoke as he turned away. 'I'm sorry.' She stopped. Sorry could never justify what she'd accused him of. Why hadn't she paused before opening her mouth? Got her chaotic thoughts in some sort of order? She still felt woozy, though how she'd come to be so drunk, she didn't know. If she'd taken a sleeping tablet, she could understand it, but she hadn't. She'd been determined to break the cycle, to not be dependent on them. Yet here she was, her memory as dysfunctional as it had ever been.

He turned back to her. Met her gaze briefly.

'Please forgive me,' she begged, a hard lump expanding in her chest. 'You've every right to be angry. I don't know what I was thinking. You're right, I did have nightmares. I always do. And every time I do, I just get more and more confused. I'm really sorry, David.' She heaved in a breath, willed the tears not to come, but they did anyway. 'Please don't go off believing I think badly of you.'

David hesitated, then, 'Hey, there's no need for that,' he said softly. Walking around the bed towards her, he hesitated again, as if uncertain how to be near her, then reached out, wiping away the tears that spilled down her cheek. 'I'm not going anywhere, Mads. I understand. I've been where you are, confused, full of grief, desperately trying to work out what's going on around me. I still am,' he admitted. 'I have bad dreams too, trust me.'

Did he understand? Maddie searched his eyes, soulful brown eyes, so full of pain. What would he do if he knew why one dream in particular left her so petrified?

'Whatever Nathan's done, you still love him, that's obvious. I guess you can't just stop loving someone, can you?' Smiling sadly, he threaded an arm around her and gave her shoulders a quick squeeze. 'What happened just now was a misunderstanding. Don't beat yourself up about it. Why don't we go and get that coffee and—'

'The nightmares weren't about Nathan,' Maddie said quickly, before her courage failed her. 'They were about me when I was young. Another where I was with Kiara, the last time I saw her.' She wavered. Would he think she was mad?

He looked at her curiously. 'And?'

She licked her dry lips. David reached past her, picking up the glass of water on her bedside table and passing it to her. She hadn't brought that in. He must have done. She didn't deserve him, his friendship, his forgiveness, his loyalty. Accepting it gratefully, she took a gulp, her teeth clinking against the edge of the glass.

David gave her a moment, and then nodded her on. 'You were saying?'

Maddie glanced at the glass, set it down, then looked back at him. 'Nathan thought I was at the apartment the night Kiara died,' she said, bracing herself to tell him the rest. She wasn't sure why she felt she had to, except she needed to know: did David think she was capable of the horrendous thing that Nathan clearly did?

He didn't respond, but she saw the flicker of doubt in his eyes and hurried on. 'You know I take sleeping tablets, or I did. They have side effects, cloud my memory sometimes and ...' She stopped and tried to calm herself. She was gabbling it out. She needed to make sense. Make sense of it herself. How she wished that she could.

David's eyes narrowed slightly, but still he didn't say anything, simply waited.

'I have gaps in my memory,' she confided, 'around events in my childhood.'

'To do with what happened to your father?' he asked, studying her carefully.

She answered with a small, defeated nod. 'I saw a psychologist,' she forced herself on, 'later, when I was in my teens. She said that at the age I was when it happened, it was likely my mind wouldn't have been able to cope with the trauma and that I'd repressed the memories.'

'Sounds possible,' David conceded.

Reassured that he did seem to understand, at least that much, Maddie pressed on. 'She told me that the memories might return over time, but that some of them might not be real. That my mind might fill in the blanks.'

He was now studying her intently. 'And Nathan thought this was relevant to the night Kiara died how exactly?'

Maddie breathed deeply, willed herself to go on. 'I drove around after visiting my mother. I do sometimes to try to clear my head. The thing is, I don't remember much after leaving the prison, where it was I drove, how long for, and Nathan lied for me. He told DS Fletcher I'd come straight home. He said later that it was because he was worried, because he thought I might have gone to the apartment to confront Kiara.'

David looked her over for a long, searching moment, his expression inscrutable.

'Do you think I might have? That I might have been capable

of hurting her?' David knew her. Next to Nathan and Kiara, he probably knew her better than anyone.

Running a hand over his neck, he glanced down. He took another second, then, 'I don't think any of us know what we're capable of until we're pushed,' he said, looking back at her. 'If you want my honest answer, though, I'm wondering why Nathan would imagine you had been there.'

Maddie looked at him quizzically. She wasn't sure she was following.

'Doesn't it strike you that he might have been worrying because he knew you had good reason to confront Kiara?'

Maddie felt her heart slide icily into the pit of her stomach. 'The affair.'

'I can't know whether you were there, Maddie,' he went on. 'It's possible, I suppose, but I doubt you would have blanked it out so completely. It might just be that your mind is filling in gaps because you're carrying guilt about the situation between you and Kiara. I can't help thinking, though, that Nathan was trying to shift the blame, knowing you would believe him. If you're honest with yourself, don't you?'

FIFTY-THREE

David

She looked good even exhausted, which she must be with all that was going on. David smiled reassuringly at her across the island as Ellie recounted her day at school; how she'd informed the boy who was bullying her that her father was the world's expert on bugs. 'I told him Daddy was going to bring a great big one home and set it on him,' the little girl said importantly. 'He didn't believe me until Josh showed him a picture of Daddy in the jungle on his iPad.'

'What picture?' Maddie's gaze flicked worriedly to David, who guessed she was wondering when it was taken. 'Can I see it, Josh?' she asked, clearly working to keep her tone light.

'The one of him holding a great big tarantula. It's really cool,' Josh said, scrambling from his stool and skidding off to fetch his iPad from the lounge.

He was back in a flash, scrolling the screen. 'It's massive,' he said, looking impressed as he handed the tablet to Maddie, whose pretty features were tinged with a mixture of hope and fear as she glanced down at the photo.

'Is it real, Mummy?' Ellie asked, her voice a worried whisper.

'It is, sweetheart,' Maddie said, sounding choked. 'But it's obviously a friendly one.'

'It doesn't look very friendly.' Ellie, whose face had paled, backed warily away.

'They *are* friendly,' Josh insisted. 'I told you they're good for the planet. They eat all the yucky bugs that eat all the crops. Without them, we'd be overrun by all the other bugs and we'd starve to death.'

Ellie didn't look appeased. 'Millions of bugs?' she asked him, her thoughts no doubt still on the playground bully.

'Quite a lot,' Josh answered diplomatically.

'They still frighten me,' Ellie whispered, her eyes filling up.

'Tell you what, why don't you go and find a film to watch before bed?' David suggested, glancing at Maddie. 'I'm sure your mum won't mind you having an extra ten minutes tonight.'

'Yay!' Josh twirled around. '*Back to the Outback.*'

'Does that have bugs in it?' Ellie asked uncertainly, sliding down from her stool to follow him to the lounge.

'Um, a few,' Josh's voice trailed back. 'But they're super cool. They look out for each other. Come and see.'

Maddie looked dubious. 'No scaring your sister, Josh,' she called after them. 'You promised, remember?'

'I'm not,' Josh called back. 'I'm trying to educate her.'

Maddie laughed at that, and then drew in a sharp breath.

David walked around to her, placing his arm across her shoulders as he looked at the photo on Josh's iPad. He'd gathered from her expression, which had gone from hopeful, albeit apprehensive, to disappointed, that she was upset.

'It's a photo from a couple of years ago for an entomology magazine,' she said. 'I thought it might be ...'

'Current?' David finished. 'I'm sorry, Mads,' he said, feeling for her. For a jarring minute, he'd also thought it might be a recent photograph. He was pretty certain, though, assuming Nathan had survived his impulsive boat trip, that he would be attempting to keep off the radar. He'd been involved in an affair with Kiara. His fingerprints were in the apartment, on a bottle of wine in the bedroom and, damningly, on the headboard. He was in the vicinity when she'd died. He'd left the kids' party. Had had ample opportunity. If he surfaced, he would be charged, and he'd know it. 'You can see he's comfortable with spiders, can't you?' he added. He was aware that the spiders being in the apartment was yet another nail in Nathan's coffin, but he couldn't bear to see her building her hopes up.

Maddie wrapped her arms around herself in that way she did when she felt troubled or lonely. 'Why don't you go and join the kids?' he suggested. 'You're probably still under the weather. You need to try and relax. I'll clear up the dinner things and then, once the kids are in bed, if you're feeling up to it, we could maybe watch something together.'

'Thanks.' Maddie climbed down from her stool and turned to the door. 'I'll just pop up and brush my teeth. Won't be a sec.'

David buried a sigh as he watched her go. He wished he could tell her how he felt, but to do that would be grossly unfair right now.

He was loading the dishwasher when his phone rang. Pulling it from his pocket, he checked it with a frown and then reluctantly answered. 'Sophie, hi.'

'Is now a good time?' she asked.

'Not sure,' he said, glancing towards the hall. 'Maddie's just popped up to the bathroom.'

'Oh, right.' She paused. 'Has Nathan surfaced yet?'

'No sign of him.' David wedged the phone against his ear and continued his task. 'He hasn't contacted her either.'

Another pause, then, 'Can you let me know if he does?'

David was about to say he doubted he would when he realised Maddie was on her way back downstairs. 'Will do,' he said instead. 'I have to go.'

Ending the call, he smiled as she walked towards him. She'd pinned her hair up. It looked nice, sophisticated. He hadn't been sure about the blonde she'd had put into it, but it suited her.

'Who was that on the phone?' she asked. 'I thought you might be discussing Nathan. I just wondered.'

She'd overheard, clearly. 'Sophie,' he said, concentrating on loading the last of the dishes. 'She wondered how things were.'

Maddie furrowed her brow. 'That was nice of her considering we don't know each other that well.'

'She probably relates.' David shrugged. 'Having children of her own, I mean.'

Maddie thought about it and then nodded. She looked distracted. She did most of the time lately, unsurprisingly. 'Thanks for clearing up,' she said, running a hand down his back. It was a friendly gesture, that was all, but still David caught his breath.

'No problem.' He smiled, watching her walk across to the bin.

'Sleeping pills.' She glanced back at him as she threw them in. 'I need to be clear-headed.'

'Well done.' David nodded, impressed, though he was surprised she'd made such a firm decision. 'Go on in and get comfy.' He indicated the lounge. 'I'll make us a coffee and join you in a sec.'

'Decaf for me.' Maddie smiled. 'Better steer clear of caffeine. Thanks, Dave.'

'No need to keep thanking me,' he assured her. 'It's the least I can do.'

Turning to flick the kettle on, he waited until she'd left the room, then went across to the bin. Glancing towards the door to check she wasn't about to wander back in, he flipped the lid and lifted the sleeping pills out. He didn't like the idea of her taking them, but there was every possibility they might be needed.

FIFTY-FOUR

Maddie

After hours lying awake watching the digits on the alarm clock click over, Maddie shuffled over to Nathan's side of the bed, clutched his pillow to her midriff and curled herself tight. She hadn't realised she'd drifted off until something snatched her back to consciousness. She'd heard a bang outside. She was sure she had. Her heart palpitating, she reached for the bedside lamp and flicked it on. She flicked it again, and again. Nothing. The bulb must have gone. Why the bloody hell had the bulb gone *now*?

Another loud crash launched her from the bed. She flew across the room and slapped her hand against the light switch, then froze, her blood running cold as she realised that wasn't working either. Her fear of the dark returning with a vengeance, she yanked the bedroom door open, stumbled out onto the landing and made her way blindly towards the spare room door.

Shit! Stubbing her toe sharply on the ladder that had been left there by the workmen, she clenched her teeth hard and limped onwards, feeling her way along the landing until she reached David's door.

It was open. Apprehension prickling the back of her neck, she pushed it wider, took a tentative step into the room, then whirled around, her heart catapulting into her mouth, as she realised there was someone behind her.

'Maddie, it's me,' David said, as a cry of fear escaped her. 'It's *me*, Mads,' he repeated. 'Christ, I'm sorry. I must have frightened the life out of you.' He hesitated for a second, then put his hands on her shoulders. 'It was just a fox,' he said reassuringly. 'It managed to knock the wheelie bin over. One of the fuses blew when I switched the outside light on. I should have thought to come up and warn you. Are you all right?'

Her heart rate slowing to somewhere near normal, Maddie nodded. 'I thought ... I didn't know where you were. The children ...'

'They're fine,' David assured her. 'They've obviously slept through the whole thing. I was just about to check on them. Jesus, you're shaking.' He drew her closer. 'It's okay, Mads. It was a bloody stupid thing to do, creeping up on you like that. You're safe, I promise you. I would never let anything happen to you or the children. You know that, right?'

She lifted her face from his shoulder. 'I know.' She smiled, feeling safe in his arms for that brief moment.

'I should go and fix that fuse,' he said, but he didn't move.

Maddie froze, too stunned to pull away as his lips found hers.

FIFTY-FIVE

Up early despite not sleeping, Maddie splashed cold water over her face and then studied herself long and hard in the bathroom mirror. Seeing how shocked she'd been last night, David had apologised for his impulsiveness, but what on earth had possessed him? Why hadn't she pulled away immediately? Allowing him to kiss her had sent out all the wrong signals. And now wasn't he bound to think that this was what she wanted, him here in Nathan's place? He was downstairs right now with Nathan's children, preparing their breakfast. Doing all the things Nathan would normally do. How had this happened?

Hopelessly confused, she showered quickly and hurried down to the kitchen to find Ellie and Josh tucking happily into scrambled eggs as they watched TV. Her heart dropped, but she made herself smile for their benefit.

'Morning,' the children greeted her cheerily. She took a step back as Boomer raced towards her.

'Hey.' David smiled at her over his shoulder, then turned quickly back to the toaster as the toast popped.

'Missed.' Josh smirked as he failed to catch it, the toaster tending to launch the bread rather than sensibly eject it.

'Again.' David sighed mock-despairingly.

'Daddy never misses, does he, Mummy? Boomer would gobble them up and get fatter and fatter if he did,' Ellie commented, munching her breakfast, seemingly unperturbed that her daddy wasn't here and there was another man in his place, oblivious to the fact that Nathan might never be coming back. She would be inconsolable if she knew what was going on – both of them would be – and Maddie didn't think she could bear it.

'I obviously need more practice.' David turned to give Maddie another smile. 'Toast?' he offered.

'No. Thanks.' She doubted very much she would be able to swallow it. 'Could I have a quick word?' She nodded towards the hall.

He scrunched his brow. 'No problem,' he said, then, 'Hang on a sec,' and he leaned to catch another flying slice of bread, to the delight of the children.

Unable to stand another second of the happy family scene, Maddie led the way to the hall.

David followed after a second, pulling the kitchen door to behind him. 'Is there a problem?' he asked, looking perplexed.

Surely he knew there was? Maddie couldn't believe he was that obtuse.

He glanced uncomfortably down. 'Look, if this is about what happened last night ...'

'It shouldn't have,' she said quickly. She'd felt so lonely, so scared; devastated at Nathan's betrayal – of her, their children, everything they'd had together. But she didn't want whatever it was David was imagining was going on here.

He nodded. 'I understand, Maddie,' he said, shrugging sadly. 'We both probably need to give ourselves a little more time.'

What? Maddie squinted at him, then, 'No.' She stepped away as he moved to put an arm around her. 'I'm sorry, David,' she said, keeping her voice low so as not to alert the children. 'I like you, but ...'

He drew in a breath. 'You don't love me.' He shrugged disconsolately again. 'It's okay, I get it. Story of my life really.'

And now Maddie felt awful. 'You're my friend, David. I love you dearly, but ...' She searched for a way to let him down lightly.

'Not in the way you love Nathan,' he finished, with a flat smile. 'I understand, Maddie, trust me. Though why you still feel that way after everything ...'

'That's just it, though, isn't it? I don't *know* everything. Nathan isn't here to tell me. I think I might be judging him too hastily.'

'Really?' David's expression was now one of incredulity.

She couldn't blame him. That Nathan had been involved with Kiara seemed indisputable. 'If he was having an affair with Kiara, that was unforgivable,' she said. 'I don't think he's capable of murder, though. I just can't believe he would be.'

'Right. Yet he believed you to be,' David pointed out bluntly. He paused, then went on tersely. 'People don't tend to wear labels advertising the fact that they're evil bastards. They present themselves as just the opposite, in fact.'

Maddie was completely taken aback. More so by the flash of fury she'd seen in his eyes. Reluctant to respond, no idea how to, she glanced away. Josh and Ellie would be engrossed in whatever they were watching on TV, but this wasn't a conversation they should be having here. 'I need to get on or we'll be late,' she said quietly instead.

Sighing heavily, David ran a hand through his hair. 'I was going to offer to take the kids to school, but I'm guessing you might not want me to now.'

Maddie felt extremely uncomfortable. 'I was going to take them in anyway this morning. I want to have a word with Ellie's teacher about the bullying.' It was true, she did, but she was thinking that allowing David to be so hands-on had been a bad idea.

'I see.' He nodded shortly. 'I'll go and grab you a coffee then, shall I, assuming that doesn't compromise you too much?'

Maddie heard the cynicism in his voice. 'David, please don't ...' She trailed off as he turned to walk back to the kitchen. She wasn't sure what she'd been going to say anyway. Please don't be hurt? It was clear that he was. Was that her fault? Thinking she'd handled the whole thing badly, she sighed in despair.

Giving herself a minute, she bent to retrieve the post from the hall floor and flicked quickly through it. Then caught herself. Did she think Nathan was going to *write* to her? She clearly was delusional. Tossing the envelopes on the hall table, she was about to go back to the kitchen to chivvy the children on when her eye snagged on one of them. A white envelope with a franked postmark, *Trailseekers Travel Agents*. Her heart missed a beat.

FIFTY-SIX

'Are we going on holiday?' Josh asked, his eyes wide with excitement as he noticed the holiday brochure that had arrived with the tickets.

'No, sweetheart, it's just advertising.' She eased it away from him, one eye on David, who was looking at the tickets, as stunned as she was. 'Take Ellie up and help her brush her teeth, will you, Josh?' she asked him.

'Aw, Mum.' He rolled his eyes grumpily. 'You know she'll only moan at me.'

'I don't need any help. I can brush my own teeth, thank you very much,' Ellie informed them, a haughty expression on her face as she headed for the door.

'Fair enough.' Maddie wasn't sure she could argue with that. 'But hurry up. You too, Josh, or we'll be late for school. Top and bottom, Ellie,' she reminded her. 'And make sure to do *all* of them.'

'I know. I'm not a *baby*.' Ellie headed off with a world-weary sigh, Boomer bounding alongside her and Josh trailing behind.

'The Maldives, hey?' David glanced from the tickets to Maddie, his expression bemused.

Maddie moved to push the kitchen door to. 'You do see what this means, though?' she asked, desperate for David to be the tiniest bit hopeful. She understood the way he must be feeling – he had every right to hate Nathan – but she didn't want to believe that he would wish him dead. 'They're dated a week away.'

'I noticed. And you're sure he booked them for the two of you, are you?'

Noting the sarcastic edge to his tone, she looked away. 'I have to go. We'll be late,' she said, retrieving the tickets from him.

'So what are you going to do with them?' David asked as she headed for the hall.

Maddie paused. 'Take them to the police station. They'll be able to check the time of the booking, prove that Nathan did leave the party for the reason he said he did.'

'Possibly,' David said.

Maddie couldn't help wondering whether he hoped they wouldn't offer any such proof. She didn't respond. She could hardly argue in Nathan's defence with the man whose wife he'd apparently had an affair with. She was unnerved by David's attitude. He was probably feeling disheartened after their conversation in the hall, but she'd never seen him like this, cynical and moody.

'Maddie, wait.' He stopped her before she reached the door. 'I'm sorry. I'm acting like a complete idiot. I don't mean to, I'm just jealous, I guess,' he admitted, clearly embarrassed. 'You obviously care a lot for him, and I suppose I'm disappointed.'

A pang of guilt climbing her chest, she turned back to face him.

'I'm sorry, Maddie. Please take no notice. I'll lick my wounds and get over it. Of course you have to take the tickets to the police, though I'm honestly not sure how much they'll help.'

Maddie nodded. It felt like he was giving her hope with one

hand and taking it away with the other. She understood why he would be suspicious of Nathan's motives, though.

'What will you do?' she asked him, assuming that after their earlier conversation, he would take the hint and go home.

'I thought I'd crack on with the garden, if that's okay with you. I've started cutting back the trees at the bottom towards the woods. I might as well finish the job.'

It *wasn't* okay with her. Maddie stared at him, flabbergasted. She'd thought he was cutting back the weeds, not the trees. He knew she didn't want those interfered with. The garden was Nathan's project. She'd wanted to keep it the way it was for when he got home. She'd told David that. It *was* Nathan, who he was, a man who respected all living things, which was one of the reasons she couldn't contemplate him ever ending a life. And now David was behaving as if he didn't care whether Nathan was coming home, didn't care about him at all. It was as if he wanted to cut him and everything that mattered to him out of her life.

FIFTY-SEVEN

Maddie had spent the whole day worrying. She'd thought she'd put the tickets in her bag, but when she'd looked for them at lunchtime, she couldn't find them. On the assumption that DS Fletcher had found out by now that Nathan had left the party, she'd rung the station instead. Fletcher had come back to her just as she was leaving school. He'd sounded incredulous when she'd told him about the tickets, but promised to follow it up, to her immense relief. She was also annoyed with herself for not being firmer with David. She hadn't wanted him to pick the children up from school. He'd woven himself into the fabric of her life somehow and now it was just too much. She had to talk to him. It was more than his being here, where Nathan should be. She was beginning to feel almost claustrophobic around him. She should suggest he go sooner rather than later. She would do it kindly, tell him he was welcome to visit but that she needed time on her own, just her and the children.

Her decision made, she pulled up on the drive, her chest tightening as she glanced towards the house. Since Nathan had gone missing, whenever she came home she would imagine she was going to find him inside, his usual smiley self, asking her if she'd had a good day. Instead, she would find David. And there might be more upset ahead when she asked him to leave, a prospect she wasn't looking forward to. She didn't want to lose him as a friend. She just hoped he really did understand that their relationship could only ever be platonic.

Bracing herself, she climbed out of her car and headed for the front door. Boomer greeted her as she let herself in, his tail wagging like a windmill. She was grateful for his pure unquestioning faithfulness, for being a constant in her life when her landscape was shifting so violently, her world becoming a darker, more frightening place.

'Mummy!' Ellie flew from the lounge, clearly also delighted to see her. 'We're going on a school trip,' she said, jiggling excitedly. 'To a wild farm.'

Maddie's eyes widened. 'Are you indeed?' Her mind boggled at the thought of what activities there might be suitable for primary school children.

'A farming and wildlife education centre,' Josh translated from the lounge in his best long-suffering voice. 'Twit.'

'Josh!' Maddie said, a warning edge to her voice.

'Sorry.' Josh, who was clearly glued to some computer game or other, sighed wearily, 'She does do my head in sometimes, though.'

Maddie's breath caught. He sounded like a seven-year-old going on seventeen. He was growing up. They both were. Would Nathan be here to see that? Would they ever see him again?

'Hi.' David smiled tentatively as he appeared from the kitchen. 'Good day?' he asked – exactly what Nathan would have said – and Maddie felt her heart plummet to the depths of her soul.

'Yes. Thanks.' She nodded quickly and took hold of her little girl's hand.

'They've had dinner,' David added as she led Ellie to the lounge so she could say a proper hello to Josh. 'I've promised them a film before bed. Hope that's okay?'

'*Wish Dragon*,' Ellie said. 'It's about a dragon that makes wishes come true. Can we watch it, Mummy?'

Maddie glanced down at her. 'I suppose,' she said, quietly annoyed with David for not consulting her, yet again. 'But straight to bed and straight to sleep afterwards.'

Ellie smiled, but she didn't look quite as jubilant as Maddie had thought she might. 'Can I ask you something, Mummy?' she said, that little furrow forming in her brow that told Maddie she was troubled.

'Of course, sweetheart. What is it?'

'If I make a wish and I'm really good, will Daddy come home?' Her huge blue eyes, once crystal clear with the innocence of childhood, were clouded with worry.

With no idea what to say, Maddie crouched down to her. 'He's working, darling,' she tried to reassure her. 'I'm not quite sure when ...' She stopped, a sharp stone she couldn't seem to swallow clogging her throat.

Josh saved her, abandoning his game to come across to his sister and slide an arm around her shoulders. 'I told you, he's had an emergency. He's helping sick people. Just because he's not here doesn't mean he doesn't love us. He'll be home soon, won't he, Mum?'

Maddie smiled, but noting the wariness in her boy's eyes, it was all she could do not to break down and weep.

Her head snapped up as David said behind them, 'He might be a while longer, but we'll make sure to have fun, hey? As long as you don't mind me standing in.'

She looked at him in disbelief. What was he doing? Did he want Nathan not to come home? To be found dead? Accused of murder? What?

Watching him walk back to the kitchen, a thought occurred.

She tried to dismiss it but couldn't. Had he taken the tickets from her bag?

FIFTY-EIGHT

Nathan

Nathan fought the deep, dark sleep that tried to reclaim him. He struggled to raise himself, but his limbs were too heavy, his mind deaf to his desperate pleas not to go back there, where the smell, a cloying scent of moisture, soil, decaying vegetation and animal musk, was so thick it almost choked him. Not the smell of life. This time it was the smell of death. *No!* he cried out again, somewhere inside his confused mind. Tried to draw air past the suffocating constriction in his chest. His breathing was shallow, the rancid river water that filled his lungs rattling his chest. He felt his body jerk, his danger antennae on red alert as nightfall descended and the sounds of the jungle beginning to ebb reached him, a cacophony of sound: birds calling, wings flapping, monkeys shrieking high in the tall trees above him. Green anacondas sliding through the lush foliage around him. *Too close.* He could sense the apprehension in the humid air. The anticipation. Feel the creatures of the rainforest, predators walking their hunting ground, preparing for the long stretch of impenetrable darkness ahead.

New sounds emerged: footfalls, low rumbling growls, grunts, snuffling and snorting. *Scuffling.* Yards away from him. The sour taste of his own fear filled his mouth as he pictured huge black caiman alligators emerging from the river. *No!* He willed his stubborn eyes to open, tried to stop his mind jerking from thought to disorientated thought, to drag himself back to consciousness. His body jolted as he felt the feather-light tickle of insect legs brushing his cheek. Terror crackled like ice through his veins as he imagined what they might be. Bullet ants, their sting capable of inflicting pain that was too excruciating to bear? Giant centipedes, multiple legs moving simultaneously, forcipules raised ready to inject highly toxic venom into his bloodstream?

It was neither of those. He knew it wasn't. Knew he was reliving it over and over, but still he couldn't stop it, couldn't block it out. Fear gripped his stomach like a vice – the debilitating fear Kiara would have felt – nausea rising like thick bile in his throat as he caught sight of the huge spider crawling purposefully from the floor of the jungle in search of its prey. One of the world's most venomous spiders, its two front legs raised aggressively, poised to strike an inch from his face.

No! Hearing the blood-curdling scream that was all around him, that came from inside him, he tore his eyes open.

'Hey,' someone called as, sucking in a life-giving breath, he yanked himself up. 'Nathan, keep calm. You're safe.' He felt firm hands on his shoulders, someone trying to prevent him from raising himself further. 'You're safe, Nathan,' the man repeated soothingly. 'We got the antivenom into you on the supply plane, remember? You're going to be okay.'

Nathan blinked hard. 'Mike,' he rasped, relief crashing through him as reality kicked in and his nightmare receded.

'Well I'm definitely not Maddie.' The medic who was travelling with him chuckled. 'You were so convinced I was at one point, I thought I might have to fend you off.'

Nathan squinted at him, his mind still a whirl of foggy confusion

'You were calling out for her,' Mike enlightened him. 'You grabbed hold of my arm and squeezed so hard I was sure you were going to stop my circulation.'

'Sorry,' Nathan apologised, though he had no recollection beyond the flimsy boat hitting the wall of water that tossed it around like a cork on the waves. No memories apart from those his unconsciousness conjured up. He saw it again, the deadly arachnid, its two-inch-thick body and seven-inch leg span. That had obviously been real. His heart rate spiked even as he thought about it, his mind going again to Kiara, how truly petrified she must have been facing her worst fear. *He's doing it on purpose. Bringing the spiders in, I mean. You know, so he can be my hero and save me.* He heard the tremor in her voice when she'd confided in him. She'd wanted him to save her. She'd reached out to him. He wasn't sure how he could live with himself knowing he hadn't taken hold of her hand.

'No problem. I was happy to stand in – up to a point,' Mike assured him with an amused roll of his eyes. 'I've asked one of the flight attendants to bring you some fluids – not alcohol, sorry. Then get some rest. You need to get your strength back. The flight's been a long haul, and we hit a few patches of turbulence, but we'll be landing pretty soon. We'll get you transported to the nearest hospital as soon as we can.'

'Thanks.' Nathan wiped the slick film of sweat from his face and thanked God for what was nothing short of a miracle. He wasn't sure how he was still alive. He assumed someone from one of the local communities had informed the medical supply team. He would have been a dead man otherwise. 'Mike.' He stopped the man as he went to sit down. 'Does Maddie know I'm okay? Did the project contact her?'

'I spoke to Melissa Bowers. She couldn't get hold of her, but she says she left a message. She's also contacted the embassy. Tell you what, why don't you call her yourself now that you're more compos?' Ferreting in his pocket, Mike pulled out his phone and handed it over.

Hands shaking, Nathan keyed in Maddie's number. Then cursed as a male voice answered. David. Cutting the call, he felt sick to the bottom of his soul. How could he have been such an idiot? He'd asked him to look out for her. Given him access to her, to his kids. *Jesus Christ.*

He couldn't be certain what had happened in his absence. One thing he was sure of, though, was that he wasn't about to allow himself to be arrested. The police had evidence against him. How much more they might have gathered since he'd spoken to Maddie, he had no idea.

He had to get home. He had to get there fast.

FIFTY-NINE

Maddie

Watching Ellie's eyelids flutter as her mind chased her dreams, Maddie pressed a soft kiss to her little girl's forehead, then crept quietly out of the room and went to check on Josh. He was still awake, his eyes on his Kindle screen rather than his tablet, which Maddie allowed in moderation. 'Okay?' she asked him.

Glancing up, he looked as if he wanted to say something, but obviously decided against it and went back to his Kindle with an 'uh huh' instead.

'Five more minutes,' Maddie said, watching him carefully.

Josh nodded. 'Night, Mum.'

'Night, little man.' She smiled and left him to it. Josh wasn't one to hide his feelings. He would talk to her when he needed to. At least she hoped he would.

She took a second on the landing to compose herself. The urge to pull her children to her, hug them and never let go was overwhelming. For now, though, she needed to be strong for them. No more bloody pills addling her brain. No more relying on other people. She'd allowed David to move into her life. He'd clearly envisaged some kind of a future with her. That wasn't a crime. That he seemed so determined to become the missing part of her family, though, to take Nathan's place so completely, was becoming more than worrying. It was frightening. Manipulative.

She has a ludicrous idea that he's bringing the spiders into the house deliberately. An icy chill ran through her as she recalled what Nathan had told her. Kiara had thought it was because David had wanted to save her, to be her hero. Now he was trying to be Maddie's hero, make her dependent on him, just as he'd done with Kiara. That thought landed with a sickening thud in her chest, and she steeled herself. She had to talk to him. She wouldn't go into the whys and wherefores. She would just ask him to leave.

Taking a steadying breath, she walked back to the stairs. She wasn't sure why she stopped outside the spare room, why she felt compelled to go in. Her thinking might be skewed, but it was growing obvious that there were parts of himself that David had kept hidden. Hesitating, she listened on the landing, then, hearing sounds of him clearing away the dinner things, went inside.

Going across to the bedside table, she opened the drawer and her eyes fell on one of the photographs she'd given him of Kiara and herself posing cheek to cheek. *I'm so sorry, sweetheart.* Her grief flooding excruciatingly back, she reached for it, running a finger softly over it before placing it back. There was a scarf in there too. Maddie's heart caught painfully in her chest as she realised it was Kiara's polka-dot scarf, the one she herself had worn on their long-ago holiday to Cornwall. She pressed it to her face. It smelled unmistakably of Kiara, a fusion of perfumes that brought the image of her friend so sharply back it was as if she were in the room here with her.

Holding her breath, trying to keep the pain stuffed down inside, Maddie was about to shut the drawer when she noticed a small brown envelope at the bottom. There was nothing written on it. She wavered, feeling like a thief in the night, then pulled it out.

The flap wasn't sealed. She glanced at the door, then, her heart thrumming a steady rat-a-tat in her chest, cautiously opened the envelope – and froze. Inside it was a locket. She and Kiara had found it in a tiny second-hand shop. It wasn't fancy, just a silver one, but Kia had loved it. Until it had been ripped from her neck.

SIXTY

She'd obviously caught him by surprise. He jumped as she went quietly into the kitchen.

'Christ,' he said, stuffing something into the drawer under the work surface, hurriedly it seemed to Maddie, and then quickly stirring the tea. 'You almost gave me a heart attack.'

Her gaze went to the drawer, then back to him as he walked towards her with a mug. 'I made it strong.' He smiled. 'I thought you could use it.'

Maddie surveyed him thoughtfully for a second, then lifted her hand. 'What's this?' she asked.

David frowned as he looked down at the locket that lay in her palm. 'No idea,' he said, offering her the tea.

Maddie didn't take it. 'It's a locket,' she informed him, her voice as cold as ice. 'It was in your bedside drawer. What was it doing there?'

David studied it, his frown deepening, then turned away, placing the mug carefully on the work surface. He studied that too, for a long moment, then turned it around as if displeased with its position. 'Like I say, I've no idea.'

'It's *Kiara's*!' she spat.

'Kiara's?' He glanced at her, his brow furrowed now with confusion. 'You mean ... Christ, Nathan?'

Maddie's heart boomed out a warning. 'I'd like you to go, David,' she said, working to keep her voice low. 'Your wallet and keys are on the hall table. I'll collect up the rest of your things and drop them at your parents' apartment.'

'I see,' he said, moving the mug another fraction, nodding slowly. 'Tell me if I've got this wrong, Maddie, but it seems to me that rather than seeing the ever-affable Nathan for what he really is, you're accusing *me* of raping my own wife.'

He turned to face her. His eyes were as dark as thunder. 'It's nothing to do with me!' he seethed, curling his fist and slamming it against the work surface. 'I didn't even know it was there!'

Maddie jumped, but she didn't look away. For a blood-freezing moment, there appeared to be a stand-off. Then David dropped his gaze.

'I didn't want to say anything, Maddie, don't you see?' Moderating his tone, he looked back at her. 'I did know the bloody thing was there, of course I did, but on top of everything else, why would I do that to you? Why would I have wanted you to tear yourself apart any more than you—'

'Now, David!' Maddie yelled as he moved towards her.

'Okay!' His voice had risen again. 'Okay,' he said more quietly, lifting his hands defensively and stepping back. 'If you really want me to—'

'I do.' She kept her gaze fixed hard on his.

He smiled sardonically. 'Right, well, I guess I have no choice then.' His expression a mixture of disappointment and fury, he shook his head, collected his keys from the hooks on the utility door and headed towards the hall.

Maddie stood aside to let him pass, looking him over as he did, seeing him clearly now for the first time. The man she'd trusted and loved for fifteen years was nothing but a coward and a liar. How gullible had she been? How shallow had her love for Nathan been that she'd trusted this controlling monster over him? He'd wanted Nathan blamed. He'd refused to corroborate his story when he could have done so easily. He'd taken the tickets from her bag. Quietly, malevolently, he'd tried to convince her that Nathan was guilty. *Dead.* It would have suited his purposes if he was. Nausea roiled inside her. If ever there was a smiling executioner, this man was the epitome of one.

He paused at the kitchen door. 'You're making a mistake, Maddie,' he warned her. 'I'm your friend. Possibly the only friend you'll have when this hits the headlines. They'll dig everything up, the present, your past.' Sweeping his gaze over her, he narrowed his eyes. 'Do you think people won't wonder whether you knew what kind of man you were married to? That the children won't suffer when the other kids at school learn what's going on? They'll be bullied mercilessly. You *need* me!'

Anger burned like corrosive acid in Maddie's chest, but she wouldn't let him goad her into retaliating. Her children were just upstairs. She wanted him gone.

She waited until his car had driven off before she went to the kitchen drawer. Fear crackled through her like ice as she realised what he'd been hiding. She might have gaps in her memory, but she hadn't put them there. Pulling out the box of sleeping pills she remembered disposing of, she felt nausea swirl inside her. He'd taken some from her cabinet and put them in her champagne on the night of her birthday, hadn't he? When had he next been aiming to feed them to her? Walking across to the bin, she banged the lid open and pushed the pills in, then picked up the mug of tea and poured it down the sink, crashing the cup in after it. *Bastard.*

The doors! She needed to lock them, keep her babies safe. Gulping back the fear clawing its way up her windpipe, she flew to the back door, making sure it was locked, then raced to the front door to throw the bolt at the top. Hearing her phone vibrate, she snatched it up to find a text from DS Fletcher. *Tried to call you. CCTV footage from the travel agent checked out. Your husband was there. Can't get hold of him on his mobile. Will try other numbers. We need to speak urgently.*

SIXTY-ONE

He wouldn't hurt her. Wouldn't hurt the children. But what if she was wrong? She had to go. She couldn't stay here where she might be putting her children at risk. Praying that DS Fletcher had got the garbled message she'd left him, she hurried up to Josh's room and gently roused him.

'What's happening?' He prised his eyes open and squinted sleepily up at her.

'You have to get up. We ...' Maddie heard her phone ringing downstairs and cursed herself for rushing up without it. 'I can't explain now, Josh. I need you to trust me. Can you do that?'

He pulled himself upright. 'You're my mum.' He blinked and rubbed his eyes. 'Course I trust you.'

Maddie hoped he could. She wasn't sure she could trust herself any more. 'Could you get Ellie up for me, very quietly, and encourage her to get dressed? But don't frighten her. Okay?'

Clearly sensing something was amiss, Josh's face grew serious. 'I won't,' he promised, shuffling his duvet down with his feet and scrambling out of bed. 'Are we going somewhere?'

'To a hotel, just for tonight. I'll explain on the way.' Maddie gave him a quick hug and headed for the door. 'I'll be two minutes. I just have to fetch my phone and grab the car keys.'

Leaving Josh pulling on his trousers and T-shirt, she went back to the stairs. Part way down, her heart skidded against her ribcage as the hall was plunged suddenly into darkness. She froze. It was the fuse again, that was all, she tried to reassure herself. The wiring had been replaced but the fuse box had been struggling. She just needed to flip the switch. At worst, she would have to replace the fuse. They kept spares on the top of the fuse box, the torch close to hand by the coat rack. She could do this. She just had to focus.

Inhaling hard, she willed herself on, her fear of the dark threatening to choke her as she felt her way down, then almost shot out of her skin as Boomer's frenzied barking reached her. Gripping the rail hard, she stumbled down another step. Where was he? The sound was coming from somewhere outside, she was sure. She wondered how he'd got out, whether in her haste to secure the back door she'd accidentally shut him in the garden.

As she listened, the barking grew fainter, muting to a pathetic whine. Maddie's throat tightened. If there was someone out there, Boomer would be in danger. His loyalty to his family would drive him to protect them. She prayed he wasn't hurt, that the person she'd believed she knew and didn't know at all had a scrap of human decency, a conscience that would compel him to stop.

Taking another tentative step down, her breath stalled, cold fear and nausea churning inside her as someone rapped hard on the front door. She glanced quickly behind her. By the light of the half-moon through the landing window, she saw her children standing barefoot at the top of the stairs, small hands clasped in each other's, fear etched into their faces. 'Go back,' she whispered.

'Mummy, I'm frightened,' Ellie whimpered, rubbing sleep and tears from her eyes.

'*Go.*' Her gaze swivelling back to Josh, Maddie willed her little boy to be as mature as she knew he could be, to look after his little sister.

Relief flooded through her as, understanding her unspoken terror, he nodded and clasped Ellie's hand tighter. Waiting until he'd persuaded her away from the top of the stairs, Maddie continued on down, cursing each creak of the floorboards, which, in the stillness of the night, was magnified a thousand times.

Her chest thudding, she slid around the newel at the bottom of the stairs, her eyes fixed to the opaque glass in the door and the dark silhouette looming beyond it. The torch was only a yard or so away, a yard closer to whoever was on the other side of that door. With no choice, she inched forward, her eyes flicking down as she groped for it. It wasn't *there*. She flailed her hand frantically around. But it was *always* there, in case of ...

Her heart lurched violently as he moved suddenly, pressing his face to the glass, trying to peer through it. 'You should open the door,' he said, his tone flat, devoid of any emotion. 'You must be petrified in there.'

He knows. Her gaze snapped back to the door. He'd known about her phobia since he'd first met her. A weakness he would use to instil deep primal fear in her – just as he had done with Kiara. Terror flooded every vein in her body. Had he tampered with the wiring from the outside? She had to get to her phone. She pictured it on the work surface in the kitchen, the knot in her stomach tying itself tighter as she realised she would have to negotiate her way there in the dark. *No choice.* She *would* keep her babies safe.

Carefully she moved away from the front door and made her way back along the hall. She'd reached the kitchen door when the letter box flapped behind her. She gulped back her racing heart and stayed where she was, eyes and ears straining for any movement or sound. She started as there was another thud behind her. The heel of a hand against the front door? A fist? Then nothing. She waited, interminably long seconds that turned into minutes. Still there was nothing. Was he regrouping? Trying to think what his next move should be? How he could trap her? Silence her?

Grasping the door handle, she pushed the kitchen door open and found her way to the work surface on the inside wall. Where was the phone? Hands trembling, she felt her way along the surface. A ragged sob escaped her as she swiped a cup to the floor. Frantically she swept both hands over the worktop, then whirled around as another bang echoed through the house. *Shit!* Turning back, she tried again – and part of her died inside as she realised the crash right next to her was her phone hitting the floor.

God, please help me. She dropped to her knees, a wretched sob escaping her as she crawled and palmed her way around. Jubilation crashed through her as her hand fell on the phone, and she snatched it up and pulled herself to her feet. Praying with all her might that it wasn't broken, she opened the casing and almost wilted with relief. Never so grateful to see blue light in her life, she turned on her torch, spun back around – and her blood froze.

Her skin crawling with revulsion, she stepped towards the jam jar in the middle of the island. The kind Josh collected his bugs in. It was full to the brim. Packed with spiders, too many to count, hunched legs and bodies entangled as they crawled over each other, searching instinctively for escape. Horror and fascination drawing her to it, she reached to pick it up. Were they poisonous? She had no way of knowing, no way of identifying them. She knew why he'd left them, though. He was delivering a clear message: *I'm not going to kill you. I'm going to corner you, petrify you until your own fear does that for me.*

It was a game. The same sick, twisted game he'd played with Kiara. Bile rose hotly inside her. She would *not* let him win. A mother's instinct was to kill before she would let any harm come to her children. He would know she would fight. She wouldn't die fighting, though. Couldn't. If need be, *he* would.

Trembling with rage and terror, she was lowering the jar back to the island when there was another loud crash behind her. The back door splintering. The jam jar shattered as it slipped from her hands, sending sharp shards of glass and scurrying spiders across the floor.

He was in. Maddie's heart stopped beating. 'Why?' she whispered, turning to face him. '*Why?*' she screamed, disbelief and deep visceral fury unfurling inside her. 'If you don't care anything for me, at least think of Josh and Ellie.'

He dropped his gaze, rubbed the thumb of one hand against the palm of his other as if considering. Finally, he looked up. 'You don't know me at all, do you, Maddie?' he said quietly. 'I would never harm the children. It's *you* I've come back for.'

SIXTY-TWO

Her phone was her only lifeline, but Maddie had no choice but to part with it. To try to fight him would be impossible. He was taller and heavier than she was. She couldn't risk being overpowered. Lowering it into his outstretched hand, she flinched as he moved closer, then froze as Josh called urgently from the landing, 'Mum, where *are* you?'

'Go back to bed, Josh,' he answered before Maddie could. 'I'm here. Everything's fine.'

'But—'

'Go back to your room!' he yelled, moving past her – and Maddie's protective instinct kicked in ferociously. Quickly, she scooped a shard of glass from the floor. It wasn't much of a weapon, but it would have to do. She didn't stop to debate the improbability of it seriously injuring him as she rammed it as hard as she could into his shoulder. She didn't look back as she heard him hiss out a curse. Didn't worry about the blood oozing from her hand. She had one thought in her head, to lead danger away from her babies. 'Josh! Hide!' she screamed, praying he would know what she meant. Then she fled.

Considering for a split second whether to head for the gate, she realised that would be locked, that she would have to climb over it, so she kept going, blundering towards the bottom of the garden. There were an abundance of bushes and conifer trees there, thick with foliage. Beyond was the fence, the woodland. If she could make it that far, it might buy her some time. It was her only chance. Her children's only chance. Her blood pumping, adrenaline and fear forcing her on, she risked a glance over her shoulder, saw him emerge from the house, and a sob of relief escaped her.

Running with only the thin light of the moon to guide her, she tripped over sawn-off branches, roots protruding like gnarled snakes from the ground. Her heart pounding so loudly she was sure it would burst through her chest, she stopped as she heard leaves rustling, twigs snapping. And then stillness.

Her ears straining, she glanced frantically around, willed him to come into view. She couldn't see him. What if he'd gone back to the house? Her gaze snapped in that direction. Where was he? Her stomach lurched as she heard scraping and scuffling in front of her. Boomer? Her hopes soared, then faded. If it was Boomer, he would come to her. Foxes. It had to be. Hearing another twig snap, she stepped warily back, then cursed as she lost her footing and fell.

Get up! For God's sake! Scrabbling in the mud, she tried to heave herself up, digging her heels in and groping around for something to give her leverage. When she looked up, David was standing over her. Feeling as if the breath had been sucked from her body, she froze.

'I'm sorry it's come to this,' he said regretfully, 'but I can't let you take that locket to the police.'

Numb with shock and fear, she twisted to face him. 'You can't hope to get away with this.' But he did, she realised. To think he could take Nathan's place, he was obviously detached from reality.

He answered with a shrug, then tipped his head to one side

and studied her silently. Suddenly his hand shot out, seizing her arm and hauling her to her feet.

Maddie squirmed and raked her fingernails down his cheek.

He didn't flinch. Silence hung suffocatingly between them for a beat, then he reached to wipe the blood from his face before calmly taking hold of her other arm. 'Why would you do this, Maddie, after all I've done for you? Do you know how hurt I was when you asked me to leave?'

'Did you honestly think you could *stay*?' she asked, incredulous.

'Is it such a bad idea?' he replied, as if he really thought it was a possibility. 'We might have been good together. We could certainly have given the house the love it needs, the children the attention they need, both of which Nathan sadly neglected to do. He did ask me to keep an eye on you, you might recall,' he went on. 'He didn't respect you very much, did he, Maddie, to ask another man to step in and look after you?'

He was insane. Nathan had had good reason to be worried about her. He'd trusted David. She had too.

'Just like Kiara didn't respect me. I can't believe I wasted so many years of my life on a woman who didn't give a damn about me, watching time slip by, my life slip by while *she* was fucking your husband!'

Maddie's stomach turned violently. Was that what this was all about? Some ludicrous act of revenge? Was it jealousy that was driving this insanity? And now that she'd rejected him, what would he do? 'Please let me go,' she begged, trying again to pull away from him.

He yanked her back, his fingers digging painfully into her flesh. 'I can't, Maddie.' He sighed sadly. 'I'm sorry. I can't allow you to go to the police. I have to consider my own future, which will be a better one, I think, without my dear wife. Sophie assures me she didn't suffer before she fell, if it's any consolation. She was drunk, wasn't she, Sophie?'

SIXTY-THREE

THE NIGHT OF THE FALL

Kiara

Stark against the white kitchen tiles they were standing stock still, huge, knotted bodies squat, eight thick legs hunched. Two of them, watching, waiting.

Oblivious to the broken glass and the pool of wine at her feet, Kiara shuffled a step back. *Please God, help me*, she prayed. She took another faltering step, and then, her flight instinct kicking in, spun around – and found the floor snatched from beneath her. She landed heavily, heard bone crack as her cheek hit the tiles. Stunned for a second, panic rising so fast it threatened to choke her, she pressed her hands against the floor, heaving herself up onto all fours. 'Get *away*! Keep *away* from me!' she screamed, crawling towards the hall, careless of the sharp shards of glass piercing her palms and grinding mercilessly into her knees, of her state of undress, of anything but her need to escape.

'*Help!* Please somebody *help me.*' Gulping back sobs, she pressed her hands to the walls, pawing her way upwards. Once shakily on her feet, she lurched towards the front door, then stopped, her eyes springing wide with unbridled fear. There couldn't be. There *couldn't* be! Scurrying towards her, this one was the size of her *hand.* Tears blinding her, she blundered towards the lounge, half limping, half stumbling to stand in the middle of it. Frantically she swept her gaze over the carpet, then, praying fervently, lifted her eyes to the walls – and her blood froze in her veins. Three, four, five, she counted in tandem with the loud boom of her heart. All motionless, poised, ready to strike.

Her whole body shaking, she moved unsteadily backwards, her eyes pivoting wildly as she watched them, willing them with all her might not to move.

She was backed against the balcony doors, groping behind her to slide them open, when one of the creatures shot upwards, scurrying up the wall and across the ceiling in an instant. A guttural scream escaped her, and she whirled around, cursing and spitting, her heart thrashing as she renewed her efforts to open the doors. *Locked.* They were locked. She tried to think above the panic consuming her senses. With trembling hands, she fumbled to open the locking mechanism, snapping a nail right down to the quick. She didn't feel it. She needed to get away. Finally, sliding the door open, she took a step out, and then stopped, turning slowly around as someone spoke behind her.

'I would say they can't hurt you,' Sophie said from the doorway, a sympathetic smile on her face, a jar in her hand. 'But I expect you've heard that before.'

Kiara fixed her gaze on the jar, a glass jar half filled with flailing legs and squirming bodies, and fear crackled through her veins.

'Shall we let them go, do you think?' Sophie asked, her smile evaporating to give way to hatred in her eyes. 'The poor things are frantic. It seems cruel not to.'

'No!' Kiara cried as the woman walked towards her, her hand on the top of the jar, her threat implicit. '*Please!* Don't.'

'You shouldn't have done it, Kiara,' Sophie growled. 'Taken him just because you bloody well could. He's not *yours*. He's mine! You shouldn't have done it!'

'I'm sorry,' Kiara blurted. 'Please ...'

'Too late. You tried to ruin my life, Kiara. You should have realised there would be consequences. There's someone else here, incidentally. Outside the door. He's too squeamish to come in. He won't save you, though. He doesn't want you, you see. He wants me. Sauce for the goose and all that.' Sophie sighed dramatically. 'The man's besotted with me.'

Kiara's shock gave way to terrifying reality. After years of being her hero, David wouldn't save her. She recalled the look in his eyes, one of near hatred, as she'd tried and failed to fight him off on that New Year's Eve that had changed the course of her life. His too. Clearly he'd found what he needed, the love, the adoration, in Sophie. She almost laughed at her own naivety. She'd thought she'd been so clever, and all the while David had been having an affair too, right under her nose. And now he wanted her gone.

She stepped further back as Sophie advanced, wrapping her arms around herself, attempting to still her incessant shaking, to stop her teeth chattering. A sharp sob escaped her as she felt the cold metal of the balustrade press against the bare flesh of her back. In that second, she knew there was no escape. No way out of the web in which she was hopelessly ensnared. It was ironic, she thought, strangely calmly, that she'd fought so hard to outrun her fear, yet here she was with nowhere left to go.

She didn't feel the impact as her bones landed, hitting the unforgiving concrete four floors below with a dull, sickening thud. Her heart had stopped beating.

SIXTY-FOUR

PRESENT

Maddie

'To the point of falling over, no pun intended,' Sophie confirmed, emerging from the foliage behind David. 'I'm pretty sure the alcohol would have numbed her pain.'

Maddie's breath stalled. She'd wondered about his sister, whether she wasn't all she seemed to be. But Sophie?

'Don't look so horrified, Maddie.' The woman laughed, shining the torch she carried towards her. 'She was shagging my husband. You can't really blame me for helping myself to hers before reminding her it's never a good idea to be on the receiving end of a woman's wrath.'

'Jake?' David's astonished gaze snapped from Maddie to Sophie. 'But ...' He shook his head in bewilderment. 'I thought you said she was ...'

'Shagging Nathan?' Sophie finished, eyeing him with mild amusement. 'I did. Luckily you didn't take much convincing. You really are gullible, David.'

He stared hard at her. 'You lied to me?'

'I had to get you to bite, didn't I?' Sophie said with an uncaring shrug. 'Would you really have found the anger you needed to do the things you did, frighten your scheming whore of a wife the way you did, if you hadn't thought it was your good friend Nathan who was shafting you? I think not. Jake's learned his lesson, by the way. He was working at the estate agent's that sold the apartment. I think he thought he could have his cake and eat it, the commission and Kiara. I lodged a complaint against him, posing as someone else, of course. I don't think they were too happy having someone accused of sexual harassment show potential clients their properties. He's lost his job and the love of his life. He's still trying to work out how. Ah well, I'm sure his broken heart will mend in time.'

Stunned, David glanced back to Maddie. He'd thought Kiara had been having an affair with Nathan. Maddie had thought the same. A turmoil of raw emotion assailed her. Anger. Acrid grief, rising so fast it almost choked her. Sophie had killed Kiara, and had implicated Nathan without a second thought. The woman didn't care. She really didn't.

'Don't do this, David,' Maddie begged, her only hope to try to get him on side. 'Don't do whatever it is she's trying to make you do.'

'He *called* me,' Sophie growled in her direction. 'The idiot had left the tickets from the travel agent in the house. That was a nice gesture Nathan made, by the way. Pity you didn't appreciate him, Maddie.'

All this to retrieve tickets the police already knew about? Maddie looked between them, uncomprehending.

David laughed ironically. 'You cruel fucking bitch,' he muttered, glancing to the skies.

'Ooh, David. Language. And you were such a nice inoffensive man as well.' Sophie made wide eyes at him, then her face hardened. 'You should be thanking me,' she went on, her tone

one of bitter indignation. 'At least I alerted you to the fact that poor, vulnerable Kiara was a lying little slut. After all you did for her too, pandering to her every need, putting up with her pushing you around. I can't believe you gave up your beautiful house to go and live in an apartment with her. Any man would be forgiven for wanting to kill a woman as selfish as that, don't you think, Maddie? The poor man was devastated, realising she was treating him like shit on her shoe. With his ego so badly bruised and his self-esteem crushed, you can hardly blame him for accepting a little sympathy and company elsewhere, can you?'

She turned smilingly towards Maddie, as if expecting her to agree. Maddie simply stared at her. 'Sadly, when push came to shove ...' Sophie shook her head despairingly. 'I'd have pushed her over the balcony in a flash if I were him, but poor sensitive David couldn't do it. He was weak. As weak as Jake. In fact, the only man with any backbone was Nathan. But *you* ...' she eyeballed Maddie accusingly, 'you weren't strong enough to believe in him, were you? You're the weakest of all of them, popping pills all over the place. Not strong enough to stand on your own two feet!'

Looking Maddie over, she sneered contemptuously, then dragged her gaze back to David. 'Oh, for God's sake, let her go, will you?' she snapped. 'She's not going anywhere. Not if she wants to ensure her children are safe.'

As Maddie staggered backwards, Sophie moved towards her and began slowly circling her, like an animal would its prey. A demented animal. Even by the light of the torch, Maddie could see the seething glint in her eyes.

'You were ready to throw away your marriage to sleep with a man who belonged to someone else, weren't you, Madeline? A man who belonged to *me*.' Sophie banged a hand against her chest, her eyes sliding to David and back. 'Just like Kiara did. She didn't suddenly decide she wanted to become my "friend".'

She made quotation marks with her fingers. 'She was already fucking my husband when I applied for the job at the salon. She wanted to keep her enemy close. If she knew where I was, she could choose her time to slip off, couldn't she? She obviously thought I was stupid. Silly cow.'

The last was spat out. Maddie stumbled backwards, desperately trying to think of a way to get past them.

'Stay!' Sophie snarled. 'There's no reason to rush off when we're all just getting to know each other so well, is there?' she added, smiling sweetly.

'Why are you doing this?' Maddie asked, the inane rubbish coming out of the woman's mouth chilling her to the bone.

Sophie ignored her. 'We thought her deceitful heart might give out, didn't we, David?' she said. Clearly she didn't care that she was doing exactly what Kiara had done to him, using him until it suited her not to, trampling what was left of his ego into the ground. 'Unfortunately, she wasn't as ill as we'd hoped she might be. She didn't feel anything, though, I promise you. There was a look of surprise on her face when she landed. It was quite comical really.'

She paused, appearing to ponder, then shook herself as if her thoughts were of little consequence. 'We hoped the detective might believe you were responsible. Nathan confided in David, you see, about your evasive memory.'

Maddie looked towards David, silently pleading with him to stop this, stop her.

'Alas, things have gone a little awry now, haven't they?' Sophie stepped in front of Maddie and held out her hand, in the palm of which were several tablets. 'You really shouldn't have gone to the police, Maddie, putting ideas in their heads. But never mind, all's well that ends well. Nathan will get the blame for everything. Who wouldn't be driven half mad and finally, tragically, to suicide, treated the way he obviously treated you? Before you think of refusing to take them, by the way, we won't hesitate to force you. We have dear Kiara's insurance to collect, you see. We can't leave any loose ends, can we, David?'

Terror gripping her afresh, fear for her children, Maddie looked beseechingly again to David. After everything he'd just heard, surely he wouldn't allow this to happen?

'David!' Sophie barked, snatching his attention to her. 'Do you want to spend the next twenty years of your life in prison, for fuck's sake?'

He appeared conflicted for a second, then glanced uncomfortably at Maddie. 'I'm sorry,' he said lamely.

Maddie searched his face, astonished. 'David, *don't*. You don't want to. You *know* you don't. Stand up for yourself.'

He looked away. 'It will be better for you this way,' he said gruffly. 'I can't go to prison. Maddie. I'm truly ...'

He stopped, his gaze snapping past her as something crashed through the foliage, launching itself at Sophie with the agility of a cougar. She screamed, flailing backwards, emitting a grunt as she crashed heavily onto her back.

Stupefied, David stared at the dog, its bared fangs and low throaty growl rooting him to the spot. Then his eyes shot wide with horror as his gaze landed on the person emerging through the trees from the direction of the woods.

Maddie sobbed out his name when she saw him. Nathan's face was rigid with fury, heavy bruising down his cheek and his hair matted with blood, making him look as feral as the animal who would die to protect him. Coming to a halt in front of David, he didn't speak, merely appraised him quietly. For a beat, it was as if the world had stopped breathing.

Then David staggered backwards. 'It's not how it looks,' he stammered. 'I was trying to ... Shit!' Realising Nathan wasn't in a listening mood, he lunged for Maddie, shoving her hard to the ground before whirling around and fleeing back through the garden.

He was going towards the house. 'Nathan!' Maddie screamed, as he hesitated by her side. 'The children!'

Nathan looked from her towards David's retreating back, then, hissing out a curse, raced after him.

Maddie's gaze flicked to Sophie, who'd levered herself to her elbows, her eyes wide with fearful apprehension and fixed on the snarling dog looming over her. 'Call it off,' she whimpered. '*Please*, Maddie. I'm sorry. It was David's idea. *All* of it. Please don't let it ...'

The words died on her lips as Maddie moved past Boomer and swung the branch she'd picked up. Swung it hard.

SIXTY-FIVE

Nathan

Fuck. Nathan kept going through the searing pain in his chest, his aim to find his children and then to kill David stone-cold dead. Clutching a hand to his side, a wheeze rattling through him, he paused briefly, watching as the man he'd once considered a friend headed for the side of the house. He was going to the back door. Obviously he was aware he could gain entrance that way. Spitting out another curse, Nathan ran on, grappling his key from his pocket and heading fast for the front.

Sweat soaking his shirt, adrenaline and blind rage driving him, he shoved the door open to be met by complete silence. Where were his kids? What might that bastard have done to them before he'd arrived? Praying to a God he was struggling to believe in to keep Josh and Ellie safe, he headed straight for the stairs.

He faltered as a dull crash reached his ears. Carefully he mounted the first step, then paused as a dark shadow flitted across the facing wall. *David*. If the kids were up there, Nathan had no doubt the cowardly piece of shit would try to use them as leverage. He *would* kill him. If he harmed one hair on either of his children's heads, he would do it excruciatingly slowly.

Determined, he forced himself on, gripping the stair rail hard and hauling himself up. There was nowhere for David to run. Nowhere up there to hide.

Reaching the landing, he tried the light switch, guessing before he did that the reason he'd seen no light from the house was that the fuse box had been tampered with. The bastard had been trying to terrify Maddie, the same way he'd terrified Kiara, deliberately, mercilessly. He deserved to die slowly, but Nathan hadn't got the time or the patience for that.

He didn't see the ladder lying across his path until he almost fell over it. Straightening up, he spotted David at the far end of the landing. He was fumbling to pull the bolt on the door leading to the top floor, spitting out profanities as he did. The man was scared. Scared enough to go up there and face his fear of heights? He should be.

Seeing him open the door and start up the stairs, Nathan followed.

'Oh Jesus.' He heard David ahead of him, his voice shaking. He would do more than that when Nathan reached him. For daring to go anywhere near his wife, his *children*, for what he'd done to Kiara, he would plead for his miserable life. And Nathan would take great pleasure in telling him, sorry, *mate*, no dice.

'It wasn't my idea,' David called back. 'None of it. Kiara wasn't supposed to *die*. It was Sophie who was in the apartment with her, not— *Fuck!*'

From the crack he heard, wood splintering, followed by a yelp of pain, Nathan gathered David's foot had gone through a rotten board. That might even things up a bit.

His breathing laboured, every sinew in his body straining to draw air into his lungs, Nathan climbed the stairs after him.

'I was trying to *help* Maddie,' David cried, his voice shrill, that of a man who'd obviously realised he was about to meet his maker. 'I would never hurt her. You know I wouldn't. For Christ's sake, Nathan, you *know* me.'

Nathan kept going. He had no intention of entering into unnecessary dialogue, wasting precious energy on vermin. He'd almost made it to the top when a plank of wood swung into his chest with the force of a freight train, sending him sprawling. His head hit the wall with a sickening crack as he landed awkwardly part way down the stairs, and for a second he was disorientated. Then he blinked hard, swiped the sweat and blood from his eyes and grabbed hold of the rail, attempting to pull himself up.

It took him a second before he realised what the scraping and scuffling was in the stairwell below him. Boomer leapt over him with the agility of a deer. And from the frenzied barking when he reached the top of the stairs, Nathan guessed he wasn't enamoured of their unwelcome guest.

David was cowering in a corner when Nathan finally reached the top. 'Call him off,' he croaked. 'Don't let the bloody thing bite me.'

Nathan surveyed him coldly, letting him sweat as Boomer's barking quieted to a threatening growl, then, 'Boomer, here,' he called.

The dog obeyed instantly, and David emitted an audible sigh of relief. 'Thank Christ,' he said, attempting to lever himself to his feet.

'You, *stay!*' Nathan warned him, moving towards him. At least he was close to the window. That was something. He wasn't sure how long he could stay standing.

David looked up with a mixture of fear and uncertainty as Nathan loomed over him. 'Whatever it is you're thinking of doing, Nathan, you don't want to,' he said shakily. 'Think of your family.'

'Where are my children?' Nathan grated, fury rising white-hot inside him.

David gawked uncertainly at him for a second. Then, 'I would never hurt your kids,' he said, his expression disbelieving. 'I love them like they were my own. I love Maddie, you *know* I do. You need to talk to her. She'll tell—'

'Where the *fuck* are my *children*?' Nathan's anger exploded. Pain sliced through him like a knife, the weight in his chest almost unbearable as he clutched two handfuls of David's shirt and yanked the spineless coward to his feet.

'What are you going to do?' David whimpered.

'Show you out,' Nathan replied simply, shoving him hard against the wall and holding him there by his throat as he reached with his free hand to open the window.

'Don't!' David gagged and squirmed, but Nathan wasn't about to let him get away. Nor, it seemed, was Boomer, who was now guarding the top of the stairs like a Rottweiler. Grabbing David by the scruff of his collar, Nathan threaded an arm around his neck and locked it tight, then steered him to the window. He wanted him to know what his fate would shortly be. He wanted him to taste his fear.

'What are you *doing*, you mad fucker?' David croaked.

'Where *are* they?' Nathan repeated, shoving him forward.

'Nathan!' Maddie screamed. 'Don't!'

Nathan looked down to where she stood on the patio below. He blinked the sweat from his eyes, and squeezed tighter, feeling David's throat gurgle.

'Nathan, *please*,' Maddie cried. 'He's not *worth* it.'

Nathan breathed in. Another sharp pain ripped through him. *Not worth it.* He repeated the words in his head. Blinked hard as the ground swam out of focus. Sirens. He could hear them. The sounds of the jungle, he could hear those too: birds calling, wings flapping, monkeys shrieking. Not monkeys. Screaming, not shrieking. His babies. Where were they?

'He'll get the punishment he deserves.' Maddie's voice cut through the cacophony of noise in his head. 'Nathan, please don't do this.'

The wail of the sirens grew louder. Nathan locked his hold still tighter.

'Nathan, *please*,' she begged. 'It won't ... Josh!' She snapped her gaze to her side. 'Go into the house. *Now*.'

Nathan's heart somersaulted in his chest as he saw his boy through the red fog in his head. He'd been in the coal bunker? *Oh Christ*. Relief flooding every cell in his body, he closed his eyes, felt himself sway.

'Dad!' Josh shouted urgently. 'Please come down. Ellie's crying. She's scared of the spiders. She won't go back inside. She *needs* you.'

His baby girl. His son. Nathan opened his eyes again. This was his biggest fear, right here. He was facing it. The prospect of his kids losing faith in him, doubting for one second that he didn't care for them, that he wouldn't always be there for them. That he wouldn't die before he would let any harm come to them.

His gaze went to Maddie. She'd watched her father die. It had damaged her. If he did this, it would break her. It would break his children.

EPILOGUE

Maddie noticed a solitary bird gliding across the sky as she and Nathan left the house. That was the second time she'd looked up to see one. Maybe it was just coincidence, but she couldn't help hoping it was a sign. *Soar high, Kia*, she willed her friend. *Leave all your cares and troubles behind you.*

Nathan squeezed her close. 'Will you be okay?' he asked her. 'It's not going to be easy.'

He was right. Visiting her mother today was going to be the hardest thing she'd ever done in her life. She glanced at him as they got into the car. 'Why didn't you tell Fletcher you'd left the party?' she asked.

Nathan hesitated. 'I panicked,' he admitted.

'Because?'

He shrugged, clearly searching for a way to explain. 'I thought it might give the police reason to start sniffing around. I was going to say something when I went to the station. But then I thought if I admitted I'd lied about that, they would assume I'd lied about other things – what time you came home, for instance.' He glanced at her, his expression guarded. 'I was scared, Mads. I thought you were convinced it was me Kiara was having an affair with, that you might have gone there that night and that maybe you'd argued. I'm sorry. I got it wrong, but having seen what visiting the prison does to you, let alone ...'

What actually being in prison would do to her. Maddie understood. It was a stupid thing he'd done, but she understood why he had: because he cared about her, because he cared about his children. 'You should have told me,' she said, careful to keep any recrimination from her voice.

'I know.' He sighed heavily. 'When we spoke on the phone, though, and I realised that David hadn't corroborated that I'd been in the bedroom on the day they moved in, even though he was aware I had, I knew the bastard was up to something. Then when I realised that you actually believed I'd been involved in Kiara's death, I just wanted to get back. I was going to call you, but ...' He stopped. 'God knows what you must have gone through.'

Maddie reached for his hand, squeezed it tight. They both had more questions, things they needed to talk through. It would wait. He needed to concentrate on getting well. They both needed to concentrate their efforts on making sure their house was a safe, happy home for their children.

They drove in contemplative silence most of the way to the prison, talking only about happier things whenever they did speak. About Ellie and Josh, and how Josh had decided he was going to look after his little sister. About the house, and the plans they were now determined to bring to fruition.

Nathan took hold of her hand as they walked together to the visitors' room. Her mother was there, looking as frail as she had the last time Maddie was here. She gave Nathan a brief curious glance as he sat down, no more.

Maddie dispensed with the niceties and got straight to the point, asking the question that couldn't wait. 'Why did you think Nathan was seeing Kiara?' She willed her mother to look at her, to tell her what she badly needed to know if she was ever to bury her ghosts.

Her mother glanced again at Nathan, and then sheepishly away. 'His friend came to see me,' she said reluctantly. 'He said he was concerned for you.'

David. Maddie sensed Nathan tense, aware as she now was of the lengths to which David had been prepared to go to convince her Nathan was guilty and manipulate his way into her life. Inhaling hard, she readied herself to ask the next question. 'Why didn't you tell me, Mum? About the matches?'

Her mother's expression was shocked at first, then she closed her eyes, drew in a breath and nodded. 'You didn't remember,' she said, exhaling shakily. 'There was only me to remind you.'

Maddie stared at her, uncomprehending.

'I'm your mother, Madeline.' Finally she looked at Maddie full on, her eyes filled with anguished tears. 'I couldn't do that to you. I thought if I said I didn't remember either, they wouldn't keep asking me questions that might trip me up. I prayed every day that your memory would never come back.'

Maddie studied her for a long, incredulous moment. 'You did it to protect me.' Realisation dawned and a confusion of emotion erupted inside her. All this time she'd thought her mother had had no feelings for her, and now ... She swallowed back a hard lump of emotion. She had loved her enough to give up her life for her.

Her mother smiled sadly. 'I didn't protect you emotionally, though, did I?' she said, deep remorse in her gaze. 'I left you with so much pain and uncertainty.'

Nathan reached for Maddie's hand again, squeezed it hard. He didn't let go of it until they reached the car, where he turned to take hold of her other hand.

Maddie could feel his eyes on her. She didn't dare meet

them. She could read his every emotion there. She didn't think she could bear it if she saw disillusionment or doubt.

He didn't say anything for an agonising moment. Then he placed a finger under her chin, gently encouraging her to look at him. 'You were a child,' he said. 'You were scared of the dark. You did what any child would have done. What Josh or Ellie might have. What I might have. It wasn't your fault, Maddie.' His tone was adamant. There was no judgement in his eyes.

He smiled encouragingly and then eased her to him. 'I love you, Madeline Anderson,' he whispered, pressing a soft kiss to her hair. 'I always will, even if you decide you'd rather not be with a man who's caused you so much pain. I just wish you would realise you're worth loving.'

A LETTER FROM SHERYL

Thank you so much for choosing to read *Do I Really Know You?*. I hope you enjoyed reading it as much as I enjoyed writing it. If you would like to keep up to date with my new releases, please do sign up at the link below:

www.bookouture.com/sheryl-browne

Have you ever had someone tell you it's all in your mind? I have.

Within interpersonal relationships sometimes we can misinterpret other people's body language or emotions and make assumptions. Maybe we will assume someone doesn't like us or is upset with us. Hopefully, through conversation, we will find that we were wrong, and it was indeed all in our mind.

Sometimes, though, in romantic relationships, if someone is habitually lying to you, phrases such as 'you're inventing things', 'you're rewriting history', 'you're mad/neurotic/too sensitive/jealous/nasty' might be hurled at you. If so, that person may well be gaslighting you.

The term comes from a play by Patrick Hamilton, later developed into the film *Gaslight* by Alfred Hitchcock, the premise of which is an abusive husband trying to convince his wife she is losing her mind with manipulative behaviours, one of which is to slowly dim the gas light, hence the term.

People who engage in gaslighting or coercive behaviour tend to never back down, even when you have absolute proof they're lying. Such behaviour can make you feel unseen and unheard. It can make you doubt yourself. You begin to realise that if you question this abusive behaviour, the arguments will escalate. You feel vulnerable, insecure and confused, unsure of the truth, particularly if the person gaslighting you is being nice to you while doing so.

Do I Really Know You? looks at gaslighting. It also looks at phobias and how they can become magnified when we feel vulnerable: fear of spiders, of heights, fear of actually being manipulated, fear of our vulnerabilities themselves. Is Kiara being manipulated or is it all in her mind? Madeline struggles with a past trauma, the details of which she's unconsciously forgotten. Her mind tends to fill in the gaps. Is she doing that now, incorrectly? Or is she too being manipulated? Are people who they seem to be? Are their actions being misinterpreted?

I sought professional help, incidentally, for my own concerns within a destructive relationship, and for my phobia. For the latter, I embarked on a cognitive behavioural therapy course. It worked. I no longer suffer from arachnophobia, which was magnified a thousand times when I was at a low emotional ebb. Rest assured, I won't be climbing through any windows to escape spiders. I now imagine them wearing pink baby bootees. I know, but it works. I hope mention of the spiders doesn't cause any readers anxiety. I love you all so much for supporting me.

As I pen this last little section of the book, I would like to thank those people around me who are always there to offer support, those people who believed in me even when I didn't quite believe in myself. To all of you, thank you.

If you have enjoyed the book, I would love it if you could share your thoughts and write a brief review. Reviews mean the world to an author and will help a book find its wings. I would also love to hear from you via Facebook or Twitter or my website.

Stay safe everyone, and happy reading.

Sheryl x

 facebook.com/SherylBrowne.Author
twitter.com/SherylBrowne

ACKNOWLEDGEMENTS

Heartfelt thanks to the fabulous team at Bookouture, whose support of their authors is amazing. Special thanks to Helen Jenner and the wonderful editorial team, who work so hard for me. Huge thanks also to the fantastic publicity team. Thanks, guys, I think it's safe to say I could not do this without all of you. To the other authors at Bookouture, I love you. Thank you for being such a super-supportive group of people.

Special thanks, too, to Dr Melissa Bell, PhD, who took time out of her life-changing work across Africa to provide invaluable insight into the life of a medical entomologist working in South America.

I owe a huge debt of gratitude to all the fantastically hard-working bloggers and reviewers who have taken the time to read and review my books and shout them out to the world. It's truly appreciated.

Final thanks to every single reader out there for buying and reading my books. Knowing you have enjoyed my stories and care enough about the characters to want to share them with other readers is the best incentive ever for me to keep writing.

Made in the USA
Las Vegas, NV
07 November 2022

58968210R00204